Penelope Nelson was born the University of Sydney and has worked in publishing, community relations, a government management development fiction, articles and poems appeared in numerous journals and anthologies.

Currently living near Narrabri, New South Wales, she writes fiction and occasional articles, and reviews paperbacks for the *Weekend Australian*.

IMPRINT

MEDIUM FLYERS

PENELOPE NELSON

Annie & Duncan,

with best wishes

Penelope Nelson
18 Dec 90

ANGUS
& ROBERTSON

A division of HarperCollins*Publishers*

AN ANGUS & ROBERTSON BOOK

First published in Australia in 1990 by
Collins/Angus & Robertson Publishers Australia

Collins/Angus & Robertson Publishers Australia
Unit 4, Eden Park, 31 Waterloo Road, North Ryde
NSW 2113, Australia
William Collins Publishers Ltd
31 View Road, Glenfield, Auckland 10, New Zealand
Angus & Robertson (UK)
16 Golden Square, London W1R 4BN, United Kingdom

National Library of Australia
Cataloguing-in-Publication data:

Nelson, Penelope.
  Medium flyers.
  ISBN 0 207 16620 X.
  I. Title.
A823.3

Typeset in Australia by Deblaere Typesetting Pty Ltd.
Printed by Globe Press, Victoria

 5 4 3 2 1
95 94 93 92 91 90

for M.J.K.

ACKNOWLEDGEMENTS

The Author gratefully acknowledges Pat Alexander for permission to quote the lines from his composition, 'Duncan', on page 51.

The Baronet lives entirely at Queen's Crawley,
with Lady Jane and her daughter; whilst Rebecca,
Lady Crawley, chiefly hangs about Bath and Cheltenham,
where a very strong party of excellent people consider her to
be a most injured woman. She has her enemies. Who has
not? Her life is her answer to them: she busies herself in
works of piety. She goes to church, and never without a
footman. Her name is in all the Charity Lists. The Destitute
Orange-girl, the Neglected Washerwoman, the Distressed
Muffin-man, find in her a fast and generous friend.
She is always having stalls at Fancy Fairs for the
benefit of these hapless beings.

William Makepeace Thackeray
from **Vanity Fair, A Novel Without a Hero**

NANKEEN KESTREL

Other names: HOVERER, MOSQUITO HAWK,
SPARROWHAWK, WINDHOVER
A distinctive small falcon often noticed hovering over
paddocks and roadsides...perches on dead trees, telephone
posts and wires: its most conspicuous behaviour is to hover
motionless before dropping on prey. Soars round city
buildings and spires, where it often breeds.

Graham Pizzey (illustrated by R. B. Doyle)
from **A Field Guide to the Birds of Australia**
© G. Pizzey and R. B. Doyle 1980
Reprinted with the permission of Collins/Angus & Robertson
Publishers.

PROLOGUE

After the last bitumen road, the town petered out in a series of vacant lots. Ramshackle sheds gave way to paddocks. Dappled and caramel-coloured ponies were grazing in the last of the sunshine. The few clouds near the hills had pink undersides. As the sun sank lower, the hills took on shades of khaki and olive green. Margot turned the front wheel of her bicycle to the right and wheeled round again. Just a few hundred metres away, a pale bird was hovering over the paddocks, almost motionless in the air.

She stared up at the bird. Twenty or thirty metres above the ground, it was fanning its wings steadily to maintain its vantage point. The bird – possibly a hawk of some kind, she must look it up – was poised and watchful, on the lookout for prey or for rivals.

Margot thought of the phrase Henry Moses had used. Medium flyers. *There was no question that the high flyers should be groomed for the top, he'd said. The puzzle was what should be done about the medium flyers.*

A kestrel. She identified it later. The Australian kestrel, light brown or grey in colour, white underneath, usually seen hovering over open fields. Known for hanging in the air, head-to-the-wind, apparently at a standstill. Named for the Latin crespare, *to rustle.*

The kestrel, Margot learnt, maintains its apparent motionlessness by fanning or rustling its wings. A common bird of prey, it floats lower and lower until it sights its target, then drops sharply to pounce on a lizard, grasshopper or mouse. Though relatively harmless, it is often shot by farmers who mistake it for a hawk.

Least savage of the eaters of living flesh, the kestrel uses its flight to reach a modest height from the ground and to survey what lies below. Its gaze does not extend to the horizon. Through skill or instinct it survives, one victim at a time. It is not the leader of a flock; it does not soar. Its grace consists in making what it does look easy. Windhover, sparrowhawk, nankeen kestrel. Mistress of the semi-rural clearing rather than monarch of the wild.

COVER STORY

Roxane knew she was in trouble as soon as she saw herself on the cover of *Business Briefing*. How could she have let that shot be taken? In the photograph she sat side-on to her desk, twirling an antique globe with one hand. Her blonde hair streamed back from her tilted head above the angled chair. Her leather skirt rode up her thighs. FLYING HIGH? asked the caption underneath. With foreboding, she turned the magazine pages to find the cover story.

She scanned the four-page article, picking out phrases. Her pulse was thudding and little dizzy specks in front of her eyes prevented her from focusing. She blinked and tried to concentrate.

Exclusive interview with Runaway executive Roxane Rowe

> *... heady days in the travel industry ... mergers and rationalisations ... poised to dominate Australia's travel industry in the 1990s ... failures ... undercapitalised timeshare ventures ... out of business ... budget packages for 'the great unwashed'.*

So long as they don't attribute that phrase to me, Roxane thought. So long as someone from some other firm said 'great unwashed'. But she could hear her own voice as she used the phrase to David Jasper. He'd laughed. They'd both been laughing. Champagne. How could she have been so naive as to let a reporter from *Business Briefing* buy her champagne?

> *Arguably the best-known name in travel,*
> *thanks to Runaway's heavy investment in the*
> *'Runaway with Roxane' series of television*
> *commercials, Roxane Rowe is not everybody's*
> *idea of a potential company director ...*

Here we go, Roxane thought. Twenty years of hard work and I am going to be described in terms of my hair and my clothes again. Then a reminder about the Runaway commercials:

> *Runaway if you dare*
> *Runaway with Roxane*
> *Glittering cities, magical islands*
> *Runaway takes you there*
> *Runaway with Roxane*
> *Runaway if you dare*
> *Runaway ...*

Alan Fisk, the twenty-six-year-old founder of Frenzy Inc. of Woolloomooloo, hailed as a musical genius for those lines, had gone on to beer and soft drink commercials with echoes of 'Waltzing Matilda'.

To Fisk's jingle, Roxane sauntered on a Pacific island beach in the sunset, wearing a bikini top and sarong printed with lilac hibiscus. In a red military jacket, she strode past the Grenadier guards outside Buckingham Palace. In a heathery tweed, she smiled dazzlingly at Irish cottagers. There was a new commercial each season. In the late 1970s Runaway's turnover doubled and redoubled. Well-fed Australians toting Runaway overnight bags with the lilac hibiscus motifs went sightseeing and shopping in all the major destinations of Europe and North America. Runaway squeezed out the student travel market and sent its younger passengers to Asian cities and Pacific islands.

> *Blonde, attractive, and in her mid-thirties,*
> *Roxane, who has been in the travel industry*
> *since her teens, is now in charge of South*
> *Pacific operations for Runaway Travel.*
> *Regarded as a shrewd negotiator and a tough*
> *competitor, though one business rival has been*
> *known to dismiss her as a 'glorified PR girl',*
> *she is widely tipped as a future appointee to the*
> *board of Runaway's parent company,*
> *Brooklands.*
> *'The secret of success in this business,' Roxane*
> *told* Business Briefing, *'is to pick the trends for*
> *the upmarket traveller without falling for*
> *something so fashion prone that you'll be*
> *deserted after a couple of seasons. That's*
> *always the risk with the real jet set — one year*
> *it's the Caribbean, then the South Pacific has a*
> *turn, and the next thing you know, the North*
> *Pole is flavour of the month.*
> *'Of course, budget packages for the great*
> *unwashed to a handful of well-known*
> *destinations where there's good shopping are*
> *likely to have a good run for a long while yet ...*

It wasn't too bad after that, so far as she could tell from a hurried reading. She went on to explain that Runaway offered a range of different tours and packages, geared to different incomes and time-frames. She took some of the credit for the market share it now enjoyed in the South Pacific and in Asia. She refused to discuss the business strategies of Brooklands, the parent company. She sounded tough and sales-oriented, but so she should in *Business Briefing*. But that line about getting on the board — would Boris assume she had planted the article to press her claims?

The phone was ringing. As long as it's not Boris, Roxane prayed. 'Des here,' her immediate boss said. 'I guess you've seen the article.' Trust Des to have got hold of an advance copy too, she thought.

'Just picked it up. I'm only on the first page.'

'It doesn't improve. Boris is beside himself. Not to put too fine a point on it, he's fucking furious.'

'Oh, Lord.'

'He wants you to go to Melbourne for next week's board meeting. Of course, the Brooklands people will issue an official retraction of the most damaging claims — phrases like 'great unwashed'. But there's not much we can do about that photo after the event, is there?'

'Des, I can't imagine how they got that photo.'

'The evidence suggests that you were there at the time. You'd have a better idea than I would.'

'Spare me the sarcasm, please. Things are bad enough as it is.'

'For someone who's always been assumed to have a future with the company, this is a bizarre sort of stunt. You've got a lot of explaining to do. If Boris gives you the chance to explain, that is.'

'If you're trying to pressure me into resigning, it won't work. I need time to think, and some good advice.'

'From a shrink or a lawyer? Only joking.'

'Yeah, hilarious. I'll talk to you again when I've had time to think things through.'

'Do that. Till the morning then.'

Roxane made herself a cup of coffee and sat on her leather sofa. The apartment was in Rushcutters Bay, but there was little consolation in the massive Moreton Bay figs and the masts of yachts.

Had she been set up? Why was her photograph chosen for the cover out of all the travel personalities interviewed? Easy. Photogenic, female, a widely recognised face. Why had she made off-the-record comments about the great unwashed when she knew the risk they'd be taken out of

4

context? She'd imagined David Jasper needed a background briefing before he could write about the industry at all. He'd used her words against her, verbatim. Damn it, they were her words. Of course Boris would be furious; he really believed all that stuff about the value of individuals. He was probably summoning her to Melbourne so he could sack her in person. She'd been angling to become a board member herself. The irony of it all.

She read the rest of the article. He'd made her sound a bitch throughout. There was a nudge-nudge reference to her connections in the business world: ... *close friends with such captains of industry as property developer Steven Szabo of Barbary Holdings.* A straight-out announcement that they were lovers might have been preferable to that. Olwyn had warned her people could accuse her of conflicts of interest through her relationship with Steven. Why had she let Jasper buy champagne? Had she fallen for something as elementary as flattery?

One consoling thought came to her: Cindy's malicious little schoolmates at Carinya would not be able to bait her daughter over the article. Her daughter must be used to having a famous mother, but this article cut deeper than most of the publicity she'd been exposed to.

Steven. She desperately wanted to talk to Steven. He would know exactly what to do. No business problem was beyond him: he had tactics for every eventuality. Besides, she could do with a little affection right now. But Steven was in Shanghai.

Who else could she turn to? Most of her friends were in the industry; she wondered if they were really friends or just associates. By morning the magazine would be on every newsstand in Australia. She could see everyone gloating over her gaffe. She would be offered sympathy, but it would be of a treacherous kind.

Twenty years. She had given her career twenty years, and when it was under threat she was all by herself. Any moment now she would start crying. Tears would be a relief, at least.

Jane Singer was a friend, but there wasn't much point turning to her. Her knowledge of the travel industry was years out of date, and she knew next to nothing about publicity or office politics. Besides, she didn't really care for the unsought advice Jane had given her about Cindy recently.

Who else could she turn to?

Since her early years in travel, Roxane had taken her lead from the woman who first gave her a job, Olwyn Tierney. The magazine article offended nearly every one of Olwyn's canons for good publicity — be positive; don't do it if there isn't something new to sell; beware of personal profiles; put the company first; don't trade on being a woman.

Olwyn had drummed all those principles into Roxane, who had imagined she knew better.

Could she still turn to Olwyn? Perhaps Olwyn would refuse to speak to her; she might be bitter about recent events. Last time Roxane had phoned her, Olwyn had her daughter say she was too sick to come to the phone. Roxane decided to take the risk.

She dialled Olwyn's home number. It was engaged. She prowled round the room, threw out some old newspapers, and dialled again.

'Olwyn? It's Roxane.'

The answering voice did not sound quite right. She tried again. 'Could I speak to Mrs Tierney please? It's Roxane Rowe.'

'I'm sorry, Ms Rowe. I'm Winifred Carswell, a friend of the family. Olwyn isn't here, I'm afraid. She's in hospital.'

'I had no idea. Is it serious? Where is she? I'd like to visit her.'

'She's in the Page Chest Pavilion at Prince Alfred. It's some type of pneumonia. And I'm afraid she's not allowed visitors at the moment.'

'I'll send flowers.'

'Well, I wouldn't do that either, really, with all the allergies and so on up there. I'm sure she'd appreciate a card or a magazine.'

6

'Oh, God, I can just imagine everyone will be giving her magazines.'

'I'm sorry, I don't quite follow.'

'Never mind. Thankyou for letting me know, Mrs Carswell. I'll write to her.'

Roxane felt desperately alone. Flying high indeed. She knew why they'd put a question mark after that. She was plummeting downwards with no parachute.

She would talk to Steven as soon as he got back. In the meantime, how was she going to face Des and the office? She re-read a postcard from her daughter which was lying on the telephone table. The photograph showed Maori warriors making fearsome faces and doing a war-dance, their huge muscular legs half-clad in grass skirts. Her daughter had no taste. Only a picture of steamy Rotorua would have been more of a cliché. Damn Cindy. If she hadn't been so anxious about Cindy she would have been more in control when she spoke to David Jasper. Weekends without Cindy were proving lonely and unsettling. She missed the wretched girl.

Steven had said he was only going to Shanghai for a few days. Who knew what that meant, once the functionaries and interpreters started showing him round mills and soft drink plants and bicycle factories? She would see him soon, but perhaps not soon enough.

Some things could not be postponed, and one of them was the Brooklands board meeting next week. She was not prone to self-pity, but the outlines of the trees blurred before her eyes.

She tried her favourite meditation: a tropical island at nightfall. Lapping water, fading light. The swoosh of a breeze through palm fronds. She remembered a comment by Truman Capote that the islands were like ships of permanent anchor where it seemed that nothing unkind or vulgar could happen to you. Her eyes were closed. She took deep breaths and exhaled slowly. She could hear the sound of her own heartbeat. The outlines of palm trees stood black against the dusky violet of night.

The muted tones of the imagined island receded as she frowned again over her current predicament. She'd been no more able to ward off the unkind or vulgar than Truman Capote had, but her travels had at least imprinted some comforting images in her memory. This time next month some other scandal would be keeping the readers of *Business Briefing* in smalltalk. If she had to, she could hide out on a tropical island in the meantime. No one was better placed to do that than Roxane Rowe, Regional Operations Manager (South Pacific).

FILE 3995

Prue Lambert was on the phone to a news clipping service. 'Everything you can get hold of on Steven Szabo and Cloudy Bay,' she said. 'I've got this morning's *Herald*, but I want anything from interstate or the financial press. All right, if extra research puts the price up, put it on the account, so long as it's itemised. The account name is CBE — Commissioner for Business Ethics.' She hung up.

Prue re-read the top letter on the file:

> *My husband didn't leave me all that much money, we were comfortable, that's all. Cloudy Bay seemed the perfect investment. If it goes into receivership, we can only expect some of our money back after the big creditors have been paid. Or if they are. It isn't fair, in my opinion. I get no pension from my late husband's superannuation, he took a lump sum. Now that is gone. What use is the key to a Golf Club that still hasn't been built? The radio ads were false advertising, so was the prospectus, if you ask me.*

Hoping, Sir, you will be able to help, as I am desperate.

Yours truly,
Mildred Lake.

The phone rang.

'Who's that?' a belligerent voice asked. Prue gave her name.

'Listen, love, I've got cockroach droppings in me cutlery drawer. Disgusting, isn't it? The landlord won't do a thing.'

Prue suggested her caller should wash the cutlery and clean out the drawer.

'That's marvellous, isn't it? That's marvellous. That's what we're paying public servants for, is it? To tell citizens they have no bloody rights at all. There's cockroach shit in my kitchen, spreading disease, and the government won't do a thing.'

'Have you had a word with the health inspector at the council?'

'Don't speak to me about the bloody council. I know your type. I've been inside. I know the types that work for the government. Screws. Bloody screws, on the take one and all.'

'Am I to take it your complaint is about cockroaches, or the prison administration?' Prue asked.

'There you go. That's the tone of voice. That's what we're up against. That's the threat.'

'I'm sorry,' Prue said. 'I have a lot of work to do. I'll give you the number of your local council.'

'I have the number of my bloody local council, lady, and this is the last fucking time I'll ring the Commissioner for Business Ethics, I can tell you.'

'Fine, then. Thankyou for your call. Goodbye.'

Prue replaced the receiver and frowned over the Cloudy Bay file. The phone rang.

'It's me,' a man announced. 'Alfred Mannix. There's an MP behind it and a Sir in front.'

'Yes, sir,' Prue said, to be on the safe side.

'It's a constitutional crisis. I need to get a message to the Prime Minister urgently. There's going to be a real political blow-up about this. Scandal brewing, believe you me. I'm well connected, I'm a knight of the realm, I'm a foundation member of parliament.'

'The House of Reps or the Senate?'

'None of your trick questions. Who's to blame me if I take direct action? I have an iron bar in my bag. I don't want to be forced to use it.'

'No. It's a constitutional crisis, you say.'

'Yes. It's the constitution. Tell the Premier. Tell the Prime Minister. Tell the Queen. There's no time to lose.'

'Have you spoken to your local MP?'

'Don't you ever listen? I am my local MP. Sir Alfred Mannix, JP, MP.'

Prue was scanning a green list of members of parliament that was stapled to her internal telephone book. There was no Mannix.

'I'm extremely grateful to you for bringing it to our attention, Sir Alfred,' she said. 'It's a timely warning.'

'A pleasure. Thanks, love.' Sir Alfred rang off.

Prue walked to the reception area, where Aileen, the receptionist, was speaking into the phone.

'So I said to her, "Mum, banlon nighties are a fire hazard. I don't want to hurt your feelings, but I have to be direct, and if you'd typed some of the reports I've typed you'd know I was just taking sensible precautions. Erica's just as happy in ski pyjamas." Look, I have to go, Sheena, someone's here.'

'Sorry to disturb you,' Prue said, 'but am I on telephone duty or what?'

'Not really,' Aileen said, 'but Col's got flu and Geoff's in Newcastle and Louise is in court all day. I put that mad caller through to you, the one who always asks for Louise. Hope you don't mind.'

'Sir Alfred Mannix?'

'Yeah. Louise says he's a sweetie if you just listen to him.'

'You could have warned me, Aileen.'

11

'Mornings like this, there isn't always time to warn everyone.' The switchboard lit up with three new calls. 'Commissioner for Business Ethics,' Aileen drawled.

Prue went back to her desk. There were three letters in the in-tray, two of them from other victims of the Cloudy Bay collapse. The business registry listed three principals for Mirabeau Acres at Cloudy Bay: Steven Szabo, Vilmos Zolnay and Melvin Hughes. She started a cross-check on them. Melvin Hughes proved to be a north coast real estate agent with a half share in a retirement village and a large holding in a building firm which specialised in clubs. Steven Szabo (she knew of him, at least) was a director of five firms, and managing director of Barbary Developments. There was no listing for Vilmos Zolnay.

Prue put a photostat of these entries in her file, then checked the telephone book. Zolnay lived in Double Bay and was listed as a doctor. Melvin Hughes's numbers appeared in the north coast directory, but Steven Szabo's were unlisted. Barbary Developments had five entries in the A–K phone book:

Barbary Holdings O'Connell Street
Barbary Properties Ltd Zetland
Barbary Commercial Leasings Ultimo
Barbary Development Corp Zetland
Barbary Financial Services O'Connell Street

Prue had not had to investigate a complaint involving anyone as powerful as Szabo before. She suspected she would not have been given this one if any of her superiors had realised who the principals of the Cloudy Bay venture were. She would have to act scrupulously, not just to satisfy her own sense of propriety or the requirements of the office manual, but to avoid being torn apart by Barbary's lawyers. Or the Commission's own legal branch, for that matter. She prised a paperclip apart as she took stock of the factors involved.

Meredith McCutcheon, who, like Prue, was an investigation officer, stood in Prue's doorway twisting at the silver chain round her neck. 'God, Prue,' she said, 'I'm so

12

unutterably depressed. Have you got time for lunch?'

'Not a chance, I'm afraid. Anything I can help with?'

'I thought you might find time to listen.'

'Yeah, well, I will, but not right now. I'm snowed under, honestly. And Aileen's been putting every loony in the city through to me, all Louise's pet screwballs.' She put down the mutilated clip and took up a pen.

Meredith's very short hair was grey at the temples. She looked as if she needed to blow her nose. 'You're the one who's always saying the crazies have to be given the benefit of the doubt,' she said.

'Oh, I know, but I have a case I really need to get my teeth into.'

'Overcompensating?' Meredith asked.

'Spare me the psychological bullshit, please,' Prue murmured, felt pen poised over her file.

'Pardon me for living.' Meredith retreated.

'Don't be like that, Meredith.' Prue felt guilty already, but the glass door had closed.

Prue and Meredith, both relatively junior investigators, belonged to the same unofficial grouping within the office. Known as the YTs (for Young Turks) they avoided various members of the old guard within the office, most of whom were in Legal Branch. There was a long-standing feud between Legal and Investigation Branches. The YTs were not as aggressive or daring in their approach as the Rambos, young men with political affiliations who carried out secret missions stemming from taped phone calls and statutory declarations to politicians. The YTs liked to finish their inquiries fast and accurately, without detours through the courts or procedural tangles in the office. They fumed when Legal Branch concluded (as happened more often than not) that there was not enough evidence to bring criminal proceedings against a person or company under investigation. At the same time, they regarded the Rambos as amateurs and cowboys. Within the group, they shared information and advice, but the overall tone of the office was guarded and uncooperative.

Prue snapped the file and a notebook into her briefcase before the phone could ring again. Szabo, yes. Everybody had a story about Steven Szabo. Someone had told her he was having an affair with Roxane Rowe. But the others — wasn't the name Vilmos Zolnay familiar too? Where had she heard of him? She couldn't recall. Run the routine checks first. That is what Malcolm Gwynne always told her.

'I'm off,' she told Aileen. 'To the library. Back in about two hours.'

'Right-oh.'

The library, Prue thought. Works every time. She knew the librarian at the *Herald*. She wanted to know a lot more about the Cloudy Bay principals before she interviewed anyone.

The bus lurched into the Haymarket end of George Street and stopped to pick up Chinese passengers with plastic bags full of vegetables: long crinkled cabbages, stalky broccoli, ginger roots. Prue had a wok but seldom got to use it.

How vegetables had changed over the last few years. The effects of immigration, she supposed. You never saw a choko any more, that was one mercy. Chokoes grew by the dozen on the thick green vine that weighed down the paling fence of the big backyard in Naremburn. Prue had grown up in a large, church-going Congregationalist family, the youngest of five. The house was fibro, with wooden verandas and sleep-outs attached at the sides and back. Chooks scratched about in the yard and the north shore trains rattled by just across the gully. Her father grew rhubarb, spinach and pumpkins too, all items that Prue avoided these days. But the terrible prickly chokoes, equally detestable steamed or mashed, remained her strongest image of childhood food. Chokoes, chooks and hymns. Prue went to the local school until she was ten, when high marks in an exam led the way to Artarmon Opportunity School. She remembered fifth and sixth class with great clarity even now. If you gave her a trumpet, she could probably still play 'When the Saints', 'Rivers of Babylon' and other specialities of the school band.

Gus Allingham used to play the cornet, Simone Greenfield led the first violins, Tony Bonaventura thumped away on percussion, and Jenola Fitzharding played flute. Great days. When they went by train to Melbourne for a national music camp, it was the farthest from home Prue had been. They were billeted with musical families all over the suburbs; her hosts, jazz friends, were the first atheists she had met.

At the end of sixth class the group broke up. While most of the boys went to North Sydney Boys' High, and most of the girls to North Sydney Girls', quite a few won scholarships to private schools further up the line, or went interstate. With the crowded timetable of high school, and the awkwardness of adolescence, life seemed to grow narrower. Prue avoided the boy-mad set: her friends were, like her, church-goers and serious students who even resisted the urge to hitch their tunics up into mini-skirts.

Some dormant hunch that life might offer more led Prue to reject a teacher's college scholarship, even though the decision meant years of part-time work as a hospital cleaner, babysitter and mail sorter. Taking the scholarship would have meant studying subjects like history and geography which could be taught at high school. Prue had decided to study sociology. Her family, imagining this was much the same thing as social work, was delighted.

University in the Vietnam era changed Prue profoundly. She became friends with Margot Tierney through a project that involved interviewing the tenants of welfare suburbs. Although Margot had had a far more privileged upbringing than Prue, they were both shocked at the extent to which welfare workers could interfere in the lives of the poor, picking on their housekeeping standards and taking their children into care. Together Prue and Margot marched for peace, went to lectures on women's rights and sexual freedom, and decked themselves out in the patched denim and flowing Indian cottons of the day. At nineteen, Prue moved away from home to share a flat with Margot and others near the university.

15

The bus picked up a bit of speed as it left Railway Square and passed the old brewery building opposite the University of Technology. When she went to work at the Commission for Business Ethics, Prue was advised to return to night classes to add accountancy qualifications to her sociology degree. To her surprise, she enjoyed working with figures, keeping records and balancing books, even though she hated the Broadway building where classes were held.

Zolnay, Zolnay ... It came to her. Damn, damn, she should have had lunch with Meredith. Zolnay was involved in a complaint about sleep treatment which Meredith investigated but which lapsed for lack of evidence. Patients were put in a deep sleep for days on end. Prue had been feeling so tense and irritable lately that the sleep cure didn't sound such a bad thing. It was ages since she had spent any time relaxing with friends. She was planning to see Margot at the weekend, anyway. And File 3995 looked as if it would prove a make-or-break case. She was determined not to lose a chance to excel. The bus had nearly reached the *Herald* building.

FURTHER EDUCATION

A beacon of light, the emblem of the Yagoona Institute of Further Education (YIFE), flickered from the salmon brick walls in a neon sign erected by the School of Electrical Engineering. The college was founded in the early seventies by a Federal Labor government keen to keep faith with its western suburbs supporters. The library, corridors and administration block were carpeted in that confident shade of emerald known as Whitlam green.

The beacon of light changed colours every ten seconds: mauve, white, gold, colours chosen by the School of Art and Design. Educational policies changed too, only a little more slowly. For a few years the college specialised in adult education, with access courses for the disadvantaged. Then it concentrated on short-term training for the young unemployed. Soon it was directed to strive for excellence in developing technologies instead. Under the Fraser government, it gave priority to vocational courses, but continued to emphasise the words equity and access in submissions to the state government. With the Hawke and Greiner governments, the rules changed again. The schools whose subjects were in the ascendant took over the courses which had fallen out of favour. Margot Tierney taught women's studies and sociology in the Branch of Contemporary Society, which was now a sub-department of the School of Accounting and Business Management.

Margot found the note on her desk, printed in green letters. WHEN YOU HAVE A MOMENT, CAN WE PLEASE TALK? BRIAN. Ominous, Margot thought. Putting it in writing. She found her head of department, Brian Lynch, in his study, underlining paragraphs of a journal article with yellow highlighter.

'How goes it?' he asked. He was a tall man, loose-limbed, and generally regarded as good-looking. Unidentified women were always telephoning him.

'Fine. How's things with you?'

'Good. Great. Now, Margot, I just think we need to be a little realistic about the budget estimates. You've asked for most of your funding for community classes. You've estimated you need eight hours a week face to face with these people.'

'Yes. Not unrealistic, when you realise that these people, as you call them, are unused to study. We have to spend a lot of time on self-esteem.'

'These women. That's what we both mean.' Brian, frowning slightly, doodled with the highlighter pen now, ringing all the paydays on his desk calendar.

'These women. Yes. Most of them need a lot of bolstering up and individual tuition. Often their husbands are hostile to their studying. We've discussed all this, Brian. It's well known that second-chance education entails a lot of counselling and personal support.'

'Sure, sure. It's not that I'm contesting that. It's just that we're under pressure at YIFE to meet vocational needs above all. There are elements on the Senate who feel your type of course should be funded by the Community Arts Board. Or some women's outfit. Not YIFE. Not necessarily. We recognise, Margot, you do a terrific job with them, but are they our first priority? Really?'

'They're mine.'

'Well, one thing I want to suggest is a research project we could get some private enterprise funds for. Feminist topic. Right up your alley. Women and success. Women in business. All the equal opportunity statistics are about public bloody servants. What's happening in industry? It's a goer as a project. We've had an approach from Synchron Mines. You could hire a part-time research assistant, and only work on it yourself two or three days a week.'

'And still be able to keep my women's class?'

'Sure. Maybe not eight hours a week. Six, maybe, or five.'

'I'll think about it, Brian. It'd be interesting. I've thought of something similar. The drawback is the time it'll take away from my oral history project.'

'If you want a working title, how about "Women at the Top"? You could interview Roxane Rowe.'

'Yes, I could. I know Roxane. My mother works for the same company. Beats me, though, why everyone's so fascinated by her.'

'No secret, surely. The commercials. Marketing. Image. One of the best-known women in the country.'

'It's the whole fame thing I object to. Why is Roxane Rowe supposed to be more important than the early women of Yagoona?'

'Funding, Margot. How fundable are the early women of Yagoona? Believe me, I'm giving you the friendliest advice. It's the difference between Roxane Rowe promoting Runaway on television, and an unshaven little creep thrusting a pamphlet on cut-price airfares into your hands at the railway station. One's upmarket, the other's decidedly down.'

'Should I tell them, do you think? My students? That YIFE regards the women of Yagoona as decidedly downmarket?'

'Christ, Margot. Give me a break. I'm doing you a favour here. Just think it over, hey?'

'I will.' Margot gave him a questioning smile, spun on her suede ankle boots, and left the room.

Nearly a decade earlier, when Margot, her husband Ted

and their son Tom returned to Australia after three years in Geneva, Yagoona College had seemed an exciting place to work. The Whitlam years saw the revival of training schemes and second-chance education for women, and when Margot joined the college staff, funds were still flowing and staff were enthusiastic. A more austere climate prevailed now, academically as much as politically. Margot realised she felt more and more remote from the projects which had the approval of the head of the faculty and the college principal. Her women's classes, which the authorities saw as insignificant, were the focal point of her work at present.

In Geneva, Ted had been working with the International Labour Organisation. Margot, at first unable to get a work permit, had mooched around with other expatriates. Taking Tom to pre-school and picking him up at lunchtime (the Swiss did not seem to approve of longday care; even school children went home for hot lunches) — these were the major excursions of her day. Occasionally they went to cocktail parties given by diplomats or international functionaries, but they could not afford babysitting on a regular basis. Margot caught up with her reading, subscribing to professional journals and wading through theoretical works she had avoided as an undergraduate. Occasionally she acted as a substitute teacher at the English-speaking pre-school.

At university Margot had been a contemporary of Prue Lambert. In the heady days of anti-war activities, women's groups and Marxist social theory, she had quarrelled frequently with her mother. Olwyn's career in travel took her away a good deal, so Margot was sent to boarding school. Coming home like a released prisoner four times a year gave her a slightly distorted view of life in Sydney: she saw it as squatters' wives must have done a couple of generations earlier, as a constellation of department stores, bookshops and dentists' rooms. School holidays sped by in a flurry of shopping trips, lunches in town and appointments with orthodontists. When she left school and shared her parents' house on a permanent basis, both she and Olwyn found it hard to adjust.

Margot's parents took little interest in her life at university. Olwyn never seemed to know whether her daughter was doing psychology or philosophy, and as for sociology ... 'Darling, it just sounds like commonsense dressed up in academic language,' was her invariable comment. Margot seldom bothered to disagree. Commonsense was one of the virtues as far as Olwyn was concerned. 'You've got no commonsense,' a remark that Margot heard more than once, was a damning judgment.

It was true that Margot preferred reading to most other activities, and that anger and hopefulness led her to embrace causes she could not always defend. 'Airy-fairy,' Olwyn would say. Or, 'Of course they're all communists.' Margot, seething, took years to learn not to rise to the bait. Her choice of boyfriends caused more rows in the Beecroft household than anything else. They were invariably campus radicals, guaranteed to enrage Derek Tierney, an executive with the Insurance Council. Margot was incapable of being polite to the suitable young men gaining actuarial qualifications as insurance industry trainees. After a couple of years of slanging matches, she and her parents agreed that it might be best if she lived away from home. She took a flat in Kingsford (Olwyn always said it was in Kensington) with Prue and two others, a move which greatly improved her relations with her parents. In due course she finished her degree and went to work in Canberra.

When she returned to Sydney to live with Ted McIver, the truce ended. Ted was an ex-Communist, ex-Catholic, and not yet divorced from his wife. He had two children from his first marriage. Ted and Margot eventually married in the registry office, six months before Tom's birth.

With the birth of their grandchild, Derek and Olwyn included Margot in their lives again. Derek was aloof and cool in his dealings with Ted, but he allowed himself moments of pink pleasure as his grandson's fist closed around his. There was still enough uneasiness in her relationship with her parents for Margot to feel jubilant when Ted's work gave him the chance to live in Europe for a few years.

Olwyn came to Europe twice while they were in Geneva. The first time, she arrived after dashing from one capital to another arranging bus tours for Australian tourists. She sat down in an overstuffed chair and slept for eleven hours. The next time, she and Margot left Tom with Ted for a few days and travelled along the Italian Riviera together. The memory of this journey remained the high point of Margot's relationship with her mother. The dazzling blue bays and pink-washed buildings were the background for sudden flashes of colour and movement. Mother and daughter were both surprised at how much fun they had in each other's company.

Derek Tierney died while Margot was in Geneva. Flying home on the next one-stop flight, Margot found her mother had turned the house into a hive of buzzing tradesmen. Someone was at the door all day. Florists, funeral directors, estate agents, landscape gardeners, the man who rolled the tennis court, the man who cleaned the pool, the man who came to quote on removal expenses. It seemed that Olwyn planned to move to a beachfront apartment as soon as she possibly could. Her friend Winifred Carswell came with two elaborate terrines. 'The funeral baked meats,' Margot quipped. Her mother did not smile.

They were not church-goers. The funeral was a ghastly, impersonal affair in a chapel on the Pacific Highway, with piped music and platitudes from a brace of insurance brokers who sounded like their own brochures. Margot felt sure that her mother must share her sense of how inappropriate and unbearable it all was, but Olwyn seemed to have suppressed grief and substituted frantic domestic activity. Margot found herself scooped up into a squad of volunteers ramming possessions into labelled cardboard boxes as if pursued by time's winged chariot. She wondered what the local doctor had prescribed for her mother: perhaps some cocktail of chemicals had spurred this frenzied action. Margot's childhood tennis racquets and Girls' Own Annuals were sent to a storage company. Travelling back to Europe, Margot wept till Singapore, then took two Valiums and dozed the rest of the way.

After they returned from Europe, Ted, Margot and Tom moved into a brick house in Abbotsford, which had a half-subsided veranda and a tantalising glimpse of the water. Olwyn and Margot entered a new phase of their relationship — never as hostile as during her student days but never as idyllic as when they travelled through Italy together.

Margot made new friends through the college, and through Ted's work in his union and at the industrial relations tribunal. Of the old crowd from university, she remained close only to Prue.

Together, Margot and Prue shared their views on men, families, politics and the ups and downs of their careers. Margot wondered what Prue would say about Brian Lynch's Synchron Mines project. She'd approve, probably. Prue was getting so conventional.

'You're miffed, somehow, aren't you?' Prue asked that Saturday as the two old friends sat under tall silky oaks in the back garden of the Abbotsford house, not quite out of earshot of the speedboats on Hen and Chicken Bay. A fringe of jasmine hung over the back porch near the kitchen door.

'Yes. Cheesed off. I don't feel it's really my project.'

'But that's the whole challenge. By the time you've finished with it, it will be yours, there'll be nothing they can do about it. And if you can get funding — well, get a research assistant, you won't have to do it all yourself. It's quite a privilege to be paid to do a feminist project.'

'That's just it. How feminist is it? The work I'm doing with the women out at YIFE, that's feminist, helping people get an education and increase their range of choices for how they spend their lives and earn their living. That's what the women's movement should be on about, not adding up how many women there are who earn more than thirty-five thousand dollars a year. That's just compiling lists.'

'You know it isn't — you know someone has to keep tabs on whether women are really making any progress in the workforce. And money's one objective measure.'

'Dear Prue. Perhaps we should trade places. You can come and work for the lovely Brian in the School of Accounting and Business Management. What an extraordinary school for Contemporary Society to report to! You know what all the boys are doing? They've formed a little consultancy co-op to do management training, and they want you to hire them privately as Profiteering Partners or whatever instead of booking them through the college. Of course, they then expect to be able to use college premises rent free, and to spend their working hours researching these courses. They get the college secretaries to type this stuff. They use the college photocopiers!'

'The ultimate white collar crime.'

'Okay, okay, you're sending me up, and maybe I do get a bit righteous, but it's not right, is it?'

'All depends. Who does the courses, what they charge, how they advertise, that sort of thing.'

'Now you're talking about the business ethics side of it — yes, so what they're doing is probably within the law, grant you that. But the sort of things they do, Prue. Three-day special courses for business executives on Time Management. You and I might have thought time management meant keeping a diary and getting to appointments on time. No, not a bit of it. It's a whole consumer science. You need a special program on your computer. Your secretary (these guys all have secretaries) needs a special program on her computer. You need a special diary with lines on it that match the spreadsheets of your computer program. Never mind that it's just a glorified appointments book anyway. You need special stationery for writing down your tasks for the day and whether they're Priority A, Priority B, or only Priority C. Listen to this crap for three days and they'll give you a certificate. For a mere two hundred dollars or so, you can have a leather diary and a few pads of printed paper.'

'But if it works, Margot? Suppose it really makes people more efficient? Why knock it? I'd go to a course like that if the office was prepared to pay. Why not?'

'I'll tell you why not. Because of the things we don't do that we could do if we didn't go in for these gimmicky fashions. Because so many adults are still illiterate. Because we haven't scratched the surface of real inequality in jobs — girls still get squeezed out of the technological areas and go to work as hairdressers and typists. Because we're doing so little about women who get bashed and raped and children who are interfered with and scarred emotionally for the rest of their lives. Because there happen to be some real social issues out there that a school that calls itself Contemporary Society should care about. Synchron Mines don't give a shit about any of that, or even about women's careers. They're forced into this project by the legislation. And, quite frankly, I suspect it's cheaper for them to fund something through the college than to hire an equal opportunity officer themselves.'

'Yes, I can see you're upset.'

'Is this the listening technique they recommend for investigators where you work? It's like a bloody psychiatrist going "Uh huh, uh huh. Yes, I can see you're upset." Yes, I bloody well am upset.'

'Sorry, Margot. I'm just so tired, or something. Maybe I have abandoned the cause, compared to you. All those women's groups ten years ago, it seems another world to me now.' In the seventies there had been consciousness-raising groups, child care centre campaigns, support groups for alcoholics and women fleeing from violence. Most of the women who'd been active in those days had demanding jobs now, and few of them gave much time to radical causes. 'You think I've sold out, don't you?' Prue asked.

'I don't know, Prue. You do what you can. Just making a success of a job like yours is an achievement in itself, I suppose. But it's a far cry from ten or fifteen years ago, that's for sure. Oh, I'll do this project, why not? As you say, it'll have some good effects. It's just the prevailing attitude. Brian wants me to interview Roxane Rowe. Now it's not that I can't get an interview with Roxane Rowe, or that I haven't heard from my mother all these years how hard-working and amazing she is and all that. But it does get on your goat a bit that people are more interested in whether someone like Roxane wears silk shirts or polyester ones than in what's happening to scores of women like the ones in my women's class.'

'Margot, you know what the media's like. People are intrigued by personalities and bored by anything more abstract or serious.'

'That doesn't mean I have to like it. Can I get you a coffee or a white wine?'

'Actually, if you've got any lemon scented tea, I'd prefer that.'

'You're in luck. Christ, how middle-aged and health-conscious we're all getting.'

They lifted the jasmine fronds and went into the kitchen. Margot looked at Prue as the jug boiled. 'You're looking tired, Prue. Depressed. How long have you been feeling low like this?'

'Since Andrew left. I feel lonely at the oddest times. I haven't felt like having a really committed relationship with any of the men I've been out with. I feel sort of numb emotionally. Perhaps depression is the word.'

'And lemon tea helps?'

'I went to a lecture on stress management, and got very frightened at the amount of coffee I was drinking. Nine cups a day, I'd got up to.'

'Christ, I hope no one tells Brian. Stress management. He'd make it a companion course to time management.'

'Cut it out, Margot. You know and I know that people working in universities and colleges, you included, have more control over their work than anyone else does. You think I get the cases I want to investigate? You think anyone acts on my recommendations unless I get someone like Malcolm Gwynne to pull strings for me? You think these women you resent who earn thirty-five thousand dollars or sixty-five thousand dollars or whatever aren't just slogging along in the rat-race trying to survive like everyone else? With just as much integrity as the victims of social ills that your heart bleeds for? Give it a break.'

Margot poured boiling water onto the Twinings bag in the dark blue mug. 'Well,' she said, 'at least I've stirred you into something more definite than "Uh huh, uh huh" for a change. That's more the old Prue we all know and love.'

Prue smiled, inhaling the lemon-scented steam. 'Don't you dare tell me I'm beautiful when I'm angry,' she said. They carried their steaming mugs back into the garden. 'If you like, I could get this group I belong to, Women in Commerce, to distribute questionnaires for you. We'd have a lot of members in the target group.'

'That'd be terrific, thanks.' Margot picked her son's bicycle off the path and wheeled it under the awning of the back porch. 'I'll need all the help I can get. I'll ask Mum, too, for help lining up an interview with Roxane.'

'That'd be great,' Prue said.

Margot put her cup down. 'Great! I've had a gutful, frankly, of everyone telling me how great that woman is.'

'But she must have ability. Look how far she's got.'

'She goes on TV a lot with a good script. But what's so great about her?'

'What we were just talking about. She's made it in her career.'

'If you say so. But I can remember when she was just a teenager. She looked quite different. There was nothing special about her. She was just a jumped-up little office girl.'

'Your mother must have thought there was something special about her.'

'Yes. Bullseye. She always did. Roxane was only a year or two older than I was. When I was growing up, nothing I did was right or interesting, and bloody little Roxane Rowe was Olwyn's idea of the cat's pyjamas. The bee's knees.'

GETTING STARTED

Twenty years, she thought again. It was surprising how vividly she remembered her first job, a holiday job at Runaway Travel, which was then housed on the second floor of a building in York Street. A counter and two interview booths, with shoulder-high partitions, were located near the door. In the crowded, noisy space of the main office, the travel consultants sat at timber desks. Pin-ups of world cities and posters from Air India and Olympic Airways provided splashes of colour. A black telephone stood on each desk. At the back of the room was a pale blue door, slightly ajar. Olwyn Tierney missed very little of what went on in the outer office.

As a Girl Friday, Roxane made tea for Olwyn and the consultants, handled some of the more straightforward counter enquiries and bustled round town collecting tickets, delivering passports and banking cheques.

With her first pay, Roxane went to Curzon's and bought a black and tan suit with a blouson top and a pleated skirt. She looked slimmer in dark colours, she believed. Each day before she left for work she shaded her round cheeks with dark brown powder and drew heavy black lines from the inside corner of her eye to a point beyond the outer corner, flicking the end slightly upwards. She covered her eyelids with green eyeshadow and put white highlighter under her eyebrows. She had copied these make-up techniques from a magazine's serialised account of the career of an Australian model who won an overseas contest called Girl in a Million. Roxane wore black winkle-picker shoes and black-toned stockings, and a copper pendant embossed with a lyrebird dangled from the leather cord around her neck. The craze for making copper bracelets and pendants in art class at school had ousted art history, painting and pottery for weeks on end.

Roxane imagined that the image she presented to the world was of an artistic, sophisticated young woman with beatnik friends, a habituée of gallery openings and artists' parties at Kings Cross. Olwyn Tierney saw an overpainted schoolgirl who had not yet shed her puppy fat. But the face was interesting: good features which would be photogenic if she lost weight. Roxane had an alert expression that could mean intelligence. Olwyn tested her out with errands that required some initiative.

Roxane was fascinated by Olwyn Tierney. More precisely, the pale blue timber door which symbolised Olwyn's authority. Claire, Daniel, Nola and Richard, who sat in the outer office, made asides about Olwyn, which Roxane filed in her memory. 'Got you on the dinner party run, has she?' 'Doesn't take any freebies, our Ol, unless of course it's London or Paris.' 'We're in a fragile mood today — be warned.' 'In the Duchess of Windsor pearls again.'

Duchess of Windsor was not a bad description of Olwyn's style. She wore slim skirts, tailored jackets, pearls and gloves. Her hair was waved high over her forehead and brushed backwards.

Roxane listened to Nola on the telephone. 'No, Jim, it's at the Stadium. No, you'd have to be real bodgies and widgies to go in the bleachers. Yeah, I know, but it's worth it ...' and, as Olwyn opened her door, 'Are you travelling alone, Madam, or would the twin share rate be the one I should quote on?'

'I went ahead and ordered the express service on Dr and Mrs Musgrove's passports,' Roxane reported. 'If we use the routine service it'll be too late. Their tickets are for Tuesday next week. What do I do about the surcharge?'

'We'll bill them for it, but write a note for Howard so the account will be properly itemised and sent out in time. Why don't you take on our regular passport run?' Olwyn suggested. 'In fact, you can go through the applications and schedule them by departure dates to check no one else is cutting it so fine.'

'Thanks, Mrs Tierney.'

'And I wonder if you could ring the Turkish Consulate and ask if we can borrow their film on the Blue Mosque. I have to give a travelogue at the Club.'

'Yes, Mrs Tierney.'

'And could you be a sweetie and get me three tubs of mixed melon fruit salad on your way back from lunch. Really, I don't know why people tolerate my dinner parties.' Olwyn Tierney smiled, confident that her parties were not only tolerated but sought after.

'Of course, Mrs Tierney.'

'We'll miss you when you go back to school.'

Roxane had known this moment would come. 'I'm thinking of not going back.'

'Not going back? A bright girl like you leaving straight after the Intermediate? And from such a good school, too. I'm sure your parents won't hear of any such thing.'

'My parents will certainly say they wouldn't hear of it, but I'm sure I can persuade them.'

'But what will you do? You can't be an office girl all your life. Someone like you should be at university.'

'But I'm good as an office girl.'

'Good, yes, but it's not a job with prospects.'

'And I'm good on the counter. I could move up to a consultant if I had the chance to learn. That's what I want to do, make a career in travel.'

'How old are you exactly?'

'Sixteen in April. I'm easily old enough to leave school. One girl I know from the Church Fellowship left at fourteen to look after her brothers and sisters.'

'Please. Let's not get into a discussion on the school leaving age. We'll discuss all this properly next week.'

'What time next week?'

'Good Lord, you want an appointment. Let's make it four o'clock on Wednesday.'

'Thanks a million.'

Olwyn Tierney smiled. She knew already what would happen on Wednesday. Roxane would come armed with provisional approval from her parents. We'll give you a year's trial, they would say. She would ring the technical colleges and be told her educational background was good enough for a travel agents' course, if combined with the right work experience.

'You'd better have a folder with you, with all your achievements to date,' she said. 'And references, from the school or wherever. And I'll have someone from our parent company here too, so do you think you could tone down the make-up a bit? A little less eyeliner? Your colouring's so attractive anyway.'

'Yes, Mrs Tierney. I will, I will.'

'In the meantime, don't forget my melon salad.'

Roxane set about making up her folder of achievements with ardour. She got together her Intermediate Certificate, her honourable mention at a craft show, a reference from the Reverend Ewan McIntyre, a reference from the family she used to babysit for, and a photograph of herself in the junior basketball team. She photocopied a favourable school report — the most recent one had to be censored — and wrote a formal letter of application for a position as a travel consultant.

She read pamphlets and price-lists and studied temperature charts. The bulk of Runaway's work was air travel to Europe, though a few shipping lines still operated. Her friends from Rowe Street talked about 'the fare for the boat'. As soon as they had a few hundred pounds, she gathered, all the talented artists and writers would be sailing off to London. Or Athens, because the fare was cheaper. One young man's departure caused such anguish that his girlfriend leapt into the water at the overseas terminal, vowing to swim to London. She was fished out by a Maritime Services launch. Roxane calculated that if she left school now, she would have the fare for the boat before she was eighteen. Or if she got somewhere in the travel business, she could go overseas for free, or at least be subsidised.

Travel. She had a vision of a traveller from a film she'd once seen. An unsmiling woman in a hat sat gazing out a train window as the porter heaved her large leather suitcase into the rack overhead. She showed her profile to advantage under the hat, impassive, as the man nodded and waited for his tip. Outside the compartment, crowds of less photogenic people swirled on their insignificant way. In the woman's handbag were secret documents and passports in several names. A financial deal in Zurich hinged on her courage and her disguises. She tipped the porter with a pound note. Power, mystery, new destinations — Roxane knew what she wanted from life.

She had achieved many of her aims. She had been made a consultant in record time. She'd travelled, even if the reality did not match her Orient Express fantasies. Commercials had made her one of the best-known people in the industry. She was always being asked to resort openings and tourist promotions, as much for her celebrity status as for the fact she was in the business. It was a good decade for being a successful woman, or an apparently successful woman, in business. She was aware that she received some of her invitations as a token woman, but that did not prevent her taking advantage of them if she saw something to be gained for herself or the firm.

The hotel publicist had made sure that the hero of O'Connell Street and the heroine of the travel promotion commercials were seated alongside one another at the Sheraton Wentworth lunchtime economics seminar. Steven Szabo, property developer and takeover specialist, a trifle too paunchy and bald to be photogenic, but a man of vigour and presence all the same, and Roxane Rowe, golden haired and wearing white, smiled for a photographer from a Sunday paper. The smiles vanished as they turned back to their food.

'I never know whether to trust the lobster mousse, do you?' Roxane asked. She hadn't met Szabo before.

'In countries with tolerable refrigeration, I countenance no fears.' A large forkful was already on its way to Szabo's mouth. He had a protruding lower jaw.

'I hear you have an interesting development planned for Cloudy Bay,' Roxane said.

'Do I indeed? What do you hear, *Mzz* Rowe?' He made the word Ms sound like a swooping mosquito.

'Partnership with Singapore hotel interests. Speedy approval by local council. Condominiums pre-sold to United States buyers.'

'Jesus. Nothing's secret, is it? Where'd you hear all that?'

'Here and there. I read some of it in the trade papers.'

'Yes, well, resorts are all the go, aren't they? Isn't my old friend Boris up to something at Indigo Island? I hear Runaway's dotting resorts all over Bali and the Pacific.'

'Not quite all round.'

'But at Indigo, yes? No?'

'Here and there. You'd have to ask Boris.'

'It won't work, you know.'

'What won't?'

'Pumping me for information and holding out yourself.'

'Excuse me,' Roxane said, 'I was trying to make conversation, that's all. Frankly, I wonder if Barbary has the expertise for resort development. It's not the same as slapping up blocks of flats and shopping centres.'

'Is that a threat or an offer, young lady?'

'Take it any way you like. I'll risk the mousse, as it doesn't seem to have done you any harm.' Roxane began eating.

'When I was young, attractive young women at luncheons discussed parties and clothes and the races.'

'We're all here for a lecture on economics.'

'Yes, but that doesn't predetermine what we discuss beforehand.' Szabo turned to the man on his left, the head of an employers' organisation, and asked him if he would be seeking pre-selection at the next Federal election. Roxane could only half hear the reply. Men can talk politics, she thought, but women get ticked off for daring to talk shop, even at a business lunch. She glanced at Szabo's profile. His eyes, from this angle, were small and colourless. Front-on, through his black-rimmed glasses, they were greatly magnified.

Lobster mousse was succeeded by fillet steak and new potatoes. The lecturer, a partner in a stockbroking firm, was on his feet before the plates had been cleared. His projector beamed half-visible graphs onto a white screen. He was not particularly optimistic about the economy. Unemployment was rising and would probably go on doing so. Export figures were not good enough. Wheat and wool prices were not getting any better. Too few of Australia's exports resulted from high technology or manufacturing. Wage levels were uncompetitively high. There was not much hope of a Liberal government in Canberra. There was too much reliance on overseas borrowing. Australia was widely perceived as having too high a level of industrial disputation and strikes.

'Perceived, he says,' Szabo snorted, lighting a cigar.

'We've been a lazy lot,' the lecturer said. 'For the first hundred and fifty years we grew wool and the sheep did all the work. Then wheat and beef. For the past twenty years or so we've turned to ripping minerals out of the ground. When are we going to do something about our other resources? An educated workforce — where are our ideas? A land of beauty — where is our tourist development?'

At these words Roxane felt a sharp blow on her thigh. She swivelled a little to the right, out of range of Szabo's knee.

'It's not that we've got to work harder,' the lecturer

concluded, 'so much as we've got to work smarter.'

A burst of applause followed the speech. Szabo leant towards Roxane. 'That wasn't a sexual assault,' he said, 'I just wanted to make sure you were paying attention.'

'Really? I'm very much obliged.'

'My dear, the last thing on my mind is to get Boris Brookstein's little Goldilocks all indignant.'

'Then don't add insult to injury.'

'Do you know, you're quite quick.'

'You're welcome. It's a well-known saying in English.'

'Fantastic. Unbelievable. You're really steamed up.' He pronounced it *fentestic*. For an instant there was something touching about this big man with the cigar in his hand. He's working on this bluster, Roxane thought, he really is.

'You must allow me to make amends,' Szabo said. 'Another English saying, yes? No? I continuously put my foot in my mouth.'

'Continually, I think you'll find,' said Roxane. Goddam it, she thought, that's his game.

'I shall get in touch.' Standing up he was an awkward man, stocky, barrel-chested.

Roxane retreated to the powder room and saw that her cheeks were the colour of red cabbage in yoghurt. She rubbed her thigh and reapplied her make-up. What's the harm if he does get in touch? she reasoned. We'll be appearing together in the Sunday papers anyway.

HARBOUR GLIMPSES

It was two weeks before he telephoned. Then she found a note at work from her secretary Di. 'Please ring Stephen Sourbow.' Unusual for Di not to have checked the spelling — he must have rung off in a hurry.

Let him call again if he's interested, Roxane thought.

That night she reconsidered. Steven Szabo was rich and powerful, and as it happened there was no particular man in her life at the moment. Besides, she'd been reading about the trend towards overseas-financed resort developments on the coast. Dozens of projects had gone broke early in the 1980s. To succeed you had to emulate the Gold Coast developers and think big, it seemed. Runaway, concentrating on cut-price tickets for the mass market and small island hideaways for the top of the middle market, had not taken much interest in developing Australian resorts. Getting Australians to travel overseas was its chief expertise. The company had put very little effort into exploring the benefits of bringing American, Swedish and Japanese tourists here.

Roxane was ambitious. Her drive to the top was souring a little, though. She often lay half awake on humid nights — she had never got around to installing air-conditioning — dreaming of ways of capitalising on her fame from television commercials. She wanted a slice of the action. It was time to grab some goodies for herself. Land, shares, capital. She needed a coach in the secrets of getting rich. Maybe Steven Szabo would be willing to take on that role.

Had she been too loyal? She'd served Runaway since she was a schoolgirl. To the ticket-buying public, she *was* Runaway. Her name and face had helped Boris Brookstein's company soar to undisputed leadership in the package tour business. And what had she got out of it herself, apart from notoriety and a fairly high salary? Concession travel, precisely the same perk that had been hers since the age of sixteen. Twenty years of airports and suitcases had taken the shine off that. A man in her position would be a partner by now; if not a partner, a board member or a major shareholder. It was not even inevitable that she would succeed Olwyn Tierney as the sole woman on the Brooklands board. Boris might be lining up some moustachioed chartered accountant with a Bachelor of Commerce and a black vinyl briefcase in his hairy fist.

She'd been reading the trade figures recently. She knew which companies were investing in holiday resorts in Queensland, Victoria, New South Wales and the outlying islands. A number of them would go broke, of course, or fail to raise the money and remain paper projects. Some would run foul of environmental legislation. But many people were going to get rich, very rich, from the ones that succeeded. Steven might even cut her into one of his ventures if he trusted her. Assuming they knew each other better, of course. Phrases from self-help books and the financial pages tossed in Roxane's mind like a salad. She gleamed with oil and vinegar. She would telephone him in the morning.

Szabo suggested lunch. 'My car will call for you,' he told Roxane. 'Be outside your building at 12.25 precisely.'

On the dot, a chauffeured white Mercedes drew up. Szabo alighted from the back seat, held the door open for Roxane, then walked round to the far side of the car and got in himself. 'I've taken the liberty of ordering a little picnic,' he said. 'I thought it might be a good day for Mrs Macquarie's Chair.'

'Wonderful,' Roxane said, although she had put on her white raw silk suit in order to impress other diners in a restaurant.

'Art Gallery Road, Dean,' Szabo said.

They drove to the end of the point and parked. A tablecloth and basket, an Esky, two large cushions and an ice bucket were produced from the boot. Szabo supervised the chauffeur as he set the gear and the food up in the shade of a Moreton Bay fig.

'What time do you have to be back?' he asked Roxane. 'Two.'

'Come back for us at ten to two, would you, Dean?'

'Very good, sir.'

'See what you can find to eat.' Szabo gestured towards the picnic basket. Roxane lifted the linen towels and discovered bread rolls, pâté, smoked salmon, three types of salad, soft cheeses and black grapes. Szabo opened a bottle of Chardonnay.

'Well, this is a surprise,' Roxane said.

'I like to do the unexpected, if it's possible. We can eat in restaurants if you prefer. Or we can organise something quieter still. But first, can you satisfy my curiosity? Your name. I notice you say Rox*ahn* rather than Rox*anne*. Why is that?'

'My parents pronounced it that way. And when I went to elocution lessons with Mirabel Blain, she absolutely insisted I stick to the French pronunciation always.'

'Elocution classes?'

'Yes. I was a private pupil of Miss Blain's, but she came to our school as well. She wore long gloves and a black cartwheel hat, I've never forgotten.'

'The rain in Spain stays mainly?' Szabo suggested.

'My dame has a lame tame crane,' Roxane said. 'And "The lowing herd winds slowly o'er the lea". You had to put your tongue under your teeth to get a special kind of "l" sound.' She demonstrated.

'Fentestic.'

'She was an actress. We were always being told how lucky we were to be taught by someone like Miss Blain who had shared the stage with Sir Ralph Richardson. Carol McCathie said she played Lois Lane in the episode where Superman was imprisoned under the slowly lowered ceiling.'

'Superman imprisoned? Why didn't he fly away?'

'He couldn't. The kryptonite robbed him of his strength of steel.'

'So this Lois Lane taught you to speak like ladies.'

'Yes. We used to call her Miss Bline, just to set her off. "That dreadful Australian accent. You'll be so ashamed when you go to England. You won't be invited to the best debutante balls or presented to the Queen. Some of my ex-pupils have had proposals from Lords or Earls. One old girl of the school is now Lady Astongarden. I need hardly tell you, she was always extremely well-spoken."'

Szabo laughed. He spread Grand Marnier pâté on pumpernickel and poured more wine. 'A picnic is a pleasant change, no?'

'Yes.'

'Tell me more about yourself. You're not married?'

'No. I have been, of course. I have a daughter who's a weekly boarder at Carinya in the southern highlands.'

'You don't live with a lover?'

'I'm away so much, what would I do with a live-in lover?'

'No need to be angry. Perhaps you resent it when I question you too much. What do you wish to know about me?'

'You're married?'

'Yes. I am fortunate in having an excellent marriage.'

'You've been married a long time?'

'Since before you were born, I imagine. Thirty-six years.'

'That's amazing.'

'Yes, it is becoming rarer to succeed with a long marriage, no? But Anna is a remarkable woman. And we grant each other a good deal of privacy, what is very important in close relationships.'

Roxane stared at the greenish waves lapping round the stone walls of Fort Denison. She was quite sure he was about to make a pass at her.

'You think I'm about to make a pass at you.'

'I thought it was on the cards.'

'My dear. That is not my way. I am waiting to hear from you that you wish to have an affair with me.'

He'd known she would return his call. He was equally confident that she would take her cue now. Perhaps there was shyness mixed with his arrogance — he was a plain man, no longer young, who'd put on a navy beret to shield his balding head from the sun — or perhaps he wanted to avoid the indignity of being refused. Again, perhaps it was another way of exercising power.

Roxane laughed. 'Of course I would, Steven,' she said. They got out their diaries, two hard-pressed business people trying to arrange a meeting. At length they found a date which did not conflict with interstate meetings, overseas inspections, Cindy's weekends or Anna's social calendar. They were not going to be spending a great deal of time together.

'It's quality what counts, not quantity,' Szabo decreed.

When Roxane had rationalised the prospect of an affair with Steven Szabo by imagining she could ask him for some financial advice, she hadn't reckoned on the way they'd make each other laugh, the tender, silent pleasure they would take in each other's nakedness, and his skill at getting her to reminisce. Lying beside him on the ludicrous violet satin sheet, she found herself dredging up childhood memories and old secrets. He was less forthcoming. She discovered he had lived with his grandmother in Budapest, had his education disrupted by the war, and during those lawless years learnt some unorthodox ways of earning the next meal or the next forged document. This outline was not accompanied by the detail or vivid scenes that characterised

40

Roxane's memories.

'Where does your office think you are now?' Szabo asked.

'I'm supposedly at home writing an article for a travel magazine on how I pack for different climates.'

'Shouldn't take you long. Warm for winter, light for summer.'

'Good heavens, that kind of simplification will never do. You don't know the fashion industry. No, it's more like "Travel expert Roxane Rowe shares her secrets of successful packing with our readers. Winter or summer, Roxane never takes more than one suitcase on her frequent overseas trips. The secret? Discipline, she says."

' " 'Once I was frightfully bad at this and took half the contents of my wardrobe,' " Roxane says. Opening the doors of her walk-in closet in her Rushcutters Bay apartment, Roxane explains that her clothes are all colour coded by season." '

'I'm right. It's not going to take you long to do. You can recite already everything what you are going to say. But you do have lovely clothes. They are important to you, no?'

'Yes. Well, no. There's only been one dress that was really important to me. It was fawn pinwale corduroy, with puffed sleeves and a brown velvet edging.'

'You were a little girl, yes?'

'Nine or so.'

'Tell me about this dress.'

'I was always a bit on the outer at primary school,' Roxane said. 'I had a working mother, and we lived with my grandmother and my cousins and my terrible aunt. And some of the girls at school were terribly rich. I was always being teased about my parents, my cousins, all sorts of things.'

'My mother doesn't work, because my mother doesn't want me to be a juvenile delinquent,' Christine Barrington sang, with the rhythm of a skipping rhyme.

'My mother doesn't work, because when I was adopted as a special chosen baby she said she would dedicate her life to me,' Josephine Buchanan said.

'My mother says mothers should be there after school when their children get home, otherwise they shouldn't have children,' Christine said.

'My mother says that, too. But she'd probably think it's all right if it's your grandmother,' Josephine said. 'Your grandmother minds you after school, doesn't she, Rox?'

'Yes. Me and my cousins.'

'What are your cousins called?'

'Barry and Roger.'

Christine and Josephine went into fits of giggling. 'Barry and Roger,' they gasped, 'Barry and Roger.'

'I don't see what's so funny about that.'

'It's not so funny ha-ha,' said Josephine, 'it's more funny peculiar.'

'My mother' (Roxane strove to imbue these words with authority) 'says that if you don't have brothers and sisters you're very lucky to be brought up with cousins. And my grandmother says it's not worth baking pastry for one, but for three, it makes sense.'

'Golly. Do you actually mean she cooks stuff for you specially after school?'

'Usually, yes.'

'My mother goes to the cake shop sometimes. But not often. Sugar's bad for the teeth,' Christine said.

'Anyway,' Roxane returned to the defence, 'my mother only works part-time.'

'What's that mean?'

'She's a part-time legal secretary — she works from ten till four so she's home fairly early.'

'What's she have to work for, if your father's an accountant?'

'Accountants aren't all rich. And they're saving up, to move out of Granny's place when the housing shortage is over.'

'My father knew some people who paid five hundred pounds key money for a flat,' Josephine said. 'But don't worry, it mightn't stay as bad as that for long.'

'I don't believe your father's an accountant at all. I think he's some ordinary old clerk in the public service,' Christine said.

'He is an accountant. He is too. He's an accounts clerk in the Lands Department.'

'Why do you say he's an accountant then?'

'Same difference.'

'Not if you really know about accountancy, it isn't,' Christine said.

'Well my father ought to know what his own job is, if you don't mind,' Roxane said.

'Does he have his own practice? Does he do tax returns? Does he have people working for him? Does he belong to Rotary? Well, then!' Christine rested her case.

'My father says he wouldn't join Rotary if you paid him,' Josephine said.

'This milk is so disgusting,' Roxane said. Every playtime they had to drink half a pint of government-supplied milk from a glass bottle. The bottles were always stored on the sunny side of the corridor, so that the cream rose to the top and the lukewarm milk smelt greasy.

'Some people really need the calcium, my mother says. Like if they were born in Europe just after the war, like Marianna Markiewicz.'

'Yeah, but Christine, we haven't all got rickets or something like Marianna Markiewicz. We shouldn't have to drink it,' Roxane said.

'I just decided something,' Josephine said. 'You're both going to be asked to my party.'

'You going to ask Barry and Roger?' Christine asked, giggling.

'Don't be silly. Only girls are coming. Daddy says we can have a magician.'

'Super.'

The invitations to Josephine's party were printed and arrived in the post. Ordinary party invitations were handed round at school, but this was to be no ordinary party.

'I'll need a party dress,' Roxane told her mother.

'You've got a party dress. Your tartan dress.'

'It's too short. Besides, it's not a real party dress. Gillian has one with ruffles and a satin sash.' Other people had lemon and pink creations with organza and lace and nylon net petticoats.

'We'll see. You don't want something tizzy and horrible like that really.' Thea had plain, conservative tastes: she wore tartan or tweed skirts with a twinset and a silk scarf.

'No, but I need something pretty. I bet Granny doesn't think that tartan dress is a party dress.'

'And don't go wheedling and whining to your grandmother behind my back.'

'Can't a person talk to their own grandmother around here without getting into trouble?'

'Roxane, you're preposterous.'

The need for a dress overrode any scruples of her mother's. She asked her grandmother's advice one afternoon before Thea got home. Barry and Roger had grabbed their slices of fruit tart and gone out to ride bicycles. Roxane did not have a bicycle: the roads were considered too dangerous for girls. 'Granny,' she said, 'I really truly do need a party dress for Josephine Buchanan's party — truly-ruly-really.'

'Josephine Buchanan is a very spoilt child,' her grandmother said. 'When she was tiny, her mother had a velvet cloak edged with ermine for her. It was one of the most vulgar things I ever heard of.'

'Do you mean common?'

'Only the common say common. It was a terrible display of wealth. But I suppose the child was lucky to be adopted into a rich family like that. And an only child. Why is the party at Chiswick Gardens, when they have that lovely house at Double Bay?'

'They're hiring a magician.'

'Roxane, just this once I might get you an early Christmas present.'

44

'Gee, Granny, that'd be beaut.' Christmas was not for months. Roxane was jubilant: she would be spared the jibes of Christine Barrington.

The party dress was in a David Jones' cardboard box, wrapped in tissue. It was fawn pinwale corduroy, tiered, with puffed sleeves, trimmed with brown velvet ribbon. Roxane paraded through the house, pirouetting for her cousins and grandmother. 'Girls are stupid, the things they make a fuss of — clothes and all that, and perfume,' Barry said.

'And silly things to put in their hair,' Roger said.

Roxane was relieved that Auntie Pammie, the boys' mother, was not home to make some crack about how Roxane was their grandmother's favourite. It was fortunate, too, that no one at school knew that Auntie Pammie worked as a receptionist at a Bondi hotel.

'It's perfectly lovely, Roxane,' their grandmother said. Even Thea said so, later, although she could not help herself saying the tartan dress would have done just as well.

One Friday night Alan Rowe took Thea and Roxane for a drive to Bondi. The seas were high, and they walked along the Promenade watching giant breakers curl and crash on the sands. Near the horizon the water was silver, against salmon-coloured clouds. 'There's too much jealousy in that house,' he said. 'I wanted to tell you two alone before I tell Mother. I'm all set to get that promotion, and I've made enquiries about a flat. I expect we'll be moving into a place in Plumer Road at the end of the month.'

'What about key money?' Roxane asked.

'Yes, I expect there'll be key money, but we've been saving up for it. We make sacrifices, you know, Roxane, for your school fees and your elocution lessons. We could have moved a lot sooner otherwise.'

'Yes I know.' Sacrifices by parents were a great theme at school assemblies. Roxane always thought of sacrifices as having something to do with giving up smoking, but on this occasion making do with old tartan dresses seemed nearer the mark.

Thea kissed Alan on the cheek and put an arm through his. 'It's wonderful, darling — our own kitchen! An end to those inedible charred chops! I can't believe it.'

'Yes, back to the meat that walks off the plate. Roxane will miss Mother's cooking, though, won't you?'

'She makes super pastries.'

'You see,' Alan said to his wife, 'she makes super pastries. And Roxane will have her own room, not just a little sleep-out like she's got now.'

'No queueing for the bathroom,' Thea said.

'Not until this young lady's a teenager, at any rate.'

Roxane watched a group of seagulls circle above the shoreline, then swoop down to scavenge, squawking and jabbering between pecks. She would be glad to get away from Barry and Roger, with their funny-peculiar names and their never-ending wisecracks. She would be an elegant person with her own room and a cupboard full of velveteen dresses and a proper desk for her homework, and no Auntie Pammie to resent her good fortune. She took off her shoes and socks and ran across the pale sand down to the water's edge. Cold, salty water snapped at her ankles and she hopped up and down in a sudden outbreak of happiness.

At Chiswick Gardens they had to show their invitations at the gate. A line of girls said good afternoon to Josephine's parents then handed their wrapped presents to Josephine, who put everything aside to be opened when they were all sitting in a circle after tea. 'What a charming dress, Roxane, how do you do?' Mrs Buchanan said. Miss Blain would not have approved of her vowels. Roxane quickly checked Josephine's outfit: no ermine this time, she was in floral silk with a purple background.

'Josephine's is very nice, too,' she said as she handed over the parcel.

'You shouldn't have — thanks a million,' Josephine said, as if getting presents was a genuine surprise.

The magician had set up his stage in a curtained booth like a Punch and Judy show.

'That's cheating,' said Carol McCathie. 'He can put things up his sleeves under the curtains.'

'Shh,' Roxane said, 'you know it's only tricks anyway.'

'It's not trickery,' Christine Barrington told them, 'only amateur magicians do tricks. This man is a professional.'

'There are professional tricks, then,' Roxane said. The lights were dimmed and suddenly the room was dark. A spotlight focused on the whitened face of the magician in his booth.

'I'm Bonzo,' he said. 'I can't help being called Bonzo, it's all my parents' fault. You'd all make me feel much better if you'd all call out to me, "Hullo Bonzo".'

'Hullo, Bonzo,' twenty voices chorused.

'Hullo, boys and girls — oh no, correction, hullo ladies and gentlemen and young ladies. I don't suppose we like boys, do we? Do we hate boys? Let's hear it — love or hate?'

'Hate! hate! hate!'

'Nobody loves boys. Boo hoo. I'm very sad about that. I'm just a boy at heart. But right now I need a volunteer — would there be a little girl here called Josephine?'

'Some coincidence,' Carol McCathie said. 'He just happens to pick Josephine.'

'Well,' said Roxane, 'her parents are paying.'

'Her parents are loaded.'

Bonzo made a red scarf held by Josephine pass through her skull and emerge on the other side of her head. He made the scarf turn blue behind her back. He asked her to pick a card and whatever card she chose and however much she shuffled the cards, he named the right one.

'This guy's not bad,' Gillian said.

Josephine sat down. Bonzo juggled; he produced a rabbit from a hat; he found a white dove in Mrs Buchanan's shopping bag; he broke tough metallic rings with a light touch.

'How's he do it?'

'He must be cheating somehow, but you'd never know it.'

'One final volunteer.' Roxane and Carol put up their

hands.

'The little girl in the pretty puffed sleeves.' Roxane went forward and held a hoop while Bonzo did a complicated juggling routine with some of the balls going through the hoop and others over the top. At the end of the act, the lights came on and everyone applauded enthusiastically. To get back to her seat, Roxane had to pass Christine Barrington.

'Wonders will never cease,' said Christine. 'Look what she's got on her feet. Black shoes and grey socks. She's got school shoes and socks on. At a party. Look — Roxane hasn't got party shoes — she's got school shoes and socks on.'

The whisper went round the room before they reached the tea table. Looking down, Roxane saw black patent shoes and lacy socks on nineteen pairs of feet. Later, when they had stuffed themselves with cream puffs and trifle and birthday cake and were sitting in a circle to watch Josephine open her parcels, Roxane did her best to squat in a yoga pose that obscured her offending shoes and socks. One day she would be somebody, really be somebody, with shoes and stockings and racks of velvet dresses, while Christine ...? She consoled herself by thinking up ignominious fates for Christine.

'What did become of Christine?' Szabo asked.

Roxane laughed. 'She married an alcoholic grazier, I'm told.'

'You want to be careful, my sweet. It can be more dangerous than what you think to make such fates come true. I must be off. Let yourself out, not to hurry.' He kissed the back of her neck and left the room.

It was the first time she had been left alone in the flat. Szabo had several properties: this one, on the fourth floor of an old building in Billyard Avenue, Elizabeth Bay, overlooked the mansion Boomerang. Roxane stretched, naked between satin sheets. Who the hell decorated this place, she wondered. Surely not his wife. She'd heard of European sophistication, but that would be going too far. Still, would a decorator have chosen this? Grey carpet, grey walls, purple and indigo curtains, sheets and cushions. Pinky-grey Mucha prints. Copies of overseas magazines on glass tables. The style was midway between dentists' waiting room and high class bordello. Not that it mattered much, Roxane thought. When the French windows were open, the harbour view dominated everything. When they were closed, she and Szabo were apt to be in bed, and purple was as good a backdrop as any.

Roxane expanded on the waiting room image. Women sat tensely, reading magazines, looking up as an elderly patient, jaw too numb for much speech, left the surgery. The dentist stood behind her, in his white jacket and rimless glasses, grinning with the inane equanimity of his profession. One by one his clients would have tête-à-têtes with this man behind the closed door, their encounters with his disquieting equipment punctuated by the high-pitched castrato of a drill, the sound of migraine headaches.

Was it like that? A succession of women coming here and leaving, no clues left behind them? Everything rinsed away with the peppermint mouthwash? There were no old tubes of make-up in the bathroom cupboard, no satin dressing-gowns on hooks, no half-used bottles of conditioner on the rail over the shower recess. Roxane herself sensed an unwritten rule, and, although she was the kind of woman seen with a drycleaned suit hanging in her Toyota Celica, she resisted the temptation to leave clothes or other belongings here.

She pushed back the satin sheets and, a little unsteadily, walked barefoot to the kitchen. She made a cup of instant coffee and spread some cream cheese on Vita Weats. Her mind seemed to be working in slow motion. It was one of the effects Steven's lovemaking had on her. She needed a good blast of caffeine and a shower to restore her control over her mind and body. Raging hormones, she thought. It was another catchphrase from a television argument about menstruation and absenteeism.

Years earlier, Roxane had debated women's role in the

workforce on the 'Mike Walsh Show'. Her opponent was a management consultant. Bra-burners was what that young man called feminists.

'I never thought I'd hear bra-burning from a management consultant,' Roxane countered, making his profession sound like typhoid carrier.

'What about the ah—menstrual—situation? Ah—hormonal changes?' the young man asked. That day he wore a grey flannel suit and a dark red silk tie. In the years since then he had become a spokesman for the Chamber of Manufacturers.

Roxane did not let her lack of statistics get in the way of a good retort.

'I've never missed a day's work for that reason,' she said, 'and nor have any of the women I know.' Her eyes swept over the studio audience and her millions of sisters in television land. If any of them were at home lolling on sofas with hot-water bottles on their stomachs and packets of Panadol at their elbows, Roxane didn't want to know.

'I have figures that suggest there is a problem,' her opponent was starting to protest. But Roxane cut in: 'You can do anything with statistics, but women won't be kept down by myths and marginalised by male authority any longer.'

They were being wound up.

Mike Walsh brought the item to a close, thanking them both. 'You're lovely,' he said to Roxane before she and her opponent were hustled away by a production assistant.

'That was naughty of you,' the young man said, 'having a go at management consultants like that.'

'What about you?' said Roxane. 'Burning bras!'

Roxane shook her head at the memory. There was nothing worse than a totally self-satisfied twenty-six-year-old male, she decided. She really did prefer older men, as she kept assuring Szabo. He was her senior by twenty-one years. She wondered how old his wife was.

COASTAL DEVELOPMENTS

Prue had approval from Ken Reynolds, the Commissioner for Business Ethics, to spend up to six days in Cloudy Bay investigating the complaints on File 3995. She drove to Cloudy Bay in the office's white Ford Laser. Once past Asquith she enjoyed the coast road, listening to the radio as she drove. When she could no longer get 2GB she settled for local stations that played country and western, a type of music she avoided but could tolerate on the open road. She sang along with Glen Campbell, Dolly Parton, John Denver and Slim Dusty:

> *I love to have a beer with Duncan,*
> *I love to have a beer with Dunc,*
> *We drink at the Town and Country*
> *And I never ever ever get rolling drunk ...*

Prue stopped at a small town and bought a vanilla milkshake. She changed into jeans and sandals in the ladies' room of a Shell garage. The air was decidedly warmer, despite the fact she had only been driving for two or three hours.

Cloudy Bay was crescent-shaped. The beach, a long new

moon of cream sand, faced due east. Cleared hillsides encircled the bay. Developers were buying up dairy farms. Inland, the ranges jutted up with brown boulder cliffs and, almost hidden behind the bends of the road, pockets of sub-tropical luxuriance. The steep platform of high land trapped clouds on the eastern side of the hills: hence the name of the beach. It was muggy.

Prue left her baggage at a motel and drove down to the beachfront, where she checked out the real estate agents' windows. Holiday flats were available for December and January at $300 a week or more. The awning was inscribed HUGHES & BLACKMORE. Good. She needed to speak to Mr Hughes. He'd been most evasive on the phone. The only staff member visible from the street was a receptionist with grey hair. Prue did not want to meet Melvin Hughes yet. She would go and see Mirabeau Acres for herself.

The route was signposted by red and white billboards which announced:

BARBARY DEVELOPMENTS PRESENTS
MIRABEAU ACRES
CLOUDY BAY'S EXCLUSIVE RESORT
RESERVE YOUR SHARE IN IT NOW!

Arrows pointed up a treeless hillside on the north-western side of the beach. The road got suddenly steeper. The Laser's engine seemed to be protesting. Prue put the car into low gear. She looked back towards the beach: from this vantage point its symmetry was beautiful.

She followed the red signs until she reached a big signpost, MIRABEAU ACRES. A handful of tawdry new buildings could be seen on a scar of cleared land. She drove over the cattle grid — there was no gate — past four new tennis courts and a rectangular hole in the ground, intended for a swimming pool no doubt. Behind the tennis courts was a building that resembled half a motel: the reception/office/family home end. Three white cabins of fibro, half-timbered in a mock-Elizabethan style, lay beyond the semi-motel. A yellow station wagon stood outside the main building.

The main door was opened by a young woman in a pink jumpsuit. Prue claimed to be interested in buying a share in the resort. 'Is Mr Hughes in?' she asked.

'Mr Hughes is in America.'

'Surely not.'

'Why? Did y'make an appointment with him or somethink?'

'Not exactly. I discussed the resort with him on the phone a couple of weeks ago and he was most insistent I should come up and see it for myself. I suppose you could show me round though, couldn't you?'

'Don't see why not.'

'Fine.'

The young woman hesitated, then went and got a bunch of keys from the inner office.

'Funny, but.'

'What's funny?'

'Him telling you to come and see the place. They're not real keen on new buyers coming out till the finance hassles are over and it's gone a bit further.'

'Really?'

'Yup. You're the first person here in ages. We used to advertise, see, on the radio in Sydney.'

'I know.'

'And television, too, last summer. But since August or so it's been real quiet.'

They were walking to the first of the three white huts. The interior was bare, airless and hot: a small bedroom, an adjoining toilet and shower; a recess with power points and an electric jug.

'All mod cons.'

'So I see.' Prue slid one of the aluminium windows open, but the air inside the hut remained hot and stale.

'When will the other fifty-seven cabins be built?' she asked.

'Like I said, when the finance is ironed out.'

'The development's in trouble financially, then?'

'No. I never said that. Mr Hughes always says, "Just look at that view — how can anything built here go wrong?"'

Prue looked towards Cloudy Bay, a glittering sapphire curve on the edge of the ocean. 'It's beautiful, yes, but from the brochure I was expecting that more of the site would have been developed.'

'It will be, sure. Just like the brochure. Sixty cabins, two swimming pools, squash, nine holes of golf, a clubhouse, horse-riding, exercise classes, health consultants. Everythink.'

'And if I want to put a deposit on a share after I've looked around?'

'I don't known that you can, like, till Mr Hughes gets back.'

'That's a pity. Are the other cabins just like this one?'

'Decor's different.' The girl led Prue through the other two cabins, identical apart from the patterns on the wallpaper: one English cottage-style, the other a riot of tropical fruit.

'And the stables?' she could not resist asking. 'The sauna and gym?'

'Look, you want to ask a lot of questions, you'd better wait till Mr Hughes gets back.'

'You're expecting him soon?'

'Two or three weeks, maybe.'

'I mightn't be here then.'

They were back in the office. Under a perspex cover was a model of Mirabeau Acres, complete with blue ponds representing artificial lakes, and a sprinkling of plastic horses. The trees, incongruously, were miniature firs and beeches.

'What's your name, anyway, if I want to get in touch?' Prue asked.

'Debbie. Debbie Hewson. Mr Hughes got your name already, has he?'

'Yes, he does. It's Munro.' Instantly Prue regretted lying. She did not do it well.

'Funny, he never mentioned you.' The first note of

suspicion in Debbie's manner.

'Well, I suppose you have so many would-be buyers.'

'Right. We do.' Debbie sat down again behind her typewriter.

'Thanks for showing me around.' Prue pushed the fronds of plastic screen aside as she went out the door.

At 2.15 Prue went to the Cloudy Bay Shire Council, showed her identification, and demanded to see the Mirabeau Acres file. The town clerk left her sitting in a vestibule for more than fifteen minutes. Prue opened a folder to check a timeline she had been developing of the different stages of the operation: the registration of the business name and the appointment of directors; the radio commercials in Sydney; the colour brochures; the charter flights for prospective buyers; the transfer of the land titles. She needed more information about the planning process. How had the property been rezoned from rural to commercial? How had Hughes and Szabo managed to secure approval in principle for the project before submitting formal plans? What did they plan to do about transport? The town had no airport.

When the town clerk returned, he was holding a number of documents, mostly folded maps and charts. A young, acne-scarred man of about twenty followed him. 'This is Adrian,' the town clerk said. 'He'll keep an eye on things while you look through the material. There's photographs in this envelope, as well as the diagrams. Well, I'll leave you to get on with it.' Adrian looked as if he had never had to supervise a visiting investigator before. Prue inspected the photographs, but they proved to be of the model of the resort development which she had already seen.

Prue found the region's tourism consultant in a small shopfront office in a shopping centre. Ian Forbes was a middle rank public servant who had been drawn by the climate and pace of the north coast.

'It's been a blow, the collapse of this Cloudy Bay venture,' he said. 'Whatever way you look at it, environmentally, socially, any other way, time-share's got a lot going for it.'

'Such as?'

'Well, it doesn't do too much damage to the environment, does it? It literally shares out resources so a couple of hundred families can get the benefit of a place instead of a couple of dozen. It doesn't pollute the air like manufacturing and scare off other tourist developments. It doesn't depend on variations in the market or the weather like crops do. We've got enough people growing bananas already, anyhow. And it provides local jobs—attracts people who'll spend money in the town.'

'So the council would be on side.'

'Not just the council,' Forbes said. 'The locals, too. They like the sort of tourist we get in Coffs, say, the family type, well off enough to rent a flat for a few weeks. No one's keen on overdevelopment, the Surfer's sort of thing. Pinball parlours and fried food all along the beachfront. Prostitution. Young lairs getting drunk and roaring round in hotted up cars. Gambling.'

'Has a casino ever been seriously considered?'

'That wouldn't be a local decision anyway. Sydney's the place to ask that question.'

'Yes, of course. How about Japanese money?'

'There's a big Japanese investment further north. Luxury hotel, that sort of thing. Not such a proposition in Cloudy Bay because of the hills. They need their own airport. Besides there's been a few snags. It's coming on very slowly. It's a case of wait and see how that gets on before anyone else tries the same thing.'

'So what are the options for the site, just as land?'

'Dairy farming. Not so good for bananas, though that's possible. Some of the new crops. Macadamia. Or tourism.'

'Caravan sites?'

'The council wouldn't be too keen on more caravan parks. They don't bring in the same class of visitor. It's more your sausages, bread and tomato sauce crowd. And they don't want the alternative lifestyle crowd either, though there's one of them on the council.'

'And time-share's more your prawns and champagne crowd?'

'That's the theory. Look, Prue, I can lend you the reports. Surveys of resident attitudes, that sort of thing. But be careful when you write up this misadventure that you don't knock the whole time-share concept. You'd be going right against government policy, and you wouldn't do the Commission any good either.'

'Meaning?'

'Meaning there's quite a few people about, and our Minister would be one of them, who feel that the Commission oversteps the mark and goes for the jugular all the time, just for its own sake.'

'For the sake of business ethics.'

'Or for personal publicity for the Commissioner. Look, don't quote me on this. None of our records is secret, we've got nothing to hide in this, but just keep a steady course, that's all.'

'If it's okay with you, Ian, I've come here for information on tourism, not for advice on how to conduct an investigation.'

'Okay. Quite right.'

'Was there ever any question of a subsidy or a grant to the Cloudy Bay syndicate?'

'Not as such, no.'

'What do you mean, *as such*?'

'No development subsidy as such was ever offered. But we did give them a sort of endorsement as to the general policy directions for the area.'

'Can I see the letters? Would you have written to the council?'

'Yes, you can, and yes, we did.'

'Why didn't you say so before, instead of just saying I could see the general policies?'

'You didn't ask, did you?'

'You mentioned there's an alternative lifestyle type on the

council?'

'Yes, Peter Potts. You won't get much out of him though.'

'I can try.'

'By all means.'

Prue went back to her motel to check through her case notes and write up what she had done so far. She wanted a shower too.

Standing under the warm water, she thought of Ian Forbes' warning about how the Commission should approach the case. Every time she had been on a major investigation, someone had told her that the Commission's reputation relied on doing things sensibly, or rationally, or with an eye to normal business practice. This was usually code for Get lost, you're making us uncomfortable. What had Malcolm Gwynne always said? 'Total enthusiasm for your investigation can mean only two things: the person who laid the complaint had all the necessary information in the first place, or someone has succeeded in sending you off on a false trail. My antennae always work overtime when I hear the phrases "total cooperation" and "nothing to hide" occurring together more than once in one conversation. Usually it's a sign the speaker wants to keep you rummaging through reams of stuff that has nothing to do with the case, while the tape or the letter or the share certificate you really need is being destroyed, or the witness you really needed is flying to South America. And people who tell you the Commission's reputation will suffer if you make an issue of something — they're worried about reputation all right, but not the Commission's.'

Malcolm Gwynne had been an Assistant Commissioner when Prue first went to work at the Commission for Business Ethics, seven years earlier, as a research assistant. With his encouragement she completed her business degree part-time at the Institute, and went to seminars run by the Society of Accountants as well. He saw to it that when she moved into investigation work, she was rotated through several sections

58

to widen her experience. Often he asked her to write case summaries for reports or staff meetings. 'Keep it short,' he would say, 'it is a myth that tedious detail is less prone to libel. Besides, we have limited privilege.'

Gossip throve at the Commission, but the fact that Gwynne had other protégés as well, male and female, saved Prue from being the target of too much backbiting. Florid, overweight, and some thirty years older than Prue, Gwynne had a voice like an actor and was admitted to the Bar. When Prue asked his advice about whether she should study law also, he boomed, 'But Prue — you can do sums. I never could. Law is for the innumerate. Stick to finance.'

Occasionally Prue and others from the office were invited to a party at the Gwynnes' place at Drummoyne. They had the downstairs flat in an old waterfront duplex, with a boatshed at the bottom of the garden and a view of the city skyline. They entertained in the garden at twilight. Sarah Gwynne had long hair drawn back into a wispy chignon, and wore long batik dresses draped with wooden beads. It was what Prue's mother would have called the Handcrafts of Asia look, but Prue thought it quite becoming for an older woman. She handed Prue a Pimm's—'Old-fashioned but thirst quenching, don't you think?' Prue had never tasted the drink before; it reminded her of the claret cup served at teenage dances. She blushed for her fifteen-year-old self, in a blue velveteen dance frock with a satin sash.

'You're Malcolm's brilliant young trainee investigator — he thinks so highly of you,' Sarah Gwynne said.

'Oh no,' Prue said. 'Brilliant is not a word anyone would ever use about me.'

'My dear, that sort of talk is so unwarranted. Accept your talents for what they are.'

'Be more assertive, you mean?'

'Not a term I'd have chosen. No. But I do remember that when we were girls, at exam time everyone used to say "I'm sure I'll fail. I'll have nightmares till the results come out. I couldn't possibly pass. I'm too stupid for Chinese or

Chemistry," all this nonsense — it was a kind of flirting really.'

'I wasn't flirting.'

'No, of course, you were being modest. But do beware of false modesty. It was a great joy to me to have sons who airily wonder if they'll get a credit or a distinction, instead of all the rubbish we went on with. That's all I mean. Do you enjoy the work at the Commission?'

'I love it.'

'And what else do you do with your life?'

'Well, I've been studying at night for years. I'm just thinking what to do now that I have more time to myself. I read and play a bit of squash. I'm thinking of joining Toastmistresses or Women in Commerce.'

'My dear, how worthy it all sounds. What about passion? Romance?'

'Maybe I'm not the romantic, passionate type, Mrs Gwynne.'

'Sarah. And that's nonsense. Everyone is, at heart.'

'Well, I do go out with people, if that's what you mean.'

'But you've never been married.'

'No, though one of my men friends suggests marriage from time to time.' They were standing apart from the other guests beside an oleander bush. The tide was low, and dark sand, patterned with long muddy ropes attached to rowboats, and a sprinkling of rusty tins, stretched out to the still water. Sarah Gwynne had extraordinary amber eyes, like an antelope, Prue thought. She was speaking intensely.

'Do think very carefully. It's so hard to combine parenthood with a career, and Malcolm sees you as a future commissioner. And marriage — we speak of it as a joy, but it's usually such an enormous struggle. Oh, I adore Malcolm. Our marriage is a good one. But there have been such dark patches. Such absolute despair at times.' She sighed. 'Here I am baring my soul, when I should be pouring the Pimm's. Do feel you can speak to me if you are doing anything rash like getting engaged?' Of course, you're such a sensible person, you'll make a success of anything you put your mind to, I'm sure.'

'I'd certainly like to keep in touch.'

'Perhaps we could have lunch at the Art Gallery one day. I'm a volunteer guide there. Tuesday is my day.'

'Sounds fantastic.'

Prue moved across to the crowd of people near the food table. 'You were having a great tête-à-tête with our hostess,' Geoff Kerin said.

'She was telling me all about the Art Gallery.'

That was only part of the truth, and she had only told Sarah Gwynne part of the truth. Intense women who talk about passion, Prue thought, do they expect people to tell them secrets wherever they turn? Her own style was so different. On investigations she was polite, quiet, and even struck some people as shy. But she had other qualities: persistence, and a memory like a tape-recorder. People underestimated her at their cost.

At the time of that party at the Gwynnes', she was still living with Andrew. He had, in fact, mentioned marriage several times, but only as their relationship began to founder. They had always said that they felt no religious obligation to marry, and did not want children, so there was no reason to get married. QED. Andrew's marriage proposals were one of the first signs of trouble. They had become tenser, together and apart, and there was a recurrent abrasiveness between them that showed up in minor quarrels about whether it was worth driving an extra kilometre to save three cents on petrol, or whether unbranded muesli from the market was really healthier than the multinationals' products. Suddenly these domestic discussions had a new potency. Prue worked longer hours, came home more exhausted, switching on the television and pouring a glass of cask white all in one movement. She would go to twilight seminars on communications law rather than go to a film with Andrew. His friends, mostly, like him, engineers, suddenly seemed boring. A rasping edginess soured their previously

61

comfortable life together. It ceased to be a case of whether they would break up, so much as when and how.

And Andrew proposed.

Lying on the yellow and brown bedspread in the Cloudy Bay motel, Prue remembered the anguish of that time, the misunderstandings, the accusations, the betrayed hopes, the tears. When Andrew left, she felt as if she would have to lie in a darkened room for a fortnight, adjusting to a new life. Yet she had got up on the Monday morning and dressed for work as usual. Life had gone on. She found other people to play squash with. She worked unpaid overtime several nights a week. After a few months, living alone seemed tolerable and the silence ceased to oppress her.

Dark patches, Sarah Gwynne had said. Absolute despair. Prue had glimpsed the darkness, and chosen work and career as her best insurance against being vulnerable through her feelings for other people.

Not that she had lived without men. She met plenty of men, one way and another. She did not subscribe totally to the theory popular with Sydney women in their thirties that all men were either gay or spoken for already. There was the occasional divorced or unmarried man. She met men in the office, at parties, through her investigations, at accountancy and management seminars, at the squash courts and in the gym.

From time to time she would have dinner with a new man.

There was Denzil Dornford, for example, who told her his marriage had been ruined by the women's liberation movement. Prue knew his ex-wife, Evelyn, by sight, and felt it would be disloyal to her sex to buy this line too uncritically. The women's movement, it appeared, had given Evelyn a focus for hostilities that Denzil believed were caused by the inadequacies of her father and the narrowness of her Catholic girlhood. She had become suddenly eloquent and vengeful, seeing men in general as the oppressors, and Denzil, as the nearest and most reprehensible member of the species, was held to blame for all the disappointments that had befallen her.

As Evelyn fumed, Denzil was accepted as a postgraduate student in an interdisciplinary course that had an intake of only ten people a year, while her application was rejected. 'That put the tin lid on it,' Denzil said to Prue, in the sorrowful tones of one who has told the same tale of woe over many meals. 'She never thought it might have anything to do with our academic records, or our motivation, or the quality of our publications. It was all a plot to keep women down and give men all the breaks. Oh, God, my life hasn't been worth living since Germaine Greer wrote that book.'

Prue knew that this was her cue to fling her arms around him and dissociate herself from Evelyn, Germaine, and all the furies, but she was finding it hard not to smile. She got him talking about the stock exchange instead, and later bade him a chaste goodnight.

Then there was Bevis Orchard, who ate salads glumly at Sportsgirl at lunchtime, trying to remain slim for the Friday night cocktail crowd. He was one of those perpetual bachelors who seek out ever-younger office workers over white wine or over-coloured cocktails in the bars and taverns of the business end of town. He was handsome, in a way, with large brown eyes and a nice boyish grin, even if he had grown heavier in recent years. Prue could not spend time with Bevis without hearing of the crimes of Philippa Orchard, his former wife. 'The woman apparently didn't have any real appreciation of what the family means,' Bevis said. 'You know how it was for our parents — stick it out through thick and thin for the sake of the children. Didn't do anyone any harm, did it, putting the family first? The concessions I made to that woman. I thought she'd appreciate being kept in a certain style. But no, she insisted on keeping up her architecture practice. Nothing sensible and modest like domestic architecture, oh, no, that wouldn't suit Philippa. Interstate shopping malls, and school halls and science labs in faraway towns in the New England ranges. There I was, at home with the nanny. Well, I'm only human. Philippa was off living her life.'

Philippa Orchard had returned from a four-day trip to Brisbane and Toowoomba to find Bevis holding hands with a Karitane nurse named Janelle. She asked for a divorce. Bevis felt she should have had more sense of proportion, should have been prepared to put the family first. 'Don't you think so?' he asked Prue.

'I hardly know enough about it to make a judgment,' Prue said, with the tact that made her a good listener and doomed her to hearing these catalogues of other women's crimes. In fact, one of the tenets of the women's movement that appealed to her was the need to break the hold of the nuclear family upon individuals. The fundamentalist Congregationalists who brought her up had seen moral values in black and white terms. Sin, blessedness. Adultery, faithfulness. Evil, good. Outer darkness, heaven. A dialectic of choices. Repentance, redemption, the second coming. Prue had had enough of certainty and repentance and the family before she turned eighteen. Guiltily, gleefully, she discovered and read library copies of Bertrand Russell and Simone de Beauvoir. She did not have to go along with all that Christian stuff about the family forever. It only provided hyprocrites like Bevis Orchard with rationalisations for the double standard, in Prue's opinion.

Then there was Sammy Glover, who was really gay, but needed to have someone to take to charity balls in aid of the foundation which funded his medical research. He was a short, slight man with a Chaplinesque charm, who happened to be a superb dancer.

There was an academic named Harvey Travis, also a wonderful dancer. He invited Prue to lunch one Friday. She took the afternoon off on flexitime. He picked her up in his battered Datsun. She noticed that the back seat was strewn with children's sneakers, floaties, flippers, sunhats and spades. 'Sorry,' he said. 'Marilyn is rather untidy, as you see. Kids' stuff all over the place. Nearly break my leg every time

I walk in the door.'

Prue wondered for a moment what a nice Congregationalist girl was doing with a married man who blamed his wife for the state of his car, but they were turning into a BP garage on the Pacific Highway. Harvey said something to the attendant. The gauge on the petrol pump clicked away beside them until the automatic shut-off operated and the attendant withdrew the nozzle from the tank. 'Twenty-two dollars forty-five,' he said to Harvey.

'Sorry,' Harvey said, 'I only asked you for four dollars worth.'

'I thought you said to fill her up.'

'You must have misunderstood me. I asked for four dollars.'

Prue was frightened she might be asked to verify this. She had no idea what had been said, but in the same circumstances she would have paid for the tankful of petrol. She avoided the men's eyes. Harvey took two creased, green, two dollar bills out of his pocket, and the garage man accepted them.

'People don't listen,' Harvey told her as they drove back onto the highway. 'I was quite specific about it. Let's forget about Chinese food. Let's go to your place.'

The lust and anticipation that had electrified Prue when she danced with Harvey Travis at the Children's Hospital Ball had suddenly waned. She was not usually a flirt, but she had, in her own eyes, flirted outrageously with Harvey Travis. It was too late to turn back. They drove to her Waverton flat.

'Nice place,' Harvey said. 'Are you the artist?'

Prue was surprised. It ought to be clear to anyone with an education in the humanities that she was not responsible for the prints and paintings and collages, which bore the signatures of many different artists. 'No,' she said, 'I've picked them up here and there.'

'Nice,' Harvey said again.

'What would you like for lunch then?' Prue asked. 'I've got some tins of soup that we could jazz up with mushrooms and sherry.'

'If you like.'

Prue had cut up the mushrooms and parsley and added them to the tinned soup when suddenly two strong arms were around her. 'Let's eat later,' Harvey suggested, kissing the nape of her neck and pulling up her blouse. 'Oh, Prue, you're such a beauty; hiding your light under a bushel in that boring old office.'

Every man who found Prue attractive suffered from the delusion that he was the first to do so. Her quiet, unassuming style — short, gleaming dark hair, eyes so brown they were almost black, glasses with clear, pale blue frames, a neat body clad in navy and white — seemed to each of them a disguise of plainness that only he had unmasked. Harvey Travis, whose wife had cascading bronze hair and a suggestive laugh, was looking at Prue's breasts with the rapture of a scholar who has unearthed a rare document. 'So beautiful, so beautiful,' he repeated.

Prue was less enraptured. Harvey's body was revealed as strong, olive-skinned, masculine, and in good shape. But the scene at the petrol station had been deeply anti-erotic. Only four dollars worth, only four dollars worth, said a chorus in her skull, as Harvey Travis leapt upon her body without preliminaries, pressed heavily into her, and moved to the rhythm of his parsimonious remark. In a minute or two, perhaps less, Harvey Travis was saying to her, 'I'm going to come soon, the first time.'

'That's fine,' Prue said politely, thinking that there would not be a second time if she had anything to do with it.

With a groan Harvey flung himself upon her recently admired breasts. Prue put her arms around him and hoped her own lack of response would go unremarked. It did.

'I'll ring you,' Harvey said. 'And if you want to speak to me, I'll give you my direct line at the Department. Don't ring me at home, needless to say. I'm not saying not to ring me, though.'

'No, I didn't think you were.' But she wouldn't. And she

would not wait like a breathless teenager for Harvey to ring her.

Being alone had its advantages, when you thought about it. Prue sighed. She took her notebook and pen from the bedside table.

Hughes and Blackmore — who is Blackmore? Where is Hughes? What was the split-up between Szabo, Hughes and Zolnay? All too smalltime for Szabo — what's in it for him? Possible to subpoena books? Transport a problem, surely. Approval in principle — local shire level only? Or Govt involvement thru Tourism, Development or both? Links between Sz & Macquarie St? Formal enquiry?

Prue shook her head and put the notebook down. No, she did not want to relinquish the file to Legal Branch and have them brief QCs at the cost of a quarter of a million or so unless there was some hope of compensation for Mildred Lake and people like her.

THE SUNSHINE STATE

Listing on its high veranda posts, the provincial Queensland town was decaying as sugar prices fell. Roxane looked down on smoking piles of cane as the plane landed. She knew this route well. She visited Shrimpton Island — co-owned by Runaway and a domestic airline — at least once a year. She boarded the light plane for the trip east.

Although her visit was a routine one, she felt a moment of excitement as she circled over Shrimpton. The dizzying turquoise sea, the ancient cycads, the imported palms and bougainvillea: the colours lifted her spirits. The nine-passenger plane bounced along the runway and came to a halt beside a mini-version of the Eiffel Tower, executed in yellow brick, barbed wire and seashells. Queensland, there's nowhere like it, Roxane thought.

The couple in charge of the island, Eric and Gillian Galston, were at the airstrip to meet her.

'How ya doin', Roxane? Too long since your last visit.' Eric loaded her hibiscus-trimmed bag into the back of the jeep. Roxane, Gillian and Eric sat three abreast, jolting along the dirt road to the resort.

'When are these roads going to be sealed? Isn't that part of the upgrading?' Roxane was holding the struts of the roof to stop her head from being bumped.

Gillian laughed. 'Eric always says you don't waste a moment,' she said.

'We hope to get a team over from the mainland before the wet season,' Eric said. 'You know there was a lot of damage in that freak rain last year. But if you're concerned about progress, wait till you see the new waterfront units.'

'Am I staying in one?'

'No, they're fully booked. We've given you a family suite in the Bougainvillea complex.'

'Fair enough,' said Roxane. 'Your new palms are doing well.'

Along the side of the road a line of palms had reached a height of about two metres. Eucalypts and banksias had been cut back to make way for them.

'Real well. And wait till you see the waterlilies.' Roxane found his anxiety gratifying.

The jeep drew up outside a bungalow-style complex. 'You're in number four,' said Gillian, handing Roxane the key. 'You'll probably want to settle in a bit first. Let us know if you want to be shown round at all. Or you may prefer to look round by yourself.'

Eric put the suitcase inside the unit. Roxane ducked under the overhanging puce flowers. She took off her sandals, enjoying the roughness of the seagrass matting under her feet. 'I'll be fine,' she said.

Eric stood hesitantly. 'I wanted to ask you something, Roxane, if it's all right with you. Since you've been promoted to Operations Manager in the South Pacific, what's Olwyn's role exactly? Is she retiring?'

Roxane laughed. 'Olwyn retire? You've got to be joking. No, she has more of an advisory role these days. You know she's on the Board. And she has such a flair for new resorts — she actually thrives on the bricks and mortar side of things. She's spending quite a lot of time at our new resort at Indigo Island.'

'Yes. Well, Gill and I just wondered, you know, how you

and she fit in.'

'You know how informal things are at Runaway. It works out fine,' Roxane said.

'Good-oh, then. Thanks, Roxane. Sing out if you want any help.'

Roxane inspected the coffee and tea sachets. The coffee was the wrong brand. It would have to be tea. She turned on the electric jug and changed into a bikini and pareo while it boiled. Then she sat down to drink.

There was a built-in radio near the bedhead, but Roxane's efforts to tune a mainland station were unsuccessful. The only channel with any strength was playing Muzak. She turned that off and lay down, exhausted. There was no need to do a full tour of the resort end of the island in her first hour after all. She would rest for a while.

At dusk she was woken by screeching birds: a flock of rosellas was being fed nearby. She had been asleep for hours. She showered, blow-dried her hair, and dressed for dinner in a black and white sundress.

Roxane was at the bar, drinking gin and tonic and listening to a police sergeant named Howard. Behind them a piano player was crooning:

> *If I said you had a beautiful body, would*
> *you hold it against me?*

'And the food?' Roxane asked. 'You're happy with the food?'

'Sure. Great tucker. Beaut. Specially prawn night. The kids love it and all.'

'Good. And the entertainment?'

'My wife was saying it's a pity you can't hire videos, seeing as the TV reception isn't that good.'

'I'll note that. Anything else?'

'If maybe the teenagers had their own rumpus room, like, for the evening.'

'Not a bad idea, Howard. Thanks.'

'Everyone back in Newcastle will think I'm conning them when I tell them not only did I meet Roxane Rowe, but I told her how to run the bloody island.'

'At Runaway we do our market research informally as well as formally. One of us visits every major destination regularly.'

'Ever get bored with travelling, Roxane?'

'Tired but not bored. It's my career after all.'

'Louise won't believe this, when I tell her she missed meeting you.'

'Where is she?'

'Putting the kids to bed.'

'Perhaps I'll meet her tomorrow.'

> *Strangers in the night, exchanging*
> *glances,*

'Care to dance?' Howard asked.

'Thanks, but no. I have to circulate.'

Roxane finished her gin and tonic. The piano player was a disgrace. He only knew a few bars of each song, and his repertoire seemed limited as well. She would have to ask Eric how long his contract was. First she would have to have words with Gillian about the plastic bags of prawn shells and heads that she'd seen stacked just outside the kitchen. She strode past a dozen dancing couples. Runaway would need to decide whether to keep Shrimpton as a family resort for people like Howard, Louise and the kids, or whether to give it the 'Indigo treatment' of the new Pacific island development. Perhaps, after all this time, Olwyn still knew better than she what direction the industry would take in the next few years.

Every client is an individual, with their own unique hopes and dreams for their annual holidays or the big trip overseas, Roxane was in the habit of telling Runaway trainees. Privately she was more cynical. The great unwashed wanted a good climate, something to do and plenty to eat. Give them that and they'd be, well, as happy as Howard.

Roxane wished Szabo could be here. He would see the joke. But at this hour she couldn't even ring him. She pictured him at home, with Anna, listening to Mahler. In fact he was at his merchant banker's, working on a takeover offer for a Queensland pastoral company whose profits had taken a recent nosedive.

If I said you had a beautiful body, would you hold it against me? There was no escaping the piano player until she closed the door of her room. Perhaps she would say in her report that Shrimpton would be fine once the current improvements were complete. Anything to keep from having to come back here regularly. Aching to be with Steven, she remembered her most recent encounter with him.

Szabo made love with deliberation. The tempo suited Roxane, who would drift into fantasies of torment and helplessness. He was going slowly to tantalise her, she told herself, to bring her to the brink and then draw back. The illusion of powerlessness heightened her pleasure. She liked to imagine herself the new bride in a harem, or a village girl subjected to *droit de seigneur*. She imagined a third person in their relationship, a panderer or a procuress, anointing her body before it was subjected to her lover's every whim. Sometimes she shared these fantasies with Szabo; he found them arousing and, it appeared, incongruous.

'They are hardly liberated, the thoughts that go through your head at these times, my darling,' he said.

'No Steven, hardly. Should I be worried?'

'Just don't tell your more radical sisters. They would not approve.'

'Stuff them.'

'I certainly will not.'

'Figuratively.'

'Hmm.' Steven Szabo lay beside her, heavy but not flabby. She liked his hands. His accent, too, had ceased to be strange. She found his, 'ebsolute gorgeous', for instance, going through her mind when she was alone or driving along in her Celica. Ebsolute gorgeous, she would repeat, you're ebsolute gorgeous. It seemed the most profound compliment anyone had paid her. Hold on, Rox, it's not like you to fall for this line, she warned herself. But the Szaboisms still reverberated.

'You look so much younger with your glasses off,' she said.

'Flettery', Szabo said, 'will get you ...'

'Don't tell me. Everywhere.'

'A long way.'

'What's the most extraordinary time you've ever made love?' she asked him. 'Present company excepted, of course.'

'Of course. Let me think. Ever? Even years back?'

'Ever.'

'I remember one time,' he said, 'just after the war. Budapest. There was a terrible housing shortage. I was just about broke. It was February. I couldn't take this girl home, the few remaining members of my family were there. I couldn't locate a single friend with an apartment. This girl and I, Gina her name was, were desperate to fuck each other. Ebsolute desperate. The snow was knee deep. No one was on the streets. God knows what the temperature was. Zero or way below. Well, Gina and I ended up screwing on a park bench. We had to sweep the snow away before we sat down. I've never forgotten that time. It still seems rather exceptional.'

Roxane laughed. 'I don't think I can compete. It's a wonder you didn't get frostbite.'

'That's exactly what we said to one another at the time.'

'Talk about ardour.'

'We were young.'

'Just think of the scandal if you tried anything like that now.'

'I am happy to say, there is no need.'

'Wonder what became of the girl. Gina.'

'No idea. I haven't thought of her for years.'

'She probably wonders whatever became of you.'

73

'She, also, must remember the temperature as much as the other person. She's probably a Librarian in Charge at Party Headquarters. Or a grandmother in Canada.'

'Or an interpreter in Vienna.'

'Or a day-care supervisor in a town on the border.'

'Or a sex educator in high schools, recommending abstinence.'

'Or dead,' Szabo sighed.

'Well, that's unromantic.'

'On the contrary, my dear, death is central to the romantic tradition. I sometimes feel — it's hard to explain — a kind of discontinuity between my European self, and my life here. It's not just the time what's passed, or the language what's changed, or the difference in the light, or the general sensibility, or lack of it. It's like two lives. I often imagine everyone I knew before is dead. Not absurd, you know. Not so far-fetched. So many of them are. My parents, my eldest brother, many of the people I knew in school and in the nearby streets. It amounted to the fact what I had a ticket out, and they didn't.'

Roxane put her arm around his shoulders, caressing the fine skin of the back of his neck. 'I'm glad you did,' she said. 'But you mustn't be morbid or guilty. There's nothing to be gained by that.'

'Part of your charm, my dear, is that it is a surprise to find the word guilt even exists in your vocabulary.'

'True. I'm not weighed down by it, am I?' Roxane was amused. 'Is it a great lack? You miss it?'

'On the contrary. I think of you as an amoral child of a country without history.'

'Well, I don't know much history,' Roxane said, 'but surely the country must have some.'

'So long as it doesn't impinge on you.'

'No worries.' Roxane was dimly aware that Szabo might congratulate her on her lack of history, but he loved his wife for their shared history. The fonder she became of him, the more she was gnawed with curiosity about Anna. In the beginning she had imagined they could have an affair quite casually, with no serious involvement and no harm to anyone. Now she felt much closer to him than she'd expected, more stirred emotionally. To Roxane any sign of vulnerability was a danger signal. She would have to be more on guard.

'Precisely,' said Steven Szabo. 'No worries. The ultimate seduction.' They laughed together and kissed again.

At Brisbane airport, Roxane bought a copy of *The Australian* to read on the trip to Sydney. Not unusually, she was the only woman in business class. She ordered a gin and tonic with a lot of ice, and looked around at her fellow passengers. The man nearest to her was filling in some type of questionnaire or survey.

Roxane leant forward, ostensibly to get a flight map from the seat pocket in front of her, but her real aim was to read over her neighbour's shoulder.

She could see only one question.

DO YOU EVER EXPERIENCE JOY?

A. FREQUENTLY B. SOMETIMES C. RARELY D. NEVER

The man had circled C. RARELY.

Poor bastard, she thought, he and his wife are probably off to some frightful weekend of marriage renewal. She could not see the scoring instructions on the man's quiz, but could imagine them. Mostly As, an excellent relationship. Mostly Cs, you and your partner will need to work hard on your marriage. Roxane had little time for counselling or attempts to patch up relationships. She moved on instead. What was the point of staying in some joyless partnership (C. RARELY) in the hope of its being transformed into passion?

She thought of Steven Szabo. He would circle A. His life would constantly be arranged to provide joy and satisfaction. He was immensely pleased with his marriage to Anna. 'A great lady — we share so much. I am very happily married. It's just that the sex is a bit stale.'

Roxane had stifled the sarcastic responses that had sprung

75

to her mind. He was not being ironic. She might think stale sex indicated failure; he clearly thought it was a sign an affair was called for. Why jeopardise what they had by objecting? Steven got what he wanted in business: the same principle applied in his emotional life. He gave the impression that although he did not flaunt his affairs in front of his wife, she was well aware they took place. His business kept him very busy. Some aspect of a Barbary takeover or share transaction took him interstate nearly every week. Roxane, the travel executive, actually spent less time out of Sydney than he did.

She finished the news section of her paper and glanced at the business page. The face of Brooklands Runaway's Managing Director, Boris Brookstein, looked at her from a story in the bottom left-hand corner. NEW DIVERSIFICATION BY BROOKLANDS, she read.

Damn it, she thought, I've been spot-testing little resorts in the Whitsundays while the whole organisation is being restructured in my absence.

Brooklands, the travel, resort and charter boat company, was to diversify into a broader range of businesses following its acquisition of Sudpac Commercial Enterprises, she read. Sudpac was a retail company which included budget grocery lines, packaging, distribution and pharmaceuticals among its activities.

Roxane visualised Sudpac's grey-striped budget labels usurping the lilac hibiscus trademark she had worked so hard to establish for Runaway. Ridiculous. Runaway would maintain its identity and functions and from day to day the Sudpac acquisition would have no effect on it. Or would it? She was extremely anxious.

> *'It's a natural expansion for Brooklands,' Boris Brookstein said in his Melbourne office yesterday. 'For some time we have been keen to establish a flexible business group with an emphasis on consumer services. Brooklands' expertise will add to the profitability of Sudpac.*

*And although the founder of Sudpac, Harvey
Stanton, will no longer be associated with the
firm, there are some fine, go-ahead people in
the Sudpac management team whose talents we
can definitely use, both in existing Sudpac
functions and in wider business within the
group, such as Brooklands Resorts and
Runaway Travel.'*

The last thing Runaway needed, Roxane thought, was
little jerks from business school with some notion of how to
sell grocery lines trying to understand the dynamics of the
travel market.

In the Runaway office that afternoon she was alert for
signs of change.

'There's a message for you to ring Mr Brookstein in
Melbourne,' the receptionist told her.

'Thanks.' DO YOU EVER EXPERIENCE PANIC? B. SOMETIMES.

'Roxane.' Boris had a very faint Berlin accent. 'You read
about our news?'

'Yes. Congratulations.'

'Yes. Gratifying. It is a big step for the firm. Everything
okay in Queensland?'

She tried a joke. 'Is everything ever okay in Queensland?'

'You know I mean Shrimpton. Isn't that where you were?
I rang yesterday.'

'Yes, fine, and they're on the phone there, you know.'

'Yes, my dear, it wasn't urgent. It's the new management
structure. I wanted to tell you before he arrives.'

'Who arrives?'

'Such a marvellous young man. From Sudpac. He has a
commerce degree and an MBA.'

'Great.'

'Yes, I'm so glad you see it that way. His name is Desmond
Hickey. He'll be the group's financial controller. All sales
and operations will report to him. And he'll be based in the
Sydney office, the Runaway office. You might check that

77

furniture and so on are being organised.'

'But what will be my relationship to him?'

'So far as Runaway marketing is concerned, you'll still be running your own race. But as financial controller he'll oversee major commitments throughout the group. And all sales.'

'But Runaway sales report to me as manager of South Pacific operations.'

'No, they'll report to the financial controller.'

'To this Desmond person.'

'To Des Hickey, yes.'

'Boris, this isn't business as usual. I'm effectively being downgraded.'

'Don't be like that, Roxane. You'll go on doing what you do best. Marketing. Promotion. You are our little golden girl of travel you know. As far as the general public is concerned, you *are* Runaway. We couldn't be more delighted with your work. I should have thought your salary package made that clear? And your last bonus?'

'Yes, Boris, that's all terrific. But this Des Hickey ...'

'Like everyone else in the group, you'll report to him for decisions requiring input from the financial controller. His qualifications are impeccable, Roxane. A few rough edges, perhaps. But a stint in the Sydney office and your example will soon fix that. Am I right?'

'I hope you are. Right now I'm feeling a little disappointed. I always assumed I'd, well — with Olwyn out of the office so much, I virtually run the Sydney office half the time. I'm hurt, Boris. I've been left out of all the plans, too. I feel as if I'm the last to know.'

'These feelings are natural. But I'm relying on you to make Des Hickey welcome and help him get the staff on side. You'd better see if the agents can rent us an extra couple of suites in the building, too. He'll be consolidating the operations of several Sudpac concerns in Sydney.'

Bitterness. It came into her voice now. 'Surely leases on suites would require the input of the financial controller.'

Boris was oblivious, or pretended to be. 'Yeah, you're right. Get some options for Des to consider. He'll be there tomorrow.'

'How does Olwyn fit into all this?'

'You can ask her. But she's quite happy.'

'I'll talk to her then. And thanks for filling me in on the Sudpac moves. And this Des Hickey.'

'I knew I could rely on you. Ciao.' Boris rang off.

Roxane buzzed her secretary. 'Get the Hookers' leasing agent for me, would you? And is Olwyn in?'

'Out just now, but we expect her back.'

Roxane was fiddling with a stapler, trying to get its spring to open so she could reload it. 'Ask Olwyn if I can see her soon as she can fit it in.'

'Yes, Miss Rowe.'

Roxane's staff called her Miss Rowe. It was a point of etiquette she had picked up from Olwyn. In twenty years, there wasn't much she hadn't learnt from Olwyn. They were not exactly close, all the same. They respected each other, but there was a touch of wariness as well. Threat, envy — it was not so simple. After all this time it was more like the subconscious rivalry of mother and daughter. Yet it was to Olwyn that Roxane habitually turned for advice, and Roxane whom Olwyn usually nominated for difficult new projects.

Olwyn walked into Roxane's office unannounced. 'Rox,' she said, 'you're looking thunderstruck.'

'Boris has just told me about this Desmond Hickey. How do you fit into the picture so far as he's concerned? Will you still be in charge of Runaway matters?'

'The company's changing a good deal, Roxane. We won't be able to keep Runaway a discrete entity in quite the same way. Sudpac's acquisition will change our operations a lot. We'll only be one of the Brooklands subsidiaries.'

'Are you saying you'll report to this Dastardly Des too?'

'Don't resort to childishness, Roxane. We haven't even met him yet.'

'So you will report to him?'

'I'm phasing myself out of the business side,' Olwyn said. 'Sudpac will be taking Brooklands into areas I really know nothing about. Motels, resorts, branch agencies, fine. But grocery distribution. Pharmaceutical franchises. It's all Greek to me. I'm too old to diversify. I've built up my reputation by being ahead of the game in travel. The first really big overseas conventions to come here. The first really good island villages. Mine. And yours, of course, Rox, you've always had very sure instincts for these things too.'

'Thanks to you.'

'So what I intend to do, for the next few months, is concentrate on the Indigo development in the Pacific. It's one I really want to put my signature on. It's a project that's really close to my heart. It'll be receiving its first guests within weeks. My time will be well and truly repaid if I base myself over there for a while.'

'I see,' said Roxane. 'Olwyn, there have been rumours you'll be retiring from the Board. I heard something about semi-retirement. And the Queensland people have got the most garbled versions of what you're doing.'

'Setting up a Pacific resort is not exactly semi-retirement.'

'But your seat on the Board? How will this Sudpac thing affect that?'

'Just curious, Rox?'

Olwyn Tierney considered Roxane, sitting before her, a picture of the successful career woman in her cream linen coat-dress and pearls. As a teenager, Olwyn remembered, Roxane had dressed in black or psychedelic colours, and had worn far too much make-up. She'd been fat, too. There was something different about Roxane's face now, not just the fact she was in her thirties. Eagerness had turned sour. Edgy, opportunistic. Roxane was tensed up like a tennis player on the baseline receiving service.

'My seat on the Board isn't affected,' Olwyn said. 'Not immediately, anyway. I'll be spending seven or eight months over at Indigo, getting that on its feet. There's a lot of negotiating to do, with the new government and the local indigenous council. More complicated than Bali.'

'I can credit it.'

Olwyn winced. Roxane was always using phrases like 'I can credit it' these days. Business convention jargon almost obscured her scanty education, except for the mispronounced French phrases.

'Quite possibly I'll decide to concentrate on Indigo, and not bother with the Board. There's a responsibility, you know — it's not fair to sit there if groceries and pharmaceuticals remain a mystery to me. Besides, I'm sixty-three. It's time I slowed down.'

'You look years younger. You're an inspiration to us all.'

'Roxane, we've known each other long enough. Can't you spare me the clichés? Inspiration to us all indeed.'

'But you are. To women of my generation you are. You're someone who made it before equal opportunity was even mentioned.'

'If you like.' Olwyn smiled and patted her grey bouffant hairdo.

'If you did step down, Olwyn, what would be my chances of getting your seat on the Board? In the eyes of the public, after all, I am Runaway. Even Boris says so. And it's important for us to have a woman on the Board. Women have been so exploited in the industry.'

'Not the ones with ability who've really stayed with it. Don't give me all that stuff about discrimination, please.'

'All right. But there are statistics on the earnings of males and females, and the number of females on Boards. And that's what I'm concerned about.'

'Roxane,' Olwyn said, 'if I support you for this, it's because I've always supported you, always acknowledged your ability and your hard work. Not because I'm striking a blow for the militant sisterhood.' Olwyn's daughter Margot was always telling her about the symbolic value of her career, that she was a role model to friends whose mothers had been housewives. And what had Margot done with all her opportunities? Taken culture to Yagoona, that's what.

'But you will support me? You're saying you will?' Blotches of colour were flaming on Roxane's cheeks.

'I will, but I have to tell you my voice may not be the one that counts. They may be looking for a distribution specialist, or someone who'll give them a bit of political kudos, or someone from an area they're about to buy into. Desmond Hickey, for instance. He rigged up some very special software to check on every aspect of Sudpac profitability from a desktop computer. I'm told it's brilliant. Now if that type of computer program can be adapted to our travel operations as well, our rivals will be completely outclassed. We need someone with those skills.'

'Some man.'

'Now, Rox. I've said I'll push for you. There may be several extra men, for all we know, representing all the new subsidiaries.'

'If you'll support me, that's the main thing. And I'll do a bit of lobbying of my own,' Roxane said.

'If you're thinking of outside pressure from women's organisations, I wouldn't if I were you — it could backfire. You have to be very cautious. And there's another source of danger. There are rumours that your private life might be putting Runaway at risk.'

'What in hell is that supposed to mean?'

'I'm not sure. But you know how Brookstein and Szabo are — old comrades but deadly rivals. Boris is paranoid about Brooklands being prey to takeovers. Szabo is an expert at them. Brooklands Sudpac would be quite a plum now.'

'For God's sake. Steven Szabo and I have a personal relationship. Underline that. We don't discuss Runaway or Sudpac or anything remotely like that.'

'Roxane, that's fine. All I'm saying is be careful.'

'I'm always careful. Or nearly always.'

'We can give Toni's old room to Dastardly Des.'

Roxane laughed. 'Exactly what I was thinking.'

Roxane's secretary, Di, stood in the doorway. 'Excuse me, Mrs Tierney, Miss Rowe. There's a gentleman to see you both.'

'I'm not expecting anyone. Did he give his name?'

A slightly overweight young man with close-cropped brown hair brushed past Di. He wore tweed trousers and a brown velour sweater.

'Don't tell me,' he said, 'I know who you both are. G'day. A privilege to be working with you. I'm Des Hickey. Not due till tomorrow, but I need to measure up the space before I get the furniture, eh?'

'How do you do, Mr Hickey?' Olwyn said. 'We were just talking about you. Welcome to Runaway.'

'May I call you Des?' Roxane asked. 'We're just delighted to have you here.' Standing up to shake his hand, she gave the smile that prompted a thousand viewers to telephone their travel agents and book a tour with Runaway.

MIDCAREER

Margot's Wednesday class was held in a scout hall overlooking a shallow gully behind a parking lot. Fifteen women who were returning to study in the hope of enrolling for degrees or diplomas the following year made up her class. All but two were mothers. The younger children were cared for in the adjacent guide hall. Women entered the scout hall blushing, their empty arms dangling. Elation and guilt succeeded one another in their smiles. Occasionally a child's cry would be heard from the adjoining building. Everyone would grow tense. If the crying persisted, one of the group would tiptoe out the back door.

Margot liked these students: their separate baskets of possessions, one lot holding cordial, wooden toys, clean nappies, sneakers; the other their biros, notebooks and plastic folders. As autumn succeeded summer, sundresses gave way to jeans and heavy sweaters, and Margot's 'Mums' class', as the college administrators called it, was hard to distinguish from any other group of students. Over the same months, the students' work became as fluent as any other group's. They progressed from *I couldn't write an essay, Ken said he'd burn my books, the kids all laugh at me, I'll never make a student, I couldn't make head nor tail of school*, to

That's not a very convincing argument, and *How should I set out the bibliography?* Margot was jubilant.

Two women in particular, Cath and Roslyn, were the driving forces behind the group. Cath was a harried looking thirty-year-old, with a frown and a permanent wave. A nonstop reader, she would shine in any tertiary course. It was Cath who took care of administrative details, advertising the course in local supermarkets and health centres, sending notices to the local press, hiring the babysitter, keeping an eye on student numbers. Roslyn was older, redheaded, a mother of six who combined an outgoing personality with a sharp mind. Roslyn bolstered the confidence of any woman who was tempted to leave the group.

Roslyn's anecdotes about her family's reactions to her return to study became a feature of Margot's mums' class. Sitting in her handknit peacock stripes, Roslyn quoted her offspring: 'Then Marlene said, "Mum has every right to develop her mind. Where's the greatest brain drain — down the kitchen sink." And Dominic said, "She ought to put her family first." And Marlene says, "You just want her to make your bed for you," and Dominic says, "Quite right, men are the hunter/gatherers and women's place is at the hearth." And Marlene says, "Who told you that crap?" and Dominic says, "Brother Macnamara." The other students were convulsed.

'Where's Wendy this morning?' Margot was checking attendance.

'I was going to talk to you about that,' Cath said. 'Wendy's got a few problems.'

'Anything I can help with?'

'I'm not sure. It's her family's attitude. Cliff seems to resent it when she's not there, or even when she's reading a book. He swept all her papers and books onto the floor the other night and said if she didn't get off her butt and clean the place up he'd burn them.'

'Poor Wendy. I had no idea.'

'And the kids. Well they pick up the attitude, don't they?

Bung on sore throats when she's due here, or demand to be driven to Homebush for hockey.'

'But she has some rights,' Margot said. 'As an individual. Why doesn't everyone see that?'

'Search me.' Cath gave a rueful smile. They took their mugs of Nescafé and went to join the other women.

'Progress reports today,' said Margot. 'Remember we were talking about original sources. Who's had any luck with local papers or diaries or letters?'

'Look what I've got,' Roslyn said. 'It's a sort of book of recipes and household hints. My aunt lent it to me. It was her mother's. It's got a certificate in it from the Easter Show in 1911.'

Everyone crowded forward. The certificate, for embroidery, had been awarded to Lily Maureen Groves.

'You'll have to think what you want to do next,' Margot said. 'Do you want to follow up on Lily Groves herself, or do you want to look at a topic like women and handcrafts?'

'Maybe I'll get my aunt talking about Lily. I could borrow my daughter's tape recorder.'

'And some of the rest of us could look at crafts.'

'And shows.'

'Not just the Easter Show. Country shows.'

'Different styles of embroidery.'

'And if women won prizes for stud rams as well as embroidery.'

Margot smiled. There was never any risk with this class that she would have to lecture formally to an unresponsive group. 'It sounds promising,' she said. 'We could aim to mount an exhibition of some kind towards the end of the year. Now let's talk a bit more about likely sources of information.'

'Why don't we ask in the local paper for people to show us things from old glory boxes?'

'And libraries.'

'Newspaper files.'

'Photo albums.'

'Historical societies.'

'This is all great,' Margot said. 'Now let's just try and be a bit systematic about who does what.'

After the class Margot drove to Wendy Grimshaw's cream weatherboard house. Wendy came to the door with a towel wrapped round her head, her face still flushed from the shower. In the living room the television was blaring.

'Turn that down, Craig, I've got a visitor.'

'I was worried about you.' Margot hesitated. Wendy would not be able to talk freely with the boy present.

'This one wasn't feeling too good,' Wendy said. 'The family comes first, doesn't it? So I give it a miss for today. Been looking at the books, but. D'you want a cup of tea?'

'I won't today, thanks, but do come and talk to me up at the college one day soon when you get a chance.'

'Yeah. Okay. But I don't know that I'm worth it, you know.'

'Of course you are.'

'No, all the others are full of ideas. They're that brainy. They know what they think and why they think it. I'm not like that. I was never any good at school.'

'Wendy, we'll discuss all this some other time, but that's nothing to do with it, how you did at school. If you burnt the first cake you made, would you decide from that that you couldn't learn to cook?'

'Yeah, well, I don't know.'

'Come and talk to me anyway.'

'Yeah, I will.' Wendy walked to the door to draw the latch on the flyscreen. The turban slipped from her hair as she bent forward, revealing a bright bruise on her right temple.

'Okay then. See you soon.' Margot walked back to her car, wondering at the protocol of silence that made her pretend not to notice Wendy had been bashed. Both Margot and the college counsellor could refer people to women's refuges if need be, but Margot was careful not to act more like a social worker than a teacher. Going to see a student who was absent

87

from class was one thing; giving unsought advice was another.

Margot got back in her car, with its *Save The Rainforests* sticker and the dented back door which she kept meaning to fix. About to start the car, she focused on her face in the rear-view mirror: a frown, deepening the little furrow between her eyebrows; tousled red-brown hair falling forward in long bangs; beads of sweat near her nose. She pulled the wings of hair back with side combs and dabbed sunscreen and powder on her nose. How did her mother manage to be so well-groomed, even in the tropics, she wondered. Margot sometimes felt that she spent her life failing to reach Olwyn's standards on a range of issues from the colour of her hair to the suburb she lived in and the friends she preferred.

Despite this almost automatic defensiveness and irritation, Margot was concerned about her mother, who was in hospital in Isantu. A French hospital apparently, or one that was French before the islands got their independence from British and French rule. Her mother had been so zestful about going to Indigo that Margot thought the months there could only be good for her health. Years of smoking were catching up with Olwyn, who was prone to lung infections. When Margot telephoned, the ward sister refused to let her mother come to the phone. It was frustrating to have to relay messages, and the nurse's heavy accent did not reassure her about standards of care. She was now waiting to hear when Olwyn could be transferred to Sydney.

Margot did not know how she would broach with her mother the need to slow down, to retire from Runaway completely perhaps, once she had recovered from this pneumonia or whatever it was. Some suitable substitute would have to go and run the Indigo Island resort. Olwyn was not just independent; she was impossibly touchy, in Margot's opinion, about any concern for her health. She would react angrily to a question like 'How are you feeling?' if it were asked too solicitously.

But then Margot had never had an easy relationship with her mother. Olwyn liked to be in charge, and Margot resisted authority. Olwyn was the scintillating, well-connected businesswoman; Margot was her dowdy left-wing daughter. Or so she was made to feel. In her student days Margot was active in the peace movement and the rebirth of the women's movement, but Olwyn saw most causes as unchic and bad for business. She saw no connection between her own success and the struggle for women's rights. Margot's husband was a trade union official; Olwyn, who thought unions were an affront to individual rights, made no attempt to disguise her irritation at Ted's job and his views. Mother and daughter shared one enthusiasm: Margot's son Tom meant a lot to Olwyn. Prickly from a lifetime of slights and misunderstandings, Margot sometimes felt Olwyn was only nice to her to make sure she could see her grandson as freely as she liked. Olwyn had never seemed impressed by her daughter's university degrees or her career in further education; Margot imagined that her touchstone for success, like so many other people's, was Roxane Rowe. Photogenic, publicity-seeking — but good at her job, or Olwyn would not have made a protégée of her.

Margot had an appointment to discuss her project with a professor of business education whose management and training consultancies were the envy of her boss, Brian. She parked her car near the loading bay of the fruit markets behind the city and found Henry Moses on the third floor of a new building nearby. A tall, good-looking man with receding hair and grey eyes, he had tanned skin that suggested a sunlamp or skiing holidays.

'Margot,' Henry Moses said, 'I had a look at your questionnaire, and I've scribbled a suggestion or two in the margins, but basically that sort of thing is not my bag, and it looks as if you're on the right track anyhow. You're getting full cooperation at Synchron, are you? Good. Good. I do quite a bit of work for them, you know, so if you need any approaches to Sir Geoffrey or to Larry Montgomery or anyone else in the hierarchy, just ask.'

'That's kind of you.'

'So what did you really want me to contribute?'

'I wondered if you had any insights into why women aren't accepted yet in executive jobs in the corporate sector.'

'There's a lot of literature on that, of course. You've read it, no doubt. Well, education, of course. Social factors. Who minds the baby; who attracts gossip. From the woman's point of view — accusations of tokenism or of screwing her way to the top. For the male executive, suspicion that he's been sexually motivated if he helps a woman get ahead. Wives — the uneasiness of wives about the women their husbands work with, or the expectations about women in general that wives generate in their husbands.'

'Yes, all of that,' Margot said. Henry Moses was not telling her anything new.

'There's a lack of authority, often. I have some great female students. Some years my best students are women. But what use is an MBA with honours and an essay prize if you can't persuade your staff to do what you tell them? I know there's this theory that women are more democratic and consultative, all that crap, but it can look to hard-headed people in the private sector as if they dither around like social workers, consulting and considering people's feelings all the time, and never getting on with the bloody job. You know the sort of thing. I have a colleague here who's rather prone to all that. *What would you think, Henry? What I think I hear you saying, Henry, is, correct me if I'm wrong ... Perhaps we could all sort of pool our ideas before we make any hasty decisions.* That sort of thing. Drives me mad. It's like Joyce Grenfell's kindergarten routine — you know it? Men get on with the bloody job.'

'And management training? Can that do anything about that difference in style?'

'Some. Not a lot. You've got to start earlier. Primary school or something. Short courses can give you insights, but it's hard to translate them into changed behaviour. There's mentoring. You can learn a lot by copying what someone you admire does. Learning on the job is more effective for an

90

executive than anything theoretical we provide, although it's my bread and butter.'

'It's like the chicken and the egg, though, Henry. You can only learn to do the job on the job, and we won't give you the job if we can help it because you've never had the job, and you might have a style we're not used to, so because you're something of an unknown quantity we'd prefer to leave it that way.'

'Hmm. Agree with you, broadly. Look, Margot, it's like this.' Henry turned to a whiteboard behind his desk and drew two lines, dividing the board into four. In the top left-hand corner he drew a star; in the bottom left-hand corner a question mark. In the top right-hand corner he drew a plus sign, and in the bottom right-hand corner a minus sign.

'You see,' he said, pointing, 'here are your stars: your top performers, the high flyers, your best executives, and your real talent for replacing those executives. That's where the real focus of your management training should go. Something between fifty and eighty per cent of your training resources should go into enhancing the skills of that sector of your workforce.

'Now.' He pointed to the plus sign. 'Here are your honest workhorses. They'll always do a good day's work for you, and they'll be very loyal to the company, even if they'll never reach the top. They deserve some topping up with training to refresh them and keep them motivated.'

He turned to the minus sign. 'This here is your deadwood. What can you do with them? Drones, incompetents, demotivated people approaching retirement, round pegs in square holes, passive aggressives who are potential saboteurs. Get rid of 'em, quick, if you can. Move 'em out. Sideways if you can't sack 'em. You do not want them in your group.'

Margot frowned. 'And the question mark quadrant?'

'Good question. Who knows? They could be potential stars or high flyers, they could just be honest workhorses. Management doesn't know enough about its question marks because they're new to the company, or maybe they haven't handled enough responsibility for judgments to be made about their individual skills. Or maybe because they're women. They could be high flyers, they could just be medium flyers — who knows?'

'Medium flyers?'

'I found the phrase on a questionnaire I'd distributed to top management when I was working in the steel industry. The general manager had written "Succession planning would be easy if we knew how to tell the high flyers from the medium flyers." '

'You're implying a lot of women are medium flyers?'

'Through no fault of their own, perhaps. A lot of them are among the unknowns in this question mark area, yes. It's harder for them to present themselves as potential high flyers, certainly. I can give you an offprint of the article I wrote on succession planning, if that's any help. Sorry I don't have time to take you to lunch.'

'That's fine. I have to get back to Yagoona anyway.'

Henry Moses smiled as if she had just said Burren Junction. 'Of course,' he said. 'Beautiful downtown Yagoona. You going to the executive development conference in Perth?' he asked as he held the door open for her.

'Not sure. The college may not be able to sponsor many of us. Budget cuts.'

'Too bad.'

'I appreciate your time, anyway, Henry.'

'Not at all.' He flicked imaginary dust off his yellow tie and closed the door.

Margot halted at the top of the iron stairs. There was one phrase she had not put in her notes. *Medium flyers*, she wrote in black felt pen in her upright handwriting.

RETREAT FROM CLOUDY BAY

In the hinterland of Cloudy Bay, Prue Lambert was in search of the one shire counsellor said to represent alternative lifestyles. She hoped that he might be more willing to talk about behind-the-scenes development deals than his colleagues were. The Windsong Commune was a cluster of old farm buildings and new cottages built of apparently random materials. Set in the hills about thirty kilometres inland, it was screened from the dirt track by tall trees.

The house nearest the road had stone foundations topped by split log walls. The windows near the front door were of stained glass. Prue struck the iron cowbell that hung beside the door. She waited three, four minutes. When no one came, she walked round behind the house. An old coachhouse had been converted into a workshop. A woman in an Indian skirt was churning butter. 'I'm looking for Peter Potts,' Prue said.

The woman went on cranking the handle. 'Peter's out at a thatching bee down past the creek.'

'Could you direct me there?'

'I can, sure, but I can't leave the butter right at this moment. Hang on. Hey, Jasmine!'

A lank-haired teenage girl came up, holding a toddler by the hand. 'Jasmine, would you show — what did you say your name was?'

'Prue. Prue Lambert. I'm from the Commission for Business Ethics.'

'Shit, eh? Is that the fuzz?'

'No. We investigate business, corporations, that sort of thing.'

'Not much in Pete's line, is it?'

'I think he could have some information from his work on the local council.'

'Yeah, well, anything's possible. Jas'll take you down.'

'Just guessing,' the girl said to Prue as they walked along a stony path, 'and no offence and all that, but you're not really into communes and cosmic stuff much, are you?'

'No, I can't say I am.'

'Who did you say you work for again?'

'The CBE. We investigate fraud, shonky companies, that sort of thing.'

'Unreal.'

'Well, it's quite interesting sometimes.'

'Too much. I'd like to get away, do something interesting like that.'

'What's stopping you?'

'Ah. Hard to say. Just people here expect you to see the city the way they did, as somewhere to come away from. You're supposed to be grateful they escaped to nature and all that. But I don't want to get into the Earth Mother scene too soon. I've seen a bit much of that.'

'But you'd be far too young.'

'Not a bit. Up in Nimbin, there's all these teenage girls, my age or even younger, pregnant, dancing round in circles saying "Om" and doing exercises for natural childbirth.'

'I wonder if it helps. Saying "Om"?' Prue and Jasmine laughed.

'And the fathers,' Jasmine said, 'they all shoot through.'

'The guy I was living with shot through,' Prue said. 'And we didn't even have kids. He just came home one day and said he was moving out. He went to a motel in Sans Souci.

Then after a few weeks he got a job in Canberra.'

'What doing?'

'He's an engineer.' Prue was giving this strange hippie girl more information about her private life than most of her colleagues had found out in years.

'What sort?'

'Electrical. He specialised in air-conditioning.'

'For office buildings and factories?'

'That sort of thing.'

'You'd need to go to uni to do that, wouldn't you?'

'Yes, university or tech, unless you were one of those technologically gifted people, who got into it by tinkering with farm machinery and so on.'

'Yeah. Well I didn't even do the HSC. Didn't seem much point.'

'If you wanted to get away, it would have opened doors. You could have gone to teachers' college.'

'That's as bad as kindergarten training. It's still the Earth Mother bit.'

'Not necessarily.'

'What do you want Peter for, then?'

'I'm investigating a development proposal at Cloudy Bay.'

'Not Mirabeau Acres — the millionaire ranch place?'

'Yes, that's the one.'

'Far out.'

'What can you tell me about it?'

'At school our careers adviser kept saying how much money there was in visitors to the area. You know, tourism and all. And for work experience he got quite a few kids to go up there. You know, answering the phone, showing visitors around and that. Well, one of the kids there, really smart kid, Warren, bit of a mathematical genius, he started looking at the books, trying to work out how many people they have to get to join the club, how much profit there's going to be in it and all that. And when Melvin Hughes found out, Pow! he sacked everyone. They had to finish the time hanging round with the council health department pretending they were learning about how to protect the environment.'

'So Warren wasn't too impressed with Mr Hughes?'

'He's just a capitalist pig. How could you be impressed?'

'Does this friend of yours, Warren, still live in the town?'

'Nah. He's away studying — Armidale, I think.'

Prue and the girl had walked down the gully and were climbing up a slope into a clearing. For a moment she stood and looked around her at the lush, wooded hills. There was no denying the beauty of the place. She was temperamentally hostile to what Jasmine called 'cosmic stuff': she harboured no romantic ideas about returning to nature, or living close to the soil, and could see no spiritual dimension to such a life. She liked order, privacy, comfort, security. She liked being paid every second Thursday. But on this brilliant morning she could see the attraction of dropping out.

The members of the thatching bee were working on the roof of a small dwelling on the side of the hill. They were using a traditional thatching method, tying bundles of dried rushes together and binding them to form a waterproof covering. They were straining and grunting at the weight of the bundles and the effort to make the weave taut. Prue's arrival provided an excuse to stop working for a few minutes. Jasmine went forward and spoke to a bearded man. As Peter Potts came towards her, Prue noticed that the other workers were all women. Two were bare-breasted; all were suntanned. Skin cancer, thought Prue. No hats. What a negative commentary I keep up about everything, she reflected, probably it's sour grapes that I wouldn't be able to saunter round unselfconsciously like that if I were half naked.

Prue explained her business to the suntanned man. Sweat ran down his cheeks and torso.

'I'd love to help you,' he said, 'but I don't know that I know anything that'd stand up in court. There are complications, too, in taking Hughes on. We've stood up to the developers on a few matters up here, and a couple of us got into local government to try and get a bit more rationality and respect for individual rights into the way things are done. But the power's still with them, see? With the capitalists. They have the lawyers, the bulldozers — you go against them once too often and they're not above reprisals. Things burn down, quite remarkably. Or trees are poisoned. Or various crops are reported to the authorities. If you don't rock the boat, like, if they have their projects and we have ours, live and let live, it's less of a hassle, get my drift?'

'I just wondered if you had any specific information about Mirabeau Acres, or if you were aware of any documents or aspects of the matter that I should be aware of.'

'Like I say, nothing specific, nothing the legal types wouldn't cut to shreds. The time-share idea at Mirabeau wasn't all that bad, you know. Let a lot of city people enjoy the coast — if they want to do it at some fancy country club, good luck to them. I only got upset when they started talking about a self-contained resort with its own airport — you know, the Japanese honeymooners' special.'

'This is the first I've heard of an airport.'

'Well the company behind it all is Barbary Developments, right? It's not just a property outfit is it? They do manufacturing, imports, all types of business under the one umbrella. What I understood was, they were hoping to extend into travel and transport, with a new airport.'

'The prospectus doesn't mention it.'

'No, but anything you've seen would have been aimed at the Australian market, right? The market they would get by having an airport that could take more than light planes would be the overseas market. Lot of capital involved. My guess is that the whole venture was undercapitalised and began to go bad long before the other components could be put in place. All to the good, if you ask me. To put in an airport, they'd have to rezone crown land, it'd be a national issue for the conservation movement, it'd be greenies versus developers like we've never seen. Any moves we've made round here towards cooperation between the new settlers and the straight community, they'd be right out the window.

97

So it's good luck all round, if you ask me, preserving the environment through lousy financing.'

'Can you tell me where to find any documentation on all this?'

'Like I tell you, sunshine, it's all just the vibes you pick up, it's not documents, it's not a court case.'

Not much of an investigation file, Prue thought. In the view of one councillor who declined to be named ... That wouldn't be much use either; Peter Potts' views would identify him immediately.

'Thanks for the information, anyway,' Prue said. 'I'll leave you my card in case you come across anything I ought to know.'

Potts grinned and looked down at his bare feet and sweating body. 'Better give the card to Jasmine,' he said, 'she can leave it down at the house for me.'

'Sorry to have interrupted you, but I'm only in the area for a couple of days.'

'No sweat, man. Peace and love.'

Prue's tongue felt numb at the prospect of returning this salutation. 'I am grateful,' she said. 'Goodbye.'

Prue, Jasmine and the toddler retraced their steps. 'If you don't want this so-called Earth Mother trip, what are you spending your time doing child care for?' Prue asked.

Jasmine shrugged. 'Valya's my half-sister,' she said. 'I felt I had to support Mum; she had two babies, at forty and forty-two. This is the youngest. It's been a very hard time for her. Brendan, my stepfather, has been doing time for possession.'

'I feel very square and stupid. You mean of marijuana?'

'Yeah. They had him on a growing charge, but they couldn't prove it, so when he went up on a possession charge for the third time they sent him to prison. Mum is having to live on social security. She can't even afford to go and see Brendan all that often. He's in Cessnock.'

They walked through a grove of bananas and light slanted through the fronds onto Jasmine's bare shoulders. She carried Valya on her hip.

'You know you could matriculate by correspondence, don't you?' Prue felt suddenly like a missionary who had to save this young woman from the alternative society.

'Yeah. I'm not into studying much, though. What I might do is, I might go and work in a restaurant a friend has in Glebe.'

'That sounds like fun.' Prue could imagine the menu. Banana yoghurt shakes, salads of unwashed alfalfa, wholewheat berry muffins. She smiled. 'Here's my card, if Peter has anything more to tell me. Or your friend Warren, if you're in touch with him at all — anything he knows about Mirabeau Acres. He must have been onto something if Hughes got so furious with him. I don't suppose you know where I'd get onto him in Armidale?'

'Wouldn't have the foggiest.' Jasmine took the child off her hip as they neared the house.

'Well, I'm grateful for your help anyway. Say goodbye to your mother for me.'

Prue drove off. On her right she passed two signs: GENUINE HONEYCOMB AVAILABLE HERE and QUARANTINE AREA — GERMAN MEASLES. She laughed and turned on the radio. She felt that commune life and quarantine were indistinguishable anyway.

Poetry in motion, you're all that I ado-or-re ... she sang with the car radio, as the road made its way from sunshine into a canopy of dappled branches, over the hills and towards the town.

Prue wondered who would assess her file when she got back to Sydney and wrote up her findings. It would have to go to Legal Branch of course, and sometimes things were held up there for months. She would not have Malcolm Gwynne there to expedite it for her. With his support, she could have made it a 'green tab' file which would have priority because of the scope of the investigation and the urgency of getting court hearings listed. But Malcolm was on sick leave and was not expected back for months.

Prue had heard about Malcolm's stroke for the first time

when Aileen greeted her one morning with 'Morning, Prue, have you given me two dollars?'

'Sorry — what are we talking about?'

'Flowers for Malcolm — he's in St Vincent's Private.'

'Good grief, I had no idea. Is he all right?'

'Serious, but improving, his wife said.'

'You've spoken to his wife?'

'Yes, she rang the Commissioner, but she told me all about it. Have you got the two dollars? We're going to have an arrangement delivered. Carnations.'

'Of course.' Prue opened her bag. 'I didn't even know Malcolm was back from Geneva.'

'This happened on the way back apparently. Some sort of stroke.'

As soon as she got to her desk Prue rang St Vincent's. 'I'll put you through to the ward sister,' the receptionist said.

'Hullo, who's that?' A male voice.

'I'm a friend of Mr Malcolm Gwynne, I was, um, enquiring ...'

'Prudence, dear child, whatever is this?'

'Malcolm, you're not the ward sister — I'm sorry, I'm confused. How are you?'

'I'm in the land of the living. Can't complain. When am I going to see you?'

'When are visiting hours?'

'Any time. Any time at all. I have my own room, and I'm bored beyond words. Sarah comes every morning, of course, but I can't read or write, you see.'

'I'll be there late this afternoon.'

'Wonderful.'

She found Malcolm Gwynne lying on a high bed listening to Haydn tapes. His woolly grey hair stood up around his high-coloured complexion. Prue went to take his hand. 'Other one, other one,' Malcolm said, squirming round to offer his left hand. Prue squeezed it. 'Sit down, dear girl. Sit just here near the window.'

'How are you? Whatever happened?'

'I'm not altogether sure. As you know, I was in Geneva at the Commissioners' Conference — those background articles you put together for me were a great help, by the way. My paper went pretty well. Well, Geneva's not the most fascinating town in the world, and I have a great fondness for luxuriating in the world's best hotels. So I took myself off to Vienna, and spent three days living like a prince. I do like service — don't mind paying for it. It was superb. I went to the opera, lay for hours in the big bath with the gold taps, wandered around in the thick towelling bathrobe, pretended to myself that I could read the newspapers ... marvellous fun. Then I took the plane to the Philippines — we don't have an extradition treaty with them, as you know, and there are a lot of overlapping villains on our files and the local police files in Manila. You can never be sure you've found a straight cop, of course, but my fellow up there seems very sincere and certainly let me look up a couple of our Mr Big Enoughs in their files. Useful time. But you know Manila?'

'No.'

'Ghastly place. Full of sex-crazed Australian yobbos who'd be turned down by any woman who wasn't desperate. But of course the poverty there — the women are desperate. And boys, too, I don't doubt. I was at the Police Administrative Centre looking at evidence when I got what seemed to be this blinding headache. Went back to the hotel shops, asked in the chemist's for something for a migraine. Went back to the files the next day. My dear, the head only got worse. I had to abandon my work there and bring my flight forward. Well, I rang Sarah and she sounded very anxious, so I agreed to come back. I don't like flying — who does? But this flight was unspeakable. Shocking headache, and no pills would stop it. And nausea as well. Couldn't even have a drink, so ill. I just sat there, half asleep, longing for the flight to end. Just before we got to Mascot, the hostess handed round landing cards. I took a pen out of my pocket, but I couldn't even get my fingers to close round the top of it. See?'

He demonstrated his half-paralysed hand.

'Frightful.'

'So I said to the hostess, "You'll think I'm an awful fool, but I'll have to get you to do this for me." She filled it out for me. Being kind, you see. Thought I was illiterate. When Sarah met me at the airport she took one look at me and brought me straight here. Well, Casualty. They're very good down there. And I was admitted from there. My doctor tells me it was a stroke, and that without treatment' — he waved at the paraphernalia around the bed — 'I'd have had a really severe stroke. And you know me, I'd hate not to be able to talk. As it is, I can't read or write. Headache. Slight paralysis. Bloody fright. Most frightening thing is, I still don't know when it happened.'

'Well, you'd have to be the toughest man I know if you managed to walk around South East Asia doing business for two or three days after a stroke.'

'So it would seem. But tell me your news. Brought any villains to book in the last few days?'

Prue laughed. 'You know it's never so simple. I think I've got a jojoba racket ready for prosecution, but heaven knows when Legal will get off their arses.'

'I do love profanity from your innocent young mouth. I wish I were there to give it a good kick along for you.'

'Aileen sent her love. Meredith's in the depths of despair again — Nadia is involved with another woman and Meredith's suddenly the odd person out in a threesome. Geoff said he would come and see you one afternoon this week when he's not going to the gym ...' Prue searched around for more office gossip. Was there a shortage of it, or was it just that people didn't confide in her? She nearly always had her head down, poring over her work. It was not an attitude that invited interruptions or confidences. She stood up and looked down on Green Park, with its old palm trees, neatly spaced benches, and notorious men's lavatory. Behind it was the wall of old Darlinghurst Gaol.

'I suppose you know,' she said, 'that this park is a great

homosexual beat. I read all about it in my sociology course. The cops used to have decoys in the toilets. Men and boys hang about in the park, or up by the wall, and as it grows darker, cars with men in them cruise by to pick them up. You've really got a bird's eye view from up here. You could see the whole bright feast of gay life being played out before your very eyes.'

'How extraordinarily sad.'

'Yes, it is sad of course.' Malcolm had pronounced 'sad' with the emphasis of an actor.

When she looked at him, his eyes were filling with tears. 'You couldn't have known,' he said. 'My marriage nearly broke up over a man. A young man. Oh, a long time ago. No regrets. I had to give all that away. The risk of blackmail, in the sort of position I'm in now, wouldn't be worth it.'

Dark patches, Sarah had said. Absolute despair. If he cries I don't know what I'll do, Prue thought.

'I had no idea,' she said. 'Really. The last thing I meant was to be hurtful.'

'No offence taken. As you say, all part of the rich tapestry of life.'

No, he wouldn't cry, but things would not be quite the same between them again either.

Prue turned into the main street and cruised along in front of the fast-food shops and beachwear boutiques. The smell of salt air, much-fried fat, and exhaust fumes reminded her that the long drive had made her hungry. She decided to buy some takeaway food and eat it in her motel room as she watched the television news, rather than go out to dinner. She drank a diet lemon drink while her chicken pieces and tabouli were parcelled up. The woman behind the counter was dark, with lank black hair, olive skin, and pronounced circles under her eyes. Why do we let people overwork us the way we do, Prue wondered. If I look as tired as that, no wonder people find me humourless. 'Four-fifty, lovey,' the woman said.

Food was not all she needed. She went into a chemist's and

bought tablets to prevent pre-menstrual cramps, juggling the food parcels and the drink canister clumsily while she located a five-dollar note. In the car she took two of the pills with the last sip of drink, and ate a slice of fried chicken breast.

Her motel room had a little alcove with an electric jug on the left of the door. She filled the jug, flicked it on, and went to the bathroom, noticing as she dried her hands that the mirror-fronted cabinet was ajar and her cosmetics and deodorant were lying in a jumbled heap.

Only then did she switch on all the lights and look at the bed. The bedcover had been neatly turned down. On her pillow, stiff, grey-black, its eyes just beginning to rot, was a large dead rat.

The whistle of the electric kettle and Prue's scream rivalled one another for shrillness. Prue dashed back to the bathroom and threw up.

No one came. This is how murders go unreported, Prue thought. People think it is none of their business, or that you're enjoying a bit of rough sex.

She switched off the frantically steaming jug, tossed the food parcels in the bin, and pushed her belongings into her overnight bag, avoiding the eyes of the rat as she moved around the room. She locked the bag in the car, relieved that she'd had her notebook, file and portable tape-recorder with her when the break-in occurred.

The motel owner said he had no idea who could have gained access to the room. He was not keen for Prue to ring the police, but offered her a discount and a new room.

'My office will be asking for a complete rebate. I couldn't possibly stay in Cloudy Bay at all at the moment,' Prue said.

'Sorry you feel that way,' he said. Customers were starting to arrive for the night, and he had little time for a woman, not a regular either, who couldn't take a joke.

Prue turned on the headlights and drove south. The road climbed away from the coast and twisted through forests and farms. On the radio someone was discussing the nature writings of Edward Thomas. It all sounded far away and long ago, a Toad of Toad Hall world of hedgehogs and badgers and moles and ... she shuddered; rats.

She turned back to the coast near Nelson Bay, and booked into a neat, pristine motel under the pseudonym of Edwina Thomas.

Back in Sydney, Prue wrote to the Lands Department requesting copies of any rezoning applications for crown land at Cloudy Bay. She had a dozen other investigations in train, so left the Cloudy Bay findings in draft while she waited for more information about proposals for an airport. She told the Commissioners about the rat incident, but, as far as they were concerned, it was a minor act of intimidation. Assaults and blackmail, if not exactly routine, were not unusual. In this case, there was no bodily harm, no subsequent legal action, and, importantly, no prime suspect. Prue listed the possibilities: someone connected with Melvin Hughes and the Mirabeau Acres venture; someone alerted by Peter Potts who was frank about not wanting trouble between new settlers and straights; or even the hostile tourism consultant, Ian Forbes, who just hadn't wanted her on his turf. The developers had the best motive, but it was a crude tactic and did not ring quite true. Prue worked on her other cases and waited for the documents.

Malcolm Gwynne was no longer in hospital. She rang the Drummoyne house, and was told by friends of the family that he and Sarah had gone to Mount Macedon, outside Melbourne, for a couple of months. There was speculation among her colleagues that he would remain on sick leave until he could retire. The prospect of never having him back in the office saddened her.

'Still feeling rattled?' Geoff Kerin's grin gave him away.

'Christ, Geoff, that's not funny.'

'No, no, it must have been awful.' He made a sobersided face, then sat down laughing.

'How's the Cloudy Bay thing coming along anyway?'

Geoff was a shrewd investigator, and she was glad of the

chance to talk the case through with someone. She sketched in the facts as she knew them, and the blank spaces she hoped to fill in.

'The Great Cloudy Bay Rip-off,' Geoff mused. 'I dunno, Prue, it all sounds a bit nebulous.'

'Very funny,' Prue said. 'Your puns go from bad to worse.' But she laughed; she was feeling buoyant again. The retreat from Cloudy Bay had unaccountably lifted her spirits. 'Did you see Malcolm before he went to Victoria?'

'Yes, he didn't seem too bad. Red in the face at the best of times, as you know. But his wife said those scan things — what do you call 'em?'

'EEGs?'

'Yeah — those. Still showing him to be at risk of a further stroke. He's supposed to take it easy for a while.'

'Some chance.'

'That's pretty much what his wife said. We'll certainly miss him here. There's all kinds of jostling at the top for his position as Deputy Commissioner, of course. There are factions and counter-factions and rumours of blood-letting. And of course, the Minister might want to make one of his advisers a permanent public servant.'

'Isn't it fun working in a nice, secure government job where nothing ever happens?'

'That's what I always say. Actually, Prue, you're looking a lot better, if you don't mind my saying so.'

'Compared to what? No, Geoff, I'll take it as a compliment. Thanks.'

It was true. She felt fine. At lunchtime she went to Sportsgirl, and, abandoning her usual navy and white colour scheme, bought a slim emerald green skirt and a toning handknit pink and green top. Instead of going to aerobics, she walked a mile or two each morning. For the first time since Andrew's departure she could take pleasure in the cacophony of galahs attacking the nearby hospital roof, or the silhouette of a cat walking up and down the M of an Edwardian roof.

INDIGO ISLAND

A tall black young man was waiting for Roxane at Isantu airport. 'Good evening, Miss Rowe,' he said. 'Brooke sent me to pick you up. Olwyn's in hospital.'

'Brooke?'

'Brooke Lake-Winton. She's deputising for Olwyn. We don't have any other Runaway guests on the flight, so I've just got the station wagon.'

'Fine. Very kind of you. I could have got a taxi if Brooke had left a message for me.'

'Not at all,' the man said. 'I'm Philippe, by the way. Philippe Desjardins.'

'Delighted to meet you.' They waited for the luggage trolley to be wheeled over from the plane. 'That one with the hibiscus.' She pointed out her suitcase.

'Yes, I recognise the Runaway design. Very loyal.'

Suspicious that she was being mocked, Roxane looked more closely at the man's face. His strong features set into a bland expression when he felt her looking at him, but there was an alertness about his eyes. He was wearing an old green T-shirt and faded jeans. Runaway rules required all staff to wear white, but perhaps Indigo was not run strictly by the book. Olwyn had lost her zest for detail lately, in more ways than one, Roxane thought. Perhaps the man — Philippe — was actually off duty, and was giving her a lift as a favour.

'And how do you fit into the scheme of things at Indigo Island?' she asked as she climbed into the passenger seat of a Citroën wagon.

'Officially, I'm a barman,' Philippe said, 'but I do various errands for Brooke. Like right now, I'm partly fetching you, but more importantly perhaps, I am bringing back the mudcrabs from the fish market. Hope you don't object to the smell.'

Roxane felt she ought to object to something, ought to give him some warning that his casual manner struck her as impertinent. But she was tired after the flight.

'How is Olwyn?' she asked.

'Brooke or Sebastien — Mr Charpentier, Olwyn's partner — they would know better than I do. I haven't been to the hospital, I'm afraid. I'm not too close to Olwyn, you know, and we're a little understaffed on Indigo right now.'

'I see.'

Isantu, the capital of the island group, had a wide shopping street near the harbour, with small streets of oriental bazaars zigzagging up the hill towards La Morne, the mountain that jutted up behind the town. The sun was setting over the harbour as they drove along the main street, pink light encircling black dots of islands on a gunmetal sea. One of these dots was Indigo.

'Been here before?'

'No, but I've stayed at the old Hilton just out of town. And of course I've seen the reports and the photographs of Indigo. It's a very special project for Olwyn, and for Runaway.'

'Not the same as seeing it. Lot of potential, Indigo.'

'Yes, I'm sure.'

'We'll get the regular six-thirty launch over,' Philippe told her. 'I didn't bring an Indigo boat over.'

'You're lucky the plane was on time.'

'Oh, I could have telephoned Brooke. There was no reason to be anxious.' Philippe lifted the two Eskies of mudcrabs out of the back of the wagon. 'If you wouldn't mind bringing one of these down to the jetty,' he suggested to Roxane, 'I can bring your suitcase and the other one.'

'So kind.' What a martyred performance, Roxane thought. How did Olwyn hire him?

They joined a small group of people in the harbour launch. Roxane noticed three Japanese couples, some Australian teenagers, and an old man with the air of a retired colonel. 'Only thing to eat over here,' he told the Japanese, 'is curry or mudcrab. Don't trust anything with a French name, it only means amateurism disguised with béarnaise sauce.'

'Please?' The young Japanese did not comprehend.

The colonel character revealed himself an old hand at charades. 'Crab?' he asked. 'Claws? Like this? You know?' Soon several Japanese people were copying his gestures and laughing. 'Crab is good. And curry. Hot! Hot! Burns the tongue. India. Good, very good.'

'Crab and curry.' Now they understood.

'You're cutting it a bit fine with those crabs,' Roxane told Philippe.

'Plenty of time. They'll have a cocktail first.'

'I sincerely hope you'll change before you serve at the bar.'

'But of course, Madame.'

The launch stopped at a small jetty near Indigo Island's main public buildings. A young woman in a sarong printed with Runaway hibiscus greeted Roxane. 'Hi, welcome to Indigo. I'm Brooke. Philippe looking after you all right?'

'Fine, but I'm getting anxious about the crabs — the kitchen should have had them hours ago.'

'Oh, no, we just wash them and slap them under the grill. No cause for concern.' Brooke Lake-Winton had tangled brown hair and a wide smile. She caught Philippe's eye and looked at him significantly, still smiling.

Philippe handed her the two Eskies. 'I'll just take Miss Rowe's suitcase down to her quarters,' he said. 'Then I'll have to change before I come up to the bar, as Miss Rowe has been kind enough to remind me.'

'Things are very casual here on Indigo, Roxane,' Brooke said. 'You don't have to dress for dinner. Would you like to come straight over to the bar or would you like me to show you your hut first?'

'Perhaps you'd be kind enough to call me Miss Rowe until we know each other better. Quite honestly, I couldn't face dinner or a drink right at this moment. Perhaps you could arrange for a chicken and mayonnaise sandwich and some mineral water to be sent to my room.'

'Yes. Of course. If that's what you'd prefer. I'll show you where it is — Miss Rowe.'

Brooke Lake-Winton (barefooted, Roxane saw) led the way along a palm-lined pebble path to a group of small salmon-coloured huts. A bed. A double bed, made up with fresh cotton sheets, and a bowl of frangipani on the dresser. Olwyn's training had done some good, at any rate. 'Great,' she said. 'I really need a rest. I'll look forward to talking to you tomorrow.'

'The sandwich won't be more than a couple of jiffs. Goodnight.'

Roxane sat in the inky night outside her hut. Wavelets of tide swirled and occasionally slapped on the shore. She found the scene reassuring: night, privacy, earth, air, water, and the packaged comforts of Runaway accommodation. People would kill for my job, she thought, and these moments of sanctuary are what it's all about. How little of my own company I get, with Cindy back from school every weekend, the office feeling free to ring me at all hours, Szabo expecting me to ditch everything for him at fifteen minutes' notice, and every second man I take to bed imagining that I want him to stay around for breakfast. What comparative bliss to be alone. The only catch was that the single occupancy rate for someone not in the industry would work out at half a week's salary. There wasn't much option but to stay in the rat race.

In the morning she would have to start flinging her weight around; jolt this backwater into action — demand the books, pick out a target or two for dismissal. But she would not think

110

about that yet. Across the water people were singing psalms. A harmony of adult voices reached her in a rhythm she did not know and must not succumb to.

There was a soft knocking at the door. Wordlessly Roxane took the tray from the Melanesian woman in the flowered smock.

In the tropical dawn Roxane heard birds calling on the roof and dreamt she was lying on a small beach in Barbados beside the turquoise sea. On the skyline a big black pirate ship listed over and began to sink. There was panic on board, with people yelling out for help, but on the shore the sunbaking white tourists were unconcerned. 'It's only the Rastafarians,' an American told her. 'Ludicrous cult, they only work for subsistence. They don't like the machine, why use motor boats to save them?' The angry men with corkscrew curls were yelling and jumping into the sea. Further down the beach someone was getting a longboat ready. 'Save the women,' he shouted. Most of the sunbathers turned their backs. Roxane dashed towards the rescued women, a boatload of pale, pearly, half-drowned creatures. As she lifted them into hospital beds, alive but dazed and weak, their tails twitched listlessly. Their silvery pallor, their tails: 'They're mermaids!' she shouted. 'Mermaids!' She staggered out of bed and turned on the jug for coffee. How could mermaids have been drowning? she wondered, shaking her head as she woke up.

At breakfast Rhonda Davidson of Eastwood was coaxing her son Shane to eat papaya. 'Pretend it's medicine,' she said. 'Just put it on the back of your tongue and swallow.'

'Yuk. Why can't we get Weet Bix or Coco Pops? Why is it all this yukky old fruit?' His sister was eating pineapple, sullenly.

'It's delicious,' their father, Don, said.

'The other day, when you were in bed, we had bacon and eggs,' Shane said.

'Dobber!' Vanessa accused him.

'Well you shouldn't have,' Rhonda said, 'the continental breakfast is included in the package, and if it's good enough for us it's good enough for you.'

'And another thing, kids, let's get this straight. There's an upper limit of three Cokes a day each to go on my account, okay?'

'But Dad, it's so hot, we get so thirsty,' Vanessa moaned.

'And it's so boring,' Shane said.

'You can swim,' Rhonda told him. 'You love swimming.'

'There isn't even a proper pool. The one here is so small and these Japanese people are everywhere. And the water's got things in it. Oyster shells and awful sea slugs.'

'And there's no TV.'

'And you can't even get the cricket scores.'

'And they don't even speak English properly.'

'And Coca-Cola is so expensive.'

'Shut up!' Don Davidson commanded through clenched teeth. 'Shut up. Your mother and I need a holiday. We couldn't give a stuff what you think. You two can just shut up and enjoy yourselves. I don't want to hear one more whinge out of either of you.'

Roxane was only half listening. The Australian family at play held little new for her. She drank black filtered coffee and ate a croissant and half a grapefruit. She must check that the Davidson kids' bacon and eggs had been added to their bill. She clinked her coffee cup onto its saucer, displacing a pink frangipani, and swept into the kitchen.

'By eleven o'clock I want to see all the restaurant accounts, itemised, for breakfast, lunch and dinner,' she told Brooke. 'And the wage books. And this afternoon I'll want the figures for the bar.' Brooke nodded. Her two Melanesian kitchen hands stood gazing at Roxane as at an emissary from another world.

Sebastien Charpentier was drinking beer on the porch with two Indigo Islanders. Roxane joined them. 'Madame,' the

Frenchman said, 'already we have the pleasure. I present Mr Isaac Pontiac and Mr Justinian Belize. Elders and shareholders.'

'Delighted,' Roxane said. 'I was hoping to meet you all before the Council meeting.'

'You intend coming to the meeting?' Charpentier was perhaps fifty, deeply tanned, with hooded eyes and the mouth of a cynic.

'Of course. I represent Runaway.'

'There are cultural considerations, Madame.'

'Meaning what?'

'It is an extension of a council of elders. It is I who represent Runaway as a rule. It is a male council.'

'Thankyou for your concern, Sebastien, but you'll find business considerations outweigh that stuff. Olwyn's in hospital, I'll be seeing her later. But as she's not here, the responsibility falls to me. Mr Pontiac and Mr Belize appreciate my position, I'm sure. I'll be attending not as a woman but as a Runaway executive.' She added, with the emphasis of one administering a dictation test, 'I'm a very senior executive of Runaway Travel.'

'I see you on the television in Sydney,' Belize said.

'Yes. Yes. In the Runaway commercials. Can you explain to Mr Pontiac?'

Belize spoke to Pontiac, who shook his head. 'It is not our custom,' he said. 'The council is for men. The spirituality is for the elders.'

'Fine, I don't want to interrupt any religious ceremony. I'll come along when you get to the Runaway lease on your agenda.'

'I talk to my people,' Belize said.

'Roxane,' Charpentier said, 'I'll speak to you later.'

'You sure will.'

Roxane looked at the can of beer that had been placed in front of her. 'It's a custom of mine,' she said, 'to use a glass. Would that be asking too much of anyone? The staff have been trained, I take it?'

Belize got to his feet and left the table.

'These are delicate matters,' the Frenchman said to Roxane. 'Believe me, one does not force the issue with these people.'

'A glass for the lady.' Belize had rejoined the group.

'How kind of you,' said Roxane, glaring at Charpentier. She turned to Belize. 'I heard singing last night. Psalms, it sounded like. There were some superb voices.'

'We are proud of our singing,' Belize said. 'We sing to honour the Lord. We go perhaps to the United States with our choir.'

'I'd like to attend one of your church services,' Roxane said, 'if there isn't any cultural sensitivity involved.'

'Women are equal before God.'

'Oh, absolutely. Will we make it Sunday morning then?'

'We worship on Saturdays.'

'Oh, you're Adventists. How wonderful. I knew the SDAs were very influential in the Pacific, of course.' Roxane held Belize with her wide, green eyes.

Isaac Pontiac looked directly at Roxane for the first time. 'The lady an Adventist?' he asked.

'The lady is coming to worship with us,' Belize said.

Charpentier drained beer from his tin. He and Roxane avoided each other's eyes. The lady is a pagan bitch, she read in his half-averted face. She continued to direct all her charm towards Belize. When the group left the table she found herself humming 'Amazing Grace'.

In the women's ward of the French hospital, Olwyn Tierney lay in a corner bed near an open window. She felt rotten. Her breath whistled through her bronchial tubes each time she exhaled. Her skin was flushed from broncho-dilator drugs. A drip was connected to her left arm. She was reading a John Fowles novel with less than full attention.

Roxane burst into the ward in a lemon and pink sundress, her sunglasses perched on the top of her head. She held out a bunch of pink frangipani. 'They'll have to put it on the other

114

side of the ward,' Olwyn said. 'Everything makes me sneeze.'

'Olwyn, darling, what's wrong with you?'

'Nothing much, Rox. I seem to have collapsed last week, but the only thing wrong with me now is a bit of trouble breathing.' She coughed.

Roxane moved the little steel chair towards the foot of the bed and sat down.

'Why this hospital? Why not the British one?'

'Why not? Sebastien brought me here. He knows the doctor in charge. I'm sure the other place is much the same.'

'I've heard some terrible things about both these hospitals. Broken legs going gangrenous, that sort of thing.'

'You must visit more often.'

'Sorry. It's just that we're concerned about you.'

'Roxane, I don't have a broken leg. And I intend to leave next week.'

'You don't look well enough to leave.'

'I'm getting better all the time. And as soon as I'm well enough to get in a plane, I'm off.'

Roxane was doing the mental arithmetic. She could go to the Indigo council meeting and still be back in Sydney well before Olwyn. 'I don't want to worry you with shop talk,' she said, 'but are you sure Sebastien can be trusted?'

'He's a bit of a rogue, the rough old colonial type, but yes, I think he's on the level.'

'How come you've never been to council meetings?'

'Tribal protocol. Women don't go.'

'And you've just accepted that?'

'Why not? Sebastien's gone for me.'

'What's to stop Sebastien knifing Runaway in the back and acting on his own behalf?'

Olwyn coughed. Her face turned purple and the wall of her chest jumped. She reached out for a glass of water. Her words came in laboured bursts.

'Look, Rox, I have to leave some things to other people when I'm out of action like this. But I've no reason not to trust Sebastien. Enjoy Indigo while you're here. You'll find it's running well, even if there are some cultural — adjustments — still to be made.' Her voice trailed away like a gramophone with a slow turntable.

'I'm wearing you out,' Roxane said. 'I'd better go.'

'Give the flowers to Madame Lelong at the end of the ward on your way out.'

'You're sure?'

'Positive. Nice of you to come. My regards to Brooke. And Sebastien. Tell him I'll see him next week.'

'You get better quickly then, okay?' Roxane said. 'We need you on deck. *A bientôt.*' Olwyn, struggling to breathe, did not have the energy to wince at Roxane's pronunciation.

'Madame Lelong?' Roxane flashed her on-camera smile although the recipient of her charity was barely conscious. '*Pour vous.*' She left the flowers on the old woman's bedside table.

She walked out onto the hospital veranda. A nurse was changing a child's dressing. Roxane turned away. Horrible skin conditions were rampant in the tropics, she'd noticed that before. Boil the water and stay in a reputable hotel, that was her advice to travellers. She felt a sudden aversion to the smells and heat of the place, the climate, the inhabitants, and to people like Olwyn who raved about natural beauty.

In the sunlight Roxane put on her dark glasses. Suddenly she was assailed by a new view of Olwyn as a fraud, a drunk, an alcoholic, an embarrassing incompetent. Olwyn believed that Indigo and places like it ought to retain local character, have some authenticity in design, and provide jobs and incomes for a developing economy. Garbage. In a few years they would deteriorate into seedy boarding houses. Why not start as they meant to go on, with multi-storeyed international hotels, a bit of style and scope? Olwyn's pseudo-native villages fooled no one. She would have to make Boris and the board see the foolishness of being guided by Olwyn. For the sake of Runaway, she had to make sure Olwyn's policies, and if necessary Olwyn herself, were ditched, fast.

TOURISM AND THE FAMILY

Roxane made her way to a hotel in the town centre where airline pilots stayed. The owner, Greg Redman, was a New Zealander who sailed north on his way round the world, never getting any further than these islands. Now he ran a charter business, two restaurants, and a hotel. Runaway sent him a lot of business: people on package tours stayed at his hotel, while the restaurants and charter boats were promoted in brochures about Isantu. On his business trips to Sydney, Greg Redman usually took Roxane to lunch.

Redman joined Roxane at the cocktail bar. 'Good to see you, Roxane, how's tricks? What's next after Indigo? How are Brooke and Sebastien making out over there without Olwyn?'

'Hey. One question at a time. And there's things I want to ask you, too.' Greg Redman had a fair moustache and scorched, fair skin. His short vowels were so narrow they were almost inaudible, while his diphthongs were those of a BBC announcer.

'What's the joke?' he asked.

'Endago. It's just the way you say Indigo amuses me, somehow.'

Roxane sat drinking with Greg Redman for two and a half

hours. He was flattered to be seen with one of the famous faces of the travel industry, while she was able to catch up on the activities of rival firms, airline gossip, local politics and scuttlebutt about her colleagues. Every scrap of scandal in the area reached Redman eventually.

'Seriously, though,' Roxane began.

'I'm always serious, baby.'

'No, Greg, really, what I need to know is, if we want to get some clout politically in Isantu — with the government, not just the council that we deal with at Indigo — who would be the main players?'

'Well, the Chief Minister.'

'Yes, but apart from him? Who really matters, in the local business scene, or as a landholder, or behind the scenes, for that matter?'

Greg Redman named a political leader from one of the northern islands, and a lawyer who ran shelf companies for a number of overseas banks.

'Any women?' Roxane asked.

'There's Marjorie Locomo, she's an interesting character. Indian, so you would expect her to be on the outer with the local leaders. Quite the reverse. She's a widow, sister-in-law of the chief minister. Runs the teacher training college up the hill. Bit of a bible-basher. Bit of a wheeler-dealer too, they say.'

'In what sense?'

'Oh, she goes on various overseas delegations representing Isantu. Stockholm, Nairobi. International women's conferences, that sort of thing.'

'So she's a feminist.'

'Roxane, dearest, I told you she's the sister-in-law of the Chief Minister. What she believes about issues has nothing to do with it.'

'Silly me.'

'Developing countries like this one are no different to anywhere else. You send someone who's close to the government, who'll do the right thing by them politically, not some dewy-eyed enthusiast who'll pick up all kinds of ideas from radical Americans.'

'You say she's a bible-basher. The people over at Indigo, our tribal co-venturers, that is, seem to be night-and-day hymn singers.'

'Yep, I'd say so. Adventists, aren't they? Of course, a few generations back missionaries were getting eaten round here.'

'Greg!'

'Don't believe me? Go and look in any of the local histories. Or the museum. One fella would get eaten and the poor old Presbyterians or whoever would send out the next bloke.'

'Like the promotion system in corporations.'

Greg Redman laughed. 'Pretty much, I guess. You doing anything tonight, Roxane? Care for dinner?'

'Thanks, that's sweet of you. But, as it happens, I'll be very busy tonight, on Runaway business.'

Roxane's dress was a frilled, full-length Mother Hubbard design, red cotton patterned with pineapples. She had spent the late afternoon with the women of the village, and for the sake of good public relations had bought two of these dresses from Esther Belize, Solomon's wife. What a triumph for the missionaries Indigo was, she thought. Even the children who dipped up and down in the water, squealing, wore pants.

It was dusk. Some of the women were in the water with their children. Others sat on the shore in their bright cottons. Roxane wanted to speak to Solomon before the Council meeting. She was finding it heavy going talking to Esther, but Solomon was still away in the town. The baby was crawling on the mud floor. He hauled himself onto a stool next to Roxane. 'How divine,' she said. 'He's so strong, your baby. How old is he?'

'Ten months.'

'Look, oh look!' said Roxane. 'All the teeth he's got. What's his name?'

'Nathan.'

'Lovely name. A lovely boy.'

'You got children?'

'Yes, I have a daughter, Cindy, short for Lucinda. She's fifteen.'

'You too young to have that big girl.'

'Flattering, darling, but I'm quite old enough.' She looked at the bookshelf beside her. A Bible, an almanac of tropical medicine, an old pile of *Reader's Digest*s, a children's encyclopedia. Bible-bashers, she thought. When it comes to wiping out local cultures, tourism isn't in it. 'You know, I'm hoping to talk to your husband before I go to the council meeting.'

'Council meeting is a men's thing. No ladies there. Ever.'

'Time for a little revolution, then — time some of the ladies did. Would you come with me?'

'No, I look after the children here.'

Solomon Belize strode into the hut and scooped up his son. 'Madame Roxane,' he began.

'Just Roxane. Please.'

'Roxane, you wear one of Esther's dresses. Good.'

His wife handed him a stubbie of beer. He sat on the stool with the beer in one hand and his son in the crook of his left arm.

'I really must come to your meeting,' Roxane told him.

'Is a men's thing, the meeting.'

'Yes, but you see, I need to discuss Runaway's proposals to build another group of cabins. It's a very modest development when you look at other things that are going up round the Pacific. It's in the best interests of the Indigenous Council as well as of my company to have the resort turn a good profit. You know what that means for Nathan and kids like him. Education. A good life.'

'Sebastien represent Runaway.'

'What about Olwyn?'

'Yes, she's the boss of the building, the restaurant, all that, but she never at meetings of the Council.'

'But Sebastien's a shareholder in his own right.'

'The tribe have fifty-one per cent. Runaway twenty-nine. Sebastien and his friends, they have twenty.'

'Well, that's a big parcel of shares. He might want things that are not the same as our company's goals. Olwyn should be there, too.'

'Olwyn a woman. Local people, they know Sebastien, they don't know Runaway.'

'What people? French?'

'Look, Sebastien work for your company, right? You ask Sebastien, he can answer all these questions.'

'Solomon, I have no wish to intrude on religious ceremonies or tribal matters or male traditions, but I have to represent my company while I'm in Indigo. I'll be at your meeting. Just tell me what time I can come.'

'I advise the lady not to come.'

'All right, thanks for the advice. I'll be there at eight forty-five. Will you tell them to expect me?'

'I tell them you coming, yes.'

Roxane found Sebastien Charpentier at the Indigo bar, tilting back on a cane stool. He was drinking Heineken beer. His skin was very tanned and he wore white. The old planter at twilight, she thought. He scowled at her outfit.

'Going native, I see.'

'Such practical wear for the tropics, aren't they? And becoming. And there are cultural reasons: I'm coming to your meeting.'

'Women never do.'

'Look, I've just been through all that with Solomon, and we've established that I'm coming. Someone has to represent Runaway.'

'That's what I do.' He lit a Gauloise.

'Yes, but you're also a shareholder with twenty per cent in your name and your associates', whomever they may be. By law the council has to have a majority holding, fifty-one per cent. Add your twenty and that's a pretty powerful voting bloc.'

'A mathematical marvel. But your distrust is unworthy of you. Olwyn trusts me.'

'That's true. She does.'

'Without my local knowledge, without my political contacts, Olwyn would be sitting up at the government offices with her plans in her hands talking about her salmon and white colour schemes and being sent from one functionary to the next. I'm the one who got things off the ground for Runaway politically.'

'And you've been overseeing the contracts, hiring the building workers, and representing Runaway at council meetings.'

'True.'

'You don't see any conflict of interest?'

'Far from it. A most harmonious partnership, Runaway and myself.'

'What safeguards do we have against kickbacks on building materials and labour costs?'

'The records are open. And you have my integrity.'

'And what sort of offers have you had for your share of the action?'

'You assume there have been offers.'

'There are rumours you'll be returning to France.'

'No, I think less and less of returning to France. The tropics get in your blood. I am a man of the sun. A man for bare feet and sunglasses.'

'That's not an answer to who's in the market.'

'Would I not keep my partners fully informed if there were anything definite on?'

'We'd have to take your word for it, wouldn't we?'

'I hear you spent half the morning at Redman's.'

'And I hear a lot about you.'

'Flattering?'

'Some of it.' Redman's speculations about Charpentier had included rumours of gun-running, import-export rackets, and backing by a consortium of right-wing European millionaires.

'I'm trying to discern your purpose, Roxane. It's a long way from Sydney. And in the tropics, rumours spread everywhere, like hibiscus.'

'It's quite simple. Olwyn's sick, and someone from head office has to keep an eye on things.'

'Admirable.' He stubbed his cigarette out in a scallop shell and lit another.

'By the way,' Roxane said, 'they're expecting me at the council meeting at eight forty-five.'

'You still intend to come?'

'Of course.'

'Against my advice, my dear, remember that.'

Roxane's taxi splashed rainwater from the unmade gutters as it sped in the dark past tropical bungalows, garden huts, straggling banana trees and warehouses screened by steel fences. She was left in a parking lot near a building that looked like a church hall. The driver seemed not to understand her when she asked him to return at ten o'clock. Static and pop music blared out of his radio. *If the lady she telephone before, the taxi come, yes?* Roxane didn't know if he was reassuring her or mocking her.

Inside the hall was a games room where a couple of teenagers were playing ping-pong while others looked on. A girl wore a pink T-shirt inscribed I ADORE JESUS. There was no sign of the council meeting.

'Excuse me,' Roxane began, 'I was looking for the meeting.'

'No ladies there,' the girl said. 'They all at home, except the ones in the kitchen.'

'The gentlemen are expecting me. Isn't this the place?'

The girl shrugged and gestured towards a door with notices pinned on it. Roxane pressed ahead, angry. Behind her someone made a loud farting noise. She stood inside the meeting room, red in the face and flustered. Eight men rose to their feet, without speaking. 'No need to get up, please,'

123

she said. Did Sebastien look sardonic? With those eyelids, it was a habitual expression.

Solomon Belize came forward and took her by the elbow. Roxane hated being elbowed, but allowed herself to be led to a chair obliquely behind the chairman's. No one moved to allow her a space at the table.

'That conclude the formal business,' Belize said, 'because we defer the decision on the extension to the Runaway development until we have a government representative here next month. But since we have here the very famous lady from Runaway Travel, Miss Roxane Rowe, perhaps she care to speak to us about her ideas about tourism in the region.'

'Thankyou.' Roxane looked around the table, leaning forward and trying to establish eye contact with the eight men. She stood up and moved to a vacant space beside Sebastien. 'I'm not sure,' she began, 'whether Mr Charpentier has ever really made clear to you just how we at Runaway see ourselves as supporting the family. The Christian family. Listening to your beautiful harmonised psalms last night — which ought, incidentally, to be recorded so they can be enjoyed all over the world — I reflected on the importance of the leisure industry to the well-being of families, both in countries like this which are tourist destinations, and in the countries such as Japan, America and Australia, where our tourists come from. Fathers of families, breadwinners, need to enjoy a well-earned break from toil, as recommended in the Bible, and where better to do it than in an island paradise such as Indigo? And honeymooners — what better foundation can there be for a happy family than a few days or weeks shared with one's chosen life partner at the outset of a Christian marriage? Tourism is not incidental to the institution, it is fundamental to it. When we talk about a possible extension of our development at Indigo, by thirty small huts, all constructed with local materials, in styles that blend in with the environment, providing work for your people, never forget that's it the protection of the decent family values that are traditional to your people that we are concerned with. The values of Christianity and the Christian family.'

Beside her, Sebastien concealed his fury with a sanctimonious expression. Roxane spoke like a lay preacher for seven or eight minutes, and was applauded by the councillors when she finished. 'Now,' Belize said, 'I believe the ladies have something for us.'

Platters of curious looking pikelets were brought in by wide-hipped women who wore long floral dresses identical to Roxane's. Declining pikelets and pineapple juice, Roxane tried unsuccessfully to get one of the male councillors alone to discuss business. People gathered around her, drinking, eating, and fingering her multiple gold bracelets which looked so out of keeping with the Mother Hubbard dress. Roxane felt desperate for air and solitude. More girls in Jesus T-shirts crowded into the room, bearing more trays of food.

'The lady intend to worship with us,' Belize told an older man.

The elderly man looked at Roxane. 'You speak of the church, the family,' he said. "What about the beer that is all our men want now? What about the white men who want to use our young women? You talk about values — our values are dying.'

'If it weren't Runaway,' Roxane countered, 'who might it be? Club Med? An American consortium? The Japanese? High-rise hotels? We are famous for the sensitivity and harmonious small scale of our resorts.'

'All resorts mean greed and drunkenness. Sin. The devil.'

'And jobs. Income. I respect your religion, I've said that. I'll be coming to your church. But the whole region needs sympathetic development to maintain its place in the economy of the Pacific. You've only got to compare Indigo with some of the other island resorts to see how lucky you are.'

'The devil speak of luck,' the old man said. 'Luck and greed, hand in hand.'

'Is there somewhere I can ring for a taxi?' Roxane asked. 'It's a little earlier than I was expecting to leave.'

'Mr Charpentier — Sebastien — have his car here.'

'Indeed I do,' Sebastien said. He gave a mock bow. 'Won't the lady do me the honour?'

'Thanks,' Roxane managed to say, 'I do need a lift.'

In the car she turned to him. 'What in Christ's name do you mean by having the meeting conclude before I got there?'

'Nothing to do with me. Local customs. Besides, it's true about waiting for a politician to come next month. It's a kind of godfather system, politics here. Old tribal loyalties come into play. They don't like to make decisions without speaking to the local representative. His father was the chief here. The old man you were speaking to is one of his uncles. And besides, they'd told you the meetings were for men.'

'It's reprehensible of Olwyn not to have challenged that, if you ask me.'

'Olwyn is a wise old woman. She has a little cultural sensitivity.'

'You're trying to tell me I shouldn't have spoken about Christian values.'

'I'm trying to tell you that people are smarter than you seem to think. You think they don't recognise hypocrisy when they hear it?'

'If you don't mind, that's an insult. How dare you imply my beliefs aren't genuine?'

Sebastien put a hand on his heart. 'Blessed are the pure in heart,' he said, 'for they shall inherit the tropical paradise.'

'I'm a little upset,' Roxane told him. 'Do you think you could keep both hands on the wheel?'

At the jetty opposite Indigo Island they transferred from Sebastien's car to the motor boat. A few lights from the tourist huts rippled on the water to their right, while a hum of voices and laughter rose from the restaurant and bar at the more brightly lit southern tip of the island. The prow of the boat reared up and slapped down as it sped through the darkness, a fan of white froth in its wake. When they beached the craft Sebastien headed for the bar. After a curt goodnight Roxane began walking towards her hut.

She had gone only a few yards along the pebble path when a series of shrill screams carried through the night air. Fear made her pulse race. She stood still on the track. The crescendo of screams was coming from the restaurant. The screams got higher and longer. The word 'bloodcurdling' went through Roxane's mind — could terror curdle the blood like custard? Anything seemed possible. She tried to breathe calmly, to stay in control.

There was silence for a moment. Then a man shouted something in another language — French? — and other male voices rang out. There was a hubbub of other people shouting advice, a dog barking, someone sobbing. Roxane ran towards the light, hampered by her long modest dress.

Before she reached the bar a figure darted out of the doorway and ran towards the beached boat. Someone was dragging Sebastien's boat into the lagoon and revving the motor. She saw his silhouette but could not see who it was. Water splashed as the man jumped into the boat and the motor started. A heavyset security guard with a German Shepherd ran after the fleeing man, shouting. The guard halted on the shoreline, shining a big orange flashlight across the water at the retreating boat. White spume glowed in the torchlight. The dog barked and leapt on the edge of the water.

Inside the bar Roxane looked around. A young woman lay on the floor in the centre of the room, weeping. She wore a bare-shouldered sarong and her long hair obscured her face. Sebastien and some of the tourists were helping her to her feet. The woman's face was swollen and bruised but it was unmistakably Brooke Lake-Winton, sobbing and gasping with pain.

'Brooke,' said Sebastien, 'it's okay, you're right now, we'll catch up with him. He can't treat you like this, we won't let him get away with it.'

There was a silence in the room as a dozen tourists watched the aftermath of the drama. Brooke stood teetering unsteadily. Tears ran down her cheeks. Suddenly she swung her right arm at Sebastien, slapping his face so hard that he cried out.

'Leave him alone!' Brooke shouted. 'Call the dogs off. You bastards, you bastards!'

Sebastien stepped forward and grasped Brooke's wrist before she could hit him again. She swivelled around, pummelling at his grip with her free hand, screaming all the while, 'Bastard, let go of me, leave him alone. Fuck off! Let me go!' She kicked at him, tossing her dishevelled brown hair.

Roxane put her arm round Brooke's shoulders. 'Brooke,' she said, 'you need to see a doctor. You're hurt, you don't know what you're doing.'

'You bitch!' screamed Brooke, squirming out of reach. 'You interfering disgusting fucking ignorant bitch, you wouldn't know what time it was. If anyone so much as comes near me, I'll get Philippe to deal with you.'

She swung round towards the onlookers. 'And you can stop gawping. I'm not a fucking sideshow.'

She broke free from Sebastien and stumbled out into the night. The tourists looked questioningly at one another. 'Shouldn't we go with her?' Rhonda Davidson asked.

'Ladies, gentlemen, please,' said Sebastien. 'There is nothing anyone can do. This is an old story. She'll recover. Leave her. It's the best thing.'

'Are you sure?'

Suddenly everyone was talking, comparing notes, offering advice.

Sebastien poured himself a cognac and brought one across to Roxane.

'As you have just seen,' he said, 'not all of Olwyn's appointments have been successful. Olwyn brought that girl over as an assistant manager, and in no time her black lover, Philippe, arrived on her heels. With no thought to the politics of our situation with the council, Olwyn put him on staff too. What an example for the kitchen staff. The local people here are very puritan, while Philippe is not only from a different island but from a quite different background, culturally. There's been trouble before, but this is the first time we've had a scene in front of the guests.'

He smiled. 'Pity you didn't wait till tomorrow to find out all the gossip at Redman's. I'm sure this little episode will keep the whole town talking for quite a while. Our security people have seen the bastard off the island. He's got my boat, but he won't go far with it. I'll just go out and check with the watchman.'

'I'd better try and calm down the guests.'

Roxane joined the Davidsons and a small group of other people. 'On behalf of Runaway,' she said, 'I must apologise for that little disturbance. As you can see, our security people have the matter in hand. I'm sorry for any distress it's caused — it's been upsetting for us all.'

'Well, quite honestly, we were just saying, it's not the sort of thing we've paid for, is it? I mean,' Don Davidson explained, 'it's not what you have in mind for a relaxing holiday, exactly.'

'It's not that I'm prejudiced,' said another man. 'Not a racist bone in my body. But when you get a young Australian girl involved with a black fellow like that, well, it's asking for trouble.'

'We were in Fiji in that cyclone, too, remember?' Don said. 'And Noumea is very unsettled.'

'Don and I are only glad the kids have gone to bed,' Rhonda said.

'Absolutely,' said Roxane. 'I'd hate to have my daughter exposed to a scene like that one. There's too much violence in the world, full stop.'

'Oh,' Rhonda Davidson said, 'you have a daughter?'

'Yes. Lucinda. She's fifteen.'

'And where's Lucinda when you're jetting around?'

'Occasionally she comes with me. But right now she's in boarding school. We've lost our barman — can I offer anyone a drink?'

129

The talk turned to the merits of various private schools. When Roxane made her exit into the quiet night some time later, she could hear behind her, 'It's not true what they say about excessive discipline at Pittwater Grammar, honestly. My sister Stephanie's children ...'

Roxane lay awake in her hut, not at all reassured by the swish of the water or the swaying of the palm fronds. What a nightmare. Philippe would have to be sacked, and Brooke would have to take leave until the bruises subsided. The virtual adjournment of the council meeting the moment she arrived was so humiliating that she felt she had been burnt with acid. A corrosive bitterness came over her in waves. Fragments of the rumours and allegations she'd heard from Greg Redman nagged at her. What if Sebastien found a co-venturer who could outbid Runaway? He could form a voting bloc with the indigenous council which would make all progress impossible until Runaway sold out to his preferred partner. And what if there was any substance to the other rumours? What if he was in league with right-wing elements in New Caledonia? What if their little island resort became a convenient offshore location for an arms cache? Worse could happen. Tribal rivalries could be fanned into something not far from civil war. Yesterday she had scorned Olwyn for her naivete. Now she realised she was out of her depth herself.

She wondered if the highly placed woman Greg Redman had mentioned, Marjorie Locomo, would be able to give her some insights into the local scene if she were approached the right way. Runaway was too vulnerable with Sebastien as its sole agent with real local connections. She was appalled at Olwyn's oversights.

Before going ashore the next morning, she checked out what Sebastien intended to do about Brooke and Philippe. Brooke had gone away to stay on a friend's yacht for a few days. Philippe would be ordered off the premises if he showed himself at the resort again. Marie-Claire would take charge in the restaurant in the meantime. 'All under control.' Sebastien adjusted his dark glasses.

'I'm grateful. I'll be over in the town for a while. Just have to check on my ticket and a few things.'

'Fine, fine. I don't trust the telephone myself.'

At the government centre Roxane made enquiries about the teachers' training college, which was situated at the top of La Morne overlooking the town. Roxane looked around for a taxi, but as none was in sight she began walking up the steep hill. A car drew up.

'Can I offer you a lift?'

The driver was an Englishwoman of about sixty. 'Terrible climb, isn't it?' she said to Roxane. 'How far are you going?'

Roxane said she was heading for the teachers' college.

'Hop in. I go right past.'

'You live here, then.'

'Yes, my husband's with the Commonwealth Development Corporation. Of course since independence they've been phasing out the overseas administrators. He's helping with that transition. He's nearly reached retirement age himself, but it's a bit traumatic for some of the younger men.'

'Where will you live when he retires?'

'We've been away from England such a long time. We've a daughter in Dunedin — we'll probably go there. Are you a tourist?'

'Not really, I'm in the travel business. I'm hoping to meet Mrs Locomo.'

'A very distinguished educator, I believe. I've only met her in passing myself. We don't mingle with the great, even in a small place like this. Marvellous view from this hill. Look down there.'

Below La Morne lay the town and port, while, offshore, Indigo and a number of other islands were green dots on a purply-blue sea, hazier towards the horizon. Roxane wondered why she had no travel posters from this vantage point.

'Here we are, the teachers' training college. Of course, you know they only go to junior secondary here. But for what it is, the standard is high.'

Roxane thanked the Englishwoman for the lift. She found herself on the outskirts of a group of buildings which looked like British military barracks. On the ground floor of a building to her left, boys were welding metal. To her right were some formal Edwardian buildings, screened by straight lines of palm trees. She walked through an open door and found herself in an empty classroom. On the blackboard was written YOU SHOULD TALK TO GOD AS IF YOU'RE HAVING FULL INTERCOURSE WITH HIM AND GETTING EVERY PLEASURE FROM THIS. IF YOU DO NOT PRAY WITH FULL SINCERITY, WITH ALL YOUR HEART AND BODY AND SOUL, YOUR PRAYERS WILL NOT BE ANSWERED. She read this message several times, trying to imagine what subject it belonged to and whether pupils were supposed to write it down. Sebastien had thought she was laying it on a bit thick at the council meeting, but the fervour of this message suggested her instincts were sound.

'Jesus loves me, this I know, for the Bible tells me so.' Roxane remembered the tune she now heard from an after-school fellowship group, where they were always unaccountably winding wool into pompoms for the poor. She'd had a persistent mental picture of the poor, in beanies, jackets, coats and accessories festooned with woollen pompoms. She followed the sound of the singing and entered a large stone vestibule. 'Can I help you? I'm the bursar.' The young woman was about twenty-three.

'Yes, please, I wonder if you could give my card to Mrs Locomo and ask if there's any chance of an interview.'

'I'm not sure about an interview — are you from the newspapers?'

'No, no, I'm a travel executive.' Roxane handed her the business card.

'One moment please. I'll enquire if the principal can see you, and even if she can't I'm sure one of the seniors will be pleased to show you round.'

A group of young people marched past her in single file

and formed a queue at a counter at the back of the vestibule. 'All those needing recorders for Compulsory Music, form a line,' an instructor shouted.

'Music is compulsory?' Roxane asked a male student.

'Music and art. For a break from the academic subjects. Not so rigorous.'

'Good idea.' Roxane found the thought of these burly black men, all built like football forwards, playing the recorder or singing 'Jesus Loves Me' somewhat incongruous. *Little ones to him belong, they are weak but he is strong.* She had learnt the piano for a few months when she was about eight, but had dropped the lessons when the teacher made fun of her for not being able to sing in tune. She formed the habit of moving her lips without making any sound, even when the fellowship group sang 'Jesus loves me'.

'Come this way. The principal will see you now.'

Roxane followed the bursar into a large office where an imposing Indian woman rose from a cane sofa.

'Mrs Rowe. I'm Marjorie Locomo. To what do we owe the pleasure of your visit to our college?'

'I've heard a great deal about the high standards of the education here,' Roxane said.

'Indeed?'

Careful, Roxane told herself, you only know what you were told by an Englishwoman who happened to be driving by, and by Greg Redman.

'We have one hundred and thirty-five students; we train them for two years for infants, junior and junior secondary teaching. The training is integrated, academic, practical and cultural. Would you like to hear our students sing?'

'I already have.'

'Of course. Religion also is part and parcel of our curriculum. What is your particular interest then?'

'I really wanted your opinion, as an influential woman of this community, about how we in the travel business can contribute to cultural self-development of your people. As you'd be aware, my company, Runaway, is the guiding force in the Indigo Island project.'

'But the law requires a majority shareholding by the tribal council.'

'Quite. We are not the major partner, but we did come up with the original plans, and we are proud of our record of making sure our developments are sensitive to the environment.'

'There is more to that than the size of buildings.'

'In what way?'

Marjorie Locomo crossed her legs. She was forty-five or fifty, and wore gold sandals and a silk sari. Her posture was very erect. Her slightly greying hair was pulled back in a chignon. There was a long pause. She looked into Roxane's eyes. 'Moral considerations.' she said.

'The indigenous council are extremely moral people,' Roxane said. 'They're Seventh Day Adventists. They're very strict about standards at Indigo.'

'SDAs who allow alcohol at the resort.'

'Well. Normal commercial practice.'

'My dear, I am no wowser, I simply point out that there is no guarantee of standards from a particular denomination.'

'I meant Christian values generally.'

'The problem confronting our nation,' said Marjorie Locomo, 'or rather the women of our nation, is maintaining their good name despite the fact that many of them can get work only as house girls.'

'They're very good workers,' Roxane said, 'certainly.'

'I don't need to tell you,' the principal said, 'that house girls, girls they are called when they are women my age, a contemptuous colonial term, housemaids are very frequently exploited by their masters. It is a step from prostitution. The associated problems, illegitimacy, venereal disease, congenital defects, our nation cannot afford them. My brother-in-law and most of his Cabinet, you may know, are Anglican. The college which I head is non-denominational evangelical Protestant. We hope, through a well-rounded training for our students, to spread respect for Christian virtues. But our numbers are small. Seventy-seven of our students are girls. Their work is good.' She handed Roxane an assignment headed 'Teaching Adolescents the Concept of Bonding Through the Use of Structured Material.' 'Merrilee, the girl who wrote that, she's very clever, she may win a scholarship to Auckland. But for the few girls we have here getting a professional training, there are hundreds, no, thousands, grateful for a job at a resort or in a private home with expatriate families or in a shop in the town. And it is difficult for us to raise our moral standards.'

'Perhaps some of the more responsible tourism companies have a role to play here,' Roxane suggested. 'We are training the local indigenous people at Indigo already, but perhaps we could emphasise the moral side more.'

'You're thinking of ...?'

'Well, talented young people, like this Merrilee, learning to manage the resort, organise the staff, deal with the agencies in town.'

'My dear, there would be one managerial position to a dozen menial ones. And the most unfortunate precedents have been set. An expatriate lass involved with an islander from a French-speaking Catholic background, not the most tactful appointment for an Adventist-owned resort. The man has children by more than one woman already — not so unusual here, or in your country, but not the right example.'

'Perhaps you could act for us as a consultant on moral and cultural issues.'

'I am so busy already, there are so many commitments at the college and in my work with the women's organisations and the family planning. And your resort is really very small, isn't it? Just a couple of dozen cabins, isn't it? A drop in the bucket.'

'But it could be more important than that, as an example. A model resort. With your input, it could be a beacon in the South Pacific. Or we could get into much bigger hotels, with the right local advisers. Do consider my suggestion.'

'Let's not rush into anything. Certainly if your company

would like to write with details of the offer, I'd be happy to consider it.'

'Of course.'

'And now, I'll have someone show you the students' art and craft.'

Roxane could not refuse. What an idiot Olwyn has been, she was thinking as she murmured praise of hand-printed fabric, what a bloody fool. Philippe was not just a black having an affair with an Australian woman, but a French-speaking Catholic working for a tight-knit English-educated protestant sect.

'Lovely colours,' she gushed. 'Quite delightful. I can see you take your inspiration from nature.'

'Leave everything to me,' Sebastien said soothingly. Roxane was far from soothed, but did not feel she had much choice.

'Brooke is resting on a friend's yacht,' Sebastien told her. 'She won't be back till Sunday night. By a happy coincidence, all the guests who witnessed that unfortunate little scene will have left by the time she returns. I'll be minding the shop myself until then, with the help of Marie-Claire and the others at the restaurant. I don't have to tell you, we won't be allowing Philippe back on Indigo. I am told it was just some lovers' quarrel, jealous accusations, but we will not condone violence. And she is part of our management — he's her subordinate, whatever their relationship.'

'He's the wrong religion for the tribe. If this trouble hadn't brewed up, there would have been other repercussions.'

'After so little time here, such an expert on local culture.'

'What about security risks, with Brooke in charge and Philippe prowling around?'

'My dear, you were nearer the mark a moment ago. Philippe wouldn't want to take on the entire tribe. The real risk is that Brooke won't want to stay without Philippe.'

'No accounting for taste. She'd have to resign, in that case. She's not everyone's idea of management material, is she? Even if she was beside herself when she abused us the other night. I'll be putting in a report when I get to Sydney, of course. Runaway may decide to put in other management in Olwyn's absence.'

'In consultation with me, of course.'

'Of course. Look, Sebastien, I hope I didn't put my foot in it at the meeting.' What am I doing? Roxane wondered. Never apologise, never explain.

'My dear, your little sermon was quite an inspiration. I shall treasure it. I was uplifted. Tourism and the family. Honeymoons and the institution of marriage. You have driven out scepticism and offered me a new spirituality.'

'Okay, it's just possible I asked for that. Runaway will be in touch, Sebastien. All the best.' She held out her hand to shake his but he clasped it like a courtier.

'Bon voyage,' Sebastien said. Roxane pulled back sharply to prevent him from raising her hand to kiss it.

SATIN AND SILK

The childish printing on the envelope with the Carinya crest was the work of Roxane's daughter Lucinda. We learnt running writing in first class in my day, Roxane thought. Whatever happened to copperplate? Irritated, she read her daughter's letter.

> *Dear Mum,*
>
> *Things are very boring staying at school over the weekends, so I hope Indigo was good. I miss you. The food is terrible as usual. The tryouts for the tennis were last week and I got in the 15Cs. I really thought I should be in the Bs but I came up against Chloe Benson in my match (she's in the As).*
>
> *I want to drop French and do Asian social studies. Please write URGENTLY saying this is okay, I need a note before they let me change. It will be a useful subject when I go to Honkers, don't say it is only a shonky subject or I'll scream. See you next weekend I hope.*
>
> > *Lots of love*
> > *Cindy.*

Roxane stuffed her daughter's letter in her handbag. She had no intention of cramping her style in Hong Kong or anywhere else by taking Lucinda along. She was planning to meet Szabo overseas next time they got the chance. On her way to work she had left her car for servicing at a Rushcutters Bay garage, so she flagged down a taxi.

'You're Roxane from Runaway, right?' the driver asked as they joined the slow line of traffic in the Kings Cross tunnel.

'Right.' Roxane was searching in her handbag for an emery board. Few things irked her so much as a ragged nail.

'Must be great getting all that free travel.'

'It is. But it's hard work too.'

'Did you see on TV about a cruise ship rip-off where people were paying hundreds for a trip on a boat that hadn't even been converted for passengers yet?'

'Yes, of course. Everyone in the industry saw that.' Roxane filed her nail. She was feeling anxious and sour.

Her tone did not deter the driver. 'How come they let those con-merchants get away with it?' he asked.

'They don't really, do they? They've had a lot of damaging publicity, and there'll probably be prosecutions, or consumer claims at least.'

'I suppose an outfit like yours wouldn't touch that sort of thing with a barge pole.'

'No indeed. All strictly above board at Runaway.' I should be paid for this, she thought.

'You've kind of staked your reputation on it, haven't you?'

'I suppose I have.'

'Did the slogan ever worry you? I mean, it's a bit of a come-on, isn't it, "Runaway with Roxane"?'

'Advertising's like that. Slick. A very talented man wrote that song. It's never worried me, no.'

'What about your husband, but? How's he take to it? Or your boyfriend?'

'I can't see that my private life has anything to do with it.' They were about to emerge into William Street.

'Well, it's your face and your name, you can't expect to keep your private life completely separate, can you?'

'I certainly do, thankyou very much. If you don't mind, I have some notes to make before my meeting.'

'Suit yourself.'

The taxi driver turned up the Co-op Intercom. 'Come in, 553,' said a nasal voice through static. '553. Jesus, don't say we've lost you again. Dja speak English, 553? Eh? Fare's waiting for ya 553.' Roxane put her nailfile back in her bag and ruffled the pages of her diary as if consulting notes.

Desmond Hickey was sitting in his office clicking the graph options on his personal computer from pie charts to bar charts and back again. Roxane tried not to be distracted by the nubbly weave of his black and white suit, which had almost an op-art effect. She had suggested to him, as subtly as she could, that he should not wear safari suits or brown suits. She might as well have saved her breath, she thought — he headed for something abominable whatever the colour.

'I didn't ring, Des, because some things are too disturbing to tell you on the phone,' she said.

'What's this?' He swivelled away from the screen, raising his eyebrows. 'You sound very serious.'

'It is very serious, Des. Our whole reputation in the South Pacific is under threat — things are in a shocking state at Indigo Island.'

'Well, of course, Olwyn is in hospital,' Desmond Hickey said.

'That's the least of it. The real trouble is the appointments Olwyn made before she got sick, and the working relationships she's let Runaway develop with its partners at Indigo.' She felt her pulse rate rising as she said this.

'How is Olwyn anyway?'

'Hard to say. Lung damage of some kind. But the real trouble, if you ask me, is alcohol. It's the only explanation.'

'Roxane, we all like a few glasses.'

'We don't all ruin our judgment and lose business from it.'

140

'Just what are you trying to tell me?'

'Simply this.' As Roxane spoke, she felt her cheeks flame and her heart beat. Treachery, treachery, her blood drummed. She felt that she was betraying her mentor, her first career idol, her old friend and colleague. But she drove the knife deeper, vindicated in her mind by the thought that she was putting the well-being of Runaway first.

'I hate to say this, Des, but Olwyn's a total liability. An embarrassment. Her appointments on Indigo have been a disaster. Brooke Lake-Winton, for God's sake, who's currently acting manager — nothing but a dishevelled little bohemian from St Kilda whose idea of haute cuisine is putting slices of kiwi fruit on turkey sandwiches. We can count ourselves lucky the clientele she's attracting wouldn't know the difference. And Olwyn's partner, Sebastien Charpentier, is a double-crosser from way back if you ask me. There's some sort of plot in the offing to sell Runaway shares back to the tribe and then go ahead with the extensions.'

'Legally impossible.'

'The law bends more easily the closer you get to the equator. Sebastien has Olwyn conned that he's the only one with the local contacts, and certainly the political ins and outs aren't simple. Suppose he forged our consent, or presented something provisional as final, what satisfaction could we look forward to getting in court in Isantu? How could we ever establish a good working relationship with the Indigenous Council without him — see, he's succeeded in getting even me to think we need him. In the short term we do, certainly. He's in charge over there till Brooke's bruises subside.'

'Bruises?'

'Yes. Now we get to the interesting part.' Roxane sketched in the events in the Indigo Bar two nights earlier.

'Christ almighty,' Des said. 'And all this happened right in front of the guests?'

'Yes, I'm afraid so. And news spreads like wildfire over there. I happened to be talking to a very influential woman, a close relation of the Chief Minister, who knew the whole story within hours. Even went out of her way to tell me it had been tactless to hire someone like Philippe from the wrong language and religious group. Of course, Philippe's been banned from Indigo after the events of the other night, but it's going to take us quite a while to get things rectified.'

'And you mean to tell me Olwyn didn't realise what was going on?'

'Olwyn's out of it. Charpentier cons her, Brooke cons her, and her boyfriend must have as well. I'm told that before she collapsed she was sitting round with guests downing gins.'

'Come on, Roxane. She got the buildings completed. She set up the deal with the local authorities, she set up the promotion package. It's thanks to her there were any guests so early in the piece.'

'That's as may be. I'm talking about what I actually found over on Indigo — what I saw with my own eyes.'

'Roxane, do be careful not to say a word about this to anyone. I'll need a full report, in writing. But make damn sure that there's only one copy of it, and that it comes to me.'

'Of course.'

Roxane sat alone in her own office, wondering if she had already told Des too much. Perhaps she should have flown to Melbourne and spoken to Boris instead. Des appeared excited at the end of their discussion: clearly he saw some opportunity in it for himself. I'd just like to see it, she thought, I'd just like to see him beat me to Olwyn's seat on the board. She had no doubt Olwyn's fellow directors would find a way to dump her. Retirement on the grounds of ill health. On the grounds of age. Of gross incompetence. There were plenty of options.

Des had tried to swear her to secrecy, but the whole of Isantu was already buzzing with rumour about Indigo Island. Not even Olwyn could prove which trails led to her.

She read the letters and messages in her in-tray. There were three requests from David Jasper of *Business Briefing* to interview her for a series of profiles on female executives. She would agree to that. A little personal publicity would not go astray right now. And if she did not get what she wanted from the Sudpac Runaway group, that was not her only option for turning the situation to her advantage.

She pressed button four on her telephone, which was permanently coded with Steven Szabo's private number.

'Darling,' Roxane drawled, 'I'm back. When do I see you?'

The soles of Roxane's feet slithered over the sheen of the satin as she slid between the purple sheets. 'These sheets,' she told Steven Szabo, 'are one of the corniest and most delicious things about you.'

'You don't like purple? It's supposed to be a woman's colour.'

'It's just such a Hollywood notion of glamour, isn't it? Late night movies have satin bedrooms. Theda Bara or Myrna Loy, they'd sit in a petticoat in front of a mirror taking five minutes to remove their earrings, surrounded by satin curtains and sheets.'

'I am not necessarily quite so dated in my tastes. I see you more as the Faye Dunaway type.'

'Okay, Clyde, you get the money, I'll keep the car running.'

Steven Szabo raced across the bedroom miming an armed holdup while Roxane, in bed, made a steering wheel out of satin sheets. Vroomm, vroomm, pow pow ... they improvised sound effects like kids in a playground. Roxane laughed and threw her arms around Szabo as he landed on the bed, straight-faced, overweight, and pretending to remove a balaclava helmet from his face. 'I've never loved you so much as this moment,' she said, tracing his spine with her fingers.

'Do that a little more and I will be your slave.' He lay face down as she caressed his neck and back, running her hands from his thighs to his spine. 'Bliss,' he murmured.

'Turn over,' Roxane said. When Szabo rolled onto his back, she bent over him, taking his erect penis in her mouth and letting her tongue circle its rim before gently taking him deeper in a moist rhythm of quiet excitement. He placed his hand between her thighs and she felt herself grow warm and wet to his touch. She moaned slightly as she moved up and down, holding his buttocks tightly and letting her hair fall lightly on the pale skin round his navel. After a time he lifted her away from his body, and placed her on her back, her face surrounded by satin pillows. She wiped saliva away from her cheeks. 'I am going to fuck you for hours,' he said.

'Threat or promise?' Roxane asked. Much as she liked to take the initiative on occasion, she thrilled to the way he took control even as she mocked him for it.

'As you wish.' He would hesitate with his penis caressing her vulva, then plunge inside her with sudden force, so that she gasped and clung on to him. He gained great satisfaction from making their sex last a long time, and Roxane, after her first orgasm, which she might not reach for some time, would find herself climaxing repeatedly with cries of pleasure, astonished and yet not astonished, expectant, exultant, while he maintained a certain aloofness, watching her, tantalising her, building her response again and again until he too chose, all in good time, to let go. They lay silently for a long time afterwards, tender with one another and relaxed.

'I missed you so much,' Roxane said. 'I had an extraordinary time over in Isantu.'

'Extra-ordinary good, or extra-ordinary bad?'

'Things I couldn't quite work out, and some very bad things. Olwyn's quite sick, she's in hospital, and the next tier of management is a bloody shambles. But I was only just beginning to suss out the local politics, how to get things through Cabinet over there, that sort of thing, when I came back.'

'Do they still have that fifty-one per cent rule?'

'Yes. You knew about that?'

'Mmmhmm. Barbary was thinking of getting into some business over there, but we thought we might be safer dealing with the French in New Caledonia. Then things got tenser between the French and the Kanak separatists and we decided to leave it for a while. We are planning something in New Zealand instead at the moment, and that could turn out to be the staging post for any move further into the Pacific.'

'Runaway's never done much with New Zealand. Our traditional routes are still more to the north. You know what a success Olwyn made of those Bali and Singapore ventures for us. And we send more bargain shoppers up to Hong Kong than any other agency. But the time is right over in Isantu: a place like Indigo could turn out to be a fantastic investment if it's properly handled.'

'Tropical islands are terribly overrated, don't you think?'

'No,' Roxane said. 'They still have magic for me. The water of course, and the colours. I love that sense of landfall, of a secret world. Indigo is actually very beautiful — you'd be very impressed if you saw it.'

'If I run away with you, Roxane, it will be somewhere a little more discreet than a Runaway resort in the Pacific. How would Switzerland grab you?'

'Not Zurich. Can't stand Zurich.'

'What would you have against Zurich?'

'Gnomes,' Roxane said. 'I like my men a little larger.' Her arm was around his broad back.

'Or Portugal. We could hire a grand old house on the shores of Portugal. Wonderful place.'

'You've been there?'

'Yes, a few times. Anna didn't want to go there while the fascists were in power, but we had English friends who had a villa there.'

'I don't want to go some place that you associate with Anna.'

'My dear, Anna and I have been together for decades — we have seen quite a bit of the globe together one way and another.'

'Yes, fine, I'm sure you have, but I don't want to retrace your steps there with you, or to lie in bed with you talking about her for that matter.'

'I thought you'd be pleased my wife has some political scruples even if I don't.'

'Yeah. Terrific. I'm over the moon.' Roxane felt awkward and guilty about Anna on several scores: she'd run into her recently without realising immediately who she was, and had not yet mentioned the incident to Steven. She hesitated to tell him because she was not sure what Anna might have said about her, or whether the marriage was one of those confusingly frank ones where the wife knows about her husband's affairs. Last and least, she felt a degree of guilt about being involved with another woman's husband.

'Come on, Roxane, I will make you a nice cup of tea if I can work out the ins and outs of this kitchen.'

'You turn right after the bathroom, I believe.'

He handed her a robe. She padded after him towards the kitchen and made toast and anchovy paste while he got the tea ready. 'Is Barbary still involved in that time-share venture up on the coast at Cloudy Bay?' she asked. 'Would that be one way to go in the Pacific — buy your own fraction of island paradise?'

'We've had our fingers burnt up there. The local man in the project, real estate chap named Hughes, got a radio campaign and a brochure going which has landed us in a bit of hot water. Of course no one at Barbary, or Vilmos or I, none of us knew what Hughes was up to. The Oxymoronics are after us.'

'I'm lost.'

'The Commission for Business Ethics. CBE. We keep getting enquiries based on complaints from little investors who feel stung. No, Barbary's pulled right out.'

'Wouldn't that be too late, if you were party to the prospectus or brochure or whatever?'

'Not if it's properly handled. That's what we pay lawyers for, after all.'

'You don't think it would work in the Pacific?'

'Touchy, politically, don't you think — rich Australians or Americans owning bits of islands in a Melanesian part of the world?'

'I suppose you're right. It doesn't seem to worry the

French, though.'

'*Le sol sacré de la France*. The French have very cleverly become the majority in New Caledonia; that's quite a different matter from these tourist propositions.'

'If Barbary does ever move into the Pacific, I would be the logical person to manage your operations there, don't you think?'

'Roxane, you would be the first to know. But we have no such intentions at present. And I'd need extremely good arguments to move capital there in the current political climate. We're thinking of Queensland again so far as our development push goes. And of course we're taking some of our manufacturing to Korea.'

'Of course.' She mimicked his accent and posture, slumped on a kitchen stool with bathrobe falling open.

'You never let me take myself too seriously,' he said. 'I enjoy that.'

'In bed I take you very seriously.'

'You'd be foolish not to.' She kissed him lightly. 'Ugh,' he said, 'fish paste — how can you eat that stuff?'

'Easy. I'm always ravenous after a particularly good fuck.'

'I won't quarrel with that.'

'Have you got any champagne in the fridge?' Roxane asked.

'What a question.' Her opened the door and produced a bottle of Bollinger. They toasted each other, toes touching on the black and white kitchen tiles. Roxane sipped her champagne and pondered whether she had succeeded in planting the idea of herself as manager of Barbary's Pacific tourism projects in Szabo's mind or not. In the meantime, she would have to concentrate on ousting Olwyn from Runaway and Sudpac.

'Have a bath with me, Steven.'

'You have a bath, my dear. I actually prefer to shower, and, besides, I have a business appointment.'

'How time flies when you're having a good time,' she said with a drawl.

'Roxane, a little Hollywood goes a long way. That simply doesn't suit you,' Szabo said. He had showered, shaved and dressed while Roxane was running her steaming hot bath. She sat in it for a long time, and did not pull out the plug until the water was turning cold and the skin on her toes and fingers had puckered into stripes. As she towelled herself dry, her pubic hair had an innocent childhood scent of Pears soap.

'By the way.' Steven stood in the doorway. 'My wife had this idea about you.'

'Your wife?'

'Yes. Anna had this notion that you'd be just the person to do some television promos for her committee's Silk Festival. She's president of Harbourside Volunteers — they support preschools for the deaf, that sort of thing.'

'But I'm under exclusive contract to Runaway.'

'Anna thinks she could get round Boris. Anna's a persuasive woman.'

'She knows about us then?'

'I'm never so coarse as to ask Anna what she knows. I have a meeting about to start.'

'It's a worthy cause I suppose. It'd be hard to say no if the request came through Boris.'

'Don't feel under any pressure because of me.'

'How could I not?'

'I must go, Roxane. Ciao now.'

Roxane thought of her encounter with Anna Szabo. It happened at Marika Gray's in Double Bay, when she was having a dress made to order. She sat on a velvet armchair near a mirrored wardrobe and did calculations on her chequebook butts. She tried not to spend more than ten per cent of her disposable income on clothes. This was a figure suggested by her accountant. Fourteen per cent, she calculated; she could live with that.

Apart from a fuchsia silk dress on a silver mannequin in the window, there were no clothes visible. Walls, furniture, light fittings and woodwork were all silver. The mirrors glinted. There was only one other customer in the shop.

Marika Gray stood in the passageway near the mirrored wardrobe. 'Where are you, Marcel?' she called to the workroom behind. 'Our client is waiting.'

The woman was in her late fifties and had short hennaed hair. While her purchases were packed in tissue-lined boxes she smoked a cigarette from a tortoiseshell holder. She stubbed out her cigarette, and as she wrote a cheque she smiled coquettishly at Roxane. 'Getting old,' she said. 'Getting fat. Running out of men. Running out of money. What more does life have to offer?' Roxane recognised the insinuating lilt of her accent as Hungarian.

'You fat? Never!' This was from Marika Gray.

Roxane smiled. 'Good question,' she said. The woman did not look as if money were really a problem.

'Marcel,' said Marika, 'would you help Mrs Szabo with her parcels?'

Roxane opened a copy of *Vogue* and looked at it intently. She hoped that she was not blushing. Anna Szabo was not at all as she had imagined her. She watched her walk away: high heeled sandals, tight linen skirt, jaunty hairstyle. Marcel followed her, his chin balancing on top of three boxes of size ten Chanel knock-offs.

'Now, Miss Rowe, it was silk you had in mind, wasn't it? A jacket dress for the late afternoon? I have some samples for you, fully imported.' Roxane looked at the silks: vivid colours, soft sheen, plain and patterned. Her mind was not on the task. She was remembering Anna Szabo's face, the roguish expression, the sign of age, the drawl in her question, What more does life have to offer? Anna would have known Roxane from television, or from the photograph with her husband in the Sunday social pages for that matter. She wondered again if Steven discussed his love affairs with his wife. In the mirror Roxane's face matched the scarlet fabric.

Cindy's train from Bowral was late. As she prowled up and down waiting, Roxane wished she had worn a scarf. The gritty air of Number 21 platform would get on her hair as well as

149

into her lungs. It was too early in the morning for conversation with other parents: the girls got up in the dark to be here for the weekend. Preoccupied with the situation at Runaway and her hours with Szabo, she had woken to the sound of the alarm clock from a dream in which she was ordering five dozen frozen chickens for a banquet she and Szabo were to host. 'Make sure they are properly thawed,' she was saying to the David Jones' caterer in her sleep as her feet hit the thick pile carpet and she reached out to still the electronic alarm. Frozen chickens, indeed: why had she not asked for fresh lobsters, she wondered. Perhaps the dream was code for a mass market resort they would open together, not a banquet at all. But Steven Szabo had made no promises when she hinted she would manage travel projects in the Pacific for him. Her hair blew over her sunglasses in the gusty wind, and she took refuge in a waiting room until the train arrived.

In a jumble of hats, bags, tennis racquets and chatter, girls in bottle-green tunics surged onto the platform. Cindy was one of the last to alight. A sullen, slightly built girl of fifteen, she had freckles and her father's sandy colouring. She did not take off her hat until they got in the car. 'Darling, what have you done to yourself?' Roxane asked.

'We were supposed to have our hair cut in the village, and I refused, so I got a friend to do it for me instead,' Cindy said.

'It's appalling.'

'Most people think it suits me. Mrs Livingstone was livid,' said Cindy with satisfaction. Her hair was shaved very short around her left ear, and fell in green fronds towards her right eye.

'It's awful. Punk-looking.'

'No, just modern, honestly.'

'Why didn't you wait till today — you could have gone to my hairdresser.'

'Big deal. At my age, go to the hairdresser's with my mother.'

'I used to love going to your grandmother's hairdresser.

They used lots of hairpins and bobby pins in those days, and apprentices used to drag magnets across the floor on a string to pick them up. And the magazines were a treat then, too. Not like these days — you're all so blasé.'

'What's blasé?'

'There you are. I don't know what they're teaching you at that school. I thought you were supposed to be learning French.'

'Mum, didn't you get my letter? I can't stand French. You have to let me swap to Asian social studies, please, please, please.'

'Don't nag, Cindy. Why should I?'

'Because Madame is so spiteful to me. She picks on me and says I can't pronounce anything properly and she doesn't like the look on my face or the group I hang around with and I will never amount to anything — she just spends half the lesson insulting me for no reason.'

'I'm sure you're exaggerating.'

'There you go; no one ever believes me. What's the use of French anyway? Asia is more our region. You're the one who's always going on about Bali and Singapore and Hong Kong and the South Pacific. I would have a bit of a start from your work if I did change.'

'It's much harder to learn a language by yourself than it is at school, but you can pick up some general knowledge about Asia without studying it as a subject.'

'You're just prejudiced. I'll have to write to Dad, too — he'd see it my way.'

'That's as may be, but I'm not going to be rushed or bullied. We'll discuss it again tomorrow afternoon before you go back. Now why don't we just stop at a chemist's and get some nice natural hair colour so you can wash out that green?'

'If all we're going to discuss is my hair, I'll get out and get the next train back to Bowral.' Cindy had her hand on the door handle.

'Stop it, Cindy. It was only a suggestion. Okay, not another word about hair for the whole weekend. How have things been otherwise? Apart from haircuts and Madame?'

'Boring as usual. I'd love to leave school, really.'

'Cindy, you know that isn't possible.'

'Double standards again. You left when you were my age.'

'Things were very different when I was your age. In fifteen years' time it will be unheard of to have a career like mine without having a degree behind you. Even now, there are times I'd like to have been to university.'

'But you're more successful than most people who did go.'

'True, but times are changing.'

'Dad doesn't think that university is the be-all and end-all of life, either.'

'Colin isn't exactly the best-informed man we know.'

'He cares about me. He knows a lot about life.'

It occurred to Roxane that she should be cautious in condemning Colin's views to Cindy, who was at an age when she might find them very attractive. Colin Bateman lived near Gisborne, New Zealand, in a little shack near a black-sand beach, and taught art at a country high school. Roxane had met him when he was the manager of an art gallery in Darlinghurst, a regular of the Rowe Street coffee bars where she had sat in her late teens, attempting to impress artists and poets with her Left Bank chic. Colin was only her second lover. She had been seduced by an artist named Axel Grimm, a libertarian whose ideas about free love seemed to her original and irrefutable. In truth she did not want to refute them. Within weeks she had found out that Axel's words were clichés, and that a different young woman from the middle-class suburbs appeared every few weeks in black stockings and pale lipstick to listen to them. She wasted little time fretting over Axel, and was glad to find Colin Bateman interested in her. Colin was quieter than Axel, and seemed to get on with everyone. Colin's gallery in Liverpool Street was the venue for some memorable art shows: happenings and performance poetry evenings were staged there. Roxane helped hand round claret and, late at night, made fondue for a few people. Colin had some spare rooms in the two-storey gallery building. Roxane moved out of her parents' Rose Bay flat and into a small room with a divan, a clothesline for a wardrobe, and seagrass matting on the floor. Thea's frisson of disgust at this decor confirmed to Roxane the rightness of the move. There was a great deal of talk in artistic circles about the impossibility of suburban taste. At times Roxane found herself wishing that her parents lived in a nasty little cottage forty kilometres from the city, furnished with net curtains and pictures of sunsets. Rose Bay was almost cosmopolitan; it could not be renounced as readily as Arncliffe or Yagoona. People from the suburbs were known as the Alphs, their customs supposedly as remote as those of the inhabitants of Alpha Centauri. Roxane adopted this jargon, and was rewarded with Colin and seagrass matting. If she did not stop making Alph remarks about punk hair, Cindy too would rush off to Colin, a righteous ageing hippie whose values had altered little since he and Roxane split up.

'What are your plans for the afternoon?' Roxane asked her daughter.

'I've been asked over to Lisa's to watch videos,' Cindy said.

'Well, that suits me. I've got a report to write.'

'Overworking, as usual.'

'I love my work, so it's hardly overwork. You reach a certain level of responsibility, and inevitably you have to put more time into it.'

'Sure, sure.'

'Don't forget you benefit from our standard of living, young lady.' In her mind were echoes of school assemblies at Fairlea: Your parents are making tremendous sacrifices for you ...

'Get off my back, Mum.'

'And a little courtesy wouldn't go astray.'

'Oh, go jump!'

'Charming. To think, Cindy, I was actually looking forward to seeing you this morning.'

'Amazing, i'n' it?'

Say nothing, Roxane told herself. One adolescent in the family is enough.

BRUNCH AT THE CROSS

Roxane pulled a sheet of paper out of her electric typewriter, scrunched it up, and tossed it into the wastepaper basket. She was not finding the report easy to write. Disastrous appointments. She crossed that out. Unwise personnel decisions. Violent incidents. Cultural insensitivity. Unsavoury rumours.

Objectively, what could she say about Indigo? The huts were well designed, built close to schedule, and the arrangements between Runaway and the Indigenous Council had been harmonious. Early bookings were good. Olwyn's deputy manager had a black lover who beat her up. One instance of physical assault, that was all the evidence she had. It could happen at the Savoy.

What about her distrust of Sebastien Charpentier? How could she put that on paper so that Des could make something of it? Des would fail to grasp the subtleties of the situation.

Olwyn's drinking. That was the hub of it. Her suspicion that Olwyn's physical collapse was due to alcohol as much as pneumonia.

'Sitting around with the guests downing gins.' Those had been Greg Redman's words. But she had drunk with the guests herself. So had Sebastien. It was normal practice.

But Olwyn's drinking could not have been normal, or she would not have collapsed. It stood to reason, didn't it? She remembered her Auntie Pam, another gin drinker, in that terrible overcrowded house in the mid-fifties, screeching drunkenly at her parents and her grandmother, ' Thea and her pampered precious daughter have always been the favourites in this house. Bunk beds are good enough for Barry and Roger, while Miss Muck has the sleepout to herself. Speech lessons. Getting a plum in her mouth. Miss High and Mighty thinks she's better than the rest of us. I know what I'd do if she was my daughter.' She usually screened Pam's shrill voice out of her childhood recollections, preferring even to remember the worst of her cousins' teasing instead.

'A drunk man is bad enough, but a woman who drinks is far worse,' Thea had said later. Roxane had no reason to doubt that maxim, and by some childish thread of logic still regarded gin as more lethal than other alcohol. Her father drank whisky and remained in good health. Her abstemious mother died of a sudden stroke when Cindy was three; just after Roxane and Colin divorced.

It was a matter of corporate image. Olwyn's drinking was reprehensible because it reflected badly on Runaway. Would Des buy that? He too thought that having a few drinks with the clients was part of good public relations.

It was too delicate a matter to trust to Des. She would have to go to Melbourne and see Boris. How? Cindy was here for the weekend and was due back in Bowral on Sunday night. Right now she was at Lisa's watching *Ghostbusters* or some such rubbish. What did she mean about wanting to leave school? She didn't have a fraction of Roxane's maturity at the same age.

It occurred to Roxane that her tactics were all wrong. She should have been far more circumspect in what she said to Des. If she put anything critical of Olwyn in writing, people other than Des would be bound to see it, and some of them would have enough loyalty to Olwyn to tip her off as to who had made the adverse report. How sharper than a serpent's tooth: Olwyn would feel betrayed by her Rox. Roxane should have said years ago that she hated being called Rox. That was one habit of Olwyn's that really got to her. So did Olwyn's assumption that she had the right to give her personal advice, like warning her about her involvement with Steven Szabo. None of her business, none of anybody's. Well, Anna Szabo's perhaps, but she had a bit of finesse.

Olwyn had hung on too long. Other women retired, left the decks clear for their successors. Olwyn loved travel, enjoyed work, and found a niche for herself creating tropical resorts. Why hadn't she crept away to the Gold Coast to play bowls or paste seashells on lampshade bases or whatever people did when they retired? Because she would be bored stiff, obviously, just as Roxane would. Just by being there, Olwyn had crowded Roxane out. Olwyn was on the Runaway board as an individual, not as a token woman, but just by being there she became 'our woman director'. Roxane could wait and wait, but she would not be invited onto the board while Olwyn was there because an unofficial quota was already filled and it would not occur to Boris Brookstein and his colleagues that there could be more than one female director.

Olwyn had not made way, that was her crime.

Roxane dialled Boris Brookstein's home number. 'The family is all at the synagogue,' she was told. She left a message asking him to ring her at home in Rushcutters Bay.

She prowled around the apartment debating what she should do. Should she get the next plane to Melbourne? Presumably planes did land in Melbourne on Saturday afternoons; a handful of the population managed to resist the football. Then what? Go out to the Brooksteins' place at Kooyong? She doubted if she could evoke the urgency of the situation at Indigo among the green hedges and secluded tennis courts of Melbourne's smartest addresses. She would be handed a cup of tea — worse, a glass of gin — and would sit there spluttering. Boris would ask his daughter, the one at the Conservatorium, to play.

No. That would not do.

She stripped the leaves of a bunch of spinach away from the stalks and ran cold water over them. She pressed the leaves into a tight bundle on a chopping block and cut them finely, green juice escaping down the sides of her serrated knife. She turned the spinach sideways and cut again, fine and straight. She put the leaves in a pan to simmer with pepper and a little butter. Domestic tasks were a comfort really; it was a pity she had married a loser like Col and had so little time at home.

What she should have done, of course, was marry someone very rich like Steven. Not Steven himself, of course; he had met Anna the year Roxane was born. And he had not always been rich. Anna had been one of the legendary European boutique owners who would take window-shoppers by the elbow, 'Won't you come inside and try it on?' Just looking. Thanks. Australian girls, intrigued by the clothes but not knowing what to make of physical contact by strangers, scurried out of the arcades as if pursued by werewolves.

No, she should have found some heir to a fortune, some Fairlea girl's brother perhaps. That was what the elocution lessons and private school fees were designed to achieve. Being somebody. What else had it meant in the 'fifties but being somebody's wife?

Yet she was of another generation. She belonged to a group of women who weren't content to sweat spinach, knit layettes and wash football jumpers forever. They wanted careers, and recognition, and personal success. She must have succeeded: Margot Tierney, that awkward, academic daughter of Olwyn's had rung up about a survey on women's careers, and David Jasper of *Business Briefing* was pursuing her to do an interview, with photographs. Market surveys had identified her as one of the most widely recognised women in Australia.

She sat at the desk again, this time making notes. The Indigenous Council. Sebastien. Olwyn's drinking. Olwyn's appointments. Losing her grip?

She walked out onto her balcony and looked across the dark tree tops at the nest of masts and the Saturday yachts on the harbour. Someone downstairs was listening to the races on the radio; an announcer's voice rose to a frenzied whine as the horses entered the straight.

The telephone rang. She lifted it on the second ring, sure it would be Boris. It was Cindy. 'Lisa's asked me to stay overnight, Mum — would that be all right?'

'Yes, fine. Thank her parents nicely, won't you? Look, Cindy, it's just possible I'll have to go to Melbourne in a hurry. Leave me the phone number. If you have to make your own way back to Central I'll leave you the taxi money on the hall table. Fine. Be in touch.'

She turned off the spinach but left it on the hotplate to stand a little longer.

She put all her tropical clothes, with the exception of the Mother Hubbards, into the washing machine. She did not trust their dye not to run. Looking again at their bulk and restrictive length, she put them in a plastic bag to wait for the next St Vincent de Paul collection.

The telephone rang again. 'Roxane, my dear. This is a surprise to hear from you at home. Didn't know you were back from the Pacific. Everything all right over there?'

'Not really. That's what I wanted to talk to you about.'

'Well, of course, with Olwyn being taken ill ...'

'There's other things, Boris.'

'Bit of trouble with a barman? Olwyn's French fellow, Charpentier, mentioned that to me.'

'I'm not sure what he told you, Boris, but the way it happened was extremely damaging to Runaway. Actually, Boris, I need to talk to you privately, not on the phone. There are really sensitive issues I want to discuss. I could come down there this afternoon.'

'But my dear, there's no need. I was just about to tell you, I am on my way up there to an inter-agency conference on refugees. I could meet you in the morning.'

'You could? That would be perfect. Where?'

'My dear, you're the expert. You suggest somewhere.'

Roxane arranged to meet him at the Bayswater Brasserie at eleven o'clock. She felt immensely relieved as she put down the phone and went to put her washing in the dryer. She was sorry now that she'd agreed so readily to let Cindy stay at her friend's place overnight. She would eat the spinach alone. It was not worth making lasagne for one.

She telephoned her father who lived in a retirement unit near Avoca. He complained that it was a long time since she had taken Cindy up to visit him. Roxane promised to do something about it but did not set a date.

'Is anything worrying you, Roxane?'

'No, Dad. Nothing. I'm fine, really.'

'I'm here if you need me.'

'Yes, I know, I know. I'll bear it in mind.'

She felt the need of someone to talk to, but her father would not do. She had no close friend who would understand the intricacies of her work situation. Szabo was out of bounds at the weekends. It was a pity she had not kept up with more of what Thea used to call her female friends. 'Don't neglect your female friends,' her mother had cautioned in the days when she hung around Rowe Street with Axel and Colin.

She rang Jane Singer's number, but there was no answer. Jane was a former Runaway consultant who was now an administrator at a boys' school. She had a daughter Cindy's age, and her family included Roxane and Cindy in various get togethers: watching the start of the Boxing Day yacht race, the odd picnic or birthday party.

Roxane decided to go for a walk along the waterfront by herself. The young, tanned sailors on the yacht club marina made her feel suddenly old and jetlagged. She sat on the edge of a timber jetty for a few minutes, watching the glint of sunlight on green water, the darker green under the hulls of tethered yachts, and listening to the way the ropes creaked as the boats swayed to and fro. It was a good place to relax, but Roxane was tired and anxious. She walked back towards the apartment building, passing a group of amateur cricket-ers whose high spirits seemed to her in very poor taste.

Early on Sunday Roxane dreamt she was at Dacca airport without a ticket. She had no money, and few papers, and no one would contact the Australian Consul or let her ring her office in Sydney. Officials treated her with disdain. The airport was filling up with veiled women, some of them carrying babies. People were lying on the floors of the bathroom, and there was a stench of urine and vomit. Soldiers with automatic weapons guarded the exits, and only passengers with boarding passes could join the waiting aircraft. Roxane was plotting the theft of a passport and ticket from a sleeping woman when the light danced onto her window boxes and allowed her to escape from her third world nightmare.

She reached the brasserie before Boris, and ordered tropical fruit salad and coffee. The table was festooned with pink frangipani. ' This is nice,' Boris said when he arrived. 'I find you all in bloom surrounded by flowers and fruits. Beautiful.'

Roxane always thought Boris looked more like a professor of international law than a travel magnate. He was a small, balding, grey-haired man with huge reserves of energy and an unexpectedly powerful voice. He was famous for both his business acumen and his work for humanitarian causes.

'Well,' he said, 'you're worried. Fire away.'

Roxane began tentatively. She described her conversa-tions with Solomon Belize and her frustrating experience at the Indigenous Council meeting. She questioned Sebastien Charpentier's loyalty. She got into her stride a little, and described Philippe's attack on Brooke, and her efforts afterwards to play down the incident to the tourists. She mentioned her conversation with Marjorie Locomo, and suggested that Olwyn had been wrong to see Charpentier as the best local connection. 'I met someone much more powerful just by walking into a teachers' college off the street,' she concluded. 'The whole thing smacks of misjudg-

160

ment, I'm afraid, and, much as I hate to say this, Boris, Olwyn's judgment these days is impaired by alcohol.'

Boris took off his steel-rimmed spectacles and looked gravely at her. His eyes were larger than they appeared through the lenses. 'But, Roxane, my dear, Olwyn's had pneumonia. It's her lungs that are the trouble.'

'Well, the hospital would say that.'

'No, not the hospital, Roxane. I've seen Olwyn this morning.'

'What? Olwyn? She's back?' Roxane heard her voice rise with the intonations of disbelief.

'Yes. I visited her not half an hour ago. She's pretty whacked from the flight back, and she's still on antibiotics, but she wanted to make sure we send suitable reinforcements over to help Sebastien run things in her absence. Actually, it's dubious whether she should go back. I've persuaded her, I think, to be guided by her doctor. She should perhaps not be too far away from a major hospital.'

'There are rumours, though, Boris, that are doing Runaway a lot of harm, about Olwyn sitting around drinking gins with clients while things go to rack and ruin.'

'By your own account, my dear, that has to be an exaggeration. The resort is doing very well, apart from one unsuitable member of staff. Look, Roxane, Olwyn has been in this business longer than I have. For as long as I've known her, I've trusted her judgment, and I've never had any reason to regret that trust. Now I can see that you've had a harrowing few days, and you've had to take a lot of responsibility over there. But you could have asked for help. You could have rung Des. He would have been only too glad to hop on a plane and sort things out for you. Instead, you seem to have been impelled to follow this red herring of the Chief Minister's sister-in-law, and you've rushed home with this extraordinary tale about Olwyn being on the gin. Now Olwyn thinks the world of you, as you know. We're all thrilled with the outcome of the Runaway with Roxane campaigns. You'd have good reason to think of yourself as the heir apparent to

161

Olwyn's place on the board. But a little loyalty to your fellow executives is called for, don't you agree?'

'Of course I'm loyal. And I certainly care about Olwyn. Are you sure she's okay?'

'She's to see a specialist later in the week. But if it's emphysema, and her lungs are permanently damaged, she might have to take things a bit easier. The slightest infection could make her very sick.'

'I see. Well, I hope you won't take what I've said to you the wrong way, Boris. I'm only thinking of the best for Runaway.'

'I'm sure you are, Roxane,' he said, with only the faintest touch of irony.

'Boris, the whole issue of cultural sensitivity. I'm not sure the Small is Beautiful approach is the best one. If we get the right people on side in these places, and it's a matter of money, mostly, isn't it, there's no reason why we can't put up top-class hotels. International stuff. Not these little villagey projects of Olwyn's. They've had their day.'

'You'll have to allow me to disagree with you. If we are in other people's countries, we don't want to put up anonymous developments. In fact the Sudpac board has had some research done on our strengths and weaknesses. These "villagey projects," as you call them, are our main marketing edge. I thought you'd have been the first to understand that.'

'Yes, I understand all right Boris, but there's no reason to move so slowly. Opportunities that we overlook will only be taken up by someone else.'

'That's the risk we run, isn't it? If you have anything specific to suggest, Roxane, as opposed to questioning current policy, why don't you and Des work out some prototypes?'

'Yes, I might.' Roxane's tone of voice revealed she had no intention of sharing her ideas with Des Hickey.

'There's another thing that's come up, too. I've had an approach from a charity committee; they want me to release you to do television promotions for them.'

162

'Why didn't they ask me first?'

'The person in question — I'm talking about Anna Szabo, the president of Harbourside Volunteers — is a very old friend. She just wanted to check with me first to see if I'd object if you did television announcements about the Silk Festival.'

'And what did you say?'

'I said Brooklands and Runaway could make you available only on the condition that it's a one-off charity promotion. No thin edges of the sandwich, Roxane. We don't want you on the screen promoting washing powders or sanitary napkins.'

'Wedge. Thin edge of the wedge.'

'Yes, exactly. Just what I said.'

'I'll never be rich, will I, Boris, while I'm in your hands?'

'It's a matter of prestige, Roxane. This particular offer is a compliment to you and to the company.'

'I'm joking, Boris. Joke, okay?'

'I would have thought we paid you quite well, by industry standards.'

'Boris, I never said otherwise. I don't want to flog soap.'

'Can I give you a lift home? I have a hire car outside.'

'No, thanks, it's walking distance for me,' Roxane said.

'Lovely to see you looking so well,' Boris said.

'And you too.' Roxane spoke without conviction, aware of having blundered from one miscalculation to another.

For once she had no idea what her next move should be.

LUCINDA

Roxane felt miserable and confused. Not only had her
attempt to warn Boris about Olwyn's mishandling of Indigo
Island misfired, but she had failed to get Steven to take her
seriously as a possible South Pacific manager for his new
ventures. Both still regarded her as a talented young thing
with a flair for marketing and good camera presence. Her
other skills — at finance, negotiation, long-term strategy —
were either taken for granted or ignored. Her major
initiatives were given to a nonentity like Des for a second
opinion. Her future at Runaway was under threat, and her
planned escape route was not working out. To cap it all, Boris
and the Szabos had come up with a cute little plan to have
her front the cameras for a charity about which she knew little
and cared less. If she told Boris she objected to this idea she
would be inviting questions about her relationship with
Szabo. She did not want to have to acknowledge to her boss
that she was having an affair with the head of a rival
corporation, particularly when Olwyn had warned her that
some people might suspect conflicts of interest. Nor did she
want to admit that she had not even met Anna Szabo. The
encounter at Marika's hardly counted.

Steven's relationship with Anna was a puzzle too. She and

164

Col, from a generation that was supposed to be much franker about sex and more willing to experiment with open marriages, had never had the kind of rapport which would have allowed them to discuss their affairs or nominate their lovers for each other's charity assignments. She'd tried to ask Steven what sort of understanding he had with Anna, but he always shrugged and gave some bluff assurance about what a marvellous woman she was. *Never so coarse as to ask Anna what she knows*, indeed. So far as she knew, Steven only had one close male friend, Vilmos Zolnay. A psychiatrist. Who could say what they might or might not confide in one another? Zolnay, Steven and Anna spoke a language she did not know. She had read somewhere that Magyar was a weird tongue, related only to Finnish.

The language spoken by Hungarians symbolised nuances of sophistication which were beyond her, beyond most people who'd studied other European languages for that matter. Its intonations were almost a taunt to the uninitiated, an unbreakable code. On the one occasion that she'd seen Anna, her posture and jaunty walk suggested someone who would land on her feet in any circumstances and take charge in most. Whereas she, Roxane, the face of Runaway, felt outfoxed and clumsy. And what did Olwyn mean by getting on a plane and coming home in the state she was in?

Suppose Olwyn found out Roxane had been putting it about she was on the gin. Suppose in revenge she had Roxane sacked from Runaway, however famous her face. What then?

There were times she regretted leaving school early. Her only post-school qualification was a travel certificate from the tech. For someone as well-known as she was, public relations must be a possibility. She could open her own consultancy. It was all too reminiscent of the cue-card ambitions of newly crowned beauty queens, though. 'I want to travel, meet people and eventually I'd like to have my own public relations company. And a big cheerio to Auntie Lindy who sewed the sequins on my dress.'

Women in their thirties did go back to study, but she knew

herself well enough to doubt whether she had the humility to put up with being assessed by academics for whom she had little time. She also doubted whether she could bear to forgo a high income for several years. No, if things didn't work out at Runaway she would go into some commercial venture or other. She had not had time to discuss this properly with Steven. She never had enough time with Steven. And some unwritten law seemed to decree that her need to confer with him should be strongest at weekends when it was impossible to push button four and be rewarded with his lilting growl.

Whatever Cindy said about school, qualifications were getting more and more important. The girl was bright enough, really. Why couldn't she see that? And where was she for that matter?

She went to the telephone and dialled. 'Hullo, Jenny. Roxane Rowe here. I'm a bit anxious about Cindy. Is she planning to go back to Central with you? Half her things are over here, and I was expecting her well before this.'

'But she left here right after lunch. We haven't seen her since about two-thirty.'

'And Lisa's with you?'

'Yes. Just a moment. I'll check whether Lisa knows where she was going ... No, Roxane, Lisa tells me Cindy got the ferry to Circular Quay at about three o'clock, and she was planning to go straight home.'

'God, this is getting worrying.'

'You know what they're like at this age. She probably called in on someone else.'

'I hope you're right. Thanks anyway. Look, I'll wait here for her, but if she's gone to the station by herself, I wonder if you could give me a call?'

'Fine. I'll do that.'

Roxane found herself gnawing at the side of a fingernail, and hastened to file it smooth before she gave way to a childhood habit of nailbiting. If Cindy wasn't here in fifteen minutes she would miss the train. She could have gone straight to the train, in which case Lisa's parents would ring up in less than an hour. So — Roxane looked at the clock under the mirror and at her wristwatch as if some minor discrepancy would solve her problems — in less than one hour she would know if there was anything to worry about.

Had the child been upset? Well, there was that tedious campaign about Asian Studies instead of French, but no intelligent girl would make herself late for school over a trifle like that, surely. Besides, Roxane had offered to discuss it all on Sunday afternoon. Well, it was Sunday afternoon now. Where was Cindy? If the stupid child really wanted to do Asian Studies, Roxane was quite prepared to capitulate.

She put Cindy's school things in order in the hallway. She tidied the Sunday papers and put out the garbage. She dusted the living room furniture. She opened the door and looked back and forth. She lifted the receiver of the phone to check it was in working order. It was. An hour passed and there was no word from Cindy.

A few minutes later, Lisa's mother rang to say Cindy had not caught the train to Bowral.

Roxane telephoned the school. Cindy's house-mistress was not there. Roxane left a message that Cindy would not be returning until the next day.

She telephoned her father at Avoca. He had heard nothing.

She rang Jane Singer. 'Give it a few hours,' Jane advised. 'You won't find the police too frantic about a girl who'll be sixteen in October. If you don't mind my saying so, Roxane, you've been very slow to make concessions to that girl's need for independence.'

'Jesus Christ, that's rich. She goes off to school and manages by herself five days out of seven. On weekends I put myself out to do what would be interesting to her. She's been at Lisa Richardson's overnight. I gave her permission the moment she asked. I was quite complimentary about this terrible punk hairdo she and her friends have concocted. I don't interfere with her friendships. What else am I supposed to do?'

'It's an attitude thing, Roxane. You assume she isn't smart enough to look after herself.'

'Well she is pretty bloody juvenile when I look back to myself at the same age. I was writing travel brochures and making group bookings when I was her age.'

'Precisely. You make it extremely clear you think she's still a kid. You fuss around about whether she's remembered her tennis racquet, or what sort of shoes she's going to wear. And she's not game to introduce you to any of the boys she knows.'

'She's just as liable to leave her tennis racquet behind if I don't remind her. And she has no idea, apparently, that you don't wear brown shoes with navy.'

'Roxane, there's no law against it. I've been meaning to say this for a long time. Why don't you ease up on the unimportant things for a while? Let her forget things and live with the consequences. Why should you worry? And who cares any more about what goes with what? Loosen the reins a bit, Roxane.'

'You sound like Colin. All this counterculture psychological crap.'

'Well, I'm sorry. What are you going to do about Colin, by the way? You'll have to get in touch with him if Cindy's missing for any length of time.'

'Thanks a fucking million. What a help you've been.' Roxane slammed down the receiver and gave way to tears. Somehow everything could be blamed on mothers. It wasn't fair. What boys did Jane mean anyway? Cindy was so tongue-tied and useless in the presence of boys that there couldn't be any serious relationships.

At eleven-thirty Roxane rang the police to report the fact that Cindy was missing. She discovered that Jane was right. The officer on duty told her to fill in the missing persons forms at the police station the following morning. There was nothing they could do in the middle of the night that couldn't wait for normal Monday to Friday office hours. 'If anything worth worrying about had happened, like an accident, you'd have heard from us,' the policeman said.

168

Roxane went to bed. She had a telephone extension in the bedroom. She was unable to sleep. What boys? What accidents? Why, in a supposedly law-abiding society, weren't the police out scouring the city for a missing fifteen-year-old instead of asking her to do the paperwork in the morning? Surely no reasonable person could accuse her of not making concessions to Cindy's need for independence. Jane was jealous of Roxane's career, that was the explanation. Everyone was jealous. Success bred savagery and bitchiness in all kinds of places, even among close friends. Jane knew about Szabo. A top job and national fame were bad enough, but a top job, national fame and a millionaire lover made an unforgivable combination. Triple whammy. This was what they meant by being lonely at the top. There just weren't enough members of the sisterhood with the same sort of prominence. So the few who had it all had to be punished. Jane was secretly pleased that she was worried about Cindy. Bitch. Even friends rejoiced at her misfortunes.

These and similar self-pitying reflections kept Roxane awake. She got up and checked that the landing light was on in case Cindy should decide to come home. She went back to bed. The bedclothes were too hot, then when she threw off the quilt they were too cold. She got up again and made herb tea. She switched on the television. A very young Katharine Hepburn was starring in a black and white film in which she tried to break into high society despite a particularly embarrassing mother. Not as embarrassing as Auntie Pammie, but bad enough. Roxane could not concentrate. She might have to take a day off work because of this emergency. Unheard of. She'd never let her family responsibilities interfere with her work; why start when her child was nearly sixteen?

In the early hours she had what seemed like a brainwave. She could ring Colin. Lucinda had two parents, after all.

She dialled the international code and the Gisborne number. Colin answered after only a few rings. Not Emily, that was one mercy.

'Col. It's Roxane.'

'Yeah. Hi. Anything wrong?'

'I hope not. But I don't know where Cindy is.'

'She's not at school?'

'No. She was home for the weekend and she stayed last night with a friend. The friends put her on a ferry at about three in the afternoon. I've no idea what she's doing or where she's been since then.'

'Not to panic. There'll be some quite ordinary explanation. You know what adolescents are like.'

'Do I? This isn't like Cindy.'

'Well, look, Roxane, think it through. If there'd been an accident or anything, the police would have told you. She's probably just in a difficult mood over something. How does she find that stitched-up school?'

'She says the French teacher picks on her. She'd like to leave, she claims.'

'Maybe she should.'

'Colin, what's the use of talking to you? That's just the kind of attitude you would take. She hasn't even got the School Certificate yet.'

'You left school at her age, if I recall.'

'So fucking what? It's a different ball game now, Colin. Why is everyone so delighted that I'm worried about something?'

'Calm down, Roxane. I'm worried myself. Maybe the kid needs a bit of a break from routine. She could come over and spend a bit of time with Em and me, find herself a little, get a bit more centred. Schooling's not the only thing, you know that. I'll keep in touch, Roxane. Ring me as soon as you hear anything. And, shit almighty, Roxane, no one is blaming you. Don't give me that trip.'

'Okay. I'm upset, that's all. I'll speak to you tomorrow.'

Dozing towards dawn, Roxane had her dream about Paul Severe. She had had this dream before. She was on a dance floor in a hall at a beachfront, a surf club perhaps. Everyone was dancing disco-style to a noisy rock band, everyone except Roxane and Paul Severe. He clasped her firmly, leading her as if ballroom dancing, and she was being guided towards the yellow light on the outside porch. Something peculiar was happening to the rhythms. Everyone else was free, dancing on their own to the four-four rhythm of the band. Roxane alone was trapped in waltz time, in the arms of a stranger. She began to realise now that the dream was a dream, and its soundtrack simultaneously parodied two Hollywood styles. *My name is Paul Severe*, a voice fit for Dr Frankenstein announced, while a Bugs Bunny falsetto repeated as a gag, *Not Paul Revere, Paul Severe: not Paul Revere, Paul Severe.* She was pinned by the man's arms, one in the small of her back, the other clasping her right hand and keeping her from getting away.

'Let me go, I have to look for Lucinda,' Roxane was struggling to tell her captor as she pushed back her bedclothes and opened her eyes.

At ten to seven Roxane telephoned the Carinya house-mistress. Miss Ikin was English, and still half asleep. 'I got your message, Mrs Bateman,' she said. 'We're not expecting Cindy until today. You will send a note, won't you?' Her young, hockey-sticks accent enraged Roxane.

'It's Miss Rowe. And no, she isn't likely to be there today, and I'm in no position to send a note. I am about to report her to the police as a missing person.'

'Oh, Lord.'

'Well might you say that. I'm relying on the school to say nothing to the girls at this time, we don't want any scandal. Cindy spent Saturday night at Lisa Richardson's, and I haven't seen her since. I expect this is just a storm in a teacup, but she's young for her age, and it's worrying.'

'Mrs Bateman, presumably the girls realise she's not back — Lisa would know you were looking for her. One of the girls may have some idea where to look for her.'

'When I want your supposedly professional advice, Miss Ikin, I'll ask for it.'

171

'Mrs — ah — Miss Rowe — I was trying to help.'

'How very considerate.'

'Miss Rowe, I know you're upset. But I'll have to inform the principal, and it's quite likely, isn't it, that the police will need to make enquiries down here in due course?'

'If one word of this reaches the media, Miss Ikin, your career will be in shreds. I'll sue you right back to whatever provincial little hockey team you escaped from. A modicum of what the prospectus is pleased to call pastoral care would have nipped all this in the bud. It's quite clear the child has decided to stay away from the school for some reason that will reflect no credit on it at all.' Roxane was beginning to sob.

'Miss Rowe, that is unnecessary. Why don't you see the police and I'll ring you again when you're less upset.'

'Don't you patronise me, Miss Ikin.'

'Goodbye until later in the day, Miss Rowe.' There was a click.

'Christ,' Roxane muttered, 'the little bitch hung up on me. How dare she? I'm not upset, I'm worried, and I have a right to be.'

She waited for a long time at the police station before anyone answered the bell at the old mahogany counter. Then a young constable with peroxided hair went away to get the appropriate form. A young uniformed man leant over the desk.

'Daughter missing, madam?'

'Yes, as I told the other officer.'

'First time she's gone missing, is it?'

'Yes, obviously.'

'Nothing's obvious to us, Madam. We just have to file an accurate report. Did you bring a photograph?'

'I should have one in my wallet.' Roxane searched through her credit cards, driver's licence and airmail stickers until she found a photo of Cindy in her school uniform.

'This is an up-to-date picture, is it?'

'Well, no, that'd be a year or two ago, and she doesn't have

172

that long hair any more, it's short and asymmetrical at the moment, with greenish bits on one side.'

'Green on which side?'

'How would I know? The left, maybe. Or the right.'

'Green on one side, short on the other?'

'Yes.'

'And was she wearing school uniform?'

'No. She disappeared yesterday afternoon — Sunday.'

'And she was wearing ...?'

'I have no idea. Jeans perhaps.'

'We need to get all this in writing. Constable Thomsett will just type it up as we go.'

The peroxided young woman wound four or five sheets of paper, separated by black carbons, into an old manual typewriter. Why weren't they using a computer? Roxane spoke through clenched teeth as she had to spell out the most elementary words: *Lucinda, hazel, Carinya, asymmetrical.* For their part, the police looked as if mothers who could not recall what their daughters wore, could not name their friends or interests, had no idea what cheap accommodation they might know of or whether they knew anyone in squats, or whether they'd taken drugs or had any approaches from older men, deserved to be filing missing persons' reports.

At her office, Roxane pressed button four on her telephone and was greeted with Steven Szabo's slurred announcement of his surname. 'It was mortifying, darling,' she said. 'They treated me with utter contempt.'

'Missing teenagers are very common-or-garden, my dear. You can't expect celebrity treatment unless she's murdered.'

'That's ...' Roxane spluttered. Tasteless? Unfeeling? Preposterous? She burst into uncertain laughter, screeched with laughter in fact, her eyes brimming with salt water.

'Yes, a tasteless remark. But keep your sense of proportion, Roxane. She will turn up quite soon. Don't worry. She's a very unimaginative young woman, from all what you say.'

'I hope you're right.'

'What does her father think?'

'He says she should go and live with him for a few months, among all that nature and sea air.'

'Perhaps he is right. Let him take the responsibility for a while. By the way, when I see you, I have some ideas for your Isantu link, the sister-in-law. Perhaps we will have luncheon later in the week? Depending on everything what's happening with Cindy, of course.'

Roxane wiped the tears away from the corners of her eyes. 'That'd be nice, Steven. I'd better go and do some work,' she said.

'Where's Des?' she asked the receptionist.

'At a meeting with someone at Pan Am. Due back pretty soon.'

'Let him know I need to talk to him, will you?'

Roxane called up the occupancy figures for the Queensland and Pacific resorts operated by Runaway on her computer screen. Queensland bookings were down a little. Indigo was doing undeniably well for a new destination. She got out the map of the Isantu group and pondered where a bigger development might be planned if Szabo was prepared to finance it. She would never agree to run it from Auckland, of course, that would be uncomfortably close to Colin. But it might be time to give Runaway the slip and join Barbary as their Pacific manager. Steven had been unresponsive when she'd raised the idea before, but if she put it more positively he would have to see the advantages.

One outer island of the Isantu group, Narewana, had very little tourism as yet, but was reputed to have fine beaches. There was no indication on the map as to whether there was a river or other source of fresh water. They could install tanks, anyhow. Her mind began to conjure up palms, swimming pools, twenty-storey hotels.

'You were looking for me?' Des smiled at her and sat down on a leather chair.

'Yes. Did Boris get onto you at the weekend?'

'No, I was out on the Hawkesbury the whole time.'

'Well, he was in Sydney for a refugee council thingummy,

174

and he insisted I have breakfast with him. He's in good form. But you knew Olwyn was back?'

'Didn't know that either. In hospital?'

'No, at home, but on medication and waiting to see a specialist. Des, I've had second thoughts about what I said about Olwyn the other day. She's not a well woman, but you know what a great person she is and how much we all owe her. How much I do in particular. I'd hate what I said about her drinking to get out. I can't stop the local gossip, of course — you know what islands are like. But I'd appreciate it if you didn't pass anything personal about her on to Boris. The Indigo thing isn't too far out of control, after all. Sebastien can hold the reins quite satisfactorily until we appoint someone to take Olwyn's place over there.'

'You have changed your tune. What did Boris say about all this?'

'Oh, nothing, really. Boris and I discussed refugees half the time. He's very involved with South East Asians, you know, as well as these Russian refuseniks.'

'What a privilege it must be for Boris,' Des said with venom, 'to be able to consult an expert in international relations over breakfast. My congratulations.' He left the room.

That's it, Roxane thought. He thinks he can beat me to a seat on the board. For a moment she wondered whether he suspected she was lying. Surely not, I'm so plausible and ingenuous, and I always put Runaway first, after all.

In the afternoon she had a call from Colin. 'Still no news?' he asked. 'In that case I'll book a ticket and come and help you. Have you got a spare bed? Look, Rox, you better keep this out of the papers. There are some terrible media angles when you think about it.' He crooned across the Tasman cable, 'Runaway, Runaway from Roxane ...'

'Colin, that is the pits. Why do I only get sick jokes from my nearest and dearest?'

'It's that amazing blonde poise. The Alfred Hitchcock heroine. No one can resist provoking her into something a bit less controlled.'

'I am right out of control at this minute, I'm warning you.'

'The Child's Father Boards A Plane,' Colin intoned. 'See you late tonight or early tomorrow.'

'Ring from the airport.'

'Fine.'

Roxane had seldom seen Colin in the past ten years or so: as a rule Cindy went to New Zealand for her holidays with her father and his wife. Roxane's dealings with her ex-husband were amicable enough; she had long been reconciled to the fact that she would contribute more financially to Cindy's upbringing than Colin could. Now that she was expecting him in Sydney within hours, she found herself thinking back to their marriage, seventeen years earlier, and the different paths their lives had taken.

They had been married in the little Rose Bay church where Roxane once made wool pompoms for the poor. No one wore pompoms to the wedding: Roxane was in cream parchment silk, and Colin had hired a morning suit. Axel Grimm stayed away, but a surprising number of supposed bohemians and libertarians put their principles to one side and came to drink their health. The reception was held at Chiswick Gardens, Edgecliff, where as a child Roxane was humiliated for wearing school shoes and socks to a birthday party. This time she had cream satin court shoes.

Roxane was twenty when she married, and twenty-one when Cindy was born. Colin's gallery was changing. Anger and political activism were replacing the self-conscious bohemianism of a few years earlier. Many of the exhibitions had an explicit anti-war theme. Colin had become active in groups opposing conscription. Roxane stayed at home with her baby for seven months, then arranged to take her to a day-care mother in Surrey Street so that she could return to work. They needed the money. Commercial success eluded the gallery, although the owner allowed it to go on operating so he could write off taxes and salve his conscience simultaneously.

Roxane's and Colin's values diverged over the next year or so, neither of them aware at first what was happening. Roxane was a senior travel consultant at Runaway by then, working long hours and coming home too tired for much conversation. She would pick Cindy up at Mrs Donnelly's, buy coleslaw, ham, rolls and cheese at the delicatessen, and stagger up the few metres to the gallery with baby, baby paraphernalia, and little white parcels of cold food in her arms. Once inside, she would kick off her shoes, deposit Cindy in a baby hammock, feed her some Heinz tinned food and let her hold her bottle herself, and put the salad things on the table. This whole routine took about fifteen minutes. Then she would watch the next episode of the Vietnam War on television and drink a glass of sherry while she waited for Colin.

Colin had more and more to do, less and less of it to do with the gallery. He attended meetings, circulated petitions, arranged billets for draft dodgers and organised demonstrations and sit-ins. *Hey, hey, LBJ, how many kids have you killed today?*

'You're reverting to student life,' Roxane had accused him. 'You spend more time up at the art school and over at the university than you do at the gallery. The openings are full of penniless politicos who'll never buy a painting. The cause may be a good one, but you're going about it in a completely childish and irresponsible way.'

'At least there's one of us who hasn't sold out to the imperialists. Those American transport companies and hotel chains you deal with are just a front for the CIA and the Republican right and the whole disgusting apparatus of United States hegemony.'

'And when are you going to spend a little time with your daughter? She scarcely sees you. When she does, she probably identifies you more with your collection of lapel badges than with your face.'

'That's great, Roxane. You're a great one to talk. The kid

scarcely sees her own mother, and I'm the one who gets criticised.'

'Do you imagine we could live on your percentage from the gallery if we didn't have my salary? To say nothing of planning for the future and saving up for a house.'

'Yeah, yeah, put in the boot. Hit me when I'm down. Make me feel worthless. Have a claret?' He opened a flagon and poured two glasses.

'You have to admit,' Roxane said, 'you're getting a bit old to wear bells on your jeans. You're nearly thirty.'

'I'm making an absurdist statement, Roxane, like a court jester. You think court jesters had a retirement age?'

'They probably had their heads chopped off when they were just jangling bells and lapel badges and stayed away at meetings every night.'

'Touché. Do have a drink. And how's my baby girl?' He lifted Cindy out of her hammock. 'Da-da-da,' she said, fingering his MAKE LOVE NOT WAR badge. 'Anyway, Cindy likes them, don't you babe?'

'The salad's on the table.'

'Roxane, other women who work full-time manage to freeze casseroles at the weekend or something. They don't serve little snacks from the delicatessen every night of the week.'

'Other men who don't work regular hours remember to go to the butcher and the greengrocer when they're asked.'

'It just goes on like this, does it?' Colin asked. 'I make some crack, you make some countercrack, on and on into the sunset of our years? Is that how you see our relationship?' Cindy was crawling on the floor at his feet, intrigued by the bells and embroidery on the cuffs of his flared jeans.

'I just don't know how I see it. When I met you, I thought you were so organised. You seemed to be someone who could handle money, do deals with other people, run things, all that stuff. On top of that you could talk about art and books and you knew everyone and I was terribly impressed. But you seem to be going backwards, there's no other way of putting it.'

'The only measure you can think of, my dear little suburban office girl, is my income.'

'Not the only one, you know that.'

Tiredness and suppressed irritation were taking their toll on their sex life. Roxane was woken once or twice each night by Cindy, who seemed to have discovered that screeching at three in the morning guaranteed an opportunity to have some time alone with her mother. Roxane and Colin made love in silence, with no humour and little tenderness. It was as if their marriage were a train with its own momentum and a mysterious destination, rattling along but not controlled by them. Roxane had once seen herself as a mysterious powerful figure on a luxury train. Now she felt like someone who would have to jump in the dark from a moving train onto an unidentified platform.

When Cindy was nearly two, Roxane was sent to Hong Kong for a fortnight on business. She arranged for Cindy to go to Thea's at Rose Bay while she was away.

In Hong Kong, Roxane had to liaise with the company which was to arrange day trips and shopping expeditions for Australian tourists. She made the most of the shopping herself, arranging for a silk suit, a jacket dress and a linen coat to be tailored at bargain prices. She met the first few contingents of visitors to take advantage of her package, escorted them to their hotels, and introduced the local couriers. Her package looked set to be one of the company's most profitable and she was pleased with her first major venture overseas.

In her off-duty hours, she avoided nightclubs and restaurants which seemed to be full of American soldiers on R and R, and Asian girls in shiny cheong-sams. She stayed at her hotel in Kowloon, reading, watching television (more war episodes, demonstrations at American universities, protest marches in many capitals), occasionally ringing Colin, and eating alone in the hotel dining room. One night she was drinking coffee after dinner when a man approached her table. 'I can see that you're not a tourist,' he said, 'and that you're here on business. This isn't a pick-up, honestly, I'd just be very grateful if you'd let me buy you a liqueur and talk to you for a while.'

Roxane looked at him. American, short hair, late thirties, navy blue silk and wool suit. 'Why not?' she asked.

'I like your silk dress,' the man said, sitting down.

'And your suit, too. We've both been patronising the local tailors.' They laughed and compared notes about the addresses of the best shops.

'I'm running a new tour package from Sydney, Australia,' Roxane explained. 'I have to tell some of our tourists very gently that Hong Kong mightn't be the best place in the world to order a three-piece lounge suite, once you add the freight.'

'Lounge suite?

'Sofa and matching armchairs,' Roxane translated.

'Who said something about divided by a common language?' Randy Millford asked.

'You must be here on R and R,' Roxane said.

'Yes. I generally pick Hong Kong for R and R. I can buy nice things for my wife, and the food is fantastic. But it can get kind of lonesome.'

'I keep watching the war on TV. I don't know how you can bear the thought of going back there.'

'Oh, don't feel too badly, ma'am, thought is something we soldiers religiously avoid.'

'You don't fool me for a second.' She smiled at him. 'Tell me about your wife and family.'

'They're in Fort Worth. There's Alexander the fourth, he's seven, and Genevieve, she's three.' He produced the inevitable photographs: blond children squinting into the sun near a turquoise swimming pool. A woman with dark wavy hair and a sunhat sat behind them.

'They're lovely. You must be very proud of them. And this is my daughter Cindy.' One of Colin's friends had taken some black and white pictures of Cindy peering through the iron railings of the gate at the foot of the gallery steps like a small, snowy-haired prisoner.

'It looks kind of old-fashioned and quaint where you live. I thought everything in Australia was new and kind of like the frontier. But then you can guess wrong from appearances. I never thought you'd be married and a mother. Your husband's a lucky man. I imagine you're very much in love with him.'

Roxane wondered. How long was it since she had felt any emotion which could be described as being in love? 'I'm not sure,' she said. 'I'm not sure how to describe how I feel about him. I feel he chose me, and we belong together somehow, but apart from that I feel terribly irritated a lot of the time.'

'That's too bad.' She hoped Randy Millford the third was not going to launch into a session of marriage guidance.

'Did you say you were in the army or the air force?' she asked.

'Army intelligence. Colonel.'

'Oh, God, you should hear what Colin thinks of the CIA and the American imperialists.'

'Radical, is he? I frankly doubt, that there's much I haven't heard of those views. We keep tabs on opinion worldwide, you know. The current generation of students is very different than mine. We were kind of patriotic, you know. Grateful to live in a rich country. More united. It's like everything that seemed solid is just fragmenting away.'

'Maybe it is.' Colin would not regard infidelity in itself as wicked; he kept some of his libertarian student notions of free love. But an American intelligence officer. Colin must never know, Roxane thought, but undeniably part of Randy Millford's charm was that he represented the militarism her husband hated.

When they left the dining room, Randy Millford shook her by the hand. 'It's been a real privilege talking with you, Roxane,' he said. 'You've made it a real pleasant evening for me.'

'Yes, it's been lovely to meet you, too,' Roxane said. 'When do you go back to ...?'

'To duty? Midday tomorrow.'

'Take care of yourself. Goodnight.'

Twenty minutes later Roxane telephoned the switchboard operator and asked to be put through to Colonel Millford. 'I wondered if I could offer you a nightcap?' she asked.

'What's the room number, honey?'

For the rest of her life Roxane would look back at the mating of strangers in an anonymous hotel room in Kowloon as one of the most extraordinary nights she had known. Randy Millford was more considerate, more conscious of her responses, more willing to wait and share than Colin had ever been. As for Axel Grimm, those encounters now seemed little better than rape. Ridiculous, she kept thinking, an American with a perfectly ridiculous name and not an original idea to bless himself with, and he turns out to be fantastic in bed.

'Fantastic,' she whispered, as his tongue made her throb with desire. He had a broad back and very little hair on his body. His eyes were blue. She had always imagined she preferred compactly built, hirsute men. But it appeared, from her sudden and intense response to the strange American's unfamiliar technique, that she knew very little about her own sexuality. He put her feet on his shoulders, and kept a gentle, insistent pressure on her clitoris as his slow, controlled rhythm continued. Roxane felt suffused with heat and anticipation. Her head tossed from side to side. When she began to climax she looked at the blue eyes of the military intelligence officer in a second of disbelief, then closed her eyes, abandoned, gasping at the sudden, indescribable waves of pleasure that flowed through her. They made love as if life held nothing else, as if they would never see the morning or their families or a uniform or a jumbo jet again, as if a room with bamboo wallpaper in a three star hotel in an overpopulated city held all the sensual secrets of the universe.

'It's never been like this,' she said.

'That's what they all say,' Randy Millford the third said.

'No, really, it's never been so extraordinary for me. You'll

182

have to believe me.'

'With your sexuality, I do find it hard to believe. But perhaps being away from the pressures of being a mother and all, that could make a difference.'

Roxane was afraid she might cry. 'Don't make me feel guilty, whatever you do,' she said. She wondered if there was some truth in what he said. Certainly, some of the intensity and excitement she had once known with Colin had disappeared once she had to worry about settling Cindy down, soothing her when she woke, changing her in the middle of the night, calming her when she cried out in dreams. She put her arms around the unfamiliar muscular body. 'You're very beautiful,' she said.

'Just don't tell my men,' the American said, smiling.

When Roxane returned to Sydney she found that Colin had allowed three young people from the peace movement to move into their building: two draft dodgers and a student named Emily Markey. She hoped that Cindy's crying would make the night intolerable for all of them, but Cindy was growing up and now preferred to stay up later in the evenings and sleep through the night.

One afternoon after work Roxane collected Cindy as usual, bought food as usual, kicked off her shoes and poured herself a drink as usual, and was about to switch on the television news when Emily Markey asked if she could talk to her about something. Emily had long, tawny hair, no make-up, a restless expression, and a slightly wheedling manner. She wore an embroidered top of thin orange cotton, and no bra. There was a slight odour of musk or incense about her, which lacked the sharp freshness of the Paris perfumes Roxane preferred.

'I suppose you realise,' Emily said with an attempt at a smile, 'that Colin and I are involved with each other?' She paused and looked at the floor before looking up again. 'I wondered if you'd mind moving into my room so I can move in with Col? He didn't know how to ask you himself.'

Cold fury made Roxane tremble. She thought for a

moment she would not find her voice. 'Sleep where you like,' she said. 'Just don't expect me to talk to you again, ever. I will, of course, have some things to discuss with Colin.'

Within weeks the marriage was over. Roxane was not exactly heartbroken, but Colin's spinelessness in letting Emily break the news to her continued to enrage her. Cindy was now the centre of Roxane's emotional life, but even in her relationship with her daughter she had a new wariness. She would do all she could to avoid giving other people the power to hurt and humiliate her again. If people found her cold, that was their problem. Roxane and her daughter went to live in Flood Street, Bondi. Emily and Colin moved to New Zealand. Cindy spent some of her summer holidays with them.

Thea died just six days after Roxane gained her *decree nisi*. Her death was sudden and unexpected. Roxane felt for her father in his grief, but her own feelings were curiously muffled. It was as if she had put all her emotions into cold storage when she broke up with Colin. Perhaps she would thaw out from those hurts one day. Her first reaction was to miss Thea as an obliging child-minder rather than as a central person in her life.

After Thea's death, Roxane relied more and more on Mrs Donnelly and her family for child care, so she was glad that Cindy could have leisurely summers with her father. The plane fare was cheaper than two months' child care would have been. When Roxane made the lucrative Runaway commercials, she bought the three-bedroom apartment in Rushcutters Bay, but by that time she only saw Cindy at weekends because she was a weekly boarder at Carinya in Bowral, returning by train on Saturday mornings.

ANNA

'I asked you to ring from the airport.'

Roxane stood at the door in a towelling robe, frowning.

'Nice welcome. Morning. No word from our daughter, I take it. Are you going to ask me in?'

'Sure. Do come in.'

Colin's beard was almost grey now, and he'd lost weight. He was becoming one of those sinewy, health-conscious middle-aged men. He wore a heavyweight navy duffle over a striped, handknit jumper, and carried an overnight bag.

'You look like a vegetarian,' Roxane said.

'Don't knock it, I just about am one.'

'Suits you, actually.'

'And what do the police say about Lucinda? What's the plan?'

'They seem to have started some paperwork, maybe put her name on a computer or something, and not much more. They did mention I could try the youth refuges at the Cross and the free food places, the Hare Krishnas and so on.'

'Have you done that yet?'

'How could I? I was at the police station, and at the office.'

'Oh, the office. Of course. First things first.'

'Don't take that tone with me, Col, it's totally unhelpful.

Can I get you some coffee?'

'That'd be great.'

Roxane brewed coffee and listened to the eight-thirty news. There were no teenage corpses, at any rate.

'Here you are,' she said. 'I do feel better now you're here. How are Crystal and Damien?'

'You can't bring yourself to ask how Emily is, even after all this time, can you?'

'No, I can't.'

'Perhaps I should find it flattering. On the other hand I suspect it's more an index of your inflexibility than your passion.'

'Colin, this is not the time to rake up all that stuff. Our daughter Lucinda is missing.'

'As the travel executive said to the police sergeant.'

'For fuck's sake, Col!'

'Okay, okay. I do have some suggestions. Why don't you stay put, stick to routine more or less, while I go out and about to make inquiries. I suppose you've had multiple copies made of photographs?'

'What? No. No, I haven't.'

'Well, whip out the album now and find a couple of recent ones. I'll get some instant photo lab on to it right away. And while I'm at the Cross I can try the Wayside Chapel and the youth workers. And the Hares. Is she into any cults or groups?'

'No, of course not.'

'Well, anything's possible, Roxane. Plenty of good vegetables, anyway.'

Roxane was sifting through photographs of Cindy — in the bath as a baby, on her first day at school, on her grandfather's lap, in a volleyball team, on horseback. Eventually she found a couple taken at a picnic with the Singers the previous summer. 'These two seem reasonable,' she said. 'Better than the one I gave the cops, anyhow. But she's got green hair, Col.'

'What shade of green?'

'Oh, an awful pea green on the ends of her hair on one side. And the other side is shaved very short.'

'She'll blend right in with the crowd then.' Roxane did not smile. Colin put an arm on her shoulders. 'I'm upset, too, sweetheart,' he said. 'But we'll find her very soon, never fear.'

Roxane sat down and put a hand to her face. 'There's this terrible assumption, Col, that if anything goes wrong it's the mother's fault. I spend every weekend with Cindy, I really care about her. I rearrange trips so as not to be away in school holidays, I do everything I can to see she's well looked after. And as soon as something goes wrong, there's this snide sort of undertone in everyone's reactions — the police, my friends ... Roxane was beginning to weep. 'I'm as anxious as bloody hell and all people do is gloat about it,' she said.

'Well, sweetheart, hell is other people. Of course there are shits out there. Don't let them get to you. Of course you're anxious; I'm anxious too. But this is so unlike you, Roxane, taking other people's stupid comments to heart. Where's that famous toughness, eh? Come on, we'll get through this together, really.'

'And even Lucinda. I don't believe she's all that distressed herself. She's out to punish me, somehow.'

'We don't know what she's on about, do we? It may have nothing to do with you.'

'The child's getting really spiteful and difficult. Snaps every time she speaks. I can't do anything right,' Roxane sobbed.

'Look, Roxane, you're tired and overwrought. Why don't you take the day off, stay here, and I'll be in touch in a couple of hours to let you know how I'm getting on.'

'You mean, stay away from work for the day?'

'Yes, actually. There are some people who would go so far as to take the day off in these circumstances.'

'I could ring in and say I'm sick.'

'You didn't say anything about Cindy, then?'

'At work? Of course not.'

'You make it hard on yourself with this superwoman stuff,

don't you? Okay, if you prefer to tell them you're sick, do that. You stay here. If you have to go out, put the answering machine on. I'll be off to get these photos done. See you later.'

When Colin had gone, Roxane rang her office and left a message that she had flu. She sat uselessly in the living room, unable either to relax or to decide what to do.

Almost out of habit, she dialled Olwyn's number. A woman answered. 'Roxane Rowe speaking — is Mrs Tierney available please?'

'Could you hold the line please?' There was a long pause. 'No, I'm sorry Roxane, my mother is not well enough to come to the phone.'

'Oh, you're her daughter. Margot, isn't it? I've got a message from you about some sort of survey or interview.'

'Yes, I did ring while you were out of the country, but don't bother about it now. I've pretty well concluded my study anyhow.'

'I would have been quite willing to help.'

'That's kind, thanks. I may see you anyway at the Women's Finance Seminar my colleague Brian Lynch is organising.'

'Oh, you work with Brian, at that college.'

'Yes. YIFE. The Yagoona Institute.'

'Well, I'm looking forward to that day of Brian's, as you say, and perhaps I'll see you then. Could you give my regards to Olwyn?'

'By all means. Thankyou for calling.'

Not well enough to come to the phone, indeed, Roxane thought. Fobbing me off as transparently as that. Whatever next? She washed up the coffee cups, filled a jug and went out onto her balcony to water her pot plants. She went downstairs and collected her morning newspaper and sat on the balcony reading about the latest trade figures.

The telephone rang, and she dashed inside, hoping it might be Cindy, imagining it was probably Colin. But a woman's voice was on the line: one that Roxane recognised immediately, although she'd heard it only once before.

'Miss Rowe. Anna Szabo of Harbourside Volunteers. I've taken the liberty of phoning you at home because your office isn't expecting you in at all. I was wondering if Steven and I might have the pleasure of your company at luncheon on Sunday? Here, at Point Piper. There are quite a number of things we ought to discuss about the Silk Festival, aren't there? And, besides, I'm longing to know you a little better.'

'This Sunday?'

'Naturally, this Sunday.' The European accent had an inflection which rose and fell like a violin being tuned.

'Mrs Szabo. This is difficult. I scarcely know you, but I have to tell you a bit about what's going on. My daughter Lucinda is missing, and I am half out of my mind — distracted with worry. Beside myself.'

'How long has she been gone?'

'Since Sunday.'

'And her age?' Anna Szabo said *etch*.

'Fifteen.'

'You are alone there?'

'Well, my ex-husband, Colin, is up at the Cross checking round the youth refuges and getting some photographs copied.'

'Tell me precisely where you are.'

'I'm at home, in Rushcutters Bay.'

'My dear Roxane, if I am on my way over there, I need the full address and the number of your apartment.'

Like an obedient child, Roxane gave these details, and then sat waiting for her lover's wife to arrive and take charge of her.

Anna Szabo felt secure in her marriage. Shared dangers and shared youth had bonded Steven and herself for life. However great his sexual passion for another woman, it would be transient and peripheral by comparison. Sex was only part of a relationship, but their lovemaking was fine, so far as it went, for two people who had been together for thirty-seven years. She knew about his involvement with Roxane. Steven was unaware of the extent to which his

189

confidant, Vilmos Zolnay, passed information on to Anna. The psychiatrist and the wife held conferences in which they discussed Steven, the source of their fortunes, as if he were a reckless seventeen-year-old who could not yet be trusted to sign his own cheques. They saw Steven's impulsiveness, and his enthusiasm for new products and new business partners as assets for Barbary: through them the business had diversified and spread. But the same qualities did not make a monogamous husband. 'You know Steven,' Vilmos would say to her on the wistaria-framed terrace outside his three-storeyed house and clinic. 'Yes,' Anna would sigh, 'I know Steven.' And they would add together — it was an old routine — 'Better than he knows himself.'

Anna Szabo looked intently at Roxane. 'My dear, you should be sitting down. Let me bring you a grapefruit juice. Did you see your doctor? How do sleeping pills affect you? You may do best to avoid them. Now, let us see whether everything that can be done is being done.'

Roxane sat back on her divan as the older woman's energy reverberated through the apartment. She began to explain what the police were doing, what inquiries Colin was making. 'The girl will be sixteen in October?' Anna asked.

'Yes.'

'Teenage girls are tougher than you think.'

'Well, yes, when I was her age I was already in the workforce.'

'When I was her age I'd travelled hundreds of miles across Europe under an assumed identity to escape from the Nazis. At one stage we were walking fifteen miles a day.'

'My God. You did it on foot. Did you sleep out? That's what's giving me nightmares, the thought of her freezing to death in these August nights.'

'Mostly we went to safe houses of one sort or another, or our guides knew of barns or disused railway sheds or something. Shelter, but very seldom any heat.'

'Your guides must have been brave.'

'Yes, some were. And they were nearly all well paid.'

'Who would have paid them?'

'Grandparents, or friends who looked after some of our parents' possessions when they were taken away. There may even have been a philanthropist or two.'

'I never realised people had to buy their way out.'

'Money saved more people from extinction than you might imagine. Does Cindy have any money?'

'I send her twenty dollars a week. Come to think of it, she has one of those automatic teller savings accounts.'

'Well, then, ring the bank and find out about any recent withdrawals.'

'Anna — can I say Anna? You're brilliant.'

Anna Szabo smiled. 'No, my dear, just logical.'

Roxane was on the telephone in seconds, but the accountant of her bank refused to give her any information on the grounds of client confidentiality. 'Fuck it all, I'm the girl's mother!' she shouted, and hung up.

'Perhaps,' Anna said gently, 'the police would be able to get access to the information in a case like this. What's the name of the officer you spoke to — have you got his number?'

'Senior Constable Collier.'

'It might be wise for me to telephone this time, don't you think?'

Mutely Roxane handed Anna the mobile phone. The police took the details and promised to report back with any information.

'You don't have children?' Roxane asked.

'No. Other things came first when I was very young. Then when I was older, well, it turned out it was not such a simple thing to have a child after all. I had all kinds of tests done. There was nothing wrong with me, so I was told. One could have drawn the conclusion that my husband was — well, the fertility problem could have been his perhaps. He was sensitive about it, of course. My interest in having children was not so great that I felt I had to exhaust every medical avenue when Steven found the whole topic somewhat

191

threatening. It is more important in the long term that people accept each other as they are, don't you feel?'

'Yes, I'm sure.' In fact Roxane was not too sure what Anna Szabo was implying.

'There are natural reactions to that kind of difficulty. One has to keep them in perspective.'

In her anxious state, Roxane was finding it hard to interpret these confidences. Is she saying Steven screws around to prove his virility? she wondered.

'I never gave it much thought, having a child,' Roxane said. 'It just seemed to be part of getting married. If the marriage had lasted, I might have had two or three. Things might have been completely different.'

'Every path we take means one we cannot travel, isn't that so?' Anna Szabo said. 'I have another item on my agenda, though you'll find it hard to give it your whole attention at the moment. You know about Harbourside Volunteers, of course. We are arguably the most significant charity committee in Sydney. Our latest project is a Silk Festival; we're importing silk fashion from all over the world, even China. I'm taking Steven to Shanghai with me shortly — perhaps he's told you?'

Roxane shook her head. She felt she was in the path of a tornado. Anna dashed on.

'Of course, I had trouble persuading Steven that imported silk wasn't going backwards economically at a time when we're supposed to be exporting more Australian goods. But we've got round that. Barbary will sponsor a series of prizes for young designers — the best hand-painted silk balldress by a designer under twenty-six – that sort of thing. The Cornucopia Committee and the Black and White ladies will be beside themselves with envy. There's never been anything remotely like what we intend to do, for scope or sheer spectacle. And of course what we do need, my dear, is the right presenter, someone elegant, recognised by television audiences, and unquestionably Australian.'

'You've ruled out Paul Hogan?' Roxane asked.

Anna laughed. 'There were several people in contention, of course, but since your name was first mentioned we've been quite sold on having you. We are used to getting our way at Harbourside Volunteers. Though I say so myself, we are quite a force to be reckoned with. There was a time when the old money, the land and wool dynasties, saw Europeans as interlopers. It happened to Steven in business, too, and to me of course, when I was selling clothes and still learning the language. People tried to freeze us out. But now, things are very different. You mustn't disappoint us, Roxane. Boris was in favour of the idea, you know.'

"Yes, so he said.'

'You must agree, no? Yes! I've brought the draft scripts for the Silk Festival announcements for you to read over, in case you want to make any minor changes in the wording to make it more natural for you. And I have some samples of Italian silk. You will, of course, need one of Nicholas Vader's drop dead creations.'

'I could never afford one. I'm still paying boarding school fees.'

'My dear, Harbourside Volunteers have arranged a great many generous sponsorships. In this case I am sure Barbary Enterprises public affairs department would be most willing to pick up the tab, don't you agree? I'd like you to go and see Nicholas this week — I've told him to expect you.'

'It's not that I'm not grateful. It's just that ... I'm not all here, really, I'm too preoccupied.'

'Just have a look at the colours.'

Again Roxane felt like a recalcitrant child. Look, a jack-in-the-box! She fingered the strips of silk — midnight blue, turquoise, emerald.

'We feel you should wear some shade of blue or green to symbolise the harbour,' Anna said.

'The dark blue is very nice,' Roxane said, without much enthusiasm.

'Just what I hoped you'd say. Now — will you see Nicholas tomorrow?'

'I don't know. I told the office I had flu.'

'In that case, you certainly can't go back there tomorrow. If I could have the phone again ... Nicholas? Anna. Yes, absolutely. Thankyou, darling. Now, Nicky, you know we discussed a television outfit for Roxane Rowe. I have her with me now – what time can you see her tomorrow? Fine. Excellent. *Au revoir.*' She replaced the receiver. 'That's all settled. You'll go and see Nicholas at ten-thirty tomorrow.'

'Thanks. This is amazing.'

'Not at all. It's just you might need a bit of a push if you're sitting here paralysed with anxiety. Oh, I might as well go on as I've begun. I generally say what's on my mind, you know. Why are you still working for that Runaway company?'

'What?'

'Why are you still with the same firm you went to work with all those years ago? Unless I'm misinformed.' Her tone of voice suggested she seldom had cause to doubt her sources of information.

'No, you're right. I'm still with Runaway. It's a very good firm — it's expanded a lot. It's given me a lot of opportunities and I've helped make it what it is, you know, define its market niche.'

'Why haven't you gone out on your own long since? What's the point of national exposure like those Runaway commercials if you don't turn them to your advantage? Start your own consultancy, your own exclusive tours. You and I could run a Silk Route tour as follow-up to the Silk Festival.'

'Sounds like fun. I wonder if you're right, about leaving Runaway. I thought the logical thing would be to stay there, and succeed Olwyn Tierney on the board when she retires.'

'Logical, but a little unimaginative, don't you think?'

'Maybe so. Perhaps you're right. I should loosen up a bit and see my options more broadly.'

'And you're so good-looking on television. Oh, very nice in real life, don't think I mean to be insulting, but sensational on the screen. You haven't begun to capitalise on that.'

'Perhaps not.'

'I'm a terrible bully. Do tell me to mind my own business if you want to.'

'It's okay. It's just that the idea of leaving Runaway is such heresy that I'm having trouble adjusting.'

There was a loud knocking on the door. Anna went to see who it was. Colin staggered inside, bearing three parcels of hot food. 'I bought a quiche for you, and a leek pie for myself, and some mixed vegetables for us to share,' he said. 'Looks like we'll have to share out the quiche too.' Roxane introduced Anna, who picked up the food parcels and went to the kitchen to organise plates and forks.

Colin raised his eyebrows. 'She's a very high-powered charity lady,' Roxane murmured. 'I scarcely even know her, but I'm making some television commercials for her committee. She seems to have taken over my life.'

'Looks that way.'

'I presume we can be informal, and do without a tablecloth?' Anna said, handing round plates of food and paper napkins.

The telephone rang, and Anna, not hesitating, picked up the receiver. 'For you,' she said to Roxane.

'Great. Great. What a relief. Thankyou, constable.' Roxane stood near the telephone, almost in a daze.

'Have they found her?' Colin asked.

'No,' Roxane said. 'But I doubt if she's sleeping rough and freezing to death. She withdrew a hundred dollars from her bank account at the George Street branch on Sunday night at eleven fifteen.'

'What's the balance in the account?' Colin asked.

'A hundred and twenty dollars.'

'Well, as you say, it's good news. And they'll let us know if there are any more transactions?'

'Yes, of course.'

'Well,' Colin said, 'that explains why they've heard nothing at any of the refuges or drop-in centres. She's still got a bit of cash; she can buy a ticket somewhere or a bed for a few nights. A great relief, isn't it?'

'I can't eat, really,' Roxane said. 'I'll just ring the office and see what messages I've received.'

She dialled the Runaway number. 'Just two messages,' Di told her. 'Dr Brian Lynch from that Yagoona college wants to discuss those financial seminars with you. And David Jasper of *Business Briefing* is still after you for an interview. Possible cover story, he says.'

'Keep them all on hold for a day or two, would you? I expect I'll shake off this flu before too long. Thanks, hon.'

'My ex-wife,' Colin announced to Anna, 'can't even tell her own secretary that she's worried stiff about something. She has to play Superwoman to the last.'

'I ebsolutely concur,' Anna said. 'Why advertise our personal concerns to our employees? It makes for a very unbecoming familiarity.'

On the Wednesday morning, Roxane woke up dreaming she was absent without leave from a European military boarding school. An inquiry was being held into the crimes of three male inmates, and she was to be questioned as an accomplice. Despite being a prefect, she had been staying away from the place in some kind of knowing fear. The District Court judge who was to head the inquiry could be heard debating whether leniency was appropriate in Roxane's case, or whether to make an example of her. 'You have to release me,' she pleaded to the cell attendant, who had dyed hair and an Eastern European accent, 'my daughter is missing.'

Struggling to her feet, Roxane wondered if she dreamt regularly or whether these nightmares were spurred by fear and anxiety about Cindy. And what was Anna Szabo doing materialising in her dreams as a custodial officer? Was she the fairy godmother who came precisely when she was needed, offering glittering ballgowns, or was she putting tabs on Roxane for a darker purpose of her own?

Where were her own friends? Why hadn't Jane Singer or the Richardson parents been in touch with her?

She rang her father on the Central Coast. 'If there's

anything I can do, darling heart,' he said, but Roxane could not think of anything he could do that was not being done already by Colin.

'Coffee,' Colin said, handing Roxane a cup. 'And I've cut up a grapefruit for you.'

'Thanks. I slept better, anyway.'

The telephone rang. 'What news of the prodigal daughter?' Jane Singer asked. 'Oh, my dear, you still haven't heard anything? This is getting quite serious.'

'It's been serious since Sunday night,' Roxane snapped.

'Look, Roxane, I'm sorry if I chose the wrong moment to speak to you about your style as a parent. I'm sure you've been an excellent mother, really.'

'I'm sure, Jane, that you meant well, but I was very hurt all the same.'

'Yes, I see that now. What can I do to help?'

'Colin's here, and between him and the police making inquiries, and my guarding the phone, we should find out where she is before too long.'

'I hope so, darling. Keep in touch.'

'Will do.'

Roxane went back to the balcony where Colin was eating breakfast. 'Who was that amazing lady who was here yesterday?' he asked.

'Her name is Anna Szabo,' Roxane said. 'She's my lover's wife.'

'Very cosy.'

'Yes, it is a bit. I'd never met her before. Then yesterday she tore around here uninvited, like some sort of avenging angel. The odd thing was, I was very pleased to see her. She has enough energy for an army. She's wasted on charity work. I couldn't help liking her, somehow.'

'Well, it doesn't do to judge others by yourself. Just because you never felt any kind impulses towards Emily doesn't mean other women can't feel well disposed towards their husband's lovers.'

'The difference is, I was expected to make way for Emily,

197

and I'm not threatening Anna and Steven's marriage in the slightest.'

'That's understood all round, is it?'

'Yes, I'd say so.'

'Well, in that case, I don't see any reason why you couldn't end up great friends with both of them, just as you could be great friends with me and Em if you cared to.'

'You're still a Make Love Not War man at heart, aren't you?'

'Yup. So it seems. And you're still a cynic.'

'What's our plan for today so far as Cindy's concerned?'

'You stay by the phone or put on the answering machine if you go out. I'll go to the Red Cross, the backpack places and the youth hostels. Then we can meet here and compare notes about two-thirty. That suit you?'

'Fine,' Roxane said.

After Colin had left, she made a slice of toast and Vegemite and sat watching breakfast television through two episodes of news, the horoscopes for the day, and the interviews in between. The weather man forecast a top temperature of twenty-one in the city and along the coast; the north coast should reach twenty-four and the Blue Mountains only fourteen. The overnight temperature had been nine degrees. At least it wasn't freezing, Roxane thought, and chances are Cindy was inside anyway. She read the paper — general approval of the Keating budget, which had been pretty much as forecast in the leaks of the preceding fortnight.

She sat by the silent phone until fifteen minutes before her appointment with Nicholas Vader. His studio was in Darley Street, Darlinghurst, a converted flat in a seedy old prune-coloured building. The studio had a calculated air of tatty chic. Framed posters from 1950s couture showings jostled with cut-outs of men in leather and bondage gear. The change rooms were partitioned off by black hessian curtains, and the uncarpeted floor was littered with bolts of fabric, shears, scissors, tape measures and piles of Italian *Vogue*. The furniture comprised a black leather sofa and several gold-framed cheval mirrors.

'Roxane Rowe,' Nicholas Vader said. 'I can't tell you how thrilled I was when Anna told me you'd taken on this silk venture for her. Such a doll of a lady, our Anna. Velvet fist in the iron glove and all that, or is it the other way around? We all eat out of her hand. Anyhow, as I said to Robert and Carol, she couldn't have made a better choice, absolutely couldn't. Now, which fabric did you choose?'

'The midnight blue.'

'Darling, that's perfect. I couldn't be more excited. You made absolutely the right choice. Stand there. Right where you are. Hold the curtain under your chin, just let me see your face and your height. Darling, you know my theory. You get precisely thirty seconds to make an impression. My dresses are made on the Drop Dead theory; every other women in sight should look nothing beside you. I'm thinking of something slim, with long sleeves, and slightly defined shoulders — a little silver stripe on the shoulderline for emphasis, what do you think?'

'I'm sure you'll think of something sensational,' Roxane said. Visualising the fabric raised into prominent sleeves, she suddenly remembered the puff-sleeved party dress her grandmother gave her.

'Darling, I always do. Leave everything to me.'

On her way home, Roxane stopped at a barrow and bought corn on the cob, pears and mandarins.

In her letterbox were a Telecom bill, a card from a real estate agent asking if she wanted to sell her property, a flyer from a hardware store, and a postcard. She dropped these items into the white plastic bag from the fruitstall, and it was only when she was putting the pears in the refrigerator that she read the postcard:

> *Dear Mum,*
> *I hope you're not worried. Couldn't face*
> *school. Am well and will probably come home*
> *soon.*

It is very pretty up here.

> *Love,*
> *Cindy.*

The postmark was partly obscured: rigo 2453 was all she could decipher. She began going through postcodes in the A-K phone book. By the time Colin returned, she had worked it out. Dorrigo. Colin took her car and set off to drive north to retrieve their daughter.

Cindy woke up in a strange room to the chiming of two grandfather clocks and a shrill chorus of birdsong, dominated by the shrieks of white cockatoos. She sat up and pulled on her jeans; she'd slept in her underwear. She walked out of the small bedroom and through a strange drawing room with seven or eight antique clocks in it, and stumbled towards the daylight which streamed in the open front door. A tiny figure was stretching up to a wooden platform, scattering birdseed, bread and honey for an extraordinary gathering of wild birds. White cockatoos circled and shrieked, a kingfisher dived, rosellas warbled, king parrots competed with lorikeets, and scrub wrens scuttled for the scraps on the grass below. The tiny woman looked up at Cindy. 'Sleep well, dearie?' she asked. 'Look, look, see the one with the glossy coat, see if we can lure him over here. He's my favourite. He's the golden regent.' The golden-crowned black bird perched on a branch overhead and cocked its head to one side.

'Makes my day when that one comes down,' the old woman said. 'Bet you don't get this many birds in New Zealand, eh?'

'No.' Cindy tried to remember what she'd said about herself. She'd said her name was Angela, she knew that much.

Cindy stood blinking at the colour and movement of birds of every variety. The chorus of weird, shrill calls was like the assault of many unknown languages. 'It was nice of you to bring me here,' she said, 'but I suppose I should find myself a room down in the town somewhere.'

'No hurry, dearie. Since Merv died and my daughter moved away, I'm a bit on the lonely side. I'd be glad of the company for a day or two more.'

The woman turned back to the platform of birds, as the black and gold bird swooped down towards the platform, then darted towards her to take a crust from her hand. 'There you are, my beauty, there, my wild prince,' she crooned. 'You know where you're loved, don't you, precious? There now, my lovely one. What you ought to do, Angela, is go down to the village phone box and call those poor parents of yours in New Zealand so they don't worry about you.'

'I sent a postcard,' Cindy said.

MUSEUM PIECE

'What was that all about?' Margot asked. 'Roxane sounded quite distressed, as if she really wanted to talk to you.'

'I'm not here on demand for anyone who wants to talk to me. I'm taking it easy on doctor's orders.' Olwyn Tierney was lying on a cane chaise longue in her Bronte flat.

'Of course, I realise,' Margot said.

Olwyn looked at her. 'You realise, do you? You imagine you realise what it's like to be stabbed in the back by someone whose career you've fostered for years? By a woman you first knew as a schoolgirl? By your own prot ...pr ...' She choked on the word and reached for her aerosol inhaler.

'What do you mean?' Margot found it distressing enough to watch Olwyn's painful breathing, without the threat of un- controlled weeping. She could only remember seeing her mother in tears two or three times in her life. Once there had been a quarrel with her father, and then, the worst of times, her father's death, that terrible week of packing cases and upheavals.

'Roxane,' Olwyn said uncertainly, 'told them...Des, even Boris, that I was an...an embarrassment to the firm. That I was a gin-sodden drunk.'

'She couldn't have,' Margot said. 'It's impossible.'

'Don't give me that. You asked what was upsetting me. Well, I'm telling you. I thought Boris was being oddly kind the other day, solicitous in a treacly way that's not a bit like him. Then Des at least had the guts to tell me what Roxane has been saying.'

'You can trust him to be truthful, I suppose?'

'Who can trust anyone?' Olwyn asked.

Margot clasped her mother's hand. 'It's slander, of course,' she said. 'Anyone can see how sick you are. Alcohol has nothing to do with it.'

'They never talk about a man who drinks with clients. It's the old double standard again.'

'It's so incredibly unfair. What does Roxane stand to gain, do you think?'

'If she wanted my seat on the board, that idea has probably misfired. But once you start a damaging campaign like this, mud sticks, whatever the truth may be. My credibility's shot to pieces.'

'That's nonsense, Mum.'

'What I'd like to do is go back to Indigo and prove them all wrong. But I'm not well enough. I have to leave it all to other people, and for the first time in my life I'm doubting whether anyone can be trusted.'

'Look, Mum,' Margot began, 'I think what you've done is terrific, not just personally but as an example to other women.'

'God damn it,' Olwyn said, 'I never intended to set an example to other women. I just tried to do a decent job, the best I could, myself.' Another coughing fit racked her.

'Yes, but you see, since I've done this research, I've come to realise just how unusual you are among women of your generation. There is still only a handful of women on boards, for instance, and you're one of them. Most women seem to run into a sort of glass ceiling and find they can't advance any further.'

'Most women run out of steam for other reasons. They put family life first — even you have tended to do that — or they prefer not to take the responsibility of the really hard jobs. Or the hours, or the confrontations.'

'It's not just that — there really is discrimination against them.'

'I'm not well enough to go over all this ground again. I'd advise you very strongly not to go ahead with your plan to interview Roxane. Just stay away from her, that's my advice. I'm casting round for a motive, apart from the obvious one of her ambition. I wonder if she's getting back at me for warning her that everyone is talking about her and Steven Szabo.'

'The Barbary Corp Szabo?'

'Of course.'

'I would have thought he was married.'

Olwyn smiled. 'Margot, you are a sweet old-fashioned girl. I'm proud of you. Of course he's married. Wife's a charity committee heavy. Real operator. They say he's had a string of affairs. She may have too, for all I know. They may have an understanding. But my concern is that there could be conflicts of interest. Szabo moved into a new field in a big way with his investments in those beef properties in the Northern Territory. What if he got a fix on Sudpac and he was getting inside information from Roxane?'

'All a bit out of my league. If I'm surprised, it's because my boss, Brian Lynch, suddenly seems very proprietorial about Roxane. They've got her to appear at some of their finance seminars. You'd have thought Margaret Thatcher was making a guest appearance from the way the boys in the department were carrying on.'

'Well, she is very well known. All the research bears that out. We may have underestimated that when the commercials started — it wasn't always our intention to have a whole series, with Roxane the star personality for years.'

'Yeah, well, she's got more than her Andy Warhol fifteen minutes worth of fame, hasn't she? Let me get you a cup of tea.'

'No, Winifred made some when she was here. I'm fine.

How are things with you really, Margot? By that, I don't mean I want a blow by blow rundown on this survey of yours.'

Margot turned to look at her mother. As a rule, Olwyn kept up a smart, almost brittle facade. It was not done to discuss health or feelings, or to show concern more than fleetingly. Margot had been inclined to take Olwyn's coolness towards her husband Ted as a personal affront. It occurred to her that she could have made more of an effort to maintain a close relationship with her mother despite their differences over Ted. She wished she could confide in Olwyn more freely, or express her love for her without taking refuge in absurd statements about how she diverged from the women in her research. Olwyn was apt to treat anything theoretical as a bore, but what Margot most needed to tell her was not theory at all.

'Actually, Mum, I'm a bit tense. When I was up in the country writing up the results, I felt a strange texture and tenderness in one of my breasts. Not a lump exactly, but my GP doesn't know what to make of it. I'm going to the breast clinic tomorrow.'

'Sweetheart,' her mother said. 'Telephone me the minute you get the results.'

'Yes, Mum, I will. I certainly will.' Mother and daughter smiled at one another.

Margot ordered a cappuccino and tried to read her paperback while she waited for Prue in the coffee shop of the museum. She'd told Prue she was coming to town for a gynaecological checkup in Macquarie Street. Some sudden diffidence had prevented her from telling Prue she had an appointment at the breast clinic. She had just had her left breast, then her right, X-rayed, pummelled, and suspended in water for ultra-sound. After the procedures, which all felt like minor assaults no matter how kind the staff were, she and three other women with tender breasts sat in an outer room to await the verdicts. A woman in her twenties, with long burgundy hair, left the consulting room in a cascade of tears, twisting up the pamphlet about self-examination. The three women in the waiting room tensed. Margot tried to do a crossword. *Sensational stories that could scare hell right out of you (9).* Lurid tales. Breastless Amazons. Surgery. Murder mysteries. Malignancies. Cancer cells. Cysts. Unexplained tenderness. Hospital dramas. Nine letters. Nine lives. Cats had nine lives. Twentieth-century women probably had a few they didn't deserve. Negative thinking. She deserved the best. Penny dreadfuls. Headlines. Screamers. Tearjerkers. Human interest. Growths. The big C.

'If you could come in now please, Mrs Tierney.'

'Ms. I use my maiden name.'

'Of course. Just take a seat.' The door between Margot and the waiting room closed. It was soundproof, that was one mercy.

The doctor was holding X-rays to the light. He spoke calmly, and the phrases that reached her seemed unthreatening. 'Not too worried …slight stringiness …normal changes in texture … hormones …regular checkups.' Margot felt relief surge through her. She began thanking the physician too effusively. The missing word came to her as she pressed the button for the lift. *Thrillers.*

She telephoned Olwyn from a public booth at Town Hall Station. Olwyn's delighted voice sounded warmer and more reassuring than Margot could ever remember it. Waiting for Prue, she felt too many surges of emotion to concentrate on her book.

'Sorry I'm late,' Prue said. 'Everything all right at the doctor's?'

'It was the breast clinic. Yes, they do think everything's all right, thank God.'

'Margot, why didn't you tell me?'

'Oh, you've been so busy, and you were away last week anyway, and I've only just got Olwyn home from Indigo Island.'

'Home to your place?'

'You're joking. Imagine Olwyn letting someone look after

206

her! No, in Bronte, but she's in bed and taking antibiotics.'

'And you're sure you're okay yourself?'

'Yes, yes. Regular checkups, that sort of thing.'

'God, Margot, I wish you'd told me.'

'I just did. How are things with you anyway? You look wonderful in those colours.'

'Thanks.' Prue told Margot a little about the Cloudy Bay investigation, and finding the rat on her pillow.

'Nauseating,' Margot said.

'Literally.'

'So what can you do about these terrible developers?'

'I'm not sure yet. I'm still waiting for more information from some other departments.'

'You're mixing it with the big league there, Prue. Steven Szabo could buy and sell all of us. Olwyn tells me he's moved into beef exports in a big way just recently. It must be complicated trying to unravel a case involving a company with so many offshoots.'

'Well, obviously the legal angles have to be covered; he'll have the best brains in Phillip Street working for him.'

'But he wouldn't stoop to that sort of caper — rats in the bed — surely?'

'You never know about his local associates, though the main one of them was supposedly overseas while I was up there. God — it's only just occurred to me to check with Immigration whether Melvin Hughes really did go to America.' Prue scribbled a note to herself on the palm of her hand.

'Every technological advance,' Margot teased her.

'I've used knots in hankies before this, too. Whoever it is, I've managed to threaten someone by asking questions. In a way it's proof that the trail is worth following. Malcolm Gwynne always taught me to look twice when all the evidence falls into your lap too neatly.'

'My project is getting more complicated, too,' Margot said. 'I've been warned off in two different directions from interviewing Roxane Rowe.'

'Why ever would that be?'

'Well, originally Brian Lynch, the head of our department, told me to make sure I included her in the interviews with successful women. In the meantime Brian and the Boys' (she made her colleagues sound like a disreputable pop group) 'have gone behind my back and signed the photogenic Miss Rowe up to speak at a Saturday seminar they're holding at the Hilton on personal finance plans for women.'

'Nothing wrong with that. They'll need a drawcard.'

'Nothing wrong with that legally, no. But they deliberately didn't mention it to me, and I find myself sidelined and excluded in spite of the fact that I know more about women's incomes than anyone else in the department. Brian now seems cool about anyone dealing with her but himself.'

'Maybe he fancies her.'

'Yeah, maybe. He's just the type to find all that promotional garbage a big turn-on. But what really hurts is the fact that they haven't even asked me to take part in these seminars.'

'You can't have it both ways,' Prue said. 'You can't go round disapproving of the expensive events their consultancy puts on and then wonder why you don't feature as an expert lecturer yourself.'

'I guess not, if you put it that way. But you've only heard half of it. I've been at Olwyn's quite a bit lately, and when I mentioned to her that I'd rung her office to try and fix up an interview with Roxane, she asked why I'd bother. And then yesterday morning Roxane telephoned her – presumably just to see how she is – and she made me say she was too sick to come to the phone. She's been quite willing to talk to other people from Runaway. Boris Brookstein was out seeing her on Sunday, and she speaks to Des Hickey willingly enough. Anyway I put Roxane off as best I could. Olwyn was quite vehement about staying away from her. Apparently the industry is buzzing with gossip about Roxane and Steven Szabo.

'Of Barbary Developments fame. My Szabo.'

'The very same. Apparently he and Roxane have been meeting secretly for quite a while. I suspect that Olwyn doesn't trust Roxane not to try and do deals with Szabo's various companies and sell Runaway out somehow.'

'Possibly,' Prue said. 'But Mirabeau Acres has been such a flop that Barbary might go quietly on the travel front for a while. Isn't he a bit old for her?'

'You know what Henry Kissinger said about power being an aphrodisiac. Age doesn't make much difference. Will you have another cappuccino?'

'Yes, I will. The coffee's terrible in the country. They think the essential feature of a cappuccino is frothed up milk. I've been served boiled milk over a teaspoon of coffee powder, topped up with froth, as genuine espresso coffee.'

'Yagoona's quite civilised, really,' Margot said. 'There's nothing wrong with the coffees out there.'

'When it comes to good coffee,' Prue said, 'Yagoona may be the last bastion of civilisation. Beyond that, the rot really sets in. Could a man that age be any good in bed, d'you reckon? He'd have to be fifty-five, wouldn't he? If not older.'

'Let's hope so, or the future could be awfully bleak.'

'Guess so. Gosh, Margot, what a relief about your breast X-rays.'

'Say that again. I'm going to give myself a bit of a break. If I swap a few classes around, I can get a four-day weekend.'

'Yes, well I guess you could do with a change of scenery if you've been worrying about cancer all by yourself, then dealing with a sick mother, and coping with Brian and the boys.'

'Heroic, when you put it that way,' Margot said, laughing. 'What about you, Prue, isn't it about time we arranged a change of pace in your life? A little romance or passion or something?'

'Thanks for your concern, but as you're aware, I'm perfectly capable of organising my own life.'

'That wouldn't be defensiveness, would it?'

'Oh, shut up, Margot. It's about time I got back to the

office.'

'Oh, don't rush. I've got someone to look up here before we go.'

'Just a little while then. I gather your mother's health is no better?'

'No, it's not great. She's been to see a specialist at Prince Alfred Hospital. She's got emphysema. Not surprising perhaps, after smoking for all those years. Anyway, what it means is, her lung capacity's about a third normal. Her stamina is wrecked; she gets breathless after any sort of exertion, and of course with that low lung capacity, she can't handle alcohol either. I gather he fairly tactfully suggested she get some sort of breathing apparatus to use at home sometimes. She was outraged. And he suggested she cut down on alcohol, or give it up or something. Whatever it was, she took it as an insult. And she's terribly upset over something that's happened at Runaway. Apparently Roxane's been saying she kept getting embarrassingly drunk while she was on Indigo Island.'

'What a bitch.'

'Yes. I used to think it was one of those conjugations. You know: I am decisive, You are tough-minded, She is a bitch. But maybe we can just stick to the third person version. She's a bitch in my book.'

'Will Olwyn have to retire?' Prue asked.

'I imagine so. Obviously the doctor suggested it. She's past normal retirement age. But she's very touchy about her health, and about her plans generally. She wouldn't actually tell me outright that the doctor had advised her to give up work. She just told me he said things like "take it easy for a while".'

'God, I wish a doctor would tell me to take it easy for a while,' Prue said. 'But what's all this about having to see someone?'

Margot looked at her watch. 'I'm going to see this bird man just before two. Why don't you come with me? I've been intrigued by the phrase "medium flyers" ever since Henry

Moses told me that lots of fairly successful women fall into that category. When I was up in the country writing up my findings on women and success, I kept seeing a kestrel hovering over the open grassland, scarcely moving, about twenty metres up. Not really high. All the time scanning the ground for movement so it can pounce on its prey. And fanning its wings slightly all the time, so it can stay in place. It struck me as an image of how hard women have to work just to maintain any position of authority they do achieve.'

'That scanning the ground is something I heard about at the stress management course. Some people — it's part of the fight or flight syndrome — are on the lookout for enemies and slights all the time. So their adrenalin is pumping away and they're in a constant state of aroused fear. Over a period of time, the stress can really lead to health problems. Who's the bird man, anyway?'

'A man named Angus Allingham. Sounds really nice on the phone.'

'It must be Gus the Goose. I knew him when we were kids. He was always into environmental things, come to think of it.'

'A bird man named Gus the Goose!'

'We used to go honk, honk, honk all the time to him too. He's probably Doctor Allingham by now. I'll behave myself, it's all right really.'

They took the lift to the basement floor and knocked on a door labelled A. Allingham. A burly, bearded man came to the door. 'Hullo,' Margot said, 'I'm Margot Tierney, I was speaking to you about kestrels. And this ...'

'But I know Prue! We've known each other — well, since we were in fifth class. Since we were ten or eleven.'

'Gus! Wherever have you been all this time?'

'I can see there's no need for introductions,' Margot began, but Prue and Gus Allingham, hugging, whooping and making worse honking noises than any gaggle of geese, could scarcely hear what she was saying.

211

That night Prue felt a curious tension, which she did not recognise for a couple of hours. Something was nagging at her, as if she had forgotten something. No — of course — she was waiting for something. She was waiting for a man to ring. She had not cared deeply about whether the telephone would ring since Andrew left. Her farcical relationships with Denzil Dornford, Bevis Orchard and Harvey Travis had never had her on tenterhooks like this.

Tonight, though, she was urgently willing the telephone to ring. She even lifted the receiver a couple of times to make sure the dial tone was audible and the phone was in working order. She knew instinctively that her relationship with Gus Allingham was one that would really matter. Her quiet, orderly life was about to alter. *Coup de foudre*, the French said. The expression suggested a brilliant electrical storm on a flat, country plain: the sky suddenly heavy and lit by eerie shades of purple and turquoise. Then the lightning itself: intense, powerful, something to fear. Zigzagging flashes and lines of light, accompanied by the deep, irregular bursts and rolls of thunder.

She hoped that Gus would not come laden with emotional luggage: grievances about other women, petulant theories about the family, righteous stories of betrayed hopes. She hoped he did not see himself as a victim of the Family Court; that he did not have three or four children being raised in another culture; that he had not let his capacity for feeling deteriorate into a self-sufficiency interrupted by occasional Friday-night adventures. Of course, a man her own age could not come to her without a history. The most she could hope was that his scars should have faded. She had had enough of the walking wounded.

If she had kept in touch with him through high school, Prue reasoned, he would have had a gang of teenage friends as witnesses. Her bra-size (12B), the colour of her underwear (white) would have been known to five or six of his peers. There was no such thing as innocence. No relationship could start totally fresh and unpolluted by previous experiences and expectations. Besides, at seventeen she had yet to escape from the surveillance of her parents, and a social life that revolved around the church. No. They would have to make the best of it in their thirties, and live with each other's lives up to now as best they could.

She read a few chapters of a novel by A.S. Byatt. She rinsed out her underwear. She washed her short, straight hair in a colourless henna shampoo that promised a remarkable sheen. She cleaned her black court shoes with cream polish. She wondered if it was time she recovered the furniture, and dreamt up colour schemes. She spent the entire evening a few strides from the cream plastic telephone, which finally, at 9.45, obliged her by bursting into shrill sound.

'Took me a while to think of anything so obvious as looking you up in the phone book under your maiden name,' Gus said.

'I'm glad you did, anyway,' Prue said, her voice a higher pitch than normal.

'Amazing to run into you after all this time,' he said.

'Quite exciting, really.'

'How about dinner?' asked Gus.

'I'd be thrilled,' Prue said, without exaggeration.

'Good. Any suggestions about where and when?'

Over antipasto and veal parmigiano, Prue and Gus the biologist played a seemingly endless game of Whatever happened to ...? as they unravelled the fates of their contemporaries at Artarmon Opportunity School. Simone became a first violinist in an orchestra in Geneva; Tony had been quite a famous draft resister; Beth had two sets of twins, one boys, one girls; Jonathan was on heroin and could be seen hanging around the back streets of the Cross; Jenola was a pediatrician; Eric a high school teacher and rugby coach. And so on, through David, Penny, Katie A. and Katie B., Warwick, Sean, Bruce and Alex.

'But whatever happened to you, Gus? Where have you been all these years?' That was the question Prue kept coming back to.

'You remember my father got that job in Tasmania? No? Well, he did. We moved to Launceston. I went to school down there, then university in Melbourne, then post-doctoral work in Arizona. Taught there for a while, then I lectured in Hobart. Then I did my first tour of duty in Antarctica ...'

'The South Pole!'

'Yes, sub-Antarctic islands, wonderful places for birds. Then I did a couple more trips down there, began moving from teaching into research and writing, and at the moment I have a temporary fellowship at the museum.'

'But you don't have to go back?'

'Back to what?'

'The South Pole.'

'I'm due back at Macquarie Island in summer, from November for about five months.'

Even before Prue and Gus became lovers, she felt the prospect of that separation from him wrenching at her. She imagined dark icy seas between herself and this man, ice floes breaking loose and floating north, their hazardous depths unseen. She pictured life at the Pole in little igloos of the kind they drew in kindergarten: men in fur tracksuits hunched over smoking stoves. This hazardous, male, alien world which loomed up in her mind already threatened to drag her man away. Her warrior, her hero, her explorer, her adventurer. Her mind grew mushy with loving epithets.

They went to his flat in Camperdown. His beard nuzzled the back of her neck. She felt his arms around her body, his hands on her breasts, his breath on her tongue. She had never known such friendliness in lovemaking, but then she had never fallen into the arms of such an old friend. Months of cool routine and sublimation vanished. She was over-whelmed with wanting him. 'Gus,' she murmured.

'Do you think you could call me Angus?' he asked. 'There's something very incongruous about that nickname — I expect a lot of goose honking to follow it.'

She smiled and began to caress his erect penis with her hand. They were gentle and unhurried. 'Angus,' she said, as

214

if attempting a word in a foreign language. She realised as they caressed one another that there might be no end to the body's betrayal of the mind: the tongue that could form the word *Angus* could equally produce *love, stay, baby, please, forever, us, couple, promise, yes.*

'God,' she murmured, 'how my body responds to yours.'

'It's supposed to,' the biologist replied.

In time Prue learnt that Angus had an ex-wife and son in the States. He had split up with Abbie when Ian was three. Now seven, Ian lived in Orlando, Florida, with his mother and her second husband, a middle manager with Disney World. Angus hoped to have Ian spend some of the northern hemisphere's summers in Australia. Prue was relieved that he spoke of Abbie without rancour, and that the negotiations over his son's visits seemed friendly.

'Would you want another child?' she asked him.

'I'm not sure. It was Abbie's idea, having Ian. Depends on whether I feel really secure in a relationship, I guess. I don't mind babies. They have more personality than people think.'

'I never even used to notice them,' Prue said. 'Now they're everywhere. Even in the supermarket. Tiny little week-old babies in bassinets or in those little carrying cocoons. Maybe in the old days they were kept at home until they were older.'

'Or maybe you were paying less attention.'

'Perfectly possible.'

BREAKFAST WITH DR ZOLNAY

Dear Miss Lambert,

I am writing to you after getting your name from Jasmine Wade at the Windsong Co-op. She told me you were following up complaints about Mirabeau Acres.

When we went up to Mirabeau Acres on a work experience placement, I was all set to learn a bit about the tourist industry, and a different type of development — not private property in the usual sense, etc. Also I thought it was good for the Cloudy Bay area to have some income, because prices on bananas, milk and so on aren't much of a living. So a lot of us who love the area go away to uni etc. and find we can't afford to go back.

If you take an accurate map of the local area, showing the crown land to the west of the Mirabeau Acres site, and the surrounding farms as well as the Mirabeau Acres site, you will see that the map shown on the prospectus is misleading in several respects. The river shown as part of the development site is actually within crown land. *The site earmarked for a light traffic airport is also crown land, and I've been told that an Aboriginal land rights claim was made a while back. No doubt you can check all this lot out in Sydney.*

When Mr Hughes saw I was delving into the interesting stuff, he threatened to charge me with trespass and theft. My mother received anonymous calls. I could have been expelled from school — forced to leave without my HSC. I didn't want it my word against his with the police, so I left off. Hughes is not a member of the Real Estate Institute; and I couldn't afford private legal action against him — he seems an odd sort of partner for a big firm like Barbary Developments to have.

My real interest in the project was the financing of it; however, as I said, Mr Hughes had us all thrown out the moment he saw I had been looking at the books. The money that was spent came from small investors, but I would expect many documents have been destroyed by now.

I hope that this is of some use.

Yours sincerely,
Warren Percival.

Prue felt elated. She read this letter several times, making notes on points to follow up with other agencies. The discrepancy between the official map and the prospectus map would be *prima facie* evidence of intent to defraud, and provide grounds for Legal Branch to launch a prosecution.

A check of Aboriginal land claims confirmed that some crown land at Cloudy Bay was involved in a claim, but it would be some time before she received copies of the documents and maps. Prue made inquiries of the Cloudy Bay police, who had no details of complaints against Melvin

Hughes.

'It's not unusual for people who don't pay the rent to have a few unexplained phone calls or odd things delivered, is it?' the sergeant asked her.

'What sort of complacent attitude is that?' Prue demanded.

'Lady, if there was anything definite to give you, you'd have it,' the police officer said. 'Just a friendly remark. Joke.'

'Yes, I see. Very amusing.' She hung up.

She checked with Immigration to see if Melvin Hughes had left the country recently. He hadn't, unless he used a false passport. She wondered if he had been in Cloudy Bay and had orchestrated the rat stunt, or if his interests were being looked after by someone who used similar tactics.

She sought an appointment with Steven Szabo, but his secretary said all inquiries were to be directed to a Martin Place law firm. Legal Branch was supposed to take charge of all contact with law firms, so Prue turned her attention to the third partner, psychiatrist Dr Vilmos Zolnay.

The receptionist at the Double Bay surgery said the doctor was out visiting patients and was not expected back until the afternoon. Prue left her name and telephone number.

She knocked on Meredith McCutcheon's office door and hovered in the doorway until Meredith finished a telephone conversation and waved her towards a chair.

'G'day,' she said, in a consciously matey style. 'Close the door. Siddown.'

'Hi, Meredith. I was wondering if you had a moment to talk about Dr Vilmos Zolnay.'

'I'm only weeks late with a major matter, working to midnight for days on end, and about to be thrown out of my own home, but don't mind me, I've got all the time in the world.' Meredith lit a cigarette in defiance of the office's supposedly voluntary policy of no smoking. She screwed up her eyes as she inhaled, and tilted back her head. Her cropped haircut gave prominence to her cheekbones. On the wall behind her was a poster of the Darling River, one of a series on waterways of New South Wales that the office had bought in a buy-up at the end of the previous financial year.

'Shit, Prue,' Meredith said, 'I'm depressed as hell.'

'It's Nadia,' Prue said. It was usually Nadia.

'Yeah. You know she got involved with Selena Benic? And how she's been trying to get me to move out so Selena can move in permanently? I've had a gutful, I really have. And you know what Nadia's like — insists on total discretion; keeps the whole thing in the closet; doesn't want her private life to impinge on her career, and so on. She expects me to be just as cool and collected as she is. It's driving me demented. Plus the fact that everyone knows Selena and it's like acting out the whole drama on stage.'

'Awful for you.' Prue looked at her frosted nails. Had it been so painful for her when Andrew left, or did women cause other women crueller heartache? 'Have you been able to tell Nadia how you feel about all this?' she asked.

'That's just it. Nadia is so controlled. She made this great speech about how we are three adult women, and I don't own her body and soul. She made out the issue is her freedom. What about my right to keep some sanity so I can get on with my work without cracking under the pressure? What about that?' Meredith was on the verge of tears.

'It's rough, isn't it?' Prue was having trouble empathising: she found Meredith's lover Nadia forbidding. Now an economist with the Futures Exchange, in upholstered gaberdine suits, Nadia talked about discretion, the corporation and professionalism. Ten years ago she'd worn black studded belts. She seldom smiled. At weekends she paraded through the Newtown shops with two greyhounds. When coming out was fashionable, Nadia came out. When separatism was the vogue, she was the first to attack those who slept with the enemy. Now she was the very embodiment of the term corporate.

'Maybe she and Selena won't last long. They hardly seem soulmates, do they?' Selena was the shy and tender-faced daughter of a Supreme Court judge.

'What's that got to do with it?' Meredith demanded, as tears coursed down her cheeks. 'They have sex in common. Passion. What else do they need?' She blew her nose. 'I have no control at all,' she went on. 'I'm all over the place. Behaving like a lunatic. Doing outrageous things. Ringing them up at three in the morning and abusing them. Ringing every half-hour. Crying. I've been beside myself. I think I've threatened violence.'

'There's a spare room at my place if you need something temporarily while you sort yourself out,' Prue said. 'I'm sorry things have been so rugged, really.'

'There's another thing,' Meredith said. 'I wish I'd had time to discuss it with you before it all blew up. Nadia was at a dinner with Selena and a whole lot of high-powered equal opportunity people and Premier's Department bods, and the Commissioner was there. Well, just as Ken launched into this rave about the marvels of equal opportunity in his office, blah, blah, women of talent like you and me, etcetera, Nadia put her oar in and said she'd heard it on good authority we don't get our fair share of the really juicy cases. Now, I may have said that to Nadia, but I haven't done the research or caucused with other women round here to the point of putting in a sex discrimination complaint or anything. But, never mind that, this terrible kitchen Cabinet discussion went on, and the next day the Commissioner and two of his bully boys came roaring in here to me and said if I have any complaints I should raise them in the office, not through my friends.'

'Hell, Meredith, we should have had a meeting of all the women in the office if we were going to do anything about this. Sometimes I only realise I'm onto something significant once I get into a case. Like this Cloudy Bay one. I really came in here to ask you about Vilmos Zolnay.'

'Psychiatrist. Hungarian. Rooms in Double Bay. Clinic there and another one at Maroubra or Matraville, somewhere down there. I had to give most of our files on him to the Health Department, because it was a matter for the medical tribunal really. There were complaints about misleading claims for sleep treatment, but they weren't really the CBE's bag. We didn't proceed. I only spoke to the good doctor on the phone. Sounds as if he could hypnotise you as soon as look at you. But what's the link?'

'He was a partner in a time-share venture at Cloudy Bay, with Steven Szabo and a real estate guy.'

'Shit, eh? Makes a change from poplar trees as a medical investment.'

'Don't forget jojoba plants.' Prue waited for Meredith to smile. She did manage to move one corner of her mouth.

'I was told that he and Szabo are very close,' Meredith said. 'But beyond that, I can't help you.'

'Let me know if you want to take up my offer of somewhere to live.'

'Thanks, pal. Sorry I don't have more information.'

Prue rang the bell on the Double Bay veranda. Wistaria hung from the veranda posts and the pergola; sandstone flagstones were weathered into soft patterns of yellow and mauve. At one end of the veranda a small table was set for breakfast: white cloth, grapefruit, dark blue china, white napkins. The heavy door opened. A woman dressed in black scrutinised Prue. 'Miss Lambert? The doctor will be with you shortly. If you could take a seat.'

Prue was shown a chair in the hallway, a carved, upright antique chair upholstered in chartreuse velvet. The hallway was dim. She noted an oval mirror, gold framed, an arrangement of yellow and white flowers on a black marble table, a mahogany grandfather clock, framed photographs of elderly people, and an incongruous smell of hospitals. Ether? Disinfectant? Chloroform? She felt suddenly nervous, and wondered where the bathroom was. The maid had disappeared. There was a small telephone table, but no telephone book.

'Miss Lambert? How delightful. So much younger than I expected. I've taken the liberty of arranging for breakfast to be brought to the terrace.' Vilmos Zolnay led Prue back to the veranda where they sat one on either side of the table in the vine-filtered sunlight.

'You're not quite what I expected either,' Prue said.

'Do elaborate.'

'Oh, I couldn't.'

'My dear Miss Lambert, I doubt that you could shock me. I am a psychiatrist, you know. People tell me the most extraordinary things.'

'It was just — well, that's it, I suppose, you don't look like everyone's idea of a psychiatrist.'

'What's that? An undersized Viennese Jew with spectacles and a diffident manner? Indeed not.'

Prue considered the man opposite her. He wore a navy Lacoste sweatshirt, white trousers and navy sneakers. He was tanned, fit and tall, with the self-conscious physicality of a body builder or a Don Juan. She knew from her research that he was in his fifties, but he looked like a younger man. He had the black eyes of a gypsy.

'Tell me what you are thinking,' he commanded.

'What is this, a word association test?'

'If you like.'

'*Montenegro*, I was thinking you reminded me of the men in a film called *Montenegro*.' Prue did not add that in the film the Montenegrans kidnapped a naive Scandinavian housewife and forced her to work in an illicit guestworkers' nightclub. Nor did she mention the murder.

'I make a point of not seeing any films from captive nations.'

'It wasn't Eastern European propaganda, I can assure you. It was a comedy, of a sort.'

'Why are you so hostile?'

'Why do psychiatrists always ask that question?'

'What do you know about psychiatrists?'

'Dr Zolnay, as you know, I'm here in connection with a Commission for Business Ethics investigation into the Mirabeau Acres at Cloudy Bay of which you are a director.'

222

Prue wiped her clammy palms on the white damask napkin. She took a portable tape-recorder out of her briefcase. 'Would you have any objection if I taped this interview?' she asked.

'Indeed I would. No, I'll rephrase that. I have no objection to your tape-recorder if we can reschedule the interview for a date when my lawyer can be present and if your Commission can meet my legal fees.'

'We never meet costs of that kind.'

'In that case, no. No tapes. I don't suppose you'd stoop to bugs.'

'Would you?' Prue squinted suspiciously at the overhanging wisteria.

Vilmos Zolnay gave a whoop of laughter. 'Good. You're tougher than I thought at first. Tell me, how does a nice suburban girl like you get into business investigations?'

'Through the most routine of channels. Research. University. Training courses. And learning on the job.'

'Admirable. The perfect *apparatchik*. Grapefruit?'

'No, thankyou.'

'Any moment now, Edith will bring the coffee. I trust you'll have some of that?' Zolnay was slicing at his grapefruit with a serrated knife, putting the pips to one side, and eating the slivers of fruit, all at great speed. His hands were long and brown, the upper sides covered with dark hair.

'You're not married, are you?' he asked.

'No, though I fail to see what that has to do with the matter in hand.'

'Defensive again. You're wise. I've had three marriages. Oh, don't be shocked. We Hungarians don't wallow in guilt over divorce. In the immigrant community, multiple marriages are more the rule than the exception.'

'I've nothing to gain by marrying,' Prue said, 'so I don't imagine I will.' Unless Gus insists, she added mentally.

'Perfect. So rational, so unromantic. Nothing to gain. So few of my patients are career women of your generation, I am terribly uninformed.'

223

'Perhaps we're a comparatively sane part of the community. We don't need to dash off to Double Bay psychiatrists.'

'Unlike the wives of North Shore stockbrokers. Yes indeed. Stay single. I see you are an intelligent young woman. A little rigid. But more than likely good at your work. Good, here's Edith. You have sugar in the coffee?'

'Thanks, no.'

'And, Miss Lambert, to risk a cliché, you are so attractive when you smile. Why don't you do it more often?'

'Dr Zolnay. I am here on an investigation into a false prospectus. I agreed to see you at this hour of the morning at your suggestion. I understand your investment in Mirabeau Acres was eighty thousand dollars.'

'Sounds right.'

'And have you recovered any of that capital?'

'You should know, Miss Lambert, that the settlement of the proceeds of the wound-up company is delayed by inquiries such as yours.'

'So at the moment you've done eighty grand pretty well cold.'

'As you so nicely put it, yes.'

'Do you invest often with your friend Mr Szabo?'

'Miss Lambert, Steven is a lifelong friend. I play golf with him, I eat with him, I listen to him, I even occasionally advise him. I am also friends with his remarkable wife. They have been cordial to all my wives, two of whom have really stretched our friendship. It was not a particularly large investment. Steven wanted someone he could trust to match the investment of the local operator, Hughes. We needed a man on the spot, but there was always some uneasiness about him. As it turns out, we were right to distrust him. It was a private venture, three-way: Hughes, myself, and Steven as the Barbary representative. It wasn't structured as a conventional Barbary undertaking. You have to realise that Steven — he is a sweet, impetuous man, a most extraordinary fellow — wanted a structure that would give me a good return for a small outlay. That's what we had every reason to expect.

We could use the capital as security on borrowings, then keep everything afloat with investment from club members. A perfect arrangement, theoretically, no?'

'If it's done lawfully, yes.'

'Yes, there you are, you say so yourself. But we chose the wrong man in Hughes. Embezzling, cooking the books, losing the records, putting cheques into fictitious names. Promising political deals that he couldn't deliver. Barbary's solicitors are onto him, don't you worry, probably with more zeal than your Commission.'

'Have they lost contact with him lately?'

'You tell me.'

'When I was on the coast, I was told he was in America. But it doesn't check out with the immigration records.'

'I'm not following this at all closely. Why don't you interview Steven?'

'Yes, people from our office will be speaking to the Barbary solicitors. But I'll have to leave that to Legal Branch.'

'You don't like that, do you, Miss Lambert? You're the little terrier type, you'd like to fasten your teeth around a shin and hang on till the end.'

'It's my job.'

'That's a discredited defence, my dear. Only obeying orders. You can do better than that.'

'What do you know about the airport?'

'It's where the planes land.' Vilmos Zolnay's whooping laughter rang out as he held his coffee cup aloft and rocked delightedly back and forth, a strand of wistaria catching on his shoulder.

'Dr Zolnay. Please stop teasing me. Terribly funny and all that. But the Cloudy Bay airport. When you last saw the plans, was it planned to cater for light planes or jets?'

'Jets, schmets. I never saw the plans. I paid my money, I went to all of two meetings. I told Steven I didn't like the look of Hughes. I check out all kinds of people for him, you know; without his wife Anna and me he'd be a babe in the woods.'

'It's hardly his public image.'

'Naturally not. And he can be tough, of course. Nevertheless, he is a very simple soul. Skims from one idea to another; the company has to set up management structures to pick up the pieces. I never saw the plans for the site. I saw the site itself. Beautiful in a way. Not enough trees, but a good outlook. I went to two meetings. I wrote a cheque. And, as you so sweetly suggest, I've done eighty grand cold.'

'Tax write-offs?'

'I let the accountants worry about that.'

'I understand your other clinic is in Maroubra.'

'Indeed.'

'Your financial records are there?'

'No, they're with my accountant, who has a standing instruction not to release any material to any government body without my lawyer giving permission.'

'I see.'

'Steven Szabo has a little joke about the Commission for Business Ethics. Well, Anna may have thought of it, she's more the literary type. He calls it the Oxymoronic Commission.'

'The what? Oh, yes, contradiction in terms. Quite good really.' Prue laughed.

'You want some advice?' Zolnay asked. 'Young women always want advice. Don't marry. Stay with the Oxymoronics. Don't try too hard with this one, the Barbary lawyers have their own ways of dealing with Hughes. They may even bring charges against him themselves. Did you imagine that it's you he's hiding from? You're not so naive, I think. No. Stay there. Write a very full report. I know you will do your best, you are the type. It won't necessarily do your career any harm. Nothing underhand will occur. Steven knows everyone, but his operation wouldn't stoop to political pressure or anything of that sort. It's been a very strange year. Allegations of every type. Commissions Against Corruption being set up that make your outfit look like a kindergarten. What can government really do about the business community, Miss

Lambert? Basically they need our enterprises and the overseas capital we attract. They may talk about ethics, but in the end you'll always hear them invoking cooperation and consensus. Consensus? We know what that means. Having a courteous little chat before the people with the power do what they were going to do all along. Same thing with Cloudy Bay, really. So there's a naughty prospectus or radio commercial or two. Tut tut. Rap on the knuckles. All the righteous words on the files. Letters. Go away and don't do it again. Just so long as they release the land for sale and I get some of my capital back. If I don't, it's no great shakes. Steven is a good friend. He'll cut me into something else before long, you can count on that. This whole little scandal is just a hiccup. You deal with your little bit of it, we'll deal with Hughes. You do see the point I am making, don't you?'

Prue did. She was being warned off by a man who made her allies look like amateurs and her powers look as flimsy as soggy tissues. She made an effort to appear calm. 'I'm terribly sorry to interrupt,' she said, 'but I wonder if I could use the bathroom?'

'Of course.' Vilmos Zolnay pressed a servants' bell, which Prue hadn't noticed before, on the sandstone wall. Edith appeared in the doorway. 'Ah, Edith,' he said, 'you'll show Miss Lambert the way to the bathroom, won't you?'

Prue followed the maid into the hallway, blinking as her eyes adjusted to the lack of light. They went through a swing door and along a passage lined with black and white tiles. Edith held open the door to a white bathroom, then left Prue alone in the sudden brightness. Prue was astonished by the size and clinical aspect of the room. There were three shower cubicles, three toilet booths and a large white bath. She dashed to the nearest lavatory and hurriedly emptied her bladder. There was a nursing-home-style metal ring on the wall for frail people to grasp. Prue found herself reaching for it with a shaking hand. She washed her hands with Cussons soap, and dried them on the paper towel from the metal canister. Another institutional touch. She powdered her nose and cheeks and brushed her short, dark hair away from her face.

Rattled. Geoff Kerin's pun came back to her. She felt distinctly rattled.

Opening the door (another big metal clasp) she found herself back in the passage, where she pushed open what she took to be the swing door to the hallway. She stood in a small bedroom with three beds crammed one against another, high, metal beds of the type found in a hospital ward. Someone was sleeping deeply in each of the beds in the dim room.

As she stood with her hand on the door to stop it swinging to and fro, a figure in one of the beds sat up suddenly, like a corpse on pulleys. She was staring into the wide-open green eyes of a middle-aged man with a bare torso. The drip apparatus strapped to his arm and tubes attached to his nose gave him the aspect of a stranded squid.

'I'm sorry,' Prue said, 'I'm terribly sorry. I came into the wrong room.'

The man's face was puffy and lined and he looked directly at Prue, who felt she had never intruded so unforgivably on someone's privacy. Then, wordlessly, the man fell backwards, turning to the side a little as his balding head hit the pillow.

Prue closed the door, found the one that led to the hallway, and dashed on to the veranda. Zolnay was reading the *Financial Review*. Prue snatched up her briefcase and stammered her thanks for the interview, adding that the office would be in touch in due course. Then she walked as calmly as she could until she was out of sight and could bolt towards her Daihatsu, which was parked in a parallel street. She sat in the driver's seat breathing deeply for a long time before she drove away from Double Bay, climbing steeply up Bellevue Road towards the more familiar territory of Bondi Junction.

On the ABC, an economic analyst was discussing the Budget. Although she tried to pay attention, she kept seeing an after-image of the sleep-treatment patient's open eyes.

'It was blatant intimidation,' Prue told Geoff Kerin when she reached the office, 'but I don't know how to prove it.'

'No,' Geoff said, 'it sounds like a sort of hypothetical threat: "If I were to set out to get you I would pull strings or find ways of discrediting you, but as it is, we've got your number so you can just write your little report and we'll deal with our own delinquents our own way".'

'That's just about what he said.'

'You'll tell the Commissioner?'

'Yes, of course, but he's in Canberra and I couldn't get an appointment till next Tuesday. I'm afraid he'll just rope in Legal Branch and it'll be the last I ever see of it. Oh, God, I wish Malcolm were here. This mob will just go to water at the very idea of mixing it with a major outfit like Barbary.'

'You've heard Malcolm's taking early retirement?'

'Yes. Sarah told me. He would have shepherded the whole case through those legal labyrinths in a few weeks. As it is, even if the Commissioner gives it a green sticker — how long would you say?'

'With no special priority, about sixteen to eighteen months. With a green sticker, well — I've got one matter that's been in there for nearly a year. And I go and rave at Carl Hirst every few weeks, to no avail. Justice delayed, mate ...you know what they'll say when it finally reaches court.'

'Yeah. Justice denied. And we'll get the blame. But I've been giving this file priority. I've got fifteen or sixteen cases of misleading advertising and dangerous goods languishing while I try and tie this one up. And I've got them on the prospectus, I really have. Their map is misleading.'

'Let me know how you go with the Commissioner. It's a top case. What do you think of this claim of Meredith's that the women in the office get the less important cases?'

'I can't make up my mind. Probably we get fewer of the ones that the Commissioners know in advance will be important cases. But we get a few cases — like Cloudy Bay — that turn out to be important even though the original

229

letter of complaint is dead ordinary. That's what makes it hard — there's an x-factor where the investigator has to decide what to pursue. And it's always possible to treat everything as minor and ordinary and miss the cases that would repay a bit of digging.'

'But sex discrimination?'

'Give Geoff this tough one and Prue this routine one? Well, sometimes it happens, doesn't it?'

'But systematically? By sex? You really think so?'

'Look, Meredith has raised a point that's worth looking at, and I'm not going to leave her out on a limb just to make everybody feel good, okay?'

'All right, don't get all feminist and shirty.'

'Shirty's an extension of feminist, is it?'

'Shit, Prue, Meredith's converted you, hasn't she? You think you only get the tough cases by coincidence.'

'Or inattention. It's very hard to distinguish neutrality from carelessness, at the best of times.'

'Okay. Let me know what line the boss takes.'

'Sure,' Prue said. 'See you.'

Prue spent the weekend with Angus Allingham. They walked along the foreshores at Ball's Head, made love all Saturday afternoon, and went to a ballet performance at the Wharf Theatre. On the Sunday morning they stayed in bed until eleven, then went for a picnic near the Lane Cove River. Prue felt some of the tension of the previous week slipping away.

The following Tuesday, she got her papers together, and read her case summary through again to memorise the main points before her meeting with the Commissioner. She was interrupted by the telephone. 'Alfred Mannix. That's got a Sir in front and an MP at the back.'

'What a privilege, Sir Alfred. It's such a long time since I heard from you.'

'Corruption, that's the name of the game, isn't it? They're putting infra-red signals into my letterbox.'

'Oh dear.'

'Yes, you can hear the hum when you walk up the street. I'm working on a system to intercept them.'

'What are you using for that?'

'An electric mixer. I put it on and press the "blend" switch, and tape it at the same time, see?'

'Yes, I think so. You will be careful, Sir Alfred?'

'Thanks for your concern, love. No risk of electrocuting meself, never fear. I expect to have results very shortly.'

'Good — you'll give us any evidence as soon as it's available, then?'

'Naturally. Tell my friend Louise I rang, won't you?'

'Of course, sir.'

'Cheerio, love.'

Prue uttered the absurd word 'Cheerio' before she knew what she was doing. She put down the phone and giggled as she wrote a note for Louise. She went back to the Cloudy Bay file. Her report, as Dr Zolnay had predicted, would be conscientious, cautious and closely argued. Her main point would be the misleading prospectus, evidence to defraud on the part of the three principals, Szabo, Hughes and Zolnay. The development depended on a new airport. Even a light airport would require the rezoning of crown land which was already under claim by the local Aboriginal land council. A jet airport, to bring tourists direct from Tokyo or Los Angeles, would mean flattening hectares of farmland and forest, with government action to acquire property. She'd found no written proof that any other government department saw Cloudy Bay as the site of an international runway or a casino, but she could not be sure what had been said informally at Ministerial level.

The Commissioner's secretary was about Prue's age, but so glossily groomed that her long, painted nails and carefully rouged cheeks seemed calculated to send Prue back to the bathroom to recomb her hair.

'Someone's with him,' Mardi said, 'but he shouldn't keep you long.'

Prue sat down and flicked through the copies of *Vogue Living* which the Commissioner's wife donated to the office from time to time. She learnt that pink, beige and apricot walls were passé, and the fashionable people were using pale grey with accents of silver, turquoise and violet. She tried to imagine her flat in those colours. Not with the cinnamon-coloured carpet, perhaps. She rehearsed what she had to say. A green sticker, a green sticker, she repeated to herself.

Gary, the records clerk, put some papers in the Commissioner's in-tray. 'Something for you, too, Prue,' he said, handing her some newspaper clippings. Prue read an item from the business pages of the *Herald*, her hand shaking. She put it underneath the other papers in her hand.

The door opened. Two men from Treasury took their leave. The Commissioner spoke to Mardi on the intercom. 'Get Carl, too, would you? Is Prudence Lambert there? Send her in.'

Prue walked into the large, curtained office. Two walls were covered with shelves of bound statutes and law journals. A similar cabinet hid a well-stocked bar, but she'd seldom been offered a drink.

'Ah, Prudence, do sit down. I've asked Carl to join us, as head of Legal Branch. This is an interesting matter you've been investigating. I've read the summary with interest. *Prima facie* evidence of intent to defraud, you believe.'

'Yes, I do. You've only got to look at the map.'

Ken Reynolds, the Commissioner, was a man of medium height, with wavy black hair over a high forehead. He had a reedy voice, and the benign, lofty manner of a High Church bishop. His brown eyes looked over gold-rimmed half spectacles.

'Picture worth a thousand words, eh?' the Commissioner said, tracing the area on the prospectus where crown land appeared as part of the Mirabeau Acres site. 'Ah, Carl, glad you could join us. I was just discussing this file of Prue's. You're aware of the Mirabeau Acres matter?'

'Not entirely, sir,' Carl Hirst said. He sat down. He was in his fifties, tall, with receding hair and, when flustered, plum-coloured cheeks. 'We've been waiting for Investigation Branch to forward the file to us. I am aware one of the principals is a very big fish indeed.'

'Mmm, Szabo,' Ken Reynolds said. 'Now, this is all pretty straightforward, isn't it, Prue? You've taken it as far as you can, and we're about to have Legal check it out for prosecution purposes.'

'I'd like you to make it a green sticker matter,' Prue said.

'Well, there may be a difference between significance and urgency, wouldn't you say, Carl? It could be a significant matter without being, as it were, necessarily, an urgent one?'

Malcolm, where are you when I need you? Prue thought.

'Indeed, sir,' Carl Hirst said. 'Most of the matters we deal with, being by definition of concern to the complainant and an implied attack on the probity of the respondent, are matters of significance. But urgency arises only if there is a danger of someone skipping the country, or if the matter has been so delayed already that there's a risk of a court throwing it out for being too far out of time.'

'But that happens to dozens of our cases,' Prue said.

'Dozens?' Carl queried. 'Accuracy is the prime requisite of an investigator, I'm bound to point out. Perhaps eight or nine in the past year.'

'Let's not get over-hasty,' the Commissioner said. 'I'm prepared to give the green sticker suggestion some consideration. Mardi gave me the impression you were distressed by other aspects of the investigation.'

'Yes. I am. When I interviewed Vilmos Zolnay, he as good as threatened me, in the guise of explaining how he wouldn't stoop to threats.' She outlined what had happened in her encounter with Zolnay.

'You taped all this, of course?' Carl asked.

'No, I didn't — he wouldn't agree to a tape-recorder unless his legal representatives were present.'

'And you didn't agree to those conditions?' asked the Commissioner.

'No, I didn't. He was demanding that we meet his legal costs, which is out of the question. Besides, it might have taken weeks to line up a time with him and his solicitors and someone from Legal Branch. I wanted to get on with it and wind up my part of the investigation.'

'You took a calculated risk, but perhaps not a wise one,' said the Commissioner.

'How would it look in court?' Carl asked. 'A young woman goes alone to a leading physician's residence one morning. How are we to be sure she is there on official business? There is no transcript of what transpires. For all we know, she may have been seeking employment or even psychological treatment. She leaves with the impression that there have been veiled threats of political interference or whatever, but she has absolutely no evidence. And she blunders into a ward of private patients, in a fashion that any barrister could show to be snooping into matters quite separate from the ones on our file, at which point she may have been seen by one of the patients, or she may have looked into the eyes of someone in an induced sleep. Sleep treatment is quite lawful in the hands of a qualified practitioner anyway. It's not as if that clinic's had any deaths. No, Commissioner, perhaps Prudence should be cautioned against the secret agent syndrome.'

'Carl has a point, Prue. There is a danger, because of our right to ask questions, subpoena documents and so on, that we get so excited by the role that we see ourselves swaggering along in cloaks and daggers and deciphering invisible ink. Successful investigations aren't like that. Very often they're boring. One fact, another fact, a painstakingly argued conclusion. When you come right down to it, all the salient points on this file could have been deduced by a moderately intelligent person sitting at a desk. Now I know it's fun claiming expenses and gadding round the countryside, and interviewing colourful identities like Zolnay, but is it necessary? That's what we must ask ourselves. What would the statute say about our powers?'

'I needed to go to Cloudy Bay to get the lead about the false map,' Prue said, unsure how to defend herself against the underlying attack.

'I would have described your work up until now as extremely sound, actually,' the Commissioner went on. 'Let's not spoil your reputation at this point with a lot of melodramatics. There's enough trouble already among the women in the office with this complaint of Meredith's that there's sex discrimination in the allocation of cases. This one goes to disprove that, anyway. It would have to be regarded as a major matter.' The Commissioner pushed his hair back from his forehead in a preening gesture. 'What's your view, Carl?'

'Perhaps a memorandum would be in order, on the need to involve Legal Branch in matters of significance where the party under investigation declines to be tape-recorded.'

'You'll draft it for me, I take it?' the Commissioner drawled.

'There's more, I'm afraid,' Prue said. 'I've only just been given this morning's clippings. Melvin Hughes, the Cloudy Bay real estate fellow, is dead. He died on Saturday at St George District Hospital.'

'Unfortunate,' the Commissioner said. 'But there's no reason why it should hold up Legal Branch's pursuit of the other principals.'

'No, Ken, it's not that. You see, when I looked at this photo I had a horrible realisation. He's the man I saw in Zolnay's sleep ward.'

'You're sure about this?'

'How could I be sure? The man I saw had tubes down his nose and drips plugged in. But his eyes were open. I'm eighty per cent satisfied the man I saw was Melvin Hughes.'

'In that case,' the Commissioner said, 'there are procedures to be followed. I'll get onto Attorney-General's and see whether an inquest has been scheduled. They'll have to move quickly and get the body to the coroner's before someone organises a nice country funeral. Carl, I want you to get Legal

Branch to take a deposition from Prue as soon as possible, and to forward it to the Coroner's court with a covering letter pointing out she is not a compellable witness. We don't want any untoward publicity flowing from this.

'I don't need to tell you, Prue, that the whole file now becomes a very serious matter. Absolute discretion and confidentiality are essential. Not a word about this to anyone. You can consider your part in the investigation complete. It's up to Legal Branch now to sift through the material you've amassed and recommend any prosecutions that should follow.'

'It should have a green sticker, though, at least,' Prue said. 'The trail will go cold if there's too much delay. Some of our matters have dragged on for years and then been thrown out of court because the time lag denies people natural justice.'

'I'm aware of how Investigation Branch feels about the effects of delay,' the Commissioner said, 'but in such a delicate matter I'll thankyou to respect the professional advice of our lawyers. I'd have thought it would be a relief to leave this murky little file to more experienced people to follow up. Aren't you on the sub-committee that's redrafting the pamphlets on dangerous products? You'll be able to give priority to things like that for a while. Okay then? Thankyou both for your time.'

'Thankyou, sir.'

Prue and Carl did not exchange a word as they left the executive area.

BUSINESS BRIEFING

On the day of her interview with David Jasper, Roxane was in a state of pent-up suspense and anxiety. Adrenalin surged through her and her cheeks were bright with colour. She had scarcely slept since the weekend, and nightmares had cut into her few hours of dozing. Cindy's postcard had reassured her there was not much to worry about, but she would be unable to relax until she saw her daughter face to face. And having lied to her colleagues, blaming flu rather than anxiety about her daughter for her absence, she was unable to confide in anyone at work. Anna's suggestions about a change of career had opened her eyes to vistas that her corporate orientation had always obscured. Renewed contact with Colin had stirred memories of the 1970s. Although she had no regrets that their marriage had ended, the basic dynamics between them had not changed greatly, so that irritation with him was mixed with affection. It was a surprise to her to feel warmth and gratitude towards Colin: the bitterness of their break-up, with its quarrels and recriminations, had been her chief memory of the marriage in recent years. Of course, he'd grown older, matured somewhat. She must have changed too: perhaps she was a little mellower. At any rate these unexpected emotions, on top of her desperation about

Lucinda, were unsettling.

She had not spent any time alone with Steven all week either: she had become used to having him as her sounding board. She consulted him about ideas for work, regaled him with anecdotes about her travels, consulted him about her wardrobe. (He was a man who noticed shoes: he praised her Italian court shoes and persuaded her not to wear lace-patterned stockings or multi-coloured sandals. Roxane, who had never known a man who cared about such things, complied with all his suggestions. She saw now that he reflected Anna's taste.) It occurred to her that her life was about to change greatly. From a situation where Monday to Friday belonged to Runaway and Steven, and the weekends to her role as a mother, she was facing the prospects of weekends without Cindy, and companionable Sunday lunches with the Szabos and their friends instead. These changes would affect the trysts in Elizabeth Bay, but she was not yet sure how. Her mind darted around like a dragonfly over a grease-spotted lake.

It was hard to concentrate on David Jasper's questions.

He was a man of about twenty-seven, dark, bearded and serious in his manner. Roxane smiled at him in her most dazzling style, but her smile was not returned. Was he hostile, sympathetic or neutral? Her usual instincts, which allowed her to identify friend and foe from tiny clues, did not seem to be operating.

'My photographer isn't due until two,' the journalist said. 'Maybe I could get you a light lunch in the meantime?'

They went to the Lobby Bar of the Sheraton Wentworth. Roxane ate the salmon from the top of an open sandwich while David Jasper poured champagne. Seaview Brüt. Szabo's flat was always stocked with Bollinger.

Roxane explained to Jasper that trends in travel are subject to fashion. He didn't seem to have done much homework on the subject. She felt bound to give him some background briefing.

'Of course,' Roxane explained, 'budget packages for the

great unwashed to a handful of well-known destinations where there's good shopping are likely to have a good run for a long while yet.'

She gave an outline of how Runaway segmented its market, of its co-ventures with other organisations, and its triumphs over rivals in specially targeted business sectors. She led Jasper to believe that she had been the architect of the company's most successful marketing coups. Oh, Boris Brookstein was a brilliant businessman of course, and she had received invaluable training in the early days from Olwyn Tierney. But in her opinion ...

'You're not still taping this, are you?'

'Yes, of course.' Jasper had a mini-cassette next to the ice bucket.

'That's a bit rugged.'

'You did give me permission.'

'Yes, back in my office.'

'You've said nothing that isn't enormously to your credit. I can't remember interviewing such a sharp-minded business-woman in any industry. Really I'd been dazzled by the PR image, perhaps. I shouldn't be surprised, given your track record. Champagne?'

'Thanks.' Roxane did not pursue the matter of the tape-recorder. She became guarded when he asked about her private life.

'You're a divorcée, Roxane?'

'Yes. I was divorced years ago when my daughter was small.'

'And you have a daughter?'

'I have just one rule when it comes to publicity, and that is: absolutely nothing about my daughter needs to be in the public domain. To an extent my face and my voice are identified with my company. Fine. My daughter, though, is another matter.' She heard her voice waver. What if this bastard, or worse, the afternoon tabloid or the radio chat shows, were to discover her daughter had run away? Colin's facetious song, 'Runaway ... from Roxane' suddenly came back to her.

'I appreciate that, Roxane, of course. Leaving that aside, then. There's a lot of talk about you, as you're probably aware, and your prominent friends. You're said, for instance, to be on very close terms with Steven Szabo. Is that the case, and if so, does it pose any problems of conflict of interest in your work?'

'Anna Szabo is a dear friend of mine — I'm delighted to be involved with her in the forthcoming Silk Festival, a fundraising event which her committee, Harbourside Volunteers, is arranging to aid deaf children. I'm afraid I know her husband only slightly. I've met him at the occasional business lunch.'

'You're denying the widespread rumours about yourself and him?'

'I never dignify rumours with comment of any kind. But I am not too sure, really, what you're alluding to. As I say, my private life has nothing to do with an article on market trends in the travel industry.'

'Fine. I don't think we have time for coffee. Our photographer will be arriving in your office very soon.'

Roxane felt rotten. Tiredness, defensiveness, adrenalin and alcohol fought for supremacy. The photographer was a burly man who puffed and heaved and complained as he searched for power points and set up lights. To Roxane's relief, Jasper abandoned his questions for a few moments. Roxane took the chance to go to the lavatory, comb her hair and repair her make-up.

When she re-entered her room, Jasper leapt guiltily away from her desk. She was pretty sure he'd been flipping through her telephone index. The computer, telephone and stationery had been rearranged. Files and papers had been moved out of sight, and an antique globe which was usually kept in the reception area as a talking point now stood on her desktop.

'If you just turn this way, we'll get a more flattering angle,' the photographer said. 'A little more relaxed? Does the chair tilt back at all? If you could cross your legs? Can we do something with that marvellous globe? Fine. Say "sex". Again. "Sex." Oh, all right, "cheese", if that's what you prefer. Fine. Good. Just one more. Twirl the globe a little. Head tilted back with the chair. Perfect. Perfect. You pose like an old trouper.'

David Jasper put his tape-recorder and notebook away as soon as the photography session was over. 'I imagine we've got a cover shot in there somewhere,' he said. 'Thanks for your time.'

'My pleasure,' Roxane said. As Jasper left her office, followed by the lumbering photographer with all his metal gear, she had a sense of foreboding. She should not have given a personal interview at a time when her defences were down. Even though she'd steered him away from her private life and tried to communicate professionally about marketing and industry trends, she sensed that he had some hidden agenda. Too late now; the horse had bolted. She carried the globe back to the reception area.

'What did they want that for?' Di asked. 'They picked it up without so much as a by-your-leave.'

'Darling, you know the manners of the press as well as I do. Let's just hope they got some reasonably flattering photographs. Now, I wonder if you can bring me the Cook Island file?'

'Right away, Miss Rowe.'

'And maybe a cup of coffee.'

'No problem.'

Roxane drank the coffee black. She tried to concentrate on her proposals for Indigo-style villages further east in the Pacific, but her mind did not seem to want to cooperate. She started checking a budget, only to find that she was using the solar-powered calculator more like a toy than a tool. It was not going to be a very productive day.

Her thoughts were suddenly interrupted by a telephone call from Colin. 'Great news, Rox! I've found Cindy. Safe and sound. Yes, truly. We're about to set off: we should be home by midnight.'

'Put her on,' Roxane told him. 'I can't believe this till I speak to her.'

'Hi, Mum,' Cindy said. 'How are you?'

'Darling, are you all right? Cindy, it's been the worst week of my life.' She felt a surge of relief, together with fury at her daughter's nonchalant tone.

'Don't do your nana, Mum, I'm okay, really. See you later, all right? Dad's bringing me home now.'

'Fine. Tell Colin to drive carefully. See you soon.'

'See ya!'

Roxane put the phone down and sat weeping quietly at her desk. She pulled a packet of Kleenex out of a desk drawer and tried to dab away the tears, but could not. Di came into the room to find her boss slumped across the desk, her face hidden by one elbow and her shoulders shaking with sobs.

'Miss Rowe. Whatever is it? Can I do anything to help?'

'It's stupid really. I don't know why I'm so upset when I finally know that everything is okay. My daughter's been missing since the weekend and I only just found out she's safe.'

Di came forward to comfort her. 'Roxane,' she said, 'you should have told me earlier.'

Roxane failed to notice that her first name had been used, in defiance of office protocol.

'I know, Di,' she said. 'I see that now. I should have told you on Monday.'

Hours later, Lucinda and Colin were on the doorstep. 'Cindy, you look quite well, darling! I've had visions of you all tired and without food and beaten up and God knows what. But you seem so — so normal.'

'I haven't changed personality since Sunday,' Cindy said.

'She's in good shape, Roxane,' Colin said. 'She seems to have fared very well, really.'

Roxane put her arms around her daughter and hugged her tight.

'Cindy, you put me through hell.' she said, straightening

up.

'Yeah, I'm sorry. I suppose I didn't think. But I've been perfectly okay, Mum, honestly.'

'More by good luck than good management,' Roxane said.

'Roxane, that doesn't help. Cindy made some quite sensible decisions by herself.'

'Really? Good. Where did you get that monstrosity of a jacket?'

'I rather like it. It's from the Woy Woy op. shop. Well, I only had my denim jacket and a sweatshirt, and the first night, Sunday, was really cold. This was only six dollars. Not bad, eh?'

'And don't say "eh" — a few days hitchhiking and you come back talking like a truck driver.'

'Your mother's been extremely anxious, as I told you,' Colin said.

'Yeah, well I'm sorry, I didn't think it was such a big deal. I did write to you.'

'With no address.'

'Yeah, but you knew I was safe, and Dad worked out how to find me. I would've come back before too long. I just suddenly couldn't face school.'

'I said we could discuss your subjects on Sunday. I was waiting for you.'

'I've been talking to Dad about school, driving home. Mum, I want to leave and go over to New Zealand for a while.'

'You can't leave school at your age, with no qualifications.'

'You did. And I can't stay there, either. If you make me go back it will be a total waste of money. I'll be off like a rocket now I know how easy it is.'

'Darling, it's so unsafe. Just because you seem to have been lucky this time doesn't guarantee you can dash all over the countryside alone at your age. You could end up in a girls' home for being exposed to moral danger. Or raped and murdered by the side of the road.'

'What I know after this week is, I don't have to stay cooped up against my will anywhere any more.'

'Carinya is a marvellous school. It's a privilege to go there. Besides, we'd forfeit a term's fees if you left without notice.'

'Big deal.'

'It's three and a half thousand dollars, Lucinda.'

'Sorry about that. But I can't go back. It's no use trying to persuade me.'

'Your father and I have made many sacrifices for you, young lady,' Roxane said, a script from her own schooldays providing the words.

Cindy laughed.

Colin looked around the apartment. 'It's not exactly a picture of self-denial, your way of life,' he said. 'Or mine, for that matter. We could try negotiating with the school over the fees. I doubt that they could insist on more than half a term's worth. Pay 'em that and just let them holler for the rest. They've got a waiting list, haven't they? Cindy and I have talked about this on the way down, Roxane, and there's a lot to be said for her coming to us over in Gisborne for a year or two. She can do her matriculation later as an adult if she really wants to go to university. In the meantime she can learn something completely different. Emily is quite a distinguished horticulturist these days, you know, and ...'

Roxane gave a snort. 'Horticulturist, my God! Spare me this crap, at least.'

'She is. She's renowned for her catalogue of rare seeds. She's got a mailing list that extends ...'

'Just spare me Emily's achievements. If Cindy goes over with you for a while, it'll be in spite of Emily, not because of her.'

'You never give up, Roxane.'

'No, I don't. That's why I'm so successful. That's why I earn four times what you do. That's why I call the shots around here.'

'Roxane, I'm not sure the Family Court would see it that way.'

'Wouldn't they? There's a little plaque on my lawyer's wall

—"The Golden Rule — He who has the gold, rules." '

'Both of you fucking well shut up! I'm too old to have my life mapped out by the Family Court or by either one of you. I'll be out that door again tomorrow if you don't stop this.'

Roxane and Colin looked silently at their daughter for a few seconds.

'Tell your mother about that amazing old bird you stayed with, Cinders,' Colin said.

'Old bird! Well, I never really found out her name. The people in the coffee shop called her Beryl the Bird Lady. I didn't know why till I woke up there the first morning. She's on top of this hill, Mum, in an old cottage, and she feeds the birds seed and bread and honey every day on this big wooden platform. You've never seen such birds.'

'Shrimpton Island is full of birds.'

'Yeah, but so many different ones. Galahs and rosellas, and Beryl's favourite was this golden regent bower bird. It was a really glossy black with the brightest yellow on its head.'

'Really?'

'Yes. Don't say "Really?" like that, it was terrific, really tops.'

'How did you meet this Beryl person?'

'I was asking at this coffee shop about the nearest youth hostel, and they said there was this old lady nearby who sometimes had kids to stay for a night or two if they didn't have any transport. And I didn't know really, I thought I might hitch up to the hostel, but while I was making up my mind Beryl came in there. She was a funny old lady, a bit hunched over, with her hair pinned in this sort of bun.'

'And you stayed in her house?'

'Yes, I stayed there for two nights. I was about to leave and go further north when Dad showed up.'

'You do seem to have fallen on your feet.'

'She's shown herself to be quite sensible, really,' Colin said.

'Sensible!' Roxane's voice rose. 'Sensible to take off

245

without a word, not to ring up, not to put an address on the postcard, to leave her mother walking round too distraught to work. Sensible!'

'Let's all discuss this when we're less tired.' Colin suggested. 'You've had a rough few days.'

'No. It's quite all right. We don't have to delay a decision for my sake. I've had enough of this argument. Cindy has my full permission to go back with you. On two conditions: I am never, never, never again, to be left without an address and a phone number, and she's got to get some good advice about ways of finishing her education as an adult if she changes her mind about qualifications.'

'She's agreed!' Cindy shouted. 'Dad, she's agreed!' Father and daughter embraced one another. Colin held out an arm and Roxane became the awkward third in a triangle of tears and rejoicing. Her neck was stiff with the tension of the past few days and she was regretting the champagne she had drunk with David Jasper. She had some soluble aspirin in the bathroom cupboard.

'I've had nightmares the whole week,' she said to Cindy. Her great affection for the child surged up again through the confusion of anxiety, joy, possessiveness, and the underlying knowledge that she had to let her go if she was to keep her.

'Yeah, Mum, I really am sorry.' Roxane pushed the green fringe back from her daughter's hazel eyes and tasted salt as she kissed her cheek.

On Saturday she woke up early, all set to meet the train. Then she realised. No train. No Cindy. In time the loneliness might become simply being alone; the uncommitted time might seem like freedom. She was surprised that she ached for the child already. The apartment seemed oddly quiet and empty. Cindy's posters were still on the walls of her room, but her clothes, sports gear and records had gone. Roxane read listlessly through the Saturday papers, even reading a few book reviews and letters to the editor. Ridiculous, she thought. The empty nest syndrome afflicts middle-aged housewives who have devoted themselves to their families. It is not something that descends on executives in their thirties who have a dozen plans for the future.

Mentally she listed her options. She could get Olwyn's place on the Brooklands board, or she could quit Runaway to run Szabo's Pacific operations, or she could, as Anna suggested, go solo. If Des got Olwyn's place on the board, she would have no choice but to quit Runaway. There might be openings in convention management, or sponsored travel documentaries. She did not want to abandon the travel and tourism field completely. When she thought of it objectively, she had plenty of choices left. Runaway had given her tunnel vision. She'd been unaware of the restrictions because she'd always been able to take off overseas on a new project. But it was time to make a break. The trick would be to make it look as if she'd been planning her moves for a long time.

On Sunday, she blow-dried her shoulder-length hair with unusual care and dressed in a bright fuchsia silk tunic over black pants. The Szabos lived in an old waterfront block at Point Piper, with an elaborate security system at the entrance. She pressed the button and waited for Anna's lilting voice. 'Yes — who is it?'

'Roxane.' She was nervous. She had never seen Steven and Anna together.

'Darling,' Anna Szabo said, embracing her, 'what a blessed relief about your little girl.'

'Yes, isn't it?' Roxane said, looking around her. Harbour vistas invaded the room through the northern and eastern windows. Inside, she saw blue-grey Persian rugs, antique chairs, flowers, mirrors, light. The paintings were contemporary, but the furniture was all antique. She didn't know the period. Steven Szabo came across to her.

'Roxane, my dear. So glad you were able to join us. Let me introduce our friends. This is Justin Hope, of Cementcrete Corp, and his wife Frances, and this is my old friend and compatriot Dr Vilmos Zolnay. And Hilary Blau, and Martin Rhys-Evans. Now. Martini? Orange juice?

Champagne?'

'Thanks, champagne.'

Roxane smiled at the circle of faces, all new to her apart from the hosts. She was the youngest person present by fifteen or twenty years.

'Of course, I know you from the television commercials,' Hilary Blau said.

'Roxane has thrilled us all by agreeing to make some TV promotions for Harbourside Volunteers,' Anna said.

'How wonderful,' Frances Hope said.

'Yes, it should be fun,' Roxane said. 'The whole Silk Festival should be.'

'You're already dressing the part, I see,' said Vilmos Zolnay.

Roxane turned to look at this man, tanned and wearing designer jogging clothes, whom she had often heard of from Steven. 'My guess would have been, though, that you were here to give some travel advice to our hosts.'

'Travel advice?' Roxane queried.

'Yes, darling, isn't it exciting? Steven and I leave for Shanghai on Tuesday morning.'

Steven Szabo caught Roxane's eye over his wife's head. 'Only for a few days,' he said with emphasis. 'In my case, anyway.'

'Yes,' said Vilmos Zolnay. 'Poor Steven. He has so many commitments at home.' He glanced towards Roxane to make sure that she had caught the significance of his remark. She had. Nothing is private, nothing at all, she thought. Steven and I might as well hold orgies: his wife and his best friend know everything he does. She looked across the room at him. He had turned his attention to the Hopes. In profile he had a double chin, his paunch bulged under his knitted shirt, and the lenses of his spectacles were thick. It was strange that he could exert such sexual power over her. He was nothing to write home about, so far as looks went.

'I hear that my favourite boy is making something really special for you,' Hilary Blau said.

'I'm sorry? Your favourite …'

'Nicky of course. The incomparable Nicholas Vader. He told me he was making a gown for you.'

'Yes. He is. It should be lovely,' Roxane said.

'If Nicky has anything to do with it, darling, it will be divine. You know what all Nicholas's creations are designed to say, don't you?'

'Yes, he did mention it. Drop dead.'

'Is this any way to speak to my guests?' Steven had come up behind her, a Bollinger bottle in his hand. She was conscious that there was no physical contact between them. When she'd arrived, Anna had kissed her but Steven had kept a distance. A conscientious host, he was refilling glasses.

'Darling,' Hilary explained, 'we were just talking about Nicky.'

And Nicky has been talking about us, Roxane reflected, as she drank French champagne. Everyone knows all about everyone else. Which may be just as well, after all, because what they'd invent would be worse.

WOMEN IN COMMERCE

Margot was writing up the results of her survey on women executives in several forms. A corporate version for Synchron Mines documented the low participation of women in technical and engineering fields and suggested changes in recruitment practices. A popular version for a women's magazine looked at the current achievements of women in the workforce and added some career advice. Finally, she was extracting the main points for her speech to Prue's group, Women in Commerce.

Never having been to a meeting of this group, Margot was not sure whether to stick to trends and facts, or loosen up and give her own interpretations of the data. Too late, she regretted asking such standard questions when doing the research: she'd concentrated on the level women reached in the organisation, how much they earned, their access to training, and what they thought of their chances of promotion. There were questions about child care and further study, and questions about marital status. But she had dodged some of the tougher issues. Do girls who play with the boys have to act like the boys? Or can women really introduce a more consultative management style and show more empathy for their subordinates? How are they viewed by those who work for them? Do women really support each other like sisters through an unofficial women's network? Or is it everyone for herself in the cut-throat world of work?

Her speech was on Women and Success. The usual notion of success was getting to the top, but did that represent success for everyone? There were undoubtedly many couples like Ted and herself, where both partners worked, who had more satisfying lives on their combined income and their middle-level jobs than they would have if they were putting all their energy into keeping one high flyer at the top. She could have been a senior lecturer by now if she'd been prepared to transfer to a country college, but what good would that have done when Ted's work kept him in Sydney? If she remained a medium flyer, it was not entirely because of some patriarchal conspiracy. It was partly that she liked to have time at home with Ted and Tom. Without the leisure to read books or to sit and talk with friends like Prue, life would be joyless for her. Success meant keeping a balance between the demands of work and home, and time to keep up with her own interests. What would Women in Commerce think of someone who saw success in those terms?

She thought of her mother, undoubtedly a high flyer. For Olwyn, work and leisure were the same thing. She would be miserable sitting under a palm tree reading magazines, yet she was in her element supervising Runaway's expansion into all those tropical paradises. Olwyn had never knitted a sock, crocheted a pot-holder or wondered whether her marmalade would set: the domestic arts left her rigid with boredom. Most of her friends were also in the travel industry. She made no conscious sacrifices when she dedicated herself to her work; she simply could not bear to contemplate retirement or the need to take it easy.

This thought prompted Margot to telephone her mother. The phone rang for a long time before Olwyn answered.

'Mum, you don't sound at all well.'

'I'm waiting for the GP to come,' Olwyn said. 'I'll be all right, really.'

'I'll come over.'

'Don't do that, Margot. Harry will be here any minute, and I'm expecting Winifred, too.'

'You're sure you'll be okay?'

'Absolutely,' Olwyn replied. Margot could hear muffled coughs.

'Ring me and tell me what Harry says, then, okay?'

'Oh, Margot, you fuss like an old woman.'

'Okay, but keep in touch. I do care about you, you know.'

'Of course, darling. Thanks.'

Although she knew it was Olwyn's way to deny pain and distress, Margot felt rebuffed as she went back to her report.

She had interviewed several managing directors, and more than 900 women, but perhaps she should have found some way of including the views of their employees as well. She did not really want to commit herself to a follow-up survey: other projects had been put aside when she decided to accept this one.

She thought again of the hovering bird she had seen when she was staying in the country. Gus Allingham had confirmed that the kestrel or windhover was quite a common bird. Typically it hovered over semi-rural clearings or golf courses, hanging in the air about twenty or thirty metres up, almost at a standstill when viewed from the ground. Closer inspection revealed that it fanned its underwings constantly to maintain that motionlessness and to survey its patch of turf for rivals or prey. It was the kind of apparently effortless grace that relied on unceasing hard work and attention to detail.

Did that bird symbolise women as medium flyers? So many reached middle management in an area they knew about, and stayed there. Their competence was fantastic, but they lacked the vision they would gain if they looked down on things from a greater height. They made their work look easy, but it cost them a lot of effort in striving to please and in warding off people — including other women — whom they saw as threats. They hung there, head to the wind,

252

motionless, at a standstill in career terms, but putting a lot of effort into maintaining their position. The least savage of the eaters of flesh, kestrels lived on grasshoppers, lizards and mice — middle-management salaries?

She knew from her questionnaire returns from Women in Commerce that the membership resembled her average female executive: a woman of thirty-five, earning a figure well above the average wage, but well below the average for thirty-five-year-old male executives. Typically this woman headed a section such as personnel or public relations, exercising a good deal of responsibility within that domain. As a rule, though, there were limitations on her budget and she had to defer to a male executive. She did not always hire and fire her own staff. She was seldom a board member, a partner, or a major shareholder. In organisations like Synchron Mines she was held back by lack of field experience compared to her male peers. The average female executive, in short, was more a highly paid handmaiden than a shaper of destinies. How could she turn this composite picture into a speech entitled Women and Success?

The more she thought about it, the more she wished she had pursued the issues of how women wove their careers around marriages, love affairs, small children, friendship, study or travel. How did they acquire powerful allies who would develop their skills and help them get ahead? Who could they emulate?

Margot herself had never lacked for a role model: she had Olwyn. In the 1950s, she remembered, a working mother was nothing to boast about. It amounted to proclaiming herself a potential juvenile delinquent. At school they'd been led to believe that working mothers were rare, far rarer than they actually were. There were very few women in management in those days, but without women the schools, factories, hospitals, shops and canteens would not have functioned. She had not been tempted to follow in her mother's footsteps; her own talents were more bookish. She had succeeded academically, without ever feeling that her degrees or publications meant much to Olwyn. It was ridiculous, at her age, still to be yearning for her mother's approval.

Another issue which Margot had failed to pursue in her survey was the power of rumour and gossip. If a man went to any trouble to foster the talent of a female employee, he ran the risk of being seen to favour her for personal reasons. Women were accused of sleeping their way to the top. Even Olwyn had made a point of telling her about Roxane Rowe's involvement with Steven Szabo, and the supposed risk of conflict of interest. Were powerful people from companies with related interests meant to forswear all personal relationships? Weren't they entitled to their privacy at some point? Her survey had revealed that women seldom succeeded without having their talent recognised by a man. They worked very hard, harder than anyone else in many cases, and in due course a male executive had the sense to see the value to himself of those efforts.

Margot made notes on cards. She would tell them about medium flyers, mentors and role models, and her own experience as Olwyn's daughter. She would point out that for every woman who joined the successful minority, a dozen women were cleaning, waiting at tables, standing at cash registers and pounding typewriters. She would talk about the problems of fostering women's talent when less than fifteen per cent of those attending senior management training courses were female. She would describe her conversation with Henry Moses, and tell them how female executives were perceived by their bosses. Somehow she would try to find an upbeat note to end on. Oh, the speech should be fine, really — perhaps her nervousness stemmed from anxiety about Olwyn.

Women in Commerce was meeting in a garishly carpeted room on the upper floor of a bowling club. The sound of silver cascading from poker machines penetrated the cantilevered side partition. Margot sat at a table at the front of the room, facing rows of blue plastic chairs. She counted how many Women in Commerce had shown up. Forty-one. The swing door at the back near the bar opened and a large woman in a tartan suit came in. Forty-two. Then two young women with severe haircuts. Forty-four.

Margot swallowed water from the glass near the microphone. Despite her years of lecturing, she was nervous in front of this group. Well-groomed — how formidably well-groomed they are, she thought, with their gold chains and their cunningly placed white handkerchiefs and silk scarves. Spots, paisleys, discreet patterns to set off navy, grey and black outfits. Margot had not polished her shoes and now knew the omission would be noticed. A memory from primary school came to her: she remembered the special assembly in the hall, which they had to leave in single file, as the senior prefect inspected the colour of each girl's bloomers. Any girl without the regulation navy blue bloomers was sent home. It's blazers now, Margot thought, looking around the room. We'd probably tolerate a bloomers inspection, too, if the president told us to line up.

But now the introductions had started. The president mentioned Margot's degrees, her job at the Yagoona Institute, and the fact that she was a friend of Prue Lambert, a long-standing member of Women in Commerce. Prue, in the front row, beamed at this reference. Margot took some deep breaths. This had better be convincing, if only for Prue's sake.

Margot told Women in Commerce she was glad to be with them and grateful for their support for her research. Several members agreed to be interviewed as part of her survey on working women and upward mobility. She hoped they would not withdraw their support on hearing the results. To begin her speech, she explained why she had chosen to call her report Medium Flyers rather than High Flyers. She pointed out how few women had yet made it beyond middle management; how equal pay still left women badly paid compared to men; how women worked as assistants to powerful men. 'In universities and colleges, a context I know from experience, most women are tutors and research assistants,' Margot said. Now that she was launched into the speech she felt more confident. The audience was attentive. Her listeners frowned as they tried to screen out the background noise of drinkers and poker machines. A couple of members arrived late, bringing a distracting wave of noise in through the folding doors with them. But so far as Margot could tell, the speech was going well. Why not? She was describing the reality of these women's working lives, interpreting the data from their own questionnaires and feeding it back to them. These were the women who were regarded by their managing directors as hard-working, trustworthy, understanding, adaptable and good at handling staff. At the same time, they were being accused of being too tentative, too compliant, of not being risk-takers or entrepreneurs. They were seen as too ready to back away from a fight. If they were aggressive, they were seen as unfeminine. On the other hand, the so-called feminine traits were seen as a handicap in management: anxiety and deference did not make for confident leadership.

Margot saw that several of the women present looked away or at the ground rather than meet her eye. Perhaps she was striking home.

She continued. 'Women who baulk at wielding power and dealing with the resulting unpopularity may become moderately successful, but doomed never to reach the top: in short, to be medium flyers. Ask a woman in power if she is tough and she hesitates; she may choose some other term like decisive or tough-minded. Ask a man and he unhesitatingly agrees — "Tough? Sure".'

She wished, looking at her audience, that she had a more optimistic message for them. Essentially she was saying that they would all have to work hard, but only a few could hope to make it to the top. Most of them could only hope to become medium flyers, controlling one little piece of turf and putting a great deal of effort into keeping rivals at bay. How did the myth of success acquire such glamour? She would have to end on a hopeful note, somehow.

She talked about the need to know oneself, and to capitalise on one's strengths. She spoke about loyalty to other women, and networking. She exhorted her listeners to give their best and demand commitment and excellence from others. She ended with the hope that in the future a greater number of women would succeed in becoming high flyers.

Margot sat down to applause from Women in Commerce, and reached for a glass of water. She'd been speaking for about fifteen minutes. Her feet seemed to have swollen, and her toes, unused to stockings, were tangled in nylon. In the front row Prue was clapping and signalling to Margot by her facial expression that the speech had gone well. Margot still felt a little ambivalent about the group for some reason, but when the president turned to her, it was not to announce a bloomers inspection, but to offer her a drink. She took a glass of white wine. Too sweet, but she was thirsty.

Prue was beside her with two more women. She introduced them as Hannah, the equal opportunity officer of the Fire Brigade, and Juliette, a management development consultant with Cementcrete Corp. Someone had reopened the cantilever doors, so that the sounds of revelry, poker machines and coin upon coin added to the clamour of voices in the meeting room. Margot, answering questions, shaking hands, laughing at jokes, began to feel like a piece of flotsam tossed in a sea of noise. A uniformed attendant from the bowling club made his way through the crush and handed a note to the club president. Margot felt someone tugging at her elbow.

'Sorry to drag you away,' the president said, 'but we have a message for you.'

RING TED URGENTLY, Margot read, her head still buzzing with the din of the room. She followed the man downstairs to a telephone booth. The coins rattled into the slot in a parody of the phalanxes of poker machines.

The unfamiliar clonks and silences of the public phone gave her the momentary impression her call was not properly connected. Then she heard Ted's voice. 'Margot? Is that you?'

'Yes. Sorry. Public phone. It's poker machine heaven in here.'

'I had a call from that friend of your mother's, Winifred Carswell. Olwyn's been taken to Prince Alfred Hospital with pneumonia. She's in intensive care in the Page Pavilion.'

'When did this happen?'

'Just hours ago.'

'You'll be home for Tom?'

'Of course.'

'I'll go straight out there. Thanks for getting a message through to me.'

Olwyn looked very small in the bed, surrounded as she was by tentacles of plastic stretching to a drip machine, oxygen gear, a heart monitor and other equipment Margot could not identify.

She took her mother's hand, the one without the drip. 'How are you?' she asked. Wrong question, you fool, she told herself.

'Not the best, as you see.' There was a hollow at the base of Olwyn's throat which deepened at the end of every gasping breath. Her hands were a beetroot colour.

'I've just been giving a talk on Women and Success for that Women in Commerce group of Prue's.'

'I was never one for those women-only shows.'

'I know. But several people sent you their regards. Prue, and someone called Hannah Berensen.'

'That's very nice.' The laboured breathing was distressing to watch.

There were three other patients in the ward, one in an oxygen tent and others attached to equipment similar to Olwyn's. Margot sat on a little steel visitor's chair. Olwyn seemed to be half asleep. Rest was probably the best thing. Margot reflected that the all-loving, all-healing conversation that she dreamt of having with her mother would probably never occur. Sickness and death remained taboo topics even though Olwyn was only just clinging to life. She squeezed the small, highly coloured hand. Olwyn returned the pressure. Margot remained seated a long time until her mother's laboured intakes of air more closely resembled the even breathing of sleep.

She walked down the corridor to the administration desk, but it was not attended. She kept walking. A glass-louvred room at the end of the corridor was labelled SOLARIUM. She looked around at the green vinyl easy chairs and went to the window, which had a view of Missenden Road and other hospital buildings. A man standing at the window looked round guiltily. Margot saw that he held a cigarette in his hand, ashing it out the louvred window.

'It's okay,' she said. 'I'm only a visitor.'

The man took another puff on his illicit cigarette, coughed pitifully, and dropped the butt out of the window. He turned back to Margot. He wore a brown, checked Sandy Stone dressing gown, and when he spoke his breathy rasp was so indistinct that Margot had to lipread.

'Visiting?' he asked. 'Husband?'

'My mother. She's got pneumonia. She's in intensive care. And you?'

The man pointed at his throat. 'Can-cer,' he articulated, one syllable at a time. 'Me voice box is half gone.' Margot's mind rushed to her recent checkup at the breast clinic.

'Tell your mother,' the man wheezed, 'when she gets out, that the sea air is no good. She should go up to the mountains.'

Margot nodded vigorously, as if silence on her part would reduce the man's effort at conversation. It was grotesque, health advice from a man whose body was rotting away from tobacco.

'I'll tell her. Thanks.' She smiled with the bland goodwill of visiting royalty and backed out of the room. This time she found the sister on duty at the desk.

'Yes, Ms Tierney,' she said, 'your mother's condition is stable, though serious, and I think you may find Dr

Farrington in the ward at the moment.'

Hurrying back to the intensive care ward, Margot found a grey-haired man bending over Olwyn, who was not replying to his questions. Sleep or coma? Margot went forward.

'Good,' the doctor said, 'you must be the daughter, I've been wanting a word with the family.' He turned back to the unresponsive figure on the bed. 'Can you hear me?' he asked. 'You're in hospital, and I'm Dr Farrington.'

There were some noisy breaths, and then Olwyn said in a half-drowned voice, 'Not worth a cracker.' She lapsed back into sleep or unconsciousness.

Margot followed the doctor up and down the corridor as they searched for a private place to talk. They ended up back in the solarium, which the cancer patient had vacated. 'Your mother will pull through this, if the antibiotics arrest the pneumonia in time,' he told Margot. 'But she'll need to alter her way of life completely. She must retire from that job. And no smoking, that goes without saying. And her lung capacity is so reduced that my advice would be no alcohol either.'

'Yes, she's been told that before,' Margot said.

'It's almost life-threatening in her condition, that's my point.'

'She sounds pretty depressed to me — "not worth a cracker".'

'You could interpret it that way, I suppose,' the doctor said.

'Oh, hell,' Margot said. 'She's such a vibrant person really.'

'We all feel the mortality of our parents as a special kind of blow,' the doctor said. 'We're used to having an older generation in the frontline between ourselves and death. It hurts to see them frail and in ill-health.'

'But you said she'll recover?'

'Other things being equal. With antibiotics, I expect her to recover. But with someone whose lungs are in such bad shape, I'd hesitate to go in for too many heroics with the life support machine if there's a crisis of any kind.'

'I'm sure she'd hate that.'

'It shouldn't come to that. Let's hope you and I aren't forced to make that decision. The hospital will get in touch if there is anything to worry about. They know where to contact you?'

'Yes. Thanks for finding the time to talk to me.'

'If we can't be bothered to talk to people, we're reducing ourselves to technocrats,' the doctor said.

'I wish you'd tell a few of your colleagues,' Margot said.

'We're not as heartless as people make out.' The doctor stood up to resume his rounds. 'You're her only family here, am I right?'

'She has a brother in Canada. British Columbia.'

"You'd better tell him how seriously ill your mother is.'

'Yes, of course.'

'I'll only go to Yagoona for my lecture,' Margot told her husband, 'then I'll go back to the hospital. There's not much point taking Tom, is there?'

'They probably won't let you anyway, unless they move her out of intensive care. Is that boy awake, by the way?'

Margot went to the hallway and shouted 'Tom!' outside her son's bedroom door. A gargle of reassuring grunts replied.

'He's just waking up.'

'There doesn't seem to be any midway point with kids, does there? They get you up before dawn for years, then they treat daylight like some sort of conspiracy.'

'It's on his head if he's late for school, not ours.'

'True enough. You'll have to put your research aside for a while, by the look of things, won't you?'

'Yes, but I've finished most of the writing up. It's a matter of editing and printing, at this stage.'

'You said your speech went well, before I had to call you away?'

'Yes, it was okay. But people prefer myths to facts, don't they — the glamour of getting to the top, everyone can do it, that sort of nonsense?'

Ted pulled a face. 'You're speaking to a socialist,' he said.

'One of the last, sweetheart,' Margot told him.

A door opened and their fourteen-year-old son stumbled to the table like a sleepwalker.

'How's Gran?' he said, shaking Sultana Bran into his bowl.

'We were just talking about her. She's in intensive care, and she was only half conscious last night. I don't think you'll be able to visit unless she's moved to a regular ward.'

'That's no good,' the boy said. The milk he was pouring overshot the plate and sloshed onto the table. He lumbered to his feet, knocking over a bowl of apples, and went to the kitchen for a sponge, pursued by the remonstrations of both his parents ('Oh, Tom!') and the sound of Granny Smiths scattering like billiard balls. Remembering their own adolescence, Margot and Ted exchanged wry smiles.

Margot listened to the radio as she drove from Yagoona to the hospital. A tour promoter and a Greenpeace spokesman were debating whether tourism should be allowed in Antarctica. She would have liked to be able to get Olwyn's views on that. Prue's friend Gus took a conservationist line, she knew, and would be spending the summer on some frozen island watching the wandering albatrosses raise their young. The Greenpeace spokesman pointed out that the small proportion of Antarctic soil which was not ice-covered all year round was vitally important for the mating and nesting of wildlife. Even modest tourism was a threat. Supposedly dedicated scientists had left piles of waste and pollution at abandoned sites. The tour promoter disagreed, mentioning hotels with two or three hundred beds. 'Any development would be extremely sensitive to the environment,' he said.

Olwyn was fond of that line, Margot reflected, but surely her projects had really been sensitive, whereas this proposal was monstrous. Runaway's projects had been different. Or had they? Olwyn's tasteful village resorts had pioneered tourism in areas which were undergoing massive change. Commercial development involved a loss of innocence, even

262

if there were improvements to the local economies. Look at Bali.

Surrounded by the intensive care equipment, Olwyn lay somewhere between sleep and unconsciousness, and did not give any sign of recognising Margot's presence. Margot sat beside her mother for more than an hour. Once Olwyn turned over, murmuring, perhaps dreaming. Her eyelids fluttered. Margot lent forward and took her mother's hand. Olwyn spoke distinctly. 'More television, Roxane,' she said. 'Saturation.' She turned on her side again.

'What?' Margot asked. 'Mum, I'm here, it's Margot.' But there was no reply from the small, unresponsive patient beside her. After another twenty minutes and a discussion with the ward sister, Margot went home.

'The doctors are still saying she could recover,' Margot told her son that night, 'but it doesn't look very good to me. Her lungs are not strong enough to handle this infection.'

'Did she talk to you?'

'No. She was unconscious or asleep all day.'

'Didn't she say anything?'

'She said something once about work. She said "More television, Roxane — saturation."'

'That'd be Roxane Rowe. I wonder what it means. Did you tell her?'

'Who? Roxane? No, darling, she was raving. You can't imagine how sick she is. She didn't know what she was saying.' Even so, Margot thought, it was hurtful that in her half-conscious state her thoughts should be of a colleague rather than her daughter.

'She didn't have any message for me?'

Margot put her arm round her son. 'No, Tom, she didn't say anything specially, but you don't need me to tell you how much she loves you. People don't often come out with those special messages television soapies and Victorian novels are full of. I couldn't help wishing she might have some special message for me, too. But life isn't like that. Or Olwyn isn't.

She belongs to the stiff-upper-lip generation. They don't say much, but it doesn't mean a lack of feelings.'

'But you're not like that — stiff upper lip.'

'No, my darling, you and I aren't.' Mother and son hugged each other in silence.

The telephone in the bedroom rang in the blackness. Margot knew what she was about to hear. She put her feet on the sheepskin rug. 'Can you find the light switch?' she asked Ted. He put on the reading light just as she lifted the receiver.

'Hullo?'

'Miss Tierney? This is the night sister. I'm sorry to wake you with bad news, but your mother died a few minutes ago. It was very peaceful. We have some of her things here. Perhaps you or one of the family would like to collect them? You don't want to see her at all, do you?'

'What? No. No, thankyou.' Monstrous visions of stiffening limbs darted across Margot's eyelids. She was still adjusting to the light.

'We don't need to discuss the other arrangements now.'

'No.' Margot was speaking with difficulty.

'Goodbye, then.'

Margot turned to Ted.

'It's your mother,' he said, putting his arms around her. She nodded, her eyes filling with tears.

'They said it was peaceful,' she said. 'Whatever that means. God, now I have to ring Doug in Canada, and Winifred, and I suppose the Runaway people. I don't feel in any state to do it. Maybe I can wait till daylight at least. Oh, Jesus, Ted, that doctor said she ought to recover.'

'Yeah, it's very sudden and distressing. Let me make you some coffee.'

'Could I have tea?'

BRANCHING OUT

Roxane bought two more copies of *Business Briefing* from the newsstand on the corner of Hunter Street. She reached the Runaway office before Des.

'Nice picture of you on the cover of that magazine,' the receptionist said.

'If you like that sort of thing,' Roxane said, trying to smile. She was now wearing a long grey woollen skirt, as if to make up for being photographed in a black leather mini.

Mentally she was rehearsing what she would say at the board meeting. She had decided an emotional appeal was justified. You have to realise, she would say, that I was under enormous pressure the week Jasper did the interview. My daughter was missing. I didn't say anything to Des or anyone else at work at the time, but what I told you was flu was actually a frightful personal crisis. I can't really be held responsible for what I said to David Jasper. I really regret any damage to the company, but I thought it was understood that much of what I said was only background briefing, not to be quoted. I have been misquoted and taken out of context. Well, yes, he taped it, but he's selected it and twisted it and made it sound altogether different.

The telephone rang. 'Roxane?' a woman asked.

'Yes.'

'Margot Tierney, Olwyn's daughter. I thought I should tell you, my mother died this morning, in hospital. She had pneumonia and didn't respond to treatment. They said it was peaceful.'

'Oh, this is terrible. I can't tell you how shocked I am.'

'Yes, it will be a loss to Runaway, of course. Actually, she said something about you yesterday. She wasn't conscious really, but she said, "More television, Roxane — saturation."'

'How extraordinary. You said she was only semi-conscious?'

'Yes. It was the last thing she said.'

'That would be Olwyn, putting Runaway first every time.'

'Yes, it would.'

'Oh, I don't mean to suggest her family wasn't important to her.'

'Of course not. I wonder if you can make head or tail of what she said, anyway. We couldn't.'

'I've just had a bit of a brainwave,' Roxane said. 'I think I understand exactly. It was very good of you to tell me at what must be a very sad time for the family. Please give my sympathy to all her relatives. Have you spoken to Boris Brookstein?'

'No, I haven't — I didn't have the number.'

'Well, don't worry, I'll do that. You will let us know about the arrangements?'

'The what? Oh, yes, the funeral. Of course.'

'My sympathies, Margot, and thankyou so much for ringing.'

For a moment Roxane was aglow with power at being the one person with a vital piece of information, something big enough to dwarf the magazine cover in Boris's priorities. Then she was assailed by other emotions.

Her secretary came in with a large sheet of cardboard. 'We've got the storyboard on the next New Caledonia promotion,' she said. 'Hey, are you upset about something?

It's not that article?'

'No, of course not,' Roxane said. 'It's Olwyn. Olwyn died this morning.' Suddenly Roxane was weeping, bawling, blubbering, overcome with tears.

'Please, Miss Rowe,' Di said, looking round for the box of tissues.

'I'll be all right,' Roxane said between sobs. 'I'll be all right. Get me Boris in Melbourne, would you?' She blew her nose on one Kleenex and dabbed at the rivulets of plum mascara with another.

'Boris?' She was proud of the grief in her voice. 'Boris? Roxane. I had to make sure you knew. You didn't? It's Olwyn. Her daughter just told me. She died this morning, in the hospital. Pneumonia. Yes, it's terrible. And you'll never guess, Boris, her last message was to me. "More television, Roxane — saturation." Those were her last words. Yes. Amazing. Oh, we will, yes. Flowers to the daughter and the grandson. No, they haven't decided yet about the funeral. No, that's fine, Boris. No, I'm okay, really. It's just the shock. Fine. All right. Yes. Okay. Bye.'

'Could you come in for a moment, Di?' Roxane said to her secretary. 'Now. Ring the David Jones' florist and have flowers sent to Margot Tierney and her son, with a personal message of sympathy from me and Boris. Oh, Des too, why not? Then I want you to get on to the agency and tell them I need a top-class film editor to work with me all the weekend. Yes, penalty rates, whatever's needed. And to have all the Runaway archival film on hand. And get me the executive producer of "Breakfast Australia", pronto.'

'Yes, Miss Rowe, right away.'

Roxane thumbed through her pocket diary. Fortunately there were no commitments for the weekend, but the 'S' on the Sunday page meant that Steven was due back from Shanghai.

'We could spend the night together, for a change,' Steven Szabo said. 'Your place or mine?'

'Let's just stick to Elizabeth Bay. I've spent too much time being anxious at home recently, and I can't go to your place, I'd feel I was intruding on Anna. I can't just barge in there while she's still OS.'

'So scrupulous, my love.'

'Yes, well, that's how I feel. Anyway, what if she came back early?'

'She won't, but I understand all what you feel. Let's eat first. I'll pick you up at seven forty-five.'

'Wonderful.'

'I almost preferred the Chinese when the Gang of Four were in power,' Steven said over dinner at Primo's. They were more amusing. They are becoming just like everyone else now. They wear very nice wool suits, Western style, and ties. They look like aspiring IBM salesmen. Of course, many of them are.'

'So you didn't set up any big new ventures?'

'Not sure. I made some contacts. I'll send Bill Guest up in due course. There are certainly opportunities and markets. It's just I didn't find the whole experience as exotic as it was in the seventies.'

'You can't have everything. Our packages still only go as far as Hong Kong.'

'Might be time you changed that.'

'Yes, it might. Heavens, we've had specialty tours up there since — well, Vietnam War days, the early seventies some time.'

'And what have you been doing in my absence, apart from appearing on magazine covers looking like an ad for something much more salacious than travel? Painting the town red?'

'Not exactly. I had a meal with one man, a professor from Yagoona if you don't mind, who wants me to extend the financial planning seminar at the Hilton into a whole series. We could make a fortune, he says.'

'Which of you could?'

'Both of us, he says.' She did not tell Steven that she had

found Brian Lynch attractive, so much so that she wondered if she really did prefer older men. Brian was about her age, or even a couple of years younger.

'Check it out, Roxane, you could do better to run it yourself — be the principal of the thing.'

'You and Anna give me almost identical advice. Isn't that odd? Anyway, mostly I've been making a television clip.'

'Commercials?'

'No, altogether different. This is a sort of retrospective. Olwyn Tierney died on Friday morning.'

'Sorry to hear that. How old was she?'

'Sixty-three.'

'How long was she in poor health?'

'She may have been sicker than anyone realised. But she was only hospitalised a few weeks ago on Indigo, and then last week here. Pneumonia. She's done me a favour in a way, with the timing. They've postponed the Brooklands board meeting because of her funeral. I was pretty nervous, after the way Des reacted to that article. And Boris, so he claimed.'

'You learnt a great deal from her.'

'Yes. I was devastated when Boris brought Des Hickey in to run the Sydney office. I'd assumed I would.'

'Boris's business has changed and diversified so much, though. The acquisitions make a greater degree of head office control inevitable.'

'I thought they'd put me on the Brooklands board, in Olwyn's place. That's what I've always aimed for, all these years. Now, with all the song and dance about the *Business Briefing* piece, I can kiss that one goodbye.'

'Anna said she was talking to you about going out on your own.'

'Yes, she was. She and I may work up a Silk Tour — Marco Polo in reverse. And I could do other speciality tours. Top-drawer stuff, targeting the top one-and-a-half per cent. The real luxury end of the market. Special interest tours to private art collections or remarkable gardens. Millionaire cruises to the Antarctic. That sort of thing.'

'Would you enjoy that?'

'Of course. With Anna's personal contacts, and my travel knowledge and marketing skills, we couldn't fail.'

'It's a relief to me, Roxane. I haven't liked your hints about the South Pacific and my operations there. Oh, things crossed my mind with this link of yours in Isantu, and I have mentioned her to Bill Guest — it's possible Barbary will use that springboard one way or another. But using you — poaching you from Boris as it were — wouldn't be ethical.'

'Ethical! You keep a whole team of lawyers busy wriggling your way out of shonky prospectuses and dishonoured contracts and minimising taxes and God knows what, and you talk to me about ethics.'

'Old friends are different. I couldn't pull a swiftie on Boris. But I'm thinking of the ethics of my company as well. It would destroy all what we have between us for you to be on the Barbary payroll.'

'Perhaps so.'

'And there's an old saying,' Steven said. 'You don't get your meat where you get your bread and butter.'

'Tacky.'

'Not tasteful, no, but there's some wisdom in these old saws.'

'Hmph!' Roxane had made up her mind to cut loose from big organisations and run her own consultancy, but she had taken it for granted Steven would create a job for her if she needed a backstop. She looked at him. Despite the glow of candlelight, his face was lined, the top of his head balding. His strangely colourless eyes were hidden by the reflection of the candle flame on the lenses of his spectacles.

Steven's Mercedes was illegally parked at a 389 bus stop, but it bore no parking ticket. 'I don't know how you get away with this,' Roxane said. 'I'm booked if I overstay a sign for ten minutes.'

'The worst they can do is fine me. But as you say, I do seem to be lucky.'

They drove up William Street, turned left just after Kings

Cross, and made their way to Billyard Avenue. 'It's funny being here at night,' Roxane said as the lights went on in the grey and violet room. 'I always used to wonder if Anna decorated this room, but now that I've met her I realise she couldn't have.'

'No, it was a demonstration unit when we revamped the building. One of our subsidiaries has renovated thirty or forty old blocks in this area. This is one of the better-situated ones. We have a decorator do up sample units in each. A job lot, virtually.'

'That figures. I used to have fantasies about a whole succession of women coming here.'

'That's not my style either. My relationships go on for years. And I don't have the time or the disposition to keep up with a lot of people."

They walked out onto the balcony together, looking down on the lights of the foreshore, some of them reflected in giddy lines on the surface of the harbour. A ferry plied across the black water in a ripple of yellow light.

Roxane and Steven kissed, but a new quality had entered their embrace. Sadness? Respectability?

'It was more fun when it was a guilty secret,' Roxane said.

'I can't keep secrets from Anna, not indefinitely. And you seem to get on so well with her. It will do you both good.'

'Yes,' Roxane said. 'It will, I see that. I like her enormously. But it will change things between you and me.'

'Does it have to?'

'And that disquietingly knowing friend of yours? Vilmos? He knows about everything too?'

'What he doesn't know, he guesses. He's a psychiatrist.'

'They're not necessarily mindreaders.'

'Don't be so sure about Vilmos.'

'If I saw him in the street I would guess he was a circus proprietor or a retired racing car driver before I thought of psychiatry.'

Steven laughed. 'You should have told him. He would have enjoyed both those identities.'

'You look more like a psychiatrist than he does.'

'Is that supposed to be flattering?' Steven asked. 'Come and let me hold you.' He took her by the shoulders and led the way to the bedroom.

'Tired?' Roxane asked. 'I'll massage your neck.'

He lay naked on the satin sheet and Roxane rhythmically stroked his spine and rubbed his shoulders. 'Mmm, that's delicious. I could go to sleep.'

'Do,' she said. 'It'll do you good.'

'Then we can spend the whole morning making love.'

'No, we can't. I have to get an early morning wake-up call if you haven't got an alarm here. I'm going on "Breakfast Australia" — a car is picking me up at my place at six-thirty.'

'How deplorable.'

'All part of a grand plan, and totally necessary. You know what Olwyn Tierney's last words were to me? "Television, Roxane," she said. "Saturation." '

'You were there?'

'No, her daughter told me.'

'But what did she mean by that?'

'I wondered about that for a moment, then I had this flash. There's the Silk Festival coming up, isn't there, with national coverage? And you'll have to watch me in the morning to see what else I think she meant.'

'I think my watch is supposed to work as an alarm,' Steven said.

They looked at the dial and knob of the watch but neither of them could work out how to set the alarm. 'I'll have to ring Telecom,' Roxane said, disappearing into the living room in a towelling robe.

'All set,' she said, 'they're ringing me at five-thirty.'

'Oh, my God.'

'Yes, it is a bit grim, but wait till you see the program.'

'Hold me, Roxane,' Steven Szabo said.

Roxane put her arms around him and he clasped her close to his pale body. 'My darling,' he murmured, kissing her neck. Roxane lent over him, caressing him, touching him and licking him until his jetlagged penis flickered with desire and grew obediently rigid. She enjoyed the intercourse that followed, but its character was changing. There was a new feeling between them; the rhythm was almost elegiac. She did not know what it was, whether they were both more conscious of Anna; whether she was actually grieving for Olwyn, or whether their affair was, little by little, losing its urgency and passion. Or perhaps they were just sleepy. They fell asleep with their arms around one another for warmth.

'Hey, Mum! Quick! They said something about Gran on television.'

Margot joined her son in the living room. 'What?'

'They just said something about after the break, Roxane Rowe will be paying her respects to Gran.'

'She's a fast worker. The poor woman isn't buried yet.' Margot had put on her seldom-worn black and grey wool dress. The funeral was scheduled for noon. 'Tell your father, too,' she told Tom.

Ted came into the room during a Toyota commercial. 'What's all this about Olwyn?' he asked.

'Tom says they said there's an item about her on next. Roxane Rowe "paying her respects".'

'Sounds like country radio. Today's funerals …dirge on the organ …these announcements come to you courtesy of Morbid & Bones, Funeral Directors and Lawn Cemetery Proprietors Extraordinaire. In the main street just up from the Blue Budgie Pet Shop.'

'I doubt that you've quite captured Ms Rowe's style,' Margot said.

'Shut *up*,' said Tom. 'It's coming on now.'

On the screen a man with a black moustache was talking intently to camera. 'Who's that?' Ted asked.

'Shut up, it's Rory Rogan.'

'A special item this morning,' the presenter said. 'Brought to us courtesy of Roxane Rowe, the most famous face in travel and cover story of this week's *Business Briefing*. It's a sad story, although it involves business triumphs. The industry has lost one of its guiding lights. I'll let Roxane tell the story.'

There was a momentary hint of tears in Roxane's eyes. 'Olwyn Tierney was my personal heroine and mentor,' she said, 'but more than that, she bequeathed the Australian travel industry a glorious legacy of vision and taste.'

'This is frightful,' Margot said.

'Shhh!' Tom said. Ted held Margot's hand.

The image had changed — Roxane in her cobalt blue dress had been replaced by footage of a liner pulling away from Circular Quay, black and white film of jets landing at Mascot, an Australian businessman in wide-legged trousers alighting from a taxi and taking leather suitcases out of the boot. 'When Olwyn Tierney built up Runaway Travel in the postwar period,' Roxane narrated, 'travel was thought of as the occasional trip "home" to Britain by sea. Now, it's more often a two-week trip to Bali for the whole family. No one in Australia can take more credit for the growing profits and changing profile of our travel industry than its pioneering genius, Olwyn Tierney, whose funeral will be held today ...' A still photo of Olwyn in about 1965 appeared on the screen.

'When I first went to work for Runaway, it operated from a small, no-frills office in York Street. After its acquisition by Brooklands, Runaway became the cog of a group of two hundred agencies in Australia and in the South East Asian region.

'With Olwyn at the helm, Runaway was the first company to package flexible tours to Hong Kong, Singapore, Fiji, and other parts of South East Asia. Her developments in Bali are a watchword for taste, sensitivity to the local environment, and awareness of what the Australian tourist wants. Her insistence on high standards enabled Runaway to sell packages wholesale to Japanese and American interests.

'I owe my professionalism and dedication to Olwyn's example. Her concern for courtesy and attention to detail made Runaway-trained consultants sought after throughout the industry.

'Olwyn's concern for the individual, her flair for marketing, her affinity with other cultures and her ability to cotton on to the consumer's need for travel as a romantic adventure made her a unique figure among travel executives.

'Olwyn never retired.

'Until just a few weeks ago she was supervising the launch of Runaway's Indigo Island resort in Isantu. The huts peek discreetly out of fronds of swaying palms, beside the blue waters of the Pacific. Already the resort is fully booked, one of our most successful ventures.'

On the screen were the salmon-pink huts, green trees, turquoise sea, duty-free shops glittering with elaborately packaged aftershave, and clips from old Runaway promotions. Roxane's assertive voice gave way to the opening chords of Albinoni's Adagio. Tom sobbed. Margot put her arms around him and rested her chin on the top of his head.

'You'd be Olwyn's logical successor at Runaway and on the Brooklands board, I suppose?' Rory Rogan asked.

Roxane looked directly at the camera, her eyes a little misty. 'No,' she said. 'I mean it about Olwyn being an inspiration to me. I intend to tell Mr Brookstein that I'll be going out on my own and forming a small company along the lines of the Runaway I joined as a teenager. It will have a more up-market focus, but it's still that small, fastidious, family feeling I want to recover.'

'So you'll be leaving Runaway?'

'I wouldn't put it so baldly,' Roxane said. 'I could never entirely leave Runaway, any more than Olwyn Tierney could.'

'But you'll be branching out?'

'Yes, Rory, branching out. I'll be forming Roxane Rowe Enterprises. I'm planning a luxury tour of the Marco Polo silk route in partnership with Anna Szabo's Harbourside Volunteers, who, as you know, are holding a Silk Festival in October. And I'll be doing some television, of course.'

'Of course.'

'Yes.' Roxane turned her right profile to the camera and looked Rory Rogan in the eye. 'Do you know,' she said, 'that Olwyn Tierney's last words were a message to me? "More television, Roxane," she said. "Saturation." '

'Well, Roxane, this has been a riveting tribute to your old mentor, if I may say so, and I hope we can extract a promise from you to come back and tell us about the Silk Festival and the silk tour.'

'Darling,' Roxane said, 'consider it done.'

'Thankyou so much for coming in at this time of personal grief.'

'It's the least I could do, Rory. I owe it to Olwyn.'

'Roxane, thanks very much for coming in today.'

'Thankyou, Rory.' The close-up showed tears welling into Roxane's eyes. A commercial followed, extolling the freshness of the fruit and vegetables at a supermarket chain. Ted switched off the television.

'The woman's preposterous,' Margot said.

'Yes,' Ted agreed. 'She is. But underneath all that sales pitch, she's genuinely feeling the loss of your mother, don't you think?'

'How would you ever get underneath the sales pitch to find out?'

Tom wrenched himself free from his mother's arms. 'You both think the worst of everybody,' he said through tears. 'She's more upset about Olwyn than either of you are. She's brokenhearted, she said so.'

'Come and let's see what you and I can wear for Rookwood,' Ted said. He led his son away from the living room, a hand on his arm.

In the crush of people in the sunlight outside the crematorium chapel, Boris Brookstein drew Des Hickey to one side.

'I don't care if you do have her resignation in writing. We need to keep her under contract for the commercials. Especially after that program this morning. The last thing we can afford is a big visible bust-up. She's our public face, and

276

a bloody photogenic one. I want you to fix it now.'

'What if she insists on the right to promote other products as well?'

'She can do her own luxury tours and a few charity numbers. Nothing else.'

'What sort of money do I offer?'

Brookstein named a figure.

'But shit, Boris, that's about what she's getting as an annual salary now.'

'Just do it, Des, before she gets an agent and really screws us.'

A woman approached and took Boris by the hand. 'You mightn't remember me, Mr Brookstein. Jane Singer. I used to work for Olwyn. What a shocking loss.'

'Irreplaceable,' he said. Jane Singer began to reminisce about Olwyn, while Boris checked from the corner of his eye that Des was singling out Roxane and making an offer to her. Roxane, who was still wearing the cobalt blue dress, had tied a black lace scarf round her head like a Spanish widow.

'Are you coming back to Olwyn's place for a drink?' Margot Tierney asked.

'Olwyn's?'

'Yes, her friend Winifred Carswell has put loads of champagne on ice. Just what she would have wanted, I'm sure.'

The funeral party began to disperse. A group of cars headed east through the congested traffic of Parramatta Road, past the turn-off to Margot's and the hospital where Olwyn had died, making its way towards the egg and asparagus brown bread sandwiches and quantities of Great Western champagne of Olwyn's wake.

EPILOGUE

In late November, Margot and Prue sat in the shade of the silky oaks in the Annandale garden. Fronds of gold blossom drooped over the galvanised iron roof of the back veranda. 'It's been a strange year,' Margot said, 'what with my mother's death, and your reunion with Gus. And the women and success project. It turned out better than I expected — remember when I was complaining about having to do it? Well, it's led to my having a role in the financial seminars I told you about.'

'But you used to disapprove of all that side of things — you thought Brian and the Boys had their priorities all wrong.'

'I'm mellowing. Even my Yagoona women aren't indifferent to money and how to handle it, after all. It's a nice positive spin-off from the research, too, instead of having it sit on the library shelves in a bound volume. I can actually help people plan some financial security so they can make the best of their talents without being anxious all the time. Besides, I stand to inherit a bit of cash from Olwyn, so I could do with some good investment advice myself.'

'Feminism reaches the world of money. Hallelujah! Remember when insurance salesman used to ring up and tell you the statistical likelihood of becoming a widow? What are you going to do with the money, Margot?'

'We'll pay off the mortgage, that'll be the main thing. And I'll travel. I've always wanted to see Scandinavia, so I think I'll work out some way of combining research with pleasure there.'

'Sounds like fun.'

'Yes. I'll tell you another thing, Prue. Brian's interest in Roxane Rowe seems to extend beyond getting her to be a figurehead at seminars. They keep going out to dinner together, not to mention anything more intimate.'

'What about Steven Szabo?'

'What about him? It's not as if he or Roxane are going to confide in me, is it?'

'I wonder if she's two-timing them or if it's over with Szabo, that's all.'

'Wouldn't have a clue. She said she's going into business with his wife, after all if she really was having an affair with him, I imagine it's over by now. Are you going to eat any more of these grapes?'

'No, thanks.'

Margot stacked the plates and cups onto a plastic tray. 'How's that case of yours, Prue?' she asked. 'The one about one of Szabo's companies?'

'It was taken out of my hands. I'm not supposed to breathe a word about it to anyone. I haven't even told Gus about it, actually. I interviewed one of the partners in the scheme, and the pieces of the puzzle were just beginning to come together when the third partner died.'

'Died?'

'Yes, died in hospital. Oh, I can't tell you about it, Margot, there's going to be an inquest anyway.'

'When?'

'It keeps being deferred. You know what the court lists are like.'

'But you don't have to do any more work on the case?'

'So the Commissioner hopes. Oh, let's just say I made some written statements and had the whole of the matter taken out of my hands. It's with our Legal Branch. They move at about the same pace as *Bleak House*, so if the poor fools who invested in the Cloudy Bay development are ever going to get their day in court, it could be years away. I've given up fretting about it. Oh, it's disillusioning when you've worked on something and can't see it through, but without Malcolm Gwynne there I'm a bit of a non-person at the Commission. The Commissioner's polite in a frosty way, but he's got me writing safety pamphlets. I'm thinking about other things, to save my sanity.'

'Yes,' Margot said. 'Whatever have you got there?'

'Don't laugh,' Prue said, 'but it's a sort of pattern book. They send you the pictures from the front of the pattern envelope as soon as the new season's designs reach the shops. I'm planning to make a whole set of silk tops and throw out my old cotton ones.'

'Silk, satin, cotton, rags. You'd better be careful, that's a marriage rhyme.'

'I don't believe in marriage, you know that. I was inspired actually, by the Silk Festival. Weren't the colours fabulous? The Italians? The Thais? And with Gus down in the Antarctic for months, well, I might as well go on with some sewing.'

'Like Penelope waiting for Ulysses. A couple of years ago you would have enrolled for a new degree or a new language if you had a bit of time on your hands.'

'Would I? Yes, I suppose you're right. But there's nothing wrong with liking beautiful things, is there? And you have to admit, old Roxane didn't look bad in that blue and silver dress the other night.'

'No, not bad at all. They'll give her a part in a television soapie next, with shoulders like that. Not to mention cleavage. Still, the fashion show had its moments, I grant you. Olwyn would have been proud of Roxane. I dreamt about her again last night,' Margot said. 'Olwyn, I mean. She was laughing. It wasn't one of those death-filled nightmares at all. She was telling wicked stories to a crony and laughing.'

280

'That's nice.'

'What do you hear from Gus? Sorry, Angus?'

'Their phone calls are rationed, so I only hear once a week. But so far so good. They got there safely, he's getting some birds on film, and they're amusing themselves at night getting up some extraordinary Christmas panto.'

'Sounds quite good fun.'

'If you like that sort of thing. Gus does, apparently.'

'You miss him a lot, don't you?'

'Yes, I do, actually.'

'You'll be getting clucky next. Joining all these women in their thirties who are suddenly desperate to have babies.'

'I have been seeing prams and strollers everywhere,' Prue said.

'Don't you want to live up to the hopes of Malcolm Gwynne and work your way up to being one of the Commissioners?'

'Yeah, and be carried off like Malcolm, in my fifties, with a stroke?'

'That'd never happen. You're so healthy. All those games of squash and gym classes.'

'Getting to the top seems to be less of an imperative for me these days. With Malcolm gone, I could be on the outer for years. I might be more one of your medium flyers after all, rather than Commissioner material.'

'Well, just think very carefully, Prue, before you chuck in opportunities like that.'

'I wouldn't be chucking it in. You've heard of maternity leave. I could quite easily have a baby and keep on working.'

'Hmm. It's a lot harder to combine the roles than you might think.'

'Anyway,' Prue said. 'It's all hypothetical. It's far too soon to say how things will work out for Gus and me. I've never faced a longer summer.'

Alone in her flat, Prue thought of the Antarctic, and of the research stations at Macquarie Island and Young Island. Her mind floated further south, to the frozen seas and the South Pole. She imagined big boulders of ice, deep paddocks of snow, frozen streams, icy ravines, and icicles hanging from the rooflines. Then she imagined a thaw. A huge iceberg with an icefall like a glacier on one side drifted away from the land, submerging and rising in the cold seas like a giant whale. It looked like a vast, delicate piece of sculpture. Ice floes drifted into the dark ocean. Icicles dripped and vanished. Green moss grew on the rocky shorelines.

On the beaches, seals were mating, the warlike bulls roaring if younger males approached the cows and their young. Little sea creatures without names multiplied in pools between rocks slimy with moss and weeds. Penguins waddled solemnly along the shore, but gained grace and speed as they took to the water.

Gus, she knew, was studying the fledgling albatrosses. After seventy-five days' incubation, and a three-day struggle to break out of the egg, one chick was born to each adult pair of wandering albatrosses. Unlike their parents, the fuzzy young birds had clownlike white faces and dark brown bodies. The parents tended the chicks for eight months, or until they could take to the skies with the broadwinged effortless soaring of their species. Gus had told Prue that these birds flew best in high winds; on still days they had to leap off cliffs to get airborne. Sometimes they comically overshot the mark when trying to land. In the air there was nothing to match them.

Prue thought of Gus cooking unhealthy fried food, smoke rising from the roof of the cookhouse. She thought of his every breath visible in the frosty air. She imagined the pale sun rising soon after midnight to shine on the brief summer. She ached for his return in the autumn.

She placed the last pin in her paper pattern. With a crisp sound, her scissors cut the crimson silk.

THE BABY-FARMER

MARGARET SCOTT

'Have you never heard of a baby-farmer? They trade in children, sir, and grow fat on human flesh.'

Terrified that her child will fall victim to the operators of a murderous racket that flourished in Victorian London, a young servant-girl pleads for help in rescuing her baby son.

She sets in train a series of mysterious and shocking events that transform the lives of the dissolute Colonel Fellowes and his family; the sinister Mrs Hartshorne; and a cast of other characters who lurk in the shadows of the richest and most hypocritical city on earth.

The Baby-Farmer, Margaret Scott's first novel, is based on the horrifying facts that emerged at a murder trial in the 1870s. A fast-moving story of crime, lust and greed, it will hold the reader spellbound all the way to its astonishing climax.

EAT MY WORDS

MARION HALLIGAN

The real excitement of ices is the ephemerality. Human nature is perverse; we like things that are difficult, delicate, that have a moment of perfection and then decline. Ices by definition are fleeting, and so they should be exquisite, sensuous, luxurious, rare. Ices and kisses.

This is a book for vicarious chefs and practised cooks; for converts to olive oil and lovers of cheese; for tasters of words and everyday cooks. For tipplers of wine; for travellers in antique lands; for reading-in-bed gourmands. Above all, it's a book for those who believe that the best food, like the best sex, begins in the mind.

In prose to seduce the weariest palate, Marion Halligan, prize-winning storyteller, writes about food and words, eating and art, cooking and reading, gardens and books. Inviting you to eat her words she tempts the fancy, nourishes the imagination, and offers the odd recipe to keep body and soul together.